Praise for Kristan Higgins

NOW THAT YOU MENTION IT

"Higgins is in top form. Many readers will relate to the family saga and rough past, and the light romance and humor sprinkled throughout will suit a wide audience. Readers won't want to put down this highly recommended read."

—*Library Journal*, starred review

"Balancing emotion, humor, and a redemptive theme, Higgins hits all the right notes with precision, perception, and panache."

—*Kirkus Reviews*, starred review

"Kristan Higgins adds humor at every opportunity to *Now That You Mention It* and proves that it is possible to deal with our past demons without losing our minds."

—*BookPage*

ON SECOND THOUGHT
An NPR Best Book of 2017

"Emotional depth is seared into every page along with wry banter, bringing readers to tears and smiles. Another hit for Higgins."

—*Library Journal*, starred review

"Higgins' complex, witty characters will seem like close friends, and readers will savor each and every page as they find that love comes in many different flavors and forms. Demand will be high for the latest from this women's-fiction star."

—*Booklist*, starred review

"A captivating read about two sisters dealing with love, loss and new beginnings."

—*RT Book Reviews*, gold review

IF YOU ONLY KNEW
An NPR Great Read of 2015
A *BookPage* Best Romance of the Year

"[An] emotionally compelling story [and] perceptive study of love, marriage, sisterhood, and loyalty. A powerful, emotionally textured winner."

—*Kirkus Reviews*

"The kind of book I enjoy the most—sparkling characters, fast-moving plot and laugh-out-loud dialogue. A winner!"

—*New York Times* bestselling author
Susan Elizabeth Phillips

"Poignant, funny and richly entertaining."

—NPR

"This emotional journey is filled with drama, laughter and tears and squeezes the heart. It should be on every bedside table in the country!"

—#1 *New York Times* bestselling author Robyn Carr

"Higgins' tender, heartfelt *If You Only Knew* bridges the gap between romance and women's fiction."

—*BookPage*

KRISTAN HIGGINS

NOW THAT YOU MENTION IT

HQN

ISBN-13: 978-1-335-04538-6

Now That You Mention It

First published in 2017. This edition published in 2020.

Recycling programs
for this product may
not exist in your area.

For questions and comments about the quality of this book,
please contact us at CustomerService@Harlequin.com.

HQN
22 Adelaide St. West, 40th Floor
Toronto, Ontario M5H 4E3, Canada
www.Harlequin.com

Printed in U.S.A.

This book is dedicated to Stacia Bjarnason, PhD—
kindness incarnate, brilliant beyond measure,
brave, funny and a dog lover to boot.
It's an honor to be your friend.

1

THE FIRST THOUGHT I had after I died was: *How will my dog cope with this?*

The second thought: *I hope we can still go with open casket.*

Third thought: *I have nothing to wear to my funeral.*

Fourth: *I'll never meet Daniel Radcliffe now.*

Fifth: *Did Bobby just break up with me?*

LET ME BACK up in an hour or so.

It was a quiet night at Boston City Hospital—for me. It usually was. While I worked at New England's biggest and busiest hospital, I was a gastroenterologist. Most of our patients were diagnosed in the office before things got too critical—everyone freaks out if they can't eat or poop, after all. So aside from the occasional emergencies—hemorrhages or burst gallbladders—it's a pretty mellow field.

It's also a field with a low mortality rate.

I had just checked the four patients my practice had

on the unit—two elderly women, both impacted, sent in by their nursing homes for enemas, basically; one small bowel obstruction, resolving nicely on a clear-liquid diet; and one case of ulcerative colitis which my colleague would operate on tomorrow.

"So more fiber, Mrs. DeStefano, okay? Lay off the pasta and add some greens," I said to one of the impacted patients.

"Honey, I'm Italian. Lay off the pasta, please. I'd rather die."

"Well, eat more greens and a *little* less pasta." She was ninety-six, after all. "You don't want to get all bound up again, do you? Hospitals are no fun."

"Are you married?" she asked.

"Not yet." My face felt weird, as it always did when I fake-smiled. "But I have a very nice boyfriend."

"Is he Italian?"

"Irish American."

"Can't win them all," she said. "Come to my house. You're too skinny. I'll cook you pasta *fagioli* that will make you cry, it's so good."

"Sounds like heaven." I didn't point out that she no longer lived in a house. And that no matter how sweet the little old lady might be, I didn't visit strangers, even strangers who thought I was skinny, bless their hearts. "Get some rest tonight," I said. "I'll check on you tomorrow, okay?"

I left the room, my heels tapping on the shiny tile floors… I always dressed for work, having come to my love of clothes later than most. I adjusted my white doctor's coat, which still gave me a thrill—*Nora Stuart, MD, Department of Gastroenterology* stitched over my heart.

I could do computer work, I supposed. The nurses would love me for it. My rounds were finished, and I was just killing time, hoping that for once, Bobby would be ready to leave at the end of his shift. He worked in the ER, so the answer was usually no.

But I really didn't want to go home alone, even if Boomer, our giant Bernese mountain dog mutt, would be there. Boomer, the bright spot in my increasingly gray life.

No. My life was fine. It was great. Best not to navel-gaze right now. Maybe I'd call Roseline, my best friend here in Boston, an obstetrician. Even better, maybe she'd be on call, and I could help deliver a baby. I texted her, but she immediately responded that she was at her in-laws' for dinner and contemplating homicide.

Too bad. Roseline understood the grayness. Then again, maybe I'd been leaning on her too much. I wrote back suggesting various ways to dispose of the bodies, then stuck my phone in my pocket.

I ambled over to the nurses' station. Ah, lovely. Del, one of my favorite CNAs, was sitting there, lollipop in his mouth, going through a pile of papers. "Hey, buddy," I said.

"Dr. Nora! How's it going?"

"Great! How are you? How'd the date go the other night?"

He leaned back in his chair, a huge smile coming over his face. "She's the one," he said smugly. "I knew it the second she smiled at me."

"Really?"

"Really. I mean, she looked up, and I practically got down on one knee. It was like we'd known each other forever. Like we were made for each other, special order, you know?"

"Sure!" I said, a bit too emphatically. "Same with Bobby and me."

Del's smile faltered just a little.

Just then, an overhead page went off. "Attention, please. Attention, please. Dr. Stuart, Dr. Nora Stuart, to ER Eleven, stat."

I jumped. "Oh! That's me!" A GI call to the ER was rare enough to still be thrilling. "Off I go, then. Bye, Del!"

I ran down the hall, feeling very badass, one hand over my stethoscope so it wouldn't bounce, wondering what the call was. Foreign body in esophagus (*choking*, in other words)? Hemorrhagic lower GI bleeding? Always exciting. More common in a city ER would be esophageal varices due to alcoholism or hepatitis— blood vessels in the throat that burst and can cause the patient to bleed to death.

I loved going to the ER. Gastroenterology was just as important as emergency medicine, but no one wrote shows about my specialty, did they? The ER was where the cool kids hung out, and my boyfriend was their king. Bobby often said there was little the emergency department couldn't fix—but if they'd paged me, well, then… *I* was the captain now.

I ran down the stairs into the ER, over to the triage nurse. Ellen looked up and said, "Twelve-year-old with a bellyache, looks sick, number eleven."

"Thanks, Ellen!" She failed to smile back. Bobby loved her, but to me, she was as charming as the Dementors in Harry Potter, always looking for some happiness to smite.

To Exam Room Eleven I went, walking briskly but not running. The ER was fairly quiet tonight; the usual suspects—the elderly, a few kids, a few addicts, a guy with a bloody hand who smiled as I walked past.

Gastroenterology…well. Someone had to do it, right? And I liked it, mostly. Ninety percent of my patients got better. The colonoscopies…believe it or not, there was a Zen to them. But yeah, it didn't make the best party chatter. I couldn't count the number of flinches I got when I told people what my field was, but they sure cared when they had an ulcer, didn't they?

Jabrielle, one of the newer ER residents, stood outside the exam room. She was a little too infatuated with Bobby, as demonstrated when she gazed deeply into his eyes at the last party we'd gone to, one of those *we can't break eye contact because this conversation is so intense* situations. Jabrielle was also irritatingly beautiful.

"Are you the GI consult?" she asked, failing to recognize me. Again.

"Yes," I said. "I'm Nora. We've met. Three times." She still looked blank. "Bobby's girlfriend?"

"Oh. Right. Anyway, I suspect appendicitis, but his pain is a little more midline. We're waiting on labs. I was going to scan him, but the attending wanted the consult to see if we can avoid the CT."

The patient looked young for twelve, his skin ashen, face drawn with pain. We didn't want to expose him to radiation from the CT scan if we didn't have to. "Hi, bud," I said. "We're gonna take good care of you, okay?" I smiled at the mother as I washed my hands. "I'm Dr. Stuart. Sorry your son is having trouble." I glanced at the chart. Caden Lackley, no trauma, eating mostly normally until today, acute abdominal pain, fever, nausea and vomiting. "Any diarrhea or mushy poop, Caden?" Like I said, not the best party chatter.

"No," he answered.

"Okay. Let's take a look."

I felt his stomach, which was tight, one of the signs for appendicitis. But the pain wasn't in the expected place; in fact, it wasn't anywhere near McBurney's point in his lower right abdomen. "It's not his appendix," I said.

Jabrielle pursed her perfect lips, irritated that she'd been wrong. All the ER docs were this way, hating when we specialists disagreed with them.

The kid sucked in a sharp breath as I palpated just under his ribs on the right side. There was no pain on the left. I rolled him to his side and tapped on his back to check for kidney problems, but he didn't react.

He was probably too young for gallstones. Pancreatitis, maybe, but again, given his age, it was a bit unlikely. It wouldn't be Crohn's disease without diarrhea. "How long has your stomach been hurting, Caden?"

"Since Sunday."

That was a nice specific answer. Today was Thursday, so five days of stomach pain. "Has it stopped and started?"

"No. It's been there the whole time."

I thought a second. "Did you eat anything different over the weekend?"

"We went to a party at my sister's," the mom said. "There was a lot of food, but nothing he hasn't had before."

"Anything with small bones in it? Fish, chicken?"

They looked at each other. "No. Nothing with bones," she said.

"How about a toothpick?" I asked.

"Yeah," he said. "Those scallops wrapped in bacon."

Bingo. "Did you maybe swallow a toothpick?" I asked.

"I don't think so," he said.

"He was eating them like popcorn," his mother said.

"Well, they *are* fantastic." I smiled. "Sometimes people can swallow things without noticing it, Caden, so I'm going to do an endoscopy. Basically, you get some nice relaxing medicine, I slip a tiny camera into your stomach and look around and maybe I'll see a toothpick. Sound like fun?"

It did to me.

I told Jabrielle to give him some Versed to relax him, then sprayed his throat with lidocaine to numb it, so he wouldn't gag. His mom sat next to him, holding his hand.

"This won't hurt a bit," I said, then I got to work, sliding the scope into his throat, talking quietly through it, looking up at the screen as Caden's esophagus and stomach were revealed. Healthy tissue, the beautiful web of blood vessels, the grayish walls of the stomach pulsing and moving with life.

And there, in the lower part of the stomach, I saw the toothpick, now black from stomach acid, sticking out of his duodenal wall. Using the endoscopy forceps, I gently grabbed it and slowly pulled it out. "Ta-da," I said, holding it up so my patient could see. "We got it, Caden. You'll feel a lot better tomorrow."

"Good call," Jabrielle murmured.

"Thank you," I said. "I'll order up some antibiotics, but he should be right as rain. In the future, big guy, eat more carefully, okay? This could've done a lot of damage. It could've slipped through into your liver, and that would've been really bad."

"Thank you so much, Doctor," the mom said. "We had no idea!"

"My pleasure," I said. "He seems like a great kid."

I pulled off my gloves, shook her hand, tousled Caden's hair and went out to write the prescription.

Felt a little heroic.

If left untreated, that toothpick could've caused sepsis. It could've been fatal. Though it didn't happen too often, I think I could firmly say I'd saved a life tonight.

Just then the doors to the ambulance bay burst open, and a pack of people ran down the hall next to a gurney. "Drive-up gunshot to throat" barked someone—Bobby, it was my honey! "Extensive blood loss in vehicle, get the Level One infuser running with four units of O positive. Call the blood bank for a mass-transfusion pack, and call trauma code for Room One, now! Stop sitting on your asses, people! Move!"

The place exploded with action, people running in every direction, doing as their lord commanded. I inched toward the room where the action was, hypnotized. Good God. It looked like half the man's throat was missing, a meaty hole about the size of a fist, Bobby's hand inside it.

"I'm clamping his carotid with my fucking fingers!" Bobby yelled. "Where the hell is the surgeon?"

Indeed, Bobby's arm was drenched in blood, his scrubs sprayed with arterial spatter. The rest of the team buzzed around the patient, cutting off his clothes, inserting lines.

"No, you can't intubate, idiot!" Bobby barked at an

intern. "Can you not see my hand in his throat? Bag him, you moron!"

I sure didn't miss residency. The ER doctors had been brutal.

Dr. McKnight from Surgery burst in, pulling on her gloves, a face shield already in place to protect her from blood-borne diseases. Someone draped her in a gown. "Clamp," she snapped. "Now!" If there was anyone more, ah, self-confident than an ER doc, it was a surgeon. "Keep your hand there, Bobby, and don't even breathe. You lose your grip, he bleeds out in five seconds. How the hell did he make it here with a pulse?"

Then a nurse saw me gaping and closed the door. I wasn't ER staff, after all.

I snapped out of my awestruck stupor and closed my mouth. Janitorial was already mopping up the trail of blood, and half the residents—including Jabrielle, who shot me a dirty look, since I made her miss the good stuff with my boring endoscopy—hovered at the exam room window to see if the guy would make it.

The other patients in the unit were quiet in their exam stalls out of respect, it seemed—a TV-worthy trauma had just passed through their midst.

I wandered back to the triage desk. "Hi again, Ellen," I said. "That's some—"

"You done with that consult?" Ellen asked.

"Oh, yeah. Um…he swallowed a toothpick. I did an endoscopy and—"

She gave me the stink eye and picked up her phone. Right. She was busy, and I was an irritating doctor who made her life harder…which was true for a lot of nurses, especially in the ER. All the more reason I bent over backward to make sure they knew I appreciated them. But Ellen wasn't the type to drink in the milk of human kindness, so I slunk to the computer and entered the report.

Just as I finished, the door to Bobby's exam room opened, and out came the team again, heading for the elevator up to the surgical floor. I could hear the beeping that indicated a regular heartbeat. Somehow, they'd saved his life or at least given him a chance.

Dr. McKnight got on the elevator with the transport team, and as the doors closed, she called, "Nice work, people. Bobby, awesome job!"

The doors closed, and applause broke out throughout the department.

The next shift of ER staff was coming on, already aware that there'd been a good save, already jealous it hadn't happened on their shift.

Bobby and his team were in no hurry to pass the torch, either. They high-fived, made much ado about their bloody clothes, their part in the drama, Dr. McKnight's speedy and delicate end-to-end anastomosis.

Bobby didn't say much—he didn't have to, because it was clear he was their god.

Finally, his eyes stopped on me. I smiled, proud of him, even as that little irritating voice said it was about time he'd seen me.

"Oh, hey," he said. We'd been together long enough that I could tell he'd forgotten I was working tonight, too. "Uh…we were gonna order a pizza and stick around to see how the patient's doing."

"Sure. Of course. Hey, Bobby, that was amazing. I saw a little bit."

He shrugged modestly. "Were you waiting for me?" he asked.

The irritation flared again. "No, I was on a consult. Twelve-year-old ate a toothpick. I scoped him, and it doesn't look perfed. Think we caught it before he got septic, too."

"Cool. Well, you want to hang out with us?"

I suppressed a sigh. I didn't. I wanted to go home and take a walk with Bobby and Boomer and get pad Thai. If we stayed here, I'd have to call Gus, our dog walker. I wanted to tell Bobby about my good call, my instincts of guessing what had caused the pain, which was what separated good doctors from mediocre ones.

But he was the one who'd had his hand in a man's throat.

"Sure," I said.

"Cool. Just let me get washed up." He left, stopping so the janitor could shake his hand.

Five minutes later, we went into the staff lounge, where the rest of the team was already in full adrenaline-junkie-chatter mode. More congratulations were given. More high fives. More jokes.

"Who's gonna get the pizza?" Jabrielle asked.

Everyone looked at me, the outsider. The boring gastroenterologist (who had also saved a life tonight, though that story wouldn't get aired).

"I'll do it," I said. "What would you like?"

Despite a magna cum laude degree from Tufts, medical degree from the same and a profession in which I earned a third more than my boyfriend, it seemed I was back in the days of waiting on customers at Scupper Island Clam Shack.

"Thanks, Nora," Bobby said. A couple other people paused in their self-praise to echo him.

"You bet." I walked through the ER, trying not to sigh.

In the hallway was a gurney. A young woman in a neck brace lay there, holding hands with a young man about the same age, also in a neck brace. College kids in a car accident, I'd guess. He leaned down so his forehead touched hers, and her hand went to his hair. They didn't speak. They didn't have to. Their love was that palpable.

Bobby and I had been like that once, right after the Big Bad Event.

But not for a long, long time.

It made me feel…gray.

Outside lurked the typical raw Boston April night—rain splattering, a cold wind gusting off the bay, the smell of ocean and trash, since the sanitation workers were on strike. It was eight-thirty, which meant a quiet night in our fair city. SoHo we were not.

I started off the curb, glanced to my left.

There, right *there*, was a giant green plastic bug on top of a van and the words *Beantown Bug Killers* painted on the windshield. In a flash I saw that the driver had one of those hideous lumberjack beards with crumbs in it, and he wore a Red Sox hat and there were Dunkin' Donuts napkins on the dashboard, and then the van hit me.

I didn't feel anything at first, but it would hurt, I knew that, and, boy, a lot of thoughts can go through your head in one second. Have they ever measured that? Brakes screeched as I sailed through the air like a rag doll, distantly aware that this would be bad. I hadn't taken one step to get away; there hadn't been time. Then the ground slammed up at me, my head bouncing on the pavement, hard. A car door slammed, followed by a thick Southie accent. "You gotta be fuckin' kiddin' me, lady. I didn't even fuckin' *see* ya. Oh, my Gawd! You okay? Fuck!"

His voice was fading.

I smelled trash, sour and sickly sweet—I lay near an overheaped garbage can. Would that be the last thing I saw? Trash? I wanted Boomer.

I wanted my mom.

The trash can was graying out. I couldn't see anymore. *I'm dying*, I thought. *This time, I'm really going to die.*

And then I was gone.

2

How will my dog cope with this?

My soul, it seemed, wasn't ready to leave just yet and was still hung up on the concerns of the material world.

Poor Boomer, the Dog of Dogs, my sweet little hundred-pound puppy, who protected me and came into the bathroom when I showered to stand guard just in case someone broke in. Boomer, who loved me with all his giant heart, who would put his head on my leg, who asked for nothing other than an ear scratch, who was afraid of pigeons but adored ducks... No one would love him the way I did. He'd be sad and confused for the rest of his life.

I *knew* I shouldn't have waited for stupid Bobby! And why the hell was *I* the one getting the pizza? Why hadn't I stood up for myself and told beautiful, snotty Jabrielle to go her damn self? She was a resident! I was a fully vested doctor, thank you!

But I hadn't, and now I was dead.

I hope we can still go with open casket.

I had often envisioned my funeral—me lying against the rose-colored satin, looking utterly stunning, the sadder songs of U2 and Ed Sheeran playing gently in the background while my friends wept and laughed over their precious memories of me. A closed casket was not part of the scenario, hit by Beantown Bug Killers or not. I wondered if my face was smooshed in. Eesh.

I have nothing to wear to my funeral.

Granted, in life I'd been a clothes whore, at least during the past fifteen years or so. But for my funeral, I wanted something special. The navy-blue-and-white polka-dot Brooks Brothers dress I'd been eyeing, or that pink floral Kate Spade. But maybe that would be too festive.

I'll never meet Daniel Radcliffe now.

It had always been a long shot, I knew that, but I'd imagined stalking him after he did a show on Broadway, waiting by the side door, our eyes meeting, his inimitable smile, going out for a drink, sharing our favorite moments from Harry Potter, me finding out that he, too, hated the destruction of Hogwarts and agreed that Ron was nowhere near worthy of Hermione. Now, with me dead, it *definitely* wasn't gonna happen.

True, no one was acting like I was dead, but I was fairly certain I was. Maybe they just hadn't noticed yet. I guessed this ER wasn't quite the be-all and end-all of modern medicine, was it? I thought I'd heard the words *dislocated patella* and *ortho consult* and *trauma alert*. I was pretty sure I'd seen the tunnel of light, but my spirit was tuning in and out.

What was that beeping? It was really hurting my head.

I'd read about this kind of thing happening. Out-of-body experiences. The soul lingering a little while before heading for the afterlife. Did I know anyone who'd greet me from heaven? My dad, maybe, if he was dead? That mean-ass grandmother of mine who used to tell me I was fat? I hoped *she* wasn't there. Who else? Maybe that sweet patient who'd died of pancreatic cancer during my fellowship. God, I had loved her. My first fatality.

"So she's your girlfriend?" someone asked. I knew that voice. Jabrielle. Couldn't miss that hint of sneer.

"Yeah." Bobby.

Was he about to start sobbing? Wait, did *Bobby* have to call the code on me? Or had he been hysterical, calling my name, having to be dragged out by two burly orderlies? Either way, the poor, poor man. Dang, I wished I remembered! I guess I'd shown up a little late to my own death. Which did seem to happen a lot in the movies.

The beeping was persistent and annoying.

"How long have you been together?" Jabrielle again.

"Oh, a little more than a year. It's funny, though. I was gonna break up with her this weekend." A pause. "She's not in the best shape, anyway." Gentle laughter.

I almost smiled.

Wait. What?

Did Bobby just break up with me?

I was barely even cold! Did he— Was he—

"So what will you do?" Jabrielle asked.

"It would be pretty shitty to dump her now, I guess."

A female purr. "Well, when you're a free man, give me a call."

"Wish I didn't have to wait so long."

Are you even kidding me?

No. No, no. I was *dead*. I didn't care about these things. Soon, I'd be floating up to the stars or something.

But just in case, I decided to try to open my eyes.

Oh, shit. I *wasn't* dead. I was in the ER. That beeping sound was the heart monitor, nice and regular, 78 beats per minute, O_2 sat 98 percent, BP 130/89, a little high, but given the pain, not unexpected.

And Bobby was fondling a piece of Jabrielle's hair.

"Do you mind?" I said, my voice croaking.

They jumped apart.

"Hey! You're awake! Take it easy, hon, you're gonna be okay." Bobby took my hand—ow, my shoulder!—and smiled reassuringly. He did have the prettiest blue eyes. "You were hit by a car."

"Beantown Bug Killers," Jabrielle added.

"Did I die?"

Bobby smirked. "You have a concussion—we scanned you, but you're fine. Bruised kidneys, broken clavicle and a patellar dislocation, which we reduced...we had to sedate you for that. You're splinted, and we're waiting on ortho to check you out. Can you feel your toes?"

Everything hurt. My back, my head, my shoulder, my knee. I was one giant throb of pain. But whatever they'd given me made it so I didn't really care.

I guess my tunnel of light had been the CAT scan.

"I want another doctor," I said.

"Hon, don't be that way."

"Bite me. You were flirting over my corpse." I pulled my hand free. Ow.

He rolled his eyes. "You weren't dead, Nora."

Fury blotted out the pain for a second. "Well, I

thought I was. Get out. Both of you. Don't be surprised if I file a complaint for unprofessional conduct. And call Gus to walk Boomer."

The tug of the sedation or concussion pulled me back under, and before the door had closed, I was asleep again.

WHEN I WOKE UP, I was in a regular hospital room, Bobby asleep in the chair beside me. Some weary white carnations were in a vase next to me, their edges brown. If that wasn't a metaphor for our relationship, I didn't know what was. I sensed that moving would be very painful, so I breathed carefully and took stock.

My left arm was in a sling. A brace of some kind was on my right leg. My back hurt, my abdomen ached, and my head throbbed, little flashes of light in my peripheral vision with every heartbeat.

But I was alive. Apparently, the concussion and drugs had given me that out-of-body feeling.

Bobby stirred, never a good sleeper. Opened his eyes. "Hey. How you feeling?"

"Okay."

"Do you remember what happened?"

"Hit by a van."

"That's right. You were crossing the street, and you got hit. Besides the patellar dislocation, your left clavicle is broken, and you've got fractures in the sixth and seventh ribs on the left. Pretty good concussion, too. The trauma team admitted you for a night or two."

"Did you call Gus?"

"Huh? Oh, yeah." He was quiet for a moment, then leaned forward. "I'm sorry about Jabrielle."

Surprisingly, my throat tightened, and tears welled

in my eyes, slipping down my temples into my hair. "At least you made it easy," I whispered.

"Made what easy?"

"Breaking up. I can't really overlook you hitting on another woman when I'm bruised and battered in the ER, can I?"

He looked ashamed. "I really am sorry. That wasn't classy at all."

"No."

"Roseline came by. I called her. She's upstairs on L and D, but she'll come down later."

"Great."

We were quiet for a few minutes.

Once, I thought I'd marry Bobby Byrne. Once, I thought he'd be lucky to have me. But somewhere in the midst of our year and change together—after the Big Bad Event—I got lost. What was once a bright and shiny penny had become dirty and dull and useless, and it was high time I admitted it.

Bobby hadn't loved me for a long time.

I was going to need help for the next few weeks. Concussions were serious business, and with my injured arm and leg, I had mobility concerns. I'd need help, and I wasn't about to stay with Bobby.

Problem was, we lived together. Roseline was a newlywed; otherwise, I'd stay with her. Other friends... No.

"I want to go home," I said.

"Sure. Tomorrow. I'll take a few days off."

"I meant *home*. To the island."

Bobby blinked. "Oh."

Strangely enough, I wanted my mother. I wanted the pine trees and rocky shores. I wanted to sleep in the room I hadn't slept in for fifteen years.

I wanted to see my sister.

Yes. I'd go home, as one does after a brush with death. I'd take a leave of absence from the practice and go back to Scupper Island, make amends with my mother, spend some time with my niece, wait for my sister to come back and…well…reassess. I might not have died, but it was close enough. I had another chance. I could do better.

"And I'm bringing Boomer," I added.

A WEEK LATER, still sore and slow, arm in a sling, leg in a soft brace, one crutch to balance me, I looked around our apartment for the last time. Bobby's apartment, really. Roseline had come over last night, and we got a little weepy, but she said she'd come see me on Scupper. Bobby had thoughtfully made himself scarce and had been sleeping on the couch all week.

I should never have moved in with him. We'd only been dating a couple of months before the Big Bad Event, after which we shacked up. Way too early. But then, going back to my place was out of the question. He said we were moving in together, I said yes. Also, we'd been in love.

And lest we forget, Bobby got off on saving people.

In the week since I was hit by Beantown Bug Killers (who had sent flowers every day), I'd done a lot of thinking. I wanted to stop being afraid, stop settling for the half love Bobby gave me, to stop feeling so gray. The time had come.

Bobby stood by the door, Boomer on the leash. There were tears in his aqua-blue eyes. "This is harder than I thought it'd be," he admitted.

"We'll still see each other. Joint custody and all that."

He smiled, petting Boomer's big head. "Thanks for that."

Yes, we were sharing the dog. After all, we'd gotten him together.

"You want to go for a ride, Boomer?" I said, uttering the most wonderful words a dog could hear. "You want to go in the car?"

Bobby drove us to the ferry station, where people could grab a boat to Nantucket, Martha's Vineyard, Provincetown, Portland or, in my case, Scupper Island, my hometown, a small island three miles off the rough and ragged coast of southern Maine. The Scupper Island ferry came to Boston almost every day; it was also the mail boat and could carry all of three cars.

Bobby unloaded my suitcases and bought my ticket. Our breakup had made him once again solicitous; he'd been a prince these past few days, fetching me my painkillers, reading to me as I fell asleep, even cooking for me.

I didn't care. He'd been fondling someone's hair in my hospital room, and that was not something I'd forget.

The ferry pulled in, a battered little thing, same as it had always been. Jake Ferriman, the eponymous captain of the boat, was a fixture. He didn't acknowledge me, just tied up the boat and jumped off, a small sack of mail in one hand.

I'd hoped my mom would come on the ferry to get me; I'd called her when I was discharged from the hospital and told her I'd be coming home, that I'd been hurt but was okay—I think I used the words *expected to recover*, always looking for attention where my mother was concerned. Her only response had been a sigh, followed by "I'll pick you up at the dock when you get here," and I bit down on all the things I wanted to say. It could wait. I was starting over, after all.

Jake returned from wherever he dropped the mail, carrying the return post in a bag in one hand. He checked his clipboard. "You travelin' alone?" he asked, eyeing Boomer.

"With the dog here."

He frowned, glanced at me again, then made a check mark on his clipboard.

"I guess this is it, then," Bobby said. "Call me when you get settled, okay?"

He hugged me carefully, then buttoned my coat over my sling. There was the lump in my throat again. "Take care," I whispered.

We'd been friends for a long time and a couple for more than a year. All that was over and done with now.

Bobby's eyes were wet, too.

Jake hefted my suitcases onto the boat, then took Boomer's leash. My dog jumped happily onto the boat and snuffled the wind. I followed more carefully.

I went inside the ferry's cabin and sat down, laid my crutch next to me. Looked at Bobby through the window and waved. Tried to smile.

"Ever been to Scupper before?" Jake asked.

I blinked, surprised he didn't know who I was. Then again, I was an adult now. I wasn't the overweight girl with bad skin and worse posture. "I grew up there. I'm Nora Stuart, Mr. Ferriman."

"Sharon's girl?"

"Yes."

"The one with the kid?"

"No. The other one." *The doctor*, I almost added,

but that would've been prideful, and Mainers didn't like that.

Jake grunted, and I sensed our conversation was over.

Then he started the engine, pulled the lines, and we were off, Boston's pretty skyline growing smaller as we headed out on the dark gray water, toward the clouds hanging on the horizon.

My hands tingled with nerves, and I petted Boomer's head. He looked up at me with his sweet doggy smile. "Sorry about this, pal," I whispered. "No one is going to be too happy to see us."

3

Scupper Island, Maine, was named for Captain Jedediah Scupper, a whaling captain who left Nantucket after he lost an election on the church council. He came to settle his own island and give Nantucket a big middle finger. Nantucket didn't seem to mind. Captain Scupper brought a wife and five kids, and those five kids found spouses, and before you knew it, there was a legitimate community here.

Over the years, its residents lived the same way as those on most Maine islands did—they suffered after the whaling industry died, then turned to fishing and lobstering.

Islanders prided themselves on survival and toughness, bonded together by hurricanes and nor'easters, drownings and hardship. When the Gilded Age hit, it gave Scupper a new industry—service. Cleaning, gardening, catering, carpentry, plumbing, nannying, taking care of the rich folks and their property.

That never changed.

I grew up with the belief that while the rich people came in June—the summer nuisance, we called them—Scupper Island was for *us*, the tough Yankees. We'd deal with the summer people, those who owned big houses on the rocky cliffs and moored their wooden sailboats in our picturesque coves. The kids were attractive and polite, but never our real friends, not when they wore Vineyard Vines and Ralph Lauren and had European nannies. Not when they ate at the local restaurants where our parents worked.

But they were our bread and butter, and lots of them were genuinely nice people. They donated to our schools, paid the taxes that kept our roads patched and plowed, fed the local economy. Still, we were glad when they left every Labor Day. Being cheerful representatives of their summer getaway was a little wearing.

Scupper belonged to *us*. To my sister and me, to our dad and absolutely to our mom.

My mother, Sharon Potter Stuart (and believe me, her maiden name was the source of great joy to this Muggle), was a fourth-generation islander, born and raised here. She was a typical tough Maine woman—able to shoot a deer, dress it and make venison chili in the same day. She cut and stacked her own wood, made her own food, viewed going to restaurants as wasteful. She knew how to do everything—fish, sail, fix a car, make biscuits from scratch, sew our dresses. Once, she even stitched up a cut when the one doctor on Scupper was attending a difficult birth.

Scupper was not just the name of our founder. It's also part of a ship—a drain, essentially, that allows excess water to flow out into the ocean, rather than puddle in the bottom. It was almost fitting, then, that so many of Scupper Island's residents left, slipping away to bigger waters. If you didn't make your life off the sea or tourism, Scupper Island was a tough place to stay.

Mom never went to college, never took a vacation. Once, I made the mistake of asking if we could go to Disney World, like just about every other American family. "Why on earth would we go there? You think it's prettier than this here?" she said once, her thick Maine accent turning *earth* to *uhth*, *here* to *heeah*.

My earliest memories of my mother were all good. She was safe and reliable, as mothers should be. Our meals were nutritious if unimaginative. She braided my somewhat-wild hair every day, patiently taming the snarls without ever pulling, and made sure we were clean. She drank black coffee all day long, the kind that she brewed in a pot on the stove, and watched us play while she did housework and chores, a hint of a smile on her face.

Our house, though plainly furnished, was clean and tidy. Homework was done at the kitchen table, under her gaze. She went to all the parent events at school. When we walked through a parking lot or across the Main Street and Elm intersection, she held my hand, but otherwise, there wasn't a lot of physical affection. When I was very little and she gave me my bath, sometimes she put the washcloth on my head and told me I had a fancy hat. Otherwise, she was simply there. And don't get me wrong. I knew how important that was.

She loved me, sure. As for my sister…well, Lily was magical.

My sister was twelve months and one day younger than I was, and different in every way. My hair was brown and coarse, not quite curly, not quite straight;

Lily's was black and fine. My eyes were a murky mix of brown and green; Lily's were a clear, pure blue. I was solid and tall, like our mother; Lily was a fairy child, knobby elbows and bluish-white skin. Lily often got carried, snuggled up on Mom's sturdy hip. When I asked if I could be carried, too, Mom told me I was her big girl.

I *loved* my sister. She was my baby, too, despite the scant year between us. I loved her chick-like hair, her eyes, her skinny little body snuggled against mine when she crept into my bed after a bad dream. I loved being older, bigger, stronger.

Those early years…they were so sweet. When I thought of them now, my heart pulled at the simplicity of it. Back when Lily loved me. Back when my parents loved each other. Back before Mom's heart was encased in concrete.

Back when Dad was here.

My father had a mysterious job, something Lily and I called "businessing." Dad wasn't an islander; he'd been born in the magical city of New York but grew up in Maine. He had an office and a secretary in town. I later learned he sold insurance.

But when I was about six, just starting all-day school, he started working from home. He took over our little den and tapped away on a computer, the first one we ever had. He was writing a book, he said, and he'd be around for us a lot more. Lily and I were thrilled. Both parents home? It'd be like the weekend all the time.

Except it wasn't. There were a lot of terse conversations between our parents; we couldn't hear the words from the bedroom Lily and I shared, but we could feel the mood, the energy between our parents brittle and tight, humming with unspoken words.

Mom took a job as manager at the Excelsior Pines, the big hotel at one end of Scupper. She'd always kept books for half a dozen local businesses, her calculator tapping into the night, but now she left the house before we got on the bus and didn't get back till suppertime.

Life changed on a dime. Before this, we'd only see Dad for an hour or two each day. Now he seemed completely dedicated to making fun for his girls. After school, he'd be waiting for the school bus, would toss us in the back of the truck, and we'd go adventuring. No *wash your hands, start your homework, here's your apple*. No, sir.

Instead, we'd hike up Eagle Mountain, pretending to be on the run from the law. We explored the tidal caves on the wild side of the island, wondering if we could live there, surviving on mussels, living like the Passamaquoddy Indians Lily and I wished we were.

In late spring, Daddy would hold our hands at the top of the ominously named Deerkill Rock, a granite precipice that jutted out over the ocean. "You ready, my brave little warriors?" he'd ask, and we'd race to the edge and jump out as far as we could, gravity separating us almost immediately, a drop so far I thought I might fly, the air rushing past my face, through my tangled hair, the thrilling, icy embrace of the ocean. We'd pop up like corks, Lily and I, coughing, shrieking, our legs already numb as we swam back to shore, our father laughing and proud, swimming beside us.

He'd take us to the top of Eastman Hill Road, that patched-up testament to frost heaves and potholes, and unload our bikes from the back of the truck. Down we'd go, the streamers from my handlebars whipping, the wind whisking tears from my eyes, my arms shuddering with the effort of staying in control. No bike helmets for us, not back then. Lily was too small and skinny to manage it, so Dad would perch her on his handlebars, the two of them soaring in front of me, the sound of their laughter lashing back, wrapping around me.

Dad would cook us the best meals, too. Travelers' food, he called it—stew cooked over the campfire, the way his Hungarian grandmother had taught him. He'd tell us stories of magical people who could hypnotize you into flying, people who could turn invisible, who could talk to animals and ride wild horses. There in the firelight, the ocean lapping at the granite rocks of the island shore, a saw-whet owl calling its lonely cry, it seemed more than just possible. It seemed true.

Then Mom would call us in and get that pinched-mouth look, shaking her head over our filthy feet, and send us to take our baths.

In the summer, we'd make forts and sleep outside, then come in covered in bug bites; grimy, happy and itchy. During the day, when Mom went to her job or did the grocery shopping on her afternoon off, Dad would let Lily and me out into the wild while he worked on his book. We'd wander, spying on the rich folks' houses, scouring the rocky shore for treasures, unsupervised and happy, returning home with Lily sunburned and me brown.

And meanwhile, my mother grew angry. Not that she showed it through anything other than terse orders about homework and chores. But the allure of all that freedom, especially with Dad's beaming approval and frequent participation…we learned not to care what our mother thought.

Sometimes, I tried to make my mother feel better—

I'd bring her lupines picked from the side of the road or find a piece of sea glass for her bowl, but the truth was, I loved having Daddy in charge. As our mother became more and more brittle, our love for Daddy mushroomed. While once I'd had friends—Cara Macklemore and Billy Ides—they didn't come over anymore, and I turned down invitations to go to their houses to play. Home was more fun. We didn't need friends, Lily and I. We had each other and Daddy. And Mom. Sure. Her, too.

So I pretended the tension between our parents wasn't there. Mom worked grimly, Dad wrote his book and played with us, and life was mostly wonderful.

Except when Mom would track us down. I don't know how she knew where we were, but every once in a while, her car would appear where we were adventuring, and she'd get out and yell at our father. "What are you doing out here? Are you out of your goddamn mind?"

"Sharon, relax!" Dad would say, grinning, panting from whatever activity we'd been doing. "They're having fun. They're outside, playing, breathing fresh air."

"One of these days, we'll be standin' over a casket if you don't stop this!"

Dad's smile would drop like granite. "You think I'd let something happen to my girls? You think I don't love them? Girls, do you think Daddy loves you?"

Of course, we'd say yes. Mom's mouth would tighten, her eyes would grow hard, and she'd either order us to get in the car or, worse, get in the car by herself and drive away, the rest of our day tainted.

"You're so brave, my girls," Dad would say. "Why be

alive if you can't have adventures, right? Who wants to end up all clenched and angry all the time?"

To prove his point, we'd go for one more swim, one more jump, one more thrilling ride down Eastman Hill. Stay out an extra half hour, have ice cream for dinner.

Lily was especially good at embracing Dad's philosophy. Once Mommy's girl, she started to avoid her, ignore her or, worse, talk about why Daddy was so much fun in front of her.

My flowers and sea glass didn't cut it. "Thanks, Nora," she'd say. But I couldn't undo the hurt—I wasn't Lily, after all, the magical, beautiful daughter.

Nothing I did seemed to make much impact on my mother, not the As on my report card, not the Mother's Day art project—a little pinch pot painted yellow with blue polka dots. (Lily said she forgot hers at school; it never came home.)

I learned to kiss my mother hello when she got home, tell her about my day so I could check the mental box that said *Talk to Mom*. Every once in a while, Mom would give me a look that said I wasn't fooling anyone. She wasn't a little black rain cloud, our mother, but her skies were unrelentingly gray.

But Daddy laughed a ton, and he and Lily and I had so many fun times, so many goofy games and adventurings and imaginative meals, long stories at bedtime or in the car when we'd take a ride to nowhere. Of course, I loved him best.

The guilt hardly ever panged at me. Lily, *she* was the one who was really mean to Mom. Not me. At least I tried.

One spring day when I was eleven, Lily and I came off the bus to find my mother sitting at the kitchen table, unexpectedly home from work, drinking her coffee. Lily buzzed right past, running up the stairs to throw her backpack on the floor and flop on the bed, as was her custom.

"Hi, Mom!" I said in my fake-cheery voice. "Guess what? Brenda Kowalski threw up during our math test, and it almost got on my desk! She had to go home early."

"Well, that's too bad." She didn't look up, just sat there, staring ahead, holding her mug. She'd changed from her work uniform of black pants and a white shirt and was wearing jeans and a flannel shirt.

No other words were spoken. Mom just sat there, twisting her wedding ring.

"Where's Dad?" I blurted, unable to take the silence anymore.

Her eyes flicked to me, then back to the middle distance. "He's gone," she said.

"Where?"

"I don't know. Off island."

Without us? That was strange. Usually, he'd wait for us, take us on the ferry to Portland, where there was a bakery filled with the most beautiful pastries, and let us get whatever we wanted.

"When will he be back?" I asked.

"I'm not sure."

My heart started to whump in my chest. "What do you mean, you're not sure?"

"I don't know, Nora. He didn't see fit to tell me."

Something was wrong. Something *big*. In that second, I felt my childhood teeter.

I pounded up the stairs. Our room had a slanted ceiling and was divided exactly in half; mine neat and tidy, as Mom requested, Lily's a snarled mess. She was lying

on her unmade bed with her headphones on, waiting for
Mom to leave, for Dad to appear with the afternoon's
entertainment, because there was always something
fun. Every single day.

I went into our parents' room, and my breath started
to shake out of me.

The closet was open, the top two drawers of the bureau—his—open, as well.

Open and empty. Our father's shoes—he had more
pairs than Mom—were gone. His socks were gone.
T-shirts. Everything, gone. Empty hangers hung like
bones in the closet.

On top of the bureau, dead center, was his wedding
ring.

I ran into the bathroom and threw up, my stomach
heaving, my whole body racked with the violent expul-
sion of my ham-and-tomato sandwich and two oatmeal
cookies, bits of apple floating on the surface.

"What's wrong with you?" Lily asked. At ten, she
already had a bit of a sneer.

"Daddy's gone," I said, my eyes streaming. I puked
again, my sinuses burning with throw-up.

"What do you mean, gone? What are you talking
about?"

"I don't know. His clothes are gone. He packed."

As I sat there, retching into the toilet, my sister ran
into our parents' bedroom, then pounded downstairs.
She screamed accusations at our mother, whose flat,
implacable voice answered questions. Something ce-
ramic broke—Mom's cup, I bet, throwing up again at
the thought of the smell of coffee.

"I hate you!" Lily screamed. "I hate you!"

Then the door slammed, and it was quiet again.

I waited for my mother to come upstairs and take care of me. She didn't.

Later that night, Lily told me what happened. Her version of it, anyway. Our mother, who was so boring and hateful and mean, had driven our father away. He'd gotten sick and tired of putting up with her, taken his novel and moved to New York City, where he was born, after all, and he was probably about to become a famous author. He'd call us and tell us to pack our things, that New York was the biggest place of all for adventuring, and we'd move, and Mom could stay here on her stupid Scupper Island.

If that was true…if our dad couldn't stand our mother anymore, I honestly couldn't blame him. He was a scarlet tanager, a rare, beautiful bird I'd only seen once in my life, flashing with red, its song happy and bright. She was a mourning dove, gray and dull, endlessly sighing the same notes over and over.

But I didn't want them to get a *divorce*.

In my version of what had happened, which I dared not tell Lily, Dad would come home with a bouquet of roses. Mom would be wearing that white dress with the red flowers on it, the only dress she had, and they'd be hugging, and we'd move to New York but come home to Scupper for summers, like the rich people.

Days passed. A week. Lily refused to go to school, and I was put in charge of breakfast while Mom went to work. At night, I listened to the suddenly scary noises of our old house, the muffled sobs from Lily's side of the room. I tried to climb into her bed to comfort her, but she shoved me away.

I waited for my father to call. He didn't.

He hadn't left a phone number, either. He had a

brother in Pennsylvania—Jeff, eight years older than my father, a man we'd only met twice before. I called him one afternoon when my mom was at a meeting at school—Lily was acting up. There was a long silence after I asked if he knew where my father might be.

"I'm sorry, sweetheart," he said. "I don't. But if I hear from him, I'll let you know."

I could tell by his voice he didn't think this would happen.

Another week crept by. Mom came home on Saturday morning and told us she'd switched her hours so she'd be able to be home with us after school.

"No one wants you here," Lily said, her voice so cold and cruel I flinched.

"No one asked you," Mom said mildly.

And that was the end of our deep family discussion.

What if Mom had *killed* Dad? Was that possible? She could lop the head off a sea bass, slide the knife down its belly and gut the thing in seconds… She could use a gun… We lived on an island, so she could dump his body anywhere and let the tides do what they would. I regretted reading the Patricia Cornwell novels I'd been sneaking out of the library, not to mention Stephen King, the patron saint of Maine. Was my father down the well, like Dolores Claiborne's husband?

We didn't have a well. Mom didn't talk to the police.

He had packed. Left his wedding ring. Sure, Mom could've faked it, but she didn't. I knew.

He was simply…gone. But Lily and I were the lights of his life. He told us that all the time. He wouldn't just leave us. He would obviously come back for us.

He didn't. He didn't come back, he didn't write, he didn't call.

The weeks turned into months. I tried to console Lily, asked if she wanted to do things together, but she ignored me, alone in her grief, which she clearly viewed as deeper than mine. I'd lost my father and his buoyant, exhilarating love, and it seemed I'd also lost Lily's.

I'd lay awake at night, heart pounding, tears slipping into my hair, missing them both with an ache in my heart that blotted out everything else. My childhood had ended, and I never even had the chance to say goodbye.

4

JAKE HELPED ME off the ferry. It was a three-hour ride, and I felt a little seasick. Or a little nauseous from my throbbing knee.

Or maybe it was just being back home.

Without a word, he got my bags and led Boomer off the boat, leaving me to crutch it alone, hobbling awkwardly up the gangplank, then onto the old dock.

Though it was mid-April, spring had not yet come to the island. My mom wasn't here yet, and the downtown was quiet. A raw wind blew the smell of fish and salt and donuts from Lala's Bakery, and with it, childhood memories. On cold winter Sundays, my father used to wake Lily and me at 5:00 a.m. to get the first donuts Lala made, almost too hot to hold, the sugar crusting our faces, the heat steaming in the wintry air.

I would see her soon, my sister. I would set things right again. That was the chance Beantown Bug Killers had given me, and I would make good on it.

And I would find out what happened with my parents. Where my father was. If he was still alive, I was going to find him, damn it.

When I was in my first year of residency, I'd stitched up a former Boston cop who did private investigations. I hired him to find my father, but he'd come up empty. With such a common name—William Stuart—and nothing else to go on since the day he left, the cop didn't turn up anything. It was time to try again, and this time, start from square one.

But for now, I had to get down the dock. One thing at a time.

With the sling, the brace and the crutch, I had to think about every step, and the rough, splintered wood of the dock didn't make matters easier. Step, shuffle, crutch. Step, shuffle, crutch. It was slow going.

Jake was already tying Boomer's leash to the bike rack; I was only halfway there. He walked back to his boat. "Thank you so much, Mr. Ferriman," I said as he passed. He grunted but didn't look at me, the charmer.

Slightly out of breath, I got to the end of the dock and patted my dog's head. A seagull landed on a wooden post, and Boomer woofed softly. Otherwise, the island was quiet, and ominously so, like one of Stephen King's towns. I missed the cheerful duck boats of Boston Common, the elegant shops of Newbury Street. Here, nothing was open.

Scupper Island Clam Shack, where I had worked for two summers, sat at the end of Main Street, right on the water. It wouldn't open until Memorial Day, if it was the same as it used to be.

I'd worked there with Sullivan Fletcher, one of the two Fletcher boys in my class. Sully had been in a car accident our senior year shortly before I left Scupper, and I wondered how he was. I'd wondered often over the years. Word had been that he'd recover, but I'd never asked for details (nor was my mother the detail type).

I looked to my right, and there was my mother's elderly Subaru turning onto Main Street. I waved, not that she could miss me; I was the only one here. She pulled over, turned off the engine and got out, looking the same as ever, and unexpected tears clogged my throat. "Hi, Mom," I said, starting to move forward for a hug.

She nodded instead, then hefted my two suitcases into the back of the car. "I didn't know you were bringing your dog," she said. Boomer wagged his fluffy tail, oblivious. "He better leave Tweety alone."

Tweety was Mom's parakeet (and favorite creature in the world). "Tweety's still alive, then?"

"Of course, he is. Where's that dog gonna sleep?"

"It's good to see you, too, Mom," I said. "I'm fine, thanks. In a lot of pain, actually, but doing okay. After being run down in the street. By a van. Sustaining many injuries, in case you forgot."

"I didn't forget, Nora," she said. "Get in the cah."

Boomer jumped in at the magical words, filling the entire back seat.

A thickly built woman with hard yellow hair approached our car. "Hey, Sharon. Who you got there?" *Who y'gawt they-ah?* Good to see the Maine accent was alive and well. The speaker was Mrs. Hurley, mother of Carmella Hurley, one of the mean girls from high school. I'd called them the Cheetos back then (not aloud, of course)—the popular, mean girls who'd go to Portland to woo cancer at tanning salons, resulting in a skin tone not found in nature.

"It's my daughter," Mom said.

"Lily, you're back, sweethaht?"

"Uh, no. I'm Nora. Hi, Mrs. Hurley. Nice to see you. How's Carmella?"

Her face hardened. Right. I was not an islander who had brought pride to my hometown. I was the girl who stole the prince's crown. Also, I looked a lot different from the olden days, when I'd been a fat, lumpy teenager with bad hair and worse skin.

"Cahmeller's wonderful," Mrs. Hurley bit out. "Well. You have a good day, Sharon. Nora."

It would soon be all over town that I was back.

Mom got into the driver's seat, and I flopped gracelessly in mine, ass first, bumping myself in the face with the crutch.

"So how *is* Carmella?" I asked, fastening my seatbelt.

"Good. Five kids. Cleans hotel rooms in the summer, bartends at Red's. Hard worker." *Hahd wehrkah.* Man, I guessed my accent had faded more than I realized. That, and I hadn't talked very much to my mom these past few years. Perfunctory phone calls, her annual twelve-hour visit to Boston.

"You'll be sharin' your room with Poe," she added.

"I will?"

"Well, where do you think she's sleepin'?" Mom pulled away from the curb.

Good point. I suppressed a sigh and looked out the window. Main Street had gentrified a bit. There was a bookstore I'd never seen, called The Cracked Spine. Cute name. Lala's Bakery, which would have a line around the corner every day in the summer, was fairly deserted now. A kitchen goods store. Huh.

"How is Poe?" I asked. I hadn't seen my niece for five years.

My mother shrugged.

"Mom, could you actually tell me?" I snapped. Five minutes, and already I was irritated.

"She's grumpy. Hates it here." She turned onto Perez Avenue, renamed for the man who'd sent a Scupper Island kid to college every year for the past quarter century...including me. We passed the ubiquitous made-in-China-souvenir shop, unimaginatively called Scupper Island Gift Shoppe (I always hated the spelling), a restaurant I'd never seen, an art gallery, another restaurant.

We'd never be Martha's Vineyard—too far, too cold, too small—but it seemed my hometown had blossomed.

"Did things go okay in Seattle?" I asked, referencing my mom's recent visit to fetch Poe.

"Dirty town," Mom said. "Lots of litter. And beggars."

Of course. Look on the dark side, that was my mother's motto. She didn't approve of panhandling, having grown up poor herself. But her version of poor was scrappy. It meant hunting and fishing for your food if you had to, knowing how to put up the vegetables from your garden, dry fish, smoke meat. If you didn't have something, you made do.

I'd been to Seattle four times to see my sister. I would've gone more, but Lily was always slippery about letting me come out there to see my niece. Once, Roseline came with me, which was a good thing, because Lily became "too busy" to see me, and I only got to see Poe for an hour. I'd been crushed, having pictured the four of us going out for pastries, visiting Pike

Place Market, eating at the top of the Space Needle. Rosie stepped up, and we did have fun—we ate crab and salmon till we just about turned pink, kayaked in Puget Sound, almost peeing ourselves when a pod of orca whales came within a hundred yards of us, giggling hysterically with fear and awe.

But in the back of my mind had been the thought, *If only Lily was here. Now* this *is adventuring! If only it was like old times.* The fact was, those old times had been old for more than a decade at that point.

"And how is Lily?" I asked, when it became apparent my mother wasn't going to mention her.

My mother's gaze didn't stray from straight ahead. "She's in jail, Nora. How do you think?"

I took a slow breath before speaking again. I knew she was in jail. My mom didn't have to be an ass about it. "Is she doing okay? Did you see her?"

"Ayuh. She seems fine."

Fine. Really? Was she devastated? Heartbroken? Remorseful? Angry? She was probably angry. She had been for the past twenty-four years, at least as far as I could tell. Since the day our father left.

Within three months of landing in Seattle at the age of eighteen, Lily had gotten tattooed, pierced and pregnant. She had a series of boyfriends; I had never met Poe's father, and to the best of my knowledge, neither had Poe. Lily's job history was spotty—barista (of course, it was Seattle), band manager for a local group, temp, barista again, tattoo artist.

My sister was also a petty criminal. Identity theft, credit card fraud and drug dealing, though the legalization of marijuana had put a dent in her business. I hadn't known about any of that until last month, when my mother told me she had to fly out and get Poe, because my sister had been sentenced to two years, out in August with good behavior.

Beantown Bug Killers had given me a plan. Stay on Scupper until Lily got out. Then she'd either come east to fetch her daughter, or I'd fly back with Poe. And I'd...fix things.

How, I wasn't sure.

We turned onto the dirt road that led to our house, and I held my arm across my chest to minimize the jostling. My collarbone ached. Mom glanced at me but said nothing. In the back seat, Boomer whined with excitement, sensing we were close to our destination. The car jolted over a pothole, and I sucked in a breath, my knee and shoulder flashing white with pain. My back ached, too, heavy and dull thanks to the bruised kidneys. Hopefully, I wouldn't be peeing blood later on.

And there it was. Home. A humble, gray-shingled Cape with a screened-in deck on one side, almost exactly as I'd left it, the bushes in front taller than I remembered.

I'd been away for so long.

My mom pulled into the unpaved driveway—we didn't have a garage—and threw the car into Park. She got out, opened the back door for Boomer, who raced off to sniff and mark his territory.

Lily and I used to think home was the most magical place on earth—the sound of chickadees and crows, gulls, the frigid ocean slapping against the rocks a few hundred yards away, the gray seals that would visit the shores with their pups. The wind would scrape and roar across the sky almost constantly, howling in the winter. The yard was just a carpet of pine needles, and beyond that, forest and ocean. The Krazinskis were our next-door neighbors, and they were half a mile away. Lily and I, and sometimes Dad, used to sit for hours in trees or makeshift forts and wait to see animals—fox and deer, pheasants and chipmunks, porcupines and raccoons.

I opened the car door, the smell of pine and wood smoke thick and rich.

Though I wouldn't go so far as saying it was good to be home—not yet—I knew this was where I needed to be.

I tried to get out of the car, but since my knee was in a brace and I couldn't bend it, I flopped right back onto the seat, jarring my collarbone, pain flashing all the way into my fingertips.

Being helpless sucked.

Also, my mother wasn't the world's most loving care-taker. She was halfway to the house with my suitcases. "Mom? Can you give me a hand?"

"Poe!" she yelled. "Get out here and help your aunt!" She went inside.

The wind gusted, cutting through my jacket, pressing me back into the seat as I struggled. The Dog of Dogs came up to check on me, and I patted his head with my good hand. Dogs beat people every time. "Are you my pretty boy?" I asked. He wagged in the affirmative, then trotted off again.

Finally, the door opened, and out came my sister.

No. It was Poe, but the resemblance was shocking.

My niece was *beautiful*. Her hair was dyed blue, shaved on one side, jaggedly cut on the other. She wore torn leggings and a T-shirt with a skull on it. As she got closer, I could see she was bedecked with black rubber bracelets and more ear piercings than I could count and had a tattoo on her neck.

She looked far, far older than fifteen. But her skin was pure and sweet, and her eyes were the same shade as blueberries, just like Lily's.

"Hi, honey," I said. "You got so big." My voice was husky. The last time I'd seen her, five years ago, she asked me for piggyback rides, which I happily gave. She'd had long black hair back then, and I taught her to French-braid it.

She gave me a dead-eyed stare, looking more like Lily than ever.

"Uh, can you just…" I held out my hand. "Take my crutch, okay."

She did, and I hoisted myself out, then hopped, grabbed onto her with my good hand and steadied myself. Took the crutch back. "Thanks, Poe."

"What happened to you?"

I blinked. "Gran didn't tell you?" Wasn't it important enough for a mention? "I was hit by a van."

"Seriously?"

"Yep. I broke my collarbone, got a concussion and dislocated my kneecap. And bruised my kidneys."

"Gross."

"Yeah."

"Can you sue them or something?" she asked with a flicker of interest. "Like, if it was FedEx or the cops?"

"It was Beantown Bug Killers, and no. I was jay-walking."

The interest faded, and the disgust returned.

We went inside, though she was faster than I was, obviously, and failed to hold the door for me. "Come on, Boomer," I said, and he trotted in, nearly knocking me over, unaware that he no longer weighed twelve pounds. I followed awkwardly. Poe was already slumped on the couch, engrossed in her phone. Mom was in the kitchen, her yellow parakeet on her shoulder.

The interior of the house was the same. I looked into the little den, almost expecting to see my father there, clacking away on his computer, or Lily, playing with her Barbies on the floor in the living room. The woodstove sat on the hearth of the stone fireplace, a more efficient way to heat the house. Same brown plaid couch, same old recliner, same coffee table where Lily and I had colored and chattered.

Of course, it was the same. My mom wasn't the type to throw things away, and she could fix anything.

I thought of my apartment—not Bobby's, but mine, the one I'd had before the Big Bad Event. The pale green couch, the balcony, the pretty throw pillows on the bed. All those lovely things, packed away in a storage unit in Brookline.

"Get away from me, dog," Poe said. "Is he really going to live with us?"

"This is Boomer. He loves people." He whined, echoing my message, and licked Poe's hand. She turned away without looking up from her phone.

I crutched it into the kitchen. Same creaky table where I'd done so much homework.

Mom was pouring herself a cup of sludge. "Want a cup?" she asked. The bird was sitting on a shelf. Near food.

"Does that bird ever go in its cage?"

"Sometimes. At night. Mostly, he flies around where he wants. Coffee?"

"Sure."

When I was in medical school, my mother came on one of her annual *Visits to Boston because I Have to See My Daughter* and informed me she'd gotten a bird. Tweety, not the most original name. She taught it (him? her?) tricks, such as eating a cracker held between her lips or sitting on her head while Mom drank coffee. Tweety could give kisses, which made me shudder and envision my mother dying an agonizing death from bird-borne encephalitis. When I called twice a month, I could often hear Tweety in the background, sounding much like a knife scraping against a plate.

But my mother loved the bird and sometimes laughed while describing Tweety's intellect, so who was I to judge?

Mom set a mug down in front of me. *Scupper Island Chamber of Commerce*, as boring and unimaginative a mug as could be. Again, I pictured my pretty things—my green-and-blue coffee cups, packed, hopefully, in bubble wrap. I hadn't been able to do it myself.

I sat down, my knee flashing with pain. "Mom, can I have an ice pack?"

"Bag a' peas okay?"

"Even better."

She got one and propped my foot up on an extra chair, then laid the frozen peas on my knee. "How's that?"

"Great. Thank you." I took a sip of the coffee (black; Mom didn't believe in half-and-half or sugared beverages) and tried not to shudder.

She sat down across from me. "So what are your plans, Nora?"

"I thought I could stay here until I was a little bit better. And then…well, I don't know, really."

I want us to be close. I miss Lily. I want to love Poe. I was hit by a car, and according to the Hallmark Channel, I'm supposed to come home.

I want to find out why Dad left us, where he's been all these years...and if he's still alive.

"How long till you get better?"

She meant how long till I could move out. Tweety screeched, probably wondering the same thing, and I eyed the bird warily. "I'll probably need help for a week or two."

She nodded. "All right. And after that? You goin' back to Boston, I imagine?"

"I thought I'd stay here for the summer. I took a leave of absence."

"Now, why'd you do that? You're a doctor, Nora!"

"I'm well aware of that. But, Mom, come on. I was hit by a van. I almost died."

"That's not what Bobby said."

"Oh, I'm sorry. Should I have gotten more hurt for you? Being knocked out cold and lying broken in the street wasn't quite dramatic enough?"

For a second, I thought about telling her about the Big Bad Event, but I doubted that would impact her. I'd lived, after all. How bad could it have been?

"Well, I'm just sayin' we don't have a lot of room here. What with Poe and all."

"I'll rent a place in a couple weeks, okay?" I took a slow breath, remembering my resolutions, my new take on life. I was going to be sunshiny again, goddamn it. "I've missed you, Mom. I want us to spend time together."

I sensed she wanted to roll her eyes, but she didn't. "So we'll hold hands and sing 'Kumbaya'?"

"Yes," I said. "It's my favorite song."

That got a tiny smile.

"I'm gonna take a shower," I said. "And a Vicodin."

"Don't get hooked on those," my mother said.

Wrong daughter to be lecturing about drug abuse. "Thanks for the advice."

I stood up, positioned my crutch and hobbled into the living room. "Poe, could you bring my suitcases upstairs?"

She inhaled a very long, slow breath, exhaled and raised her eyes to the ceiling. "Sure."

I went up the stairs, one at a time, Boomer trying to help, running up and down, nearly killing me. The bird flew right at my head, either attacking me or trying to nest in my hair. "Jesus! Get away, Tweety!" He zoomed past again, and Boomer lunged. "No, Boomer! Down." Imagine if my dog ate my mother's favorite living creature on my first day home.

"No bird," I told him, and he looked deeply ashamed. Luckily, my mom called for Tweety, and the creepy little thing whizzed past again, diving at Boomer, who ducked, this time and went into the kitchen.

By the time I made it to the top, I was drenched in sweat and in a bonfire of pain. God, my ribs were killing me! And my back. And my knee! And my stupid collarbone. I was one giant ball of hurt.

I went into my room. Poe had taken my old bed, based on the snarl of sheets. The other bed, once Lily's, was covered in clothes, magazines, makeup.

Poe came in with my suitcases and dropped them.

"You'll need to clear off that bed," I said.

"Then where am I supposed to put my stuff?"

"The bureau? The closet? The trash? I don't know,

honey, but I have to sleep there. Let's try to get along, okay? I'll be here all summer."

"I have to share a room with my elderly aunt all summer? Do I have to rub lotion on your feet and Tiger Balm on your shoulder, too?"

"I was hoping you'd shave off my corns."

"Jesus!"

"Poe. I'm kidding. And I'm not elderly, okay? I'm thirty-five. I'll rent a place as soon as I can get around on my own. If I sleep well and don't break another bone tripping on your crap, I'll get out of here sooner. See? Clearing off the bed works in both our interests."

"Whatever."

My eye twitched. "Would you please get me a glass of water?" I asked sweetly. "I have to take some medication." I cleared a spot on the bed, then used my crutch to snag my purse as Poe went into the bathroom. She returned instantly with a slightly grubby glass filled with water which, if experience was an indicator, would be tepid, since she didn't run the water beforehand.

It was lukewarm, all right, but my knee was on fire, and my left arm felt like lead. I swallowed a pill. Poe picked up the bottle. "Oh, the good stuff," she said. "No generics for you doctors, I guess. Can I have one?"

"Put that down and stay away from it."

"I was *kidding*. Jesus." She stomped down the stairs.

Boomer came up and nuzzled my hand. "You love me, right?" I asked. He licked my hand in affirmation.

The travel and stress of my injuries caught up with me. I lay back against Poe's clothes and closed my eyes. To my surprise, tears leaked out. Though he didn't deserve it, I missed Bobby. I missed Boston. I missed

Roseline and the hospital and Dr. Breckenridge, that old flirt.

I missed my old life and the old me, the way things were before, when Bobby and I were still new and life seemed so perfect and clean and pure.

I wasn't wanted here. There was a pretty huge chance that coming back had been a big mistake.

5

WITH ALL THE speed of an elderly slug, the first week passed. Poe had a habit of sleeping through her alarm (a lovely little ditty called "Black Dying Rose," which consisted of someone screaming so hard I imagined he'd eventually cause variceal hemorrhaging). Somehow, Poe wasn't jolted into a state of terror as I was, so I had to throw my pillow at her every morning.

"What? God!" was her customary greeting. Then she'd stumble about the room, tossing clothes, grumbling, accusing me of moving her stuff, before using up all the hot water in her way-too-long shower. She'd stomp downstairs like Hagrid the giant, refuse to eat breakfast, then get in the car with my mother, who dropped her at school on the way to the hotel. At least they let Boomer out on their way.

My dog loved it here. He'd come in after a half an hour of romping in the woods, burs or twigs stuck in his feathery fur. I'd brush him as best I could with my good arm, Boomer crooning as I did so, going into his doggy trance.

My knee was already a lot better, though too much weight on it still made me see stars. The collarbone would take a little longer, but the pain had subsided to a dull ache.

I napped. I read. I watched three seasons of *House of Cards*. I was recovering from a shock, I told myself, and not just lazy. Tweety watched my every move and, if my guess was right, whispered my activities to my mother later in the day.

But being lazy felt pretty good. I was also starting to feel…safe. Since the Big Bad Event, I'd put a lot of effort into life, especially where Bobby was concerned—trying not to be too much of a downer, to have something interesting to say, to save pajamas for actual bedtime, to pretend I didn't mind his nights out with friends, when Boomer and I would lock every window no matter what the weather was and stick a chair in front of the door, too.

Here, it was surprisingly great to do nothing. Being alone in my childhood home didn't freak me out the same way being alone in Boston had.

At night, after a supper of *Food That Would Keep Us Alive*, Tweety occasionally eating a piece of bread from my mother's lips, as I struggled not to dry heave or mention bird-borne pathogens, I'd ask Poe if she wanted to play Scrabble or Apples to Apples or Monopoly. Shockingly, she did not and would go upstairs to listen to more screamo music. I'd take a Vicodin in lieu of a glass of wine, put an ice pack on my knee and watch *Wheel of Fortune* with my mother. Chatting was not allowed, though shouting out the answer was. Mom beat me every time.

On the eighth night of my exciting new life, Boomer and I were on the couch. Bernard from Duluth, Georgia, had finally managed to figure out CITY THAT NEVER SLEEPS four letters after my mother had, winning a vacation to Hawaii. Mom clicked off the TV and went into the den, Tweety swooping in from somewhere to land on her head. Gah.

Fun was over. I decided to seek out company and distraction in cyberspace.

Shit. My laptop was upstairs. "Poe?" I called over the music. "Would you mind bringing me my computer, honey?"

Nothing. I waited ten seconds.

"Poe?"

"I'm *coming*! I answered you already. Jesus." Eight angry thuds shook the house as she came down the stairs. She practically threw the computer at me.

"Thank you so much, sweetheart."

She stomped back upstairs.

Was it wrong to want to kick one's niece? It probably was. I forced myself to smile, stroked Boomer's ears, took a cleansing breath and reminded myself that Poe was going through a hard time. Her whole life had been hard. Maybe. I didn't really know, did I?

But my sister was in jail, Poe was far, far away from her friends, and last night, I'd forgotten to bring a towel into the bathroom, so she had to see me lying in the tub with only a washcloth for cover, which is pretty much every teenager's most horrible nightmare.

One of these days, though, I'd win her over (pause for laughter).

I opened my email. Ah, there was a funny note from Roseline asking me about hot lobstermen (none), my mother, Boomer, my niece. She'd also attached a picture of herself with a huge smile on her face, holding up a little voodoo doll of Bobby—I could tell, because he was wearing scrubs and a mask, and Roseline had written *Bobby* on his shirt. Adorably, he was stuck full of pins.

My ancestors have your back! read Roseline's note. Bobby should be coming down with explosive diarrhea any second.

I snorted. Aw! You're the best, I typed. Also, Harvard wants their degree back. Everything is fine here. I heart Vicodin! My mother's bird is trying to kill me. Send help.

I started to type more, then realized I didn't have a lot to say. The truth about my mom and Poe would concern her—*We barely talk, but they're tolerating me!* Besides, I had a stiff upper lip now. I didn't whine or complain, because I wasn't a smear on the pavement with a bouquet of flowers marking the spot I'd died. I was alive! Yay. Besides, it was only my first week (plus one day). So I just asked her questions about Amir and married life and if she'd had any fun baby deliveries lately.

My computer pinged. Another email…this one from Bobby.

Hey there. Missing you. The place seems too big without you and Boomer. Are you doing okay? Doing your PT? Sleeping all right? Maybe we can talk tomorrow. Bobby

Damn. I wanted to hear his voice, and I absolutely didn't want to hear his voice. Was he dating Jabrielle already? Why was he saying he missed me? I hoped he missed me. I was so glad he missed me. I hoped he was suffering *and* had explosive diarrhea.

But no. I was a bigger person now. Near-death experience, et cetera, et cetera.

Doing fine here! I typed. Boomer loves the island and finds something dead to bring home almost every day. I'm feeling much better and really love getting to know my niece again. She's fantastic!—Lies, all lies—Boomer misses you, too—Truth—Mom sends her best—Lie—Sure, give me a call tomorrow. I have plans for dinner—to eat survival food with Mom and Poe—but am mostly free in the afternoon.

I hit Send.

It seemed so long ago that Bobby and I had been *that* couple. That couple in neck braces I'd seen in the ER—okay, fine, not the most romantic image, but you know what I mean. That couple who's connected by a shimmer of energy. Whose love made other people disappear so that they were the only two people in the world.

He dumped you after you were hit by a car, Nora, said my smarter half.

Chances were pretty high that he'd blow off tomorrow's call. If history was an indicator, he'd have a patient or coworker who needed him.

I sighed. Then I glanced in the den, where my mother was still working, opened Google and typed in the same words I'd typed a hundred times before.

William Stuart, Maine, obituary. From the little den, Tweety screeched, channeling Edgar Allen Poe's raven. Boomer whined. Tweety had pecked him on the head the other day, and now he was terrified of the bird. Like owner, like dog.

For some strange reason, my father didn't have a middle name, something Lily and I had tried to remedy, everything from Toad, as in *Frog and Toad Are Friends*, to Denzel, as in Washington. It would've been helpful in tracking him down, that was for sure.

There were plenty of dead William Stuarts out there and Bills and Wills. But the ones who had the same birth year as my father never seemed to fit.

This time was no different. If my father was dead, I had no way of knowing.

Sitting here, in the house where I had once felt so loved and safe, it was hard to believe that my father had never come back at all.

Never even called.

But maybe, now that I was back on the island, I could find out what happened.

6

ON THE NINTH night of my convalescence, my mother told Poe and me to get out of the house. "I have something going on here," she said. "Can you two go out for ice cream or something?"

"I'm injured," I said. "And I just took a Vicodin, so I can't drive." Also, *Game of Thrones* was on, and like any good viewer, I was in love with Jon Snow.

"Then go upstairs and close your door," she said.

"I'm a little old to be sent to my room."

"Believe me, you'll want to go," Poe said.

"Why?"

"It's work," my mother said. But her cheeks flushed.

Now that was odd. My mother never blushed. Ever. Nothing embarrassed her. Once, when I was in high school and Mom was in the throes of a particularly gruesome menopause (or meno-go, as the case was), she'd bled so much at the grocery store that she left a red trail in her wake. She'd opened a package of paper towels, cleaned up and added an economy-size box of adult diapers to our cart. Didn't so much as flinch.

So her blushing now… Was this one of those sex-toy parties? "What kind of work?" I asked.

"It's a new venture," she said, putting Tweety in the cage. At least there was that.

"What *kind* of new venture?"

"Nora, just get upstairs," she growled.

"It's hug therapy," Poe said.

I snorted. No one else cracked a smile. "Seriously?" No answer. "Mom, if you need a hug, I'm right here." I tried to remember our last hug. Failed.

"I *give* the hugs, Nora. I don't get them."

"Really?"

"People pay for it," Poe said.

"Like prostitution?"

My mother frowned. "It's a recognized therapy—"

"Recognized by whom?"

"—and people are pathetic and will pay for just about anything," my mother said.

"That's beautiful."

"And sometimes, they take a nap here."

"Are you kidding me?"

"Just fix your face and get upstairs. Take your dog with you."

"Don't you want him for pet therapy? Which *is* actually a recognized therapy?"

"Nora, get."

I glanced at Poe, who, for once, made eye contact. "Does she turn into a pillar of salt when someone touches her?" I asked.

"Get!" my mother said, her face redder now.

Boomer raced up the stairs, then back down, then up

again as I hobbled up the stairs. Rather than going into our room, I paused. "Let's spy," I suggested.

"It's gross," Poe said.

"All the better."

I stationed myself just off to the side of the stairs, where I was hidden but could peek. Poe went into our room and emerged with the pink velour beanbag chair, sat in it, then looked at me. She sighed, hauled herself out and shoved it my way.

"You're a good kid," I whispered.

She rolled her eyes.

"So Gran does this every week?" I asked.

"Just in the last month."

A few minutes later, there was a knock on the door. "Hello there, Hazel," Mom said. "Bawb. Jawn."

Who were Bob and John? I peeked down. Holy crap! There were eight or nine people there. For hugs! From my mother!

"How much does she charge?" I whispered.

"Twenty bucks," Poe whispered. She almost smiled.

My mother was about to make almost two hundred dollars giving hugs? Huh. Maybe she was onto something.

"You're all very welcome here," she said. Holy crap, there was Amy, who'd dated Sullivan Fletcher in high school! She needed a hug from my mother? And Mrs. Downs, who had the best example of resting bitch face I'd ever seen. I worried for my mother; Mrs. Downs seemed like the type to bite the head off a baby polar bear and eat it. Mr. Dobbins, the first selectman of Scupper Island for the past twenty years. A widower, if I wasn't mistaken.

A thought occurred to me.

My mother needed a man.

"Does Gran have a special someone?" I whispered to Poe.

"A what?"

"A boyfriend?"

"Oh, Jesus, Nora. No."

"I think we should find her one."

Poe's phone buzzed, and she stood up and went into our room, closing the door. I guess we weren't going to bond over making fun of hug therapy.

I sighed, then turned my attention back downstairs. This was the same spot where Lily and I would spy from on Christmas Eve, waiting for Santa Claus to come. We never did manage to stay awake.

A yearning for my sister squeezed me so hard I couldn't breathe for a second. My skinny little sister of the milky-white skin and big blue eyes, who used to always be so affectionate, always touching me in some way—snuggled at my side or holding my hand or with her arm around my shoulders, her sweet, sleepy smell that made my heart swell with love every time.

Lily. My little flower.

How had we lost that? How had so many years passed without us being close?

My mom started talking, jolting me out of my memories.

"Welp, you're all here for hug therapy, so let's get stahted." Mom's accent thickened. "Amy, sweethaht, ovah heah." I saw slim legs clad in skinny jeans and ballet flats make their way over to my mother's sturdy Naturalizers. I tilted my head down, making my collarbone flare with pain, but I had to see.

Yes. My mother was hugging a human. It was a long

hug, too. "You're a good person," she said. "You're a nice girl."

Actually, Amy had been a raging bitch—Queen of the Cheetos—who'd made my mother's daughter utterly wretched, but hey. Maybe people changed. Probably not, but still.

They were still hugging. Amy was getting more affection in this hug than I'd gotten from my mother in the past twenty years. Was I jealous? You bet your life I was.

"What's her deal?" I whispered to the dog. He didn't know, either.

Mom released her, and Amy sniffled and moved toward the kitchen.

Next up was Mr. Dobbins. "Bawb. You're a good man. You have a good haht." He bent down to hug my sturdy mother, and she hugged him tenderly, firmly.

This was really freaky. Maybe it was the Vicodin. Maybe I should cough up twenty bucks and get a hug, too.

I looked at Boomer, who lowered his head to lick my hand. Nah. Who needed a mother when I had the male version of Nana from *Peter Pan*? Plus, I was pretty sure that somewhere in the mother's handbook, it said your kids shouldn't have to bribe you to get hugged.

My mother moved through the crowd, hugging people and telling them nice things. I pulled my phone out of my pocket and texted Roseline that I was either hallucinating on painkillers, or my mother was offering hugs for twenty dollars apiece in our living room.

Video or it didn't happen, was her answer.

Mr. Dobbins came back for another.

Yep. My mother needed a man. It seemed very clear.

Maybe this was for her sake, too. Alone all these years (Hello, guilt, how've you been?). And since I was here on the island for the summer, I might as well find her someone. Why not, right? Another text to Roseline. Am going to find my mother a boyfriend.

Don't make rash decisions while on powerful narcotics, she responded. Go to bed.

I *was* pretty dizzy. And while I did want to see my mother tuck some people in with blankies on our old couch and chairs, I also knew I was too jealous to watch.

7

THE DAY AFTER hug therapy, I took a little crutch walk, as I'd been doing, a little farther every day. The sun was hard and bright, the oak trees topped with fuzzy, pale green buds, and the salty air filled my lungs and woke parts of my soul I'd forgotten about. Sure, Boston was on the water, but it wasn't like this. Here, the air was both clean and alive with scents, sometimes thick with the promise of rain, sometimes carrying smells of pipe tobacco—presumably from Burke Hollawell, a lobsterman from my childhood (and potential bae for my mother?). Last week, I got a whiff of blueberries—somewhere, a pie was fresh out of the oven. And always, the smell of pine.

I hobbled to a rock at the shore and sat down to catch my breath. Boomer ran up, smiling his doggy grin, and dropped a pinecone at my feet. "Oh, good boy!" I said and threw it. He bounded off, forgot his mission and chased a squirrel into a tree.

I slid out of the backpack straps, took out my water

bottle and drank. Then I dug out a notebook and pen
and started writing to my sister.

Dear Lily,
I hope things are going okay for you. I don't know
if Mom or Poe told you, but I'm back on the island
for a while after I had a little accident. Poe and I
are sharing our old room. You've done an amazing job raising her. She's really great and smart,
and I love talking to her.

Well, that would be a lie. I tore off the sheet, crumpled it up and stuck it in my bag.

Dear Lily,
I'm back on the island for a while, and I want
you to know I'll try to keep an eye out for Poe.
Even though you stopped answering my emails
and texts and letters, I still love you and will try
to help Poe in any way I can.

Too condescending, with that healthy slosh o' bitter-
ness. I crumpled up that one, too.

Dear Lily,
You'll never guess where I'm sitting right now.
Lookout Rock. I'm back on Scupper for a while
and will probably spend a few months here; I took
a leave from the hospital after I got banged up in a
car accident. Home is the same. Mom's bird is trying to kill me. Kind of creepy, the love they share.
    A cormorant just popped up in front of me,
then slipped back under the water. The ocean is

choppy today, making lots of noise against the shore.

Mom and Poe are doing well. I hope you are, too.

Love,

Nora

That one I could send. At least I had an address for her now. Washington State Women's Correctional Facility.

For reasons unknown, my sister had given me up long ago. Granted, I hadn't been a whole lotta fun after Dad left, but neither had she. Why didn't we become even closer after his desertion? God knows I wanted to. But sisters who didn't get along was hardly an original problem. There was the ugly sister/beautiful sister thing, of course. The fat/thin issue. There was the fact that I made it off the island into a better future, and she'd made it off into... well, single motherhood, borderline poverty and now jail.

She did have Poe. From what I'd been able to tell on the few visits I was granted, my sister loved her child.

That night, as Poe and I were lying in our beds, I decided to go for it. It was dark, and the night was cold and clear. Through the skylight, I could see the brilliant smear of the Milky Way.

"Have you talked to your mom recently?" I asked.

Poe didn't answer for a minute. "What's it to you?"

"Just wondering how she is."

"She's fine." Poe rolled over to face the wall.

"If you ever want to talk about it, I'm here, honey."

She muttered something.

"What's that?"

"I don't need to talk to you," she said, enunciating clearly, her voice loud, as if talking to a room full of slightly deaf simpletons. "Though my circumstances are challenging, I am quite well-adjusted."

"That's great," I said. "I'm glad." I took a long, slow breath, still staring at the stars. "Your mom and I were really close once."

"Whatever."

"I loved her more than I loved anyone."

"Hooray for her."

"And I love you, no matter what. I would love to be closer, and I'd—"

"Could you shut up now? I'm trying to sleep."

I reached down to pet Boomer, who slept next to me, since we both couldn't fit on the twin bed. His tail thumped, letting me know I was loved. *God, grant me the serenity to not tell my niece she's a royal pain in the ass.* "Good night, Poe. Sleep well."

THE SECOND WEEKEND after I returned to Scupper Island, my mom asked if I wanted anything in town. It was Saturday, her day to do the grocery shopping.

"Can I come with you? Please? Please?"

"Sure, but only if you calm down." She kissed Tweety on the beak—I suppressed my scream—and went to the bottom of the stairs. "Poe, you need anything?"

"No."

"Text me if you think of anything."

There was no answer.

"Give me a few minutes," I told my mom. "I need to brush my hair." And change and put on makeup. Without a doubt, I'd run into someone I knew.

Half an hour later, I was shiny and clean and ready to go. "Go see Poe," I told my dog. Given time, I knew he'd win her over. He obeyed, galumphing up the stairs, the genius.

I'd graduated to a plain old runner's brace, which made my knee look lumpy but was a vast improvement over the soft cast. My mom was waiting by the front door, puss on her face, arms crossed.

We drove into town, my mom grumbling about the "crowds" that would be at the market, now that it was 10:00 a.m. By *crowds*, she meant four to six people.

We pulled into the store's parking lot. "I think I'll take a hobble around, if that's okay with you," I said.

"Suit yourself."

"Here, let me give you some money for groceries." I took out my wallet.

"Save it."

"I make a good living, Mom. Let me help."

She gave me a dirty look, then threw the car into Park. "I can afford to put food on the table, Nora."

"Well, I'm an extra mouth to feed, and—"

She got out the car and walked off, her canvas bags flapping indignantly.

"Thank you!" I called. She didn't look back.

I would definitely be needing that rental place, fast. Otherwise, there'd be blood everywhere, and soon. I hated to use words like *killing spree*, but between Poe talking on the phone at 3:00 a.m. this morning, then using all the hot water again and my mother's refusal to have a conversation of more than two sentences, I was getting a little homicidal.

I maneuvered myself out of the car. Sammy's Grocery was behind Main Street, the heart of our happening downtown, and it was probably time for me to start walking without the crutch.

And you know... I didn't want to look quite so pathetic. Bad enough that I was still limping.

Slowly and carefully, I wobble-walked up the slight incline. It was the end of April now, and in the years I'd been away, the town had planted crab apple trees along Main Street. They were thinking about blooming—the little pink buds were still clenched, but giving a sweet glow. A restaurant—Stone Cellar—had window boxes of pansies. I peeked inside. Wooden beams, dark floor, nice-looking bar. And looky here—it was open on weekends in the off-season. That was something. Only Red's, the bar frequented by the hard-core drinkers, had been open year-round when I was a kid.

I stopped at the corner. The gray-shingled building here was, conveniently, a real estate office, pictures of houses in the windows.

Time to be independent and all that.

Suddenly, I missed Bobby. I missed him so much it wrapped around me like a lead blanket, heavy, tugging me down. He *had* called the other day, at two-fifteen in the afternoon, and his voice had made my eyes well up. We'd talked gently and sweetly to each other, asking about work, what the other was doing. We'd listened to each other breathe, and it was...nice.

If he was dating Jabrielle, he didn't say so.

Once, I'd imagined marrying Bobby. Before we started dating even, and once we'd started, I couldn't imagine anyone more perfectly suited to me. We had so much fun together! Life had seemed impossibly wonderful.

Then the Big Bad Event happened, but even that showed me how great he was. About three months after the BBE, he'd said, "When we make it official someday," just an offhand remark that had made me so embarrassingly happy I almost floated. I'd told Roseline, who was already engaged, and she'd brought me to the posh bridal salon where she'd bought her gown, and we played dress-up for an hour.

Now I was getting a place of my own, back in the hometown I never wanted to return to.

At least I didn't have to remember our fun times here. Bobby had never been to the island. I'd never let him come. *I* hadn't come, always making the case that Mom should come to Boston, which she did, stoically, without a lot of fuss, never staying more than a day.

The man in the real estate office saw me standing there and opened the door. "Can I help you?" he asked.

"I'm looking to rent a place for a couple of months," I said. *Until Lily comes back. Until I make things right again.*

"Come on in!" he said with such good cheer that I knew he was an island transplant. "I'm Jim Ivansky. We handle lots of rentals here. What brings you to Scupper?"

I filled him in, mentioned Boomer, and he smiled and smiled as Realtors do. "We have some great places. You'll be renting during the summer, so the price will go up after Memorial Day, but I'm sure we can find you something."

The first few houses he showed me were the summer people's McMansions—five-bedroom, six-bath places on the water, complete with boathouses.

"It's just me and my dog," I said. I paused. "Maybe something with two bedrooms, in case my niece wants to stay with me once in a while."

He scanned his listings. "How about this?" he asked, swinging the computer screen around to show me. It was the Krazinskis' place, an unremarkable ranch on

Route 12, the closest house to Mom's. I wondered why their house was vacant. The interior pictures showed a pretty bland, somewhat-careworn place and a kitchen last updated in the 1970s, based on the Harvest Gold appliances.

"Got something with a little more…character?" I asked, feeling guilty. Lizzy Krazinski—or Lizzy Krizzy, as she'd been known—had been a year behind me in school. We'd ridden the school bus together. She'd been okay, Lizzy.

"I know what you mean," Jim said. He scrolled down. It seemed that it was McMansion or meh.

"Oh, hold on, what was that one?" I asked.

"This? It's a houseboat."

"In Maine? Isn't the water a little rough for that?"

"It is, but it's moored in Oberon Cove," Jim said. "Some rich tech goober had it built over at WoodenBoat and then bought most of the Cove to moore it. Built a nice dock, too. To the best of my knowledge, he hasn't even lived here yet. One of those guys who has houses all over the world."

"Think he'd rent it?" I asked.

"It's not for sale; I just have the listing for tax reasons. I'm on the assessment board here in town. But let me give him a call. I think he's in New Zealand on a spirit quest."

"Of course." I smiled. Rich tech goobers did things like that.

Jim punched in a string of numbers, and miraculously, the guy picked up. "Collier, Jim Ivansky from Island Real Estate here. I've got a beautiful young lady here who's absolutely in love with your houseboat." He put his phone on speaker. "You're on with Nora Stuart. Nora, meet Collier Rhodes."

"Hi there!" I said in my Cute Nora voice. "It's such a pleasure to talk to you! Jim's right, I'm madly in love. What an amazing place you've built!"

"Thank you so much!" he said. "So you're looking for shelter and inspiration, is that it?"

Not really, but… "You got it." I told him my story of returning home after an accident, the siren call of the sea, the rugged beauty of Maine. "I wonder if you'd consider renting it to me. It's so lovely, and I'd take excellent care of it. Something about it just spoke to me."

"I hear you. Returning to your roots, taking time to breathe in the cosmic power that saved your life. Absolutely get it. I'd be honored to rent it to you. You know what? You don't even have to pay me."

Jim winced. There went his commission.

"No, no," I said. "I'm more than happy to pay."

"All right. I totally respect that. Okay, then. I'll let Jim work out the details. Namaste, Nora Stuart." He hung up.

"Ah, tech geniuses," I said, and Jim laughed.

Ten minutes later, the houseboat was mine until mid-September, though I planned to go back to Boston in August. But maybe Poe and Lily would like to stay there when Lily got out of jail. In the meantime, it was all mine. It was even furnished. I couldn't wait to see it. Maybe my mom and Poe would like to come with me. Or not.

Boomer, I was sure, would love it.

I went out of the office, keys in hand, and started down the street, feeling rather pleased with myself. No more Tweety giving me the evil eye.

I'd be living alone again. First time since the Big Bad Event.

My heart suddenly went into A-fib, a hummingbird trapped in my chest, buzzing frantically, trying to get out. My mouth was sand, palms sweaty.

I'd be okay. It was fine. I had Boomer now. And it was Scupper Island. A very safe place.

Shit. I couldn't do it. I'd have to stay with my mom. She wouldn't kick me out. I turned to go back in the real estate office, then turned around again.

No. Now or never. No more gray, no more fears. Plus, when Lily came back, she could stay with me.

"Time for a donut," I muttered. I took a deep breath and let it out slowly. Lala's was four shops (or shoppes) down the street. I could use a sugar boost, since my mother didn't believe in dessert, viewing it a moral weakness like her Calvinist ancestors before her. Poor thing. I mean, sure, I was a GI doc and believed in good nutrition, but I also had a beating heart.

There. The thoughts of donuts had helped. I was calmer.

"Let me get the door for you," said an older gentleman, approaching with a newspaper under his arm. Mr. Carver, who did handyman work for the summer people—opening their houses, clearing their lawns, letting them know if a tree fell during the winter.

My dad used to help him out once in a while.

"Hi, Mr. Carver," I said.

"Ah…hello there, young lady."

"Nora Stuart. Bill and Sharon's daughter." I glanced at his left hand. Married, and therefore not a contender for Mom.

"Is that right? Jeezum crow, you got big. Have a good day, now." He smiled and headed off.

Not everyone hated me. That was nice to know. "Hey,

Mr. Carver," I said, gimping out after him. "Do you have a minute?"

"Sure thing." Steam rose from his coffee.

"Um…" It was embarrassing that I had to ask someone I hadn't seen in almost two decades a deeply personal question. "Do you remember my dad, Mr. Carver?"

"Of course. He was a nice fella."

"Did you ever hear from him? After he left the island?" *Because he never bothered getting in touch with me.* My face felt hot.

"Cahn't say that I did, sweethaht." He thought another second or two. "No. I don't think so." His weathered blue eyes were so kind that I had to look away.

"No, I figured it was a long shot. But thank you."

"You're welcome. Nice to see you."

So. The first stone had been overturned and revealed nothing. It wasn't exactly a surprise, but…well.

The humid, sweet air of Lala's was like a much-needed hug.

Standing in line was a mother with three little kids. The older two stood silently, staring down at their phones, their necks curved in that unmistakable posture that said, *Don't bother me, I'm emotionally dead inside.* The littlest kid, about six, blond with a puffy winter coat on, pulled on his mother's hand. "I want a cookie," he said.

"You're not *getting* one. I already *told* you that." She adjusted her purse strap and sighed.

The little boy pushed out his lip, then saw me looking. "What happened to you?" he asked, eyeing my sling.

"I didn't look crossing the street, and I got hit by a

car," I said. "So you make sure you look both ways and always hold a grown-up's hand."

The mom looked back at me.

It was Darby Dennings, sidekick of Amy Beckman, Queen of the Cheetos, receiver of hugs. Amazing how I knew everyone instantly, as if I hadn't been gone for fifteen years.

"Sorry if he's bothering you," Darby said with a smile. Her eyes flicked up and down, assessing my injuries, her gaze lingering on my purse. "That's a great bag," she said. "Mind if I ask where you got it?"

"Oh, um… I think I got it at—"

I'd bought it at a snooty boutique on Newbury Street after I was hired by Boston Gastroenterology Associates. Roseline, who had a serious shopping addiction, believed that every woman needed to own a purse that was way too expensive. We'd made a day of it, both of us still heady with our salaries, and settled on this one, made of buttery brown leather so smooth and supple I wanted to date it.

It had cost an amount that still embarrassed and thrilled me.

"I got it at T.J. Maxx," I said.

"You can get great stuff there," she said. "The one in Portland?"

"Boston."

"Is that where you're from?" There wasn't so much as a flicker of recognition in her eyes.

"Mommy, I want a cookie!"

She ignored the little guy, smiling at me, and I saw myself through her eyes for one deeply satisfying second. Granted, the sling. But still, my hair was shiny from the straightening iron and the high-end products

I used to tame it. Makeup was Chanel. I wore a blue cashmere sweater and Lucky Brand jeans and buttery leather Kate Spade flats.

"I'm from here, actually," I said. "Nora Stuart. How are you, Darby?"

Her jaw dropped, and her face went from pleasant to flushed, her smile fading. "Well, holy crap."

"These are your kids?"

"Yeah. Uh, Matthew, Kaylee and Jordan."

"Hi, kids," I said. "I went to school with your mother."

The children didn't respond or notice or care.

"You lost weight. Christ. I didn't even recognize you." Her eyes narrowed as if I'd played a trick on her.

"Whatcha want there, Darby?" asked Lala.

Then the door opened again, bringing a gust of cold air, and in came a good-looking guy.

Darby glanced at him, too. "Hey, Sully."

Good God. Sullivan Fletcher. Twin brother of Luke Fletcher, god of high school. For a second, I wobbled on my bad knee.

He did a double take when he saw me.

"Nora! Hey. How are you?" He didn't smile, but he didn't scowl, either.

"Hi," I breathed. "Fine, thanks, Sullivan. Um…how are you?"

He looked good, thank God. I never did learn exactly what had happened to him in that car accident senior year…just that he'd had a brain injury. I remember they said he was expected to recover, but you never knew what that truly meant.

But the years had been kind to Sullivan Fletcher. Once, he'd been an ordinary-looking boy, brown hair, brown eyes. Now age had given him character. His face had lost its boyish softness, and his jaw and cheekbones were hard and well-defined. Curling hair, on the shaggy side. He was tall, maybe six-one and rangy and...well, interesting.

And he was *normal*. My adrenaline burst was followed by relief. Those words—*traumatic brain injury*—had haunted me. Every time we'd had a TBI case in residency, I'd thought of Sullivan Fletcher.

But here he was, looking completely healthy and... well...good.

Really, really good. My mouth was dry with relief.

"I heard you were back," he said.

"Yep. I am." So much for witty repartee.

I wondered if Luke had turned out, as well. Once upon a time, I had loved Sullivan Fletcher's twin...right up until I hated him.

"Darby, what do you want? I don't have all day," said Lala.

"A loaf of rye. Jesus. Do I ever get anything else?"

"I want a cookie, Mommy!" said the little guy. The other two had yet to look up from their phones.

Lala put the bread through the slicer, wrapped it and handed it over, taking Darby's money at the same time. "Help you?" she said to me.

"Could I please have a donut?"

"Just one?"

"Yes, please."

"You're in Boston now?" Sullivan asked.

"That's right," I said, nodding. "Here for a little while. Are you getting donuts? I love them. I mean, you know, who doesn't, right? Donuts should be the uni-

versal sign of happiness. We could win wars with donuts. And, hey, no one makes donuts like Lala, right?"

You are a highly trained physician, my brain told
me. *Snap the fuck out of it.*

Sullivan's eyebrows drew together a little.

"What do you do for work?" Darby asked, making
no move to leave.

I dragged my eyes off Sully, trying to regain my
cool. "I'm a doctor."

"A doctor?" she said. "A *real* doctor?"

"Yep. I'm a gastroenterologist."

"What's that?"

"Stomach and digestive track."

"Gross," Darby said.

I usually had a reply for that, some alleged Mark
Twain quote about the joys of pooping, but my mind
was blank. Was Sullivan mad at me? What had happened to Luke? Did he still live here? Should I apologize? Maybe I should just get out of here.

Yes. That one.

"Here you go," Lala said, and I handed over a couple dollars, then hobbled out, my bad leg locked, the
other feeling weak.

Sully held the door for me. "See you around," he said.

"Yes," I said. Another eloquent answer.

Then, before I made more of an ass of myself than
I already had, I stiff-legged it down the street. I kept
my head down, the fear that had splashed at me earlier
now rising like a fast tide.

Luke Fletcher would definitely know I was back now.

8

WHEN IT FINALLY became clear that my father wasn't coming back anytime soon, I did what unhappy girls do all over the earth, and especially in America.

I ate.

That first, joyless summer crept past in inches. A new school year started, and I was hungry all the time. Loneliness for my father was like a sinkhole, and I couldn't find enough food to fill it, despite always taking seconds, always scraping my plate.

Then I started eating in secret, sneaking down to the kitchen at night when my mother was in bed to stuff a leftover meatball in my mouth, chewing the cold, tasteless wad, reaching for another before I even swallowed. I told my mother I could make my own lunches now and added extra slices of American cheese, folding one in quarters, pushing it into my mouth while I slathered the bread with mayonnaise.

At school, I started stealing dessert from the cafeteria, even though I was a brown-bag kid. Pudding or Jell-

O with fake whipped cream on it, the big hard cookies that spattered crumbs everywhere. I'd go through the lunch line, pretending I needed an extra napkin, and subtly grab a little bowl or cookie or Twinkie, then slip off to the gym, which was always empty at lunchtime, and swallow my treat in gulps, tasting only the first bite, shoving the rest in as fast as I could.

I didn't have friends anymore. All those years of rushing home to see what Dad and Lily and I were going to do (because it was better than anything in the world) had left me outside the harsh world of junior high, where cliques were carved in stone, and cafeteria seating was more complex than the British peerage.

At home, I helped myself to seconds of my mother's boring, unvarying dinners. Monday night: chicken, baked potatoes, carrots and peas. Tuesday night: meat loaf, mashed potatoes, green beans. Wednesday night: pork chops, rice, peas again. You get the idea. But I ate and ate and ate.

"You're getting fat," Lily accused. She remained elf thin. Soon, I knew, she'd start to become beautiful. "Stop eating, Nora. It's gross." She pushed back her own untouched dinner, superiority and disgust shining from her blueberry-colored eyes. One of our shared chores was after-supper cleanup. I always volunteered to do it solo. That way, I could eat her meal, too.

"Go do your homework, Lily," our mother said, her eyes on me.

My father wasn't the only one who'd left, it seemed. The day he packed up was the day my sister stopped loving me.

I ate and waited out the year, trying to be as invisible as possible in school that year, counting the weeks till summer, when I prayed Lily and I would recapture the magical times we'd had with Dad. When she would love me again. When I'd once again have a place in the world.

When summer finally arrived, I tried to re-create some of the things we'd done before—draw little maps in the dirt of the secret ancient Mexican cities Dad told us about or make birds' nests that a real bird might want to live in, shinny up the saplings that lined the rocky shore, make forts.

It didn't work.

Lily wanted nothing to do with it. One time, I brought up the subject of our father and put my arm around her to reassure her—I was the big sister, after all. She shrugged it off like my arm burned. "Get over it, Nora," she said bitterly and went back inside.

In a lot of ways, Lily seemed older than I was. She had a sharpness about her, a complexity that I lacked. While I had hidden in sixth grade, Lily started the year off by talking to the prettiest, richest girls in our school without fear, without hesitation, as if she was one of them. And they accepted her.

Everyone knew about our father leaving. In Lily's case, it made her edgy and badass. In my case, it made me a loser.

My solitude continued into the next school year. I worked hard, because homework could fill up hours, because if I was hunched over a math work sheet at our kitchen table, I didn't have to see my younger sister, once so loved, glaring at me. I asked for extra-credit projects so I could spend more time at the library, sitting in the cool, dim stacks, reading, scribbling notes, so I didn't have to go home to the home where my father no longer lived. The one bright spot in my life was straight As every semester.

I worried that our dad called Lily, that he was coming to get her, but he'd leave me with Mom. Every day when I got home, I checked the answering machine. Every day, a zero sat unblinking.

One time, I screwed up my courage when my mother was driving me to the dentist. Somehow, talking in the car was always easier. "Do you think Dad will ever come back?" I asked, looking out my window.

There was a pause, then, "I don't know."

Thus ended our conversation.

So I had homework, I had my secret food (which wasn't that much of a secret really). And then came puberty. Overnight, it seemed, the plagues of Egypt visited my body. I went from a chubby adolescent to someone with breasts and a beer belly, thick thighs that chafed, a butt that was both wide *and* flat. The hair on my legs was as thick as on my head. I had to shave my armpits daily, or the stubble would prick my skin. I had a 'stache. I had bacne. I got warts on my knuckles.

There was no indignity too great. My first period— white pants. My second period left a puddle in my chair in math class. During that special time of the month, I would sweat like I'd just finished the Boston Marathon during a heat wave. I had inexplicable halitosis, despite flossing and brushing three times a day. A new clumsiness happened upon me when I grew boobs, throwing me off balance, causing me to trip and stumble more than anyone else in the world, it seemed.

I started researching witchcraft to see who had done this to me.

And as I had predicted, my sister grew beautiful.

For a while I just existed, watching my sister live without me, even if she did sleep four feet away. My mother went to and from work at the hotel, did the books for her freelance clients in the evenings, made our dinners, packed our lunches. She didn't say anything about my weight gain. If she knew I was wretched, she didn't say anything. Told me I did well on my report card, resting her hand on my shoulder for a second, which made me just about cry.

Every day, I prayed my father would call. Would come back. Would bring happiness back into our lives.

Then came ninth grade, and I fell in love.

It was ridiculous, really. There I was, a "husky" girl in a world of beautiful waifs, wearing my homemade jumpers (because jeans cut into the soft fat around my waist), turtlenecks to cover up as much skin as possible, sturdy shoes and knee socks to mask the fact that the warts had spread to my feet. My hair was a horrible combination of frizzy, wiry, curly *and* straight, and because spitballs were good at hiding in there, I wore it in a ponytail most of the time. I looked like the definition of *spinster*, even at the age of fourteen.

Of course, Luke Fletcher wouldn't notice me.

But love is stupid, isn't it? My brain couldn't stop the free fall of my heart. I knew even the idea was a joke, but my insides leaped and wriggled when he walked by. He'd always been cute—the better-looking, funnier, more athletic Fletcher twin. Sullivan wasn't hideous or anything…just average.

Luke, on the other hand, was breathtaking. My lungs literally stopped working at the sight of him. He had tawny blond hair, green eyes, dimples. A flashing, easy smile, and a laugh that echoed in the chambers of my swollen, empty heart.

He was great at sports, already six feet tall, and had gone from lean to muscled over the summer. He was tan from working outside—his father owned Scupper Island Boatyard, and both boys worked there, and now Luke's skin was golden and perfect, hypnotic. He was on the soccer team, a starter his freshman year.

My crush was horrible, absurd, embarrassing. I wished with all my heart that it would wither and die, but it didn't. It grew. It was a virus.

If God hadn't already blessed Luke enough, he was *smart.* As smart as I was, smarter even, because my grades came from studying and reading, and his came from simply being. He and I were the only two kids from our class to take Algebra II as freshmen. The only two kids who got put into the Honors English class. The only two who got an A+ on our biology midterm.

He was nice, too.

When it suited him, he was nice.

I knew I'd never have a chance with a boy like that. Of course, I didn't. But my stupid, ridiculous heart lived for any notice, any opportunity just the same. Once, I sat next to him in assembly by some miracle and sweat and blushed for the entire hour, drunk with the smell of him—shampoo and sweat. His arm brushed mine, and my whole body clenched with lust.

Twice a week, Mr. Abernathy, the English teacher, *made* us (like it was a sacrifice for me) stay after school to do college-level writing prompts. The math teacher wanted us to compete as a team in the Math Olympiad, and in the two glorious weeks leading up to it, we crammed together at the library, four nights in all.

Sitting with him at the competition, scribbling notes, looking at each other with smiles when our answer was correct… It was magic. We took third in the state. When the principal broadcast our results in the morning announcements, I blushed so hard my face hurt.

"Way to go, Fletcher!" Joey Behring called. "Too bad it had to be with the Troll."

Did I mention my nickname? Yeah. My physical appearance wasn't unnoticed by my peers. Did I have some good features? Who cared at that age?

"She's okay," Luke said, and my face burned hotter from the gallant defense.

Sullivan Fletcher paused at my desk as homeroom let out. "Good job, Nora," he said.

"Thanks," I mumbled.

And so went high school. Study, savor every second my academic achievement let me have with Luke. More than college, more than the urge to do well, his presence was my motivation.

The summer between freshman and sophomore years, I got a summer job at the Scupper Island Clam Shack, which meant I deep-fried a lot of seafood. Ate a lot of seafood, too. Working there was a relief; most of the customers were the summer nuisance, and I tried to be cheerful and sunny and pretend I wasn't fat when I waited on them. I gave my mother my paychecks—money was always tight—and she told me I was a good kid.

Sullivan Fletcher worked at the Clam Shack as well as at his father's boatyard. He was not as blessed athletically as his twin, not particularly brainy, though not dumb, either. He wasn't mean, didn't talk much, and I might've liked him, had he not dated Amy Beckman,

Queen of the beautiful Cheetos, one of Lily's pack. Amy went out of her way to mock me, and Lily pretended not to notice (or didn't mind).

Lily…sharp-tongued, model thin, blue-eyed and graceful, carelessly sexual, an expert at conveying everything with a look. Her grades were in the toilet, but she didn't care. When Mom suggested I tutor her, Lily made a face of such disgust that tears came to my eyes.

Worst of all, we still shared a room. Our little house only had two bedrooms. Every day, Lily would dress in front of me, totally unselfconscious about her body, her ribs striating through her skin, her vertebrae rippling as she pulled on pants. She was tiny and perfect, still so beautiful to me, as she had been when she was little. I tried not to look, but her body fascinated me. What would it be like to bend over and not have a stomach bulge? To not have to wear a bra? To have arms as long and slim as a ballerina's, an ass that was both round and shapely but still fit into size 00 jeans?

At night, I'd cry sometimes, fully embracing my misery like any teenager worth her salty tears. I lacked my mother's ironclad pragmatism, lacked Lily's sense of self-preservation. Instead, I wrapped myself in melancholy, remembering when my sister and I were little, when we were close, when we were happy. I missed my father and hated him and loved him and hated him some more for ruining everything. Tears would slip into my ears as I listened to Lily breathe.

Or listened to her sneak out, slipping open the window, out onto the roof, down onto the lawn, as light and silent and beautiful as a dragonfly.

I missed her so much my bones hurt with it. The fact was, my sister had become a bitch, and it would've

served me well to tell her that and show some gump-
tion, as my mother would say…but that was the gift of
hindsight. As it was, I yearned for her love, the friendship that I had never once questioned before our father
left. "When will you be done in there?" was about the
lengthiest conversation we had in years.

So Luke Fletcher was my heaven and hell. Any excitement in my life came from occasionally being paired
with Luke in school. Every time was a mixed bag—we'd
do a calculus problem on the board, extra credit going
to the person who finished first; me acutely aware that
my arms jiggled as I wrote, that the whole class was
pulling for Luke.

But either way, if he won or I won, he'd smile at me,
and it was everything.

Until senior year, that was.

Twenty years before I started high school, Scupper
Island had produced a super genius named Pedro Perez,
son of a fisherman, who was off-the-charts brilliant. He
went to Tufts, then Harvard, then Oxford, then Stanford,
and before he was thirty, he had three PhDs and had
invented a computer algorithm that tracked consumer
data and changed marketing forevermore. He had sev-
enty-nine patents on all sorts of things, from agricul-
tural tools to advanced rocket engines (and time-travel
machines, if you listened to the rumors). Like any good
billionaire hermit, he owned a ranch in Montana and
moved his family out with him.

But once a year, Dr. Perez came back to Scupper to
show his appreciation to his hometown by sending the
kid with the highest GPA to Tufts. This Scupper Island
slot at the university may or may not have had something to do with the fact that Dr. Perez had given the

school tens of millions of dollars. It might simply have been a testament to our good public schools, funded by the tax dollars of our summer residents. But each year, a Scupper Island kid went off to Medford, Massachusetts and never looked back.

The scholarship covered everything. Tuition, room, board, books, a generous allowance that, rumor had it, covered everything from dorm-room furnishings to eating out. Dr. Perez's only requirement was that the recipient finish college; dropouts would have to repay him.

No one ever dropped out.

Scupper Island was so grateful they renamed a street after him—Maple Street became Perez Avenue, and every year at the start of the second semester, Dr. Perez left Montana, returned to the island and announced the winner. He asked that grades not be posted after December midterms, so the winner could be kept a secret until the first week of January, when the entire school assembled to see who the lucky senior would be.

Most years, it was obvious who'd win, but occasionally, it would be suspenseful.

Going into our senior year, Luke and I were neck and neck. I had a 4.115 GPA, thanks to the weighted grades from my AP classes (an A in those meant a 5.0, not a 4.0).

Luke's GPA was 4.142, because he got A+es in gym... And every year, for that miserable semester, as if changing in the locker room in front of my slender female classmates wasn't punishment enough, I got an A−.

I tried, I was a good sport, cheering on my classmates even if they ignored me. I sweat and ran and played volleyball, diving for balls, trying my best, and I still got an A−. I wondered if that had been deliberate; the gym teacher was also the soccer coach. If Luke went to Tufts, he'd almost certainly play soccer, which would be a feather in Coach's cap.

"An A– is a good grade," Coach said when I meekly approached him freshman year and asked what I had to do to bump that grade up. His eyes scanned me. "For a girl with your physique, I'd say it's a very generous grade. You work hard. You're doing fine." The implication was clear. Only the really fit kids got As.

Luke, of course, was a god.

In the spring of my junior year, my mother sat me down and told me if I wanted to go to college, I'd have to get there myself, a fact I already knew. She didn't want me to get my hopes up that there was money "lying around for that."

If I won the Perez Scholarship, I'd go for *free*. To *Tufts*! The name itself was beautiful, light and sunny, full of promise.

Only 0.027 of a grade point average stood between Luke and me.

And so, shit got serious…at least, for me. Luke and I took the same AP classes. If I could get even half a grade higher than Luke, I could erase my deficit.

He didn't seem concerned. Luke was gifted at English and history; I had to sweat over those subjects to get my grades. But I had an edge in science, and it was a weighted class. AP bio was my chance.

I pictured going to Tufts. I sent away for information, and Luke's mother, who ran the post office, snarled at me when I collected the fat catalog, knowing full well why I wanted it. She ignored me when I thanked her, but I barely cared, inhaling the sharp, rich scent of the catalog before going to the park bench to pore over the pictures and course descriptions.

Oh, the campus! The brick buildings and unnaturally green lawns! I could see myself in one of the dorm rooms, a puffy white comforter on my bed, throw pillows and…and whatever else people brought to college. I'd be in the beautiful city of Boston (well, Medford, but practically Boston). I could see my future self: slim and pretty with better hair, at ease, laughing with friends— friends!—treating them to pizza with Dr. Perez's expense account.

I would get an A+ in AP bio. I didn't think Luke could.

But he pulled a rabbit out of a hat…or a human, more accurately. Xiaowen Liu was a Chinese girl whose family had just moved to Maine from Boston and lived in a big house on the cliff. On the first day of school, Luke asked her to be his lab partner.

"Hey, Nora," he said with a grin. "Guess who got a perfect score on her biology SATs?" He gave Xiaowen a one-armed hug, making her blush. I didn't blame her. I understood. She had an accent; the Cheetos had immediately pretended not to understand her and didn't even try to pronounce her name—*She-ao-wen*, not terribly hard. But they insisted on calling her "Ex-Ee-Oh-whatever," the feral, skinny bitches.

I said hi to Xiaowen on her first day, and she said hi back, but that was it for the "Outsiders Bonding" moment. I lacked the confidence to ask if she wanted to hang out sometime, and besides, her mother chauffeured her to and from school in a new Mercedes. The money thing, you see. I was an islander; she was a rich person from away. She had what I wanted to pull off and failed—quiet confidence.

All three of us got an A+ on the first big bio test. There went my edge in science.

Then came the English class speeches.

Luke knew he'd ace his. I was the Troll, after all; he was Apollo.

Public speaking was my greatest dread—standing in front of my peers, their judgment and disdain enveloping me like a poison gas. I'd have to suck in my stomach. I'd break out in hives on top of acne. I'd sweat. My scalp would ooze oil. Seriously, I was cursed.

But I needed every A+ I could get. We were assigned topics; mine was the failure of the juvenile justice system in Maine. Luke's was on genetic engineering, an unfairly interesting topic.

I worked on that speech for *weeks*. Researched and studied, outlined and organized. I went to the library to watch speeches by MLK and Gandhi and Maya Angelou for body language and rhythm. Practiced in front of a mirror. Filmed myself. Memorized. Tweaked. Memorized again.

Luke gave his speech, and it was an unsurprising success. He was relaxed and confident, friendly and informative. Was it one for the ages? Not really, but if I'd been his teacher, I'd have given him an A. Maybe an A+.

Mr. Abernathy congratulated him fondly and told the class that tomorrow, we'd be treated to mine. Sweat flooded my armpits and back at the mention of my name. There were groans and sighs from the Cheetos.

"Don't worry, Nora," Mr. Abernathy said absently as I left the class. "You'll do fine."

"That's a tough act to follow," I said.

"I'm sure you've worked hard, dear. Try not to worry." Ha.

I *thought* Mr. A liked me. Maybe he was even rooting for me. He was the classic English teacher—rumpled and kind, disorganized and eloquent. His classroom was cheerfully messy, books overflowing from the back bookcase, faded posters of great authors hanging on the walls, a few straggling plants on the windowsill. His desk was covered in papers and books, and the huge dusty blackboard (which was actually green) was crowded with homework assignments he never managed to erase, quotes from literature and abbreviations like GMC for *goal, motivation, conflict*, or KISS for *keep it simple, stupid* and doodles of Walt Whitman and Emily Dickinson. Though I was a science geek, he made me love reading.

"Don't worry," he repeated, sensing my insecurity. "I have every faith in you."

At least someone did. I went home and practiced the speech again and again and again in the cellar, so Lily and Mom wouldn't overhear me. I slept horribly, having nightmares about getting lost, missing my speech, then giving it, only to realize my legs were covered in fur. I couldn't eat that morning (a rarity, let me tell you), and my heart thudded and twisted all morning.

I slid into English and slunk to my desk. "All right, then," Mr. Abernathy said. "Nora, you're up, dear."

I went to the front of the class, and before the sweat could start oozing from every pore, I began.

The class was about to be stunned. So was I.

That saying about practice makes perfect? It worked.

Rather than give statistics (as Luke had), I had chosen a fellow student to use as an example.

"Sullivan Fletcher was convicted of underage drinking and illegal drug use after a devastating car accident in which he was the driver," I began. "Tragically, his twin brother, Luke Fletcher, was also in the car at the time and suffered the complete severing of his penis."

The class burst out in surprised laughter. Except for Luke.

The rest of the speech followed the fictional life of juvenile delinquent Sully Fletcher, his poor-quality education, the violence he would encounter in our woefully underfunded correctional facilities, his difficulties in getting a job, finding a wife, his high odds of divorce and becoming a deadbeat dad. I talked about his struggles with drug use and alcoholism.

I walked between the rows of desks, addressing the students by name. "Picture that, Lonnie. Seven out of ten. What if you were in the bunch? Caroline, you have a little sister. Imagine if she had to visit you in State."

I ended by stopping by Sullivan's desk. "I hope you're never in an accident, big guy," I said fondly, as if I could actually have a conversation with a Fletcher boy, let alone call him by a nickname. Then I turned to his twin. "And, Luke, I hope your parts stay intact." Another big laugh. "But now you all know what to expect once you start down the dark road of a criminal."

Then…shockingly…applause. I think Xiaowen started it.

"Very entertaining, Nora," said Mr. Abernathy. "Well done."

I went back to my seat, my face now burning, the sweat now drenching me, my face so slick with oil that I could write my name in it, but the speech was *over*. I had faked my way through that composed, relaxed, funny persona, and it worked. The minute class was over, I bolted for the bathroom before my bowels melted.

I had to miss my next class, thanks to nervous diarrhea.

The next week, when our speech papers came back, there was a big fat A+ at the top of mine.

I covered my grade with my hand, but Luke saw mine…and I saw his. A−.

He gave me a cool, assessing look. In that moment, it seemed like Luke Fletcher realized that he might not get something he wanted. Something he felt was his due.

Later that day, he hip-checked me in the hall, sending me sprawling, my corduroy jumper riding up over my thick thighs, my books splaying all around me. "Watch where you're going, Troll," he said, his voice the same sneer the Cheetos used, slashing like a razor because it came from his perfect mouth.

He stepped on my notebook and pivoted, tearing the cover.

He had never called me Troll before.

It was November; the semester would be ending in December, just before Christmas. Per Dr. Perez's request, our grades would not be posted from now until the announcement. We had midterms coming up, and based on what I knew, I ran the numbers.

Despite the A− on his presentation, Luke was more than likely going to pull an A, if not an A+, in English. Because of my stupid gym grade, even if I got a perfect score on every test (as I fully intended to do), Luke's GPA would be 0.008 higher than mine. He'd get the scholarship. He'd go to Tufts.

I'd have to go somewhere else. I'd be saddled with debt, have to take on a couple of jobs, try for every merit scholarship there was. It was possible. I could do it.

I'd applied to the colleges like Harvard and Yale

that had huge endowments for kids in my shoes, but I wasn't likely to get in. All their applicants had fabulous grades, too, and grades were the *only* thing I had going for me. I lacked any extracurriculars aside from the Math Olympics, too busy studying. No sports to sweeten the pot, no hours of community service, no trips abroad to dig wells.

I wanted to be a doctor—I loved science, and I could see myself in surgery, saving lives, beloved by my peers, not having to worry about clothes because of scrubs. For that career to come true, I needed great grades from a great college to help me get into med school, which would cost at least another quarter of a million dollars.

It would be a long, long road without the Perez Scholarship.

The Fletcher boys had everything. Two parents who loved them and each other. Their father owned the boatyard, his mother was not only the postmistress of our town but also ran the general store (same building, very cute, a must-visit if you were a tourist). As year-rounders went, they were set. They weren't wealthy but they were solid. I imagined that Luke would be accepted at many colleges, get plenty of merit *and* sports scholarships.

But I *needed* the Perez Scholarship. And it looked like I wasn't going to get it.

One day in early December, as I sat in the cafeteria, not eating (chubby girls didn't eat in public), reading *The Scarlet Letter*, Luke approached me, his sycophants trailing behind him.

"Hey, Troll, guess who called me yesterday?"

Even as he insulted me, I couldn't help the blush of attraction that burned my chest and throat. "I don't know."

"The soccer coach from Tufts. Said he can't wait to have me on the team. Guess the scholarship's mine. Nice try. But you knew it would go to me, didn't you? Deep down inside that fatty heart of yours?"

His fan club laughed. He rapped his knuckles on my table, making me jump, getting another laugh, then left.

Tears stung my eyes, and hatred—for Luke, for high school, for myself—churned in my stomach. There had to be *something* I could do. Something that Luke couldn't. What that was, I had no idea.

Finals were approaching, and both Luke and I knew we had to ace every damn test. Uncharacteristically, he was studying, no doubt to make sure he wouldn't hand me the win. Every day after school, I saw him in the library, once my refuge, and he'd mouth, "Sorry, Troll."

I was doomed.

With two weeks left in the semester, with the January announcement of the Perez Scholarship recipient coming just after break, I was desperate. I pored over my report cards, doing the math again and again. Even if I got an A+ on every exam, if Luke did the same, he'd win.

But there was that matter of the A+ on my speech to his A−. The tiny ray of hope. It was possible that one A− could drop his term grade to an A, and if that happened…well, shit. Even if that happened, he'd still be the tiniest bit ahead.

On the last day of classes before exams, Mr. Abernathy wished us luck, told us to study hard. "Won't make a difference," Luke said as he passed my desk, bumping it with his hip.

I sat there, my face burning, pretending to take a few last notes, waiting for everyone to leave. It didn't take long.

"Everything okay, Nora?" Mr. Abernathy asked, gathering up his own stuff from his cluttered desk.

"Oh, sure," I lied.

"I have a meeting, I'm afraid. Do you mind turning out the lights?"

"Not at all, Mr. A."

He smiled and left, and I sat there for another minute. Told myself I'd done all I could. That the University of Maine would give me a good package. Or maybe I'd go to community college for a couple of years and then transfer somewhere. I told myself that while the road to my adult life would be longer and harder without the scholarship, it was still a road I could travel.

But my heart, that stupid organ, ached. My stomach, that bottomless pit, growled. I'd go home, stuff my face, have a cry and a binge before Lily came back from whatever she did after school.

Tufts had been *so* close. A free ride. The beautiful dorm room. Expenses. The pizzas. The friends.

I got up to turn off the lights.

Then I saw it.

There, on the messy, dusty blackboard filled with quotes from Shakespeare and Frederick Douglass and Sojourner Truth and homework assignments from the last two months, was my chance.

It had been there all along, written in Mr. A's messy scrawl on the very first week of school, on the far left-hand side of the board. Underneath a caricature of Edgar Allan Poe and above a quote from *Heart of Darkness*, was my future.

The words were faded and smudged, but still mostly legible.

ECP: 12 Great Works

ECP stood for *extra-credit project*.

Now I remembered. Mr. Abernathy, his eyes twinkling from beneath his bushy eyebrows, had told us on the first day of the school year, back when the board was still clean, that if anyone had extra time, he or she could do a twenty-five-page essay on any common theme running through twelve great works of literature. In the twenty-nine years Mr. Abernathy had been teaching at Scupper Island High School, no one had ever taken it on, he told us. Not even Dr. Perez. Nevertheless, Mr. A had passed out a list of a hundred suggested titles, all in addition to the ones we already had to read, from Homer's *Odyssey* to *We Were the Mulvaneys* by Joyce Carol Oates. It was due at the end of the semester.

Ten days from now.

Even I hadn't had the time to tackle that project. Not with all my other advanced classes and AP workload.

Twelve books, a twenty-five-page paper during finals. That was freakin' impossible.

My heart began a sickly roll in my chest. Already, I knew I *would* do the project, and I'd get an A, goddamn it. And Luke would *not* do the project.

I wasn't going to let him.

If he hadn't called me Troll…if he hadn't told me the scholarship was his…if he hadn't made me fall that day…if I hadn't once loved him with all the fervor that every fat, ugly, ignored girl has nurtured…

I poked my head out the door. School was over, and the halls were empty. From far away, I heard Mr. Paul, the nice janitor, start to whistle. The sharp smell of disinfectant was barely detectable. He was washing floors over by the gym, then. I was alone.

ECP: 12 Great Works

My heart felt huge and sick, heaving now.

Carefully, I pressed my arm against the already-fuzzy words. Just a little smear—didn't want to be too obvious. I erased the round part of the *P*, subtly added a line to the *C*. I faded out the 1 of the 12… Just a little rub. Smeared the *k*, picked up a stub of chalk and added a squiggle, then topped the whole thing off by tapping the eraser so a shower of chalk dust antiqued my efforts.

Just in case.

I stepped back and took a look. I was pretty sure the extra-credit assignment had been there long enough to be virtually invisible—it had been to me—but if someone looked now, it looked more like *EGI 2 Great Words*.

Just in case.

Was I proud? No. But the hate burned white-hot in my chest, outweighing morality.

It was possible that Luke had already done this project, but I was almost positive he hadn't. He was a braggart, and if he'd whipped off a twenty-five-page paper and read a dozen extra books on top of our already-heavy syllabus, he would've said something.

Also, I imagined Mr. Abernathy would've given me the heads-up that my competitor had done the assignment. A gentle, "Don't forget that extra-credit project, Nora. Luke finished his." He was like that, Mr. A.

But he would *not* be able to give Luke the heads-up, because I was going to hand mine in at the last possible second. It was due the last day of the semester—De-

cember 23, and December 23 was the day Mr. Abernathy was going to get it.

Because I was organized, I still had the list of books
in my English folder. I went to the Scupper Island Library and did something I'd never done before—I stole
six books, stuffing them into my backpack. If I checked
them out, it might get back to Luke. His girlfriend's
mother worked at the library. Everyone wanted Luke to
get the Perez Scholarship. No one was pulling for me.

I didn't know if the project would make a difference,
but I had to try.

For the next ten days, I worked like a fiend. I read
and studied constantly, when I was fixing a snack, eating, sitting on the toilet. I only allowed myself two hours
of consecutive sleep a night, sleeping on the couch,
claiming I was sick and didn't want to give my germs to
Lily. If Lily was home in the afternoon, I slipped down
to the cellar to read those damn books. Truth was, I was
afraid she might rat me out.

I read, I scribbled notes, I studied for exams, I stole
six more books from the library. I read some more.
Wrote. Studied. Read. Wrote. Crammed.

"You okay?" my mother asked. "You look tired."

"Exams," I mumbled. "I'm fine."

She knew something else was going on, but she
didn't press it. She never did. I didn't have time to
wish she were the type of mother to sit down and say,
"What's wrong, honey?" I was on a mission.

By the time my last exam rolled around, I was a
wreck, literally shaking with fatigue. Five minutes before the end of the last day of the term, I handed my
paper in to Mr. Abernathy.

He looked at me in surprise. "My heavens, Nora,"

he said. "I can't believe it. You're the first student ever to complete this."

"And, boy, am I tired," I said. And I leaned against the blackboard and sighed dramatically, smearing what I had done in case Mr. A took a closer look. "Phew."

It was sleeting out, the sky heavy and dark as I walked home. Tears slid out my eyes, and I didn't bother wiping them away. I went straight upstairs, crawled into my bed and slept for seventeen hours straight.

Christmas came. Lily was civil for an hour as we exchanged gifts but didn't stay for dinner. Mom and I ate alone, then watched TV. I slept most of break, watched TV, stayed in my pajamas.

I didn't know how I did on my exams, because the teachers hadn't posted the grades, per Dr. Perez's request. I didn't know how much extra credit I'd get from Mr. Abernathy, or if it would make a difference. All I knew was that I tried, and there was an ugly, hard part of me that hadn't existed before.

Technically, I hadn't cheated. Morally, I knew I had. I told myself I didn't care, that it would be worth it, that Luke Fletcher didn't deserve every single bright and shiny thing in the world.

On January 4, the first day of the new term. Dr. Pedro Perez came to school, and the entire student body and faculty gathered in the gym at nine o'clock sharp. I sat in the back, closest to the door, because if Luke won, I knew I would cry.

Xiaowen sat next to me, and I broke out in an icy sweat.

Xiaowen Liu. Holy crap on a cracker, what about Xiaowen? I didn't even know what her GPA was! Forget my AP classes, forget Luke… What about Xiaowen?

I hadn't even thought about her. It had been Luke and me for three years, and now this transfer student would nab our town's most distinguished honor.

"Hi, Nora," she said.

"Hey," I said, my voice choked.

"Good luck," she said.

"You, too."

Luke walked past with his posse, his arm around Dara, his hand in her back pocket. I looked at my feet, not wanting to see his triumphant, perfect face. I heard the words *lard ass* and a ripple of ugly laughter.

My heart was beating so hard I could barely hear as the principal kissed up to Dr. Perez, thanked him, praised him, all but leg-humped him as the billionaire genius sat in a folding chair next to the podium, looking at the floor, a faint smile on his face.

Finally, *finally*, he stood up. "Hello, kids," he said. "It's my honor to present the Perez Scholarship to the Scupper Island student with the highest GPA. This year's winner, with a GPA of 4.153, is Nora Stuart."

There was a collective gasp. For a second, I didn't know why.

It was because Luke hadn't won.

And neither had Xiaowen.

I had.

There was some applause. Not much, probably just the teachers.

"Nora, come on up here," said the principal, a touch of impatience in her voice. Another Luke fan. She went to every soccer match.

"Congratulations," Xiaowen said. I looked at her, my eyes feeling stretched open too wide. "Go," she added.

On wobbling, watery legs, I went up to where Dr. Perez waited. "Well done," he said, shaking my damp hand.

"Thank you," I breathed. "Thank you, Dr. Perez. I… I… Thank you." Tears streamed down my face, and Dr. Perez chuckled.

If only Daddy could see this.

It had been six and a half years since I had seen him or talked to him, yet that was my first thought.

My eyes found Lily in the crowd. She was staring at me, listening as Janelle Schilling whispered in her ear.

There might've been a trace of a smile on her face.

Suddenly, Luke stood up and strode out of the gym, fury in every step. Dara, his girlfriend, followed, then Tate Ellister, who also played soccer, then the rest of the team. They said nothing. Amy got up and left, too.

"Well, now," the principal said. "Uh, congratulations, Nora. Hard work pays off. You juniors and underclassmen, you listen up, all right? Next year, this could be you."

With that, our assembly was over. "If you need anything, let me know," Dr. Perez said, handing me his card. "Good luck."

A man of few words. "Dr. Perez," I said as he turned away. "You…you've changed my life." I paused. "And it needed changing."

He looked at me for a long second. "Make the most of it." Then he winked, let the principal glad-hand him again and left me trembling, elated…and alone.

My sister made her way up to me. "Congrats," she said. She looked me up and down, but there was some amusement in her eyes. "You look like you're about to pee yourself."

"I feel like it, too," I said. My voice was still weird, legs still shaking.

"So I guess you'll be in Boston next year."

"Yeah." I *would* be. I'd be sitting on that perfect lawn. I'd have friends.

I wouldn't be the Troll. Maybe. In fact, maybe... maybe I could be someone else entirely.

"Gotta run," Lily said.

"Bye," I said belatedly, but she was already halfway across the gym.

A few teachers congratulated me in the hall. In homeroom—Luke was conspicuously absent—our report cards were passed out.

I'd gotten perfect grades in everything except gym, which was the expected A−.

Perfect exam scores.

Mr. Abernathy, who was also our homeroom teacher, handed me my twenty-five-page paper. There were a few notes in the margins, but at the end, he'd written *I'm proud of you, Nora.* And the grade—an A.

"Nora Stuart, please, come to the office," said the school secretary's voice over the PA. "Nora Stuart, to the office, please."

I had a phone call—the admissions officer from Tufts, congratulating me, telling me they looked forward to seeing me at Accepted Students Day and how well all of the Perez Scholars had done. They had no doubt I would do the same.

It was really happening.

At lunch, rather than risk the cafeteria, where supervision was thin, I power walked down to the hotel, where my mother worked. "Mom, I got it!" I said, bursting into her office, sweat trickling down my back, thighs stinging from chafing the whole way there.

"Got what, Nora?" She looked up expectantly from her desk.

My God. She didn't know, because I hadn't told her. This whole semester, and I had never told her I was ranked second in our class.

"The Perez Scholarship. I'm going to Tufts." I started to cry. "They called me. Tufts. I got in, and Dr. Perez is paying for everything."

Her mouth opened, then shut. "Is that right?"

"Yes. I have the highest GPA at my school."

"Oh, Nora!" She got up and gave me an awkward hug. "Good girl. You've always been a hard worker. I'm proud of you." She paused. "Well. You'd best get back to school, hadn't you?"

So that was it for celebration. It didn't matter. I was leaving this hellish little place, just like my father. And maybe, once off island, he'd find me. Okay, that was far-fetched, but anything was possible today.

I walked back to school, hoping this wasn't a dream. I would make the most of it. I'd become a doctor. I'd reinvent myself, lose weight, have fun, maybe even have a boyfriend. I'd sit in the front of every class and raise my hand and not be shy about being smart. I'd introduce myself to my professors on the first day, and—

"Think you're hot shit, huh?"

It was Luke, waiting for me with his gang in front of the school. The cold wind gusted, cutting through my puffy winter coat.

"Hi," I said, my eyes darting around.

"Hi," he mocked in a whiny voice. "Don't say hi to me, fat ass. That scholarship was mine."

"Apparently not." Seemed my confidence had been given a boost.

"You cheated, didn't you? I don't know how, but you cheated."

"I studied, Luke." My cheeks started to burn.

"I studied, Luke," echoed Joey Behring.

"You know what?" Luke said, a snarl twisting his face. "You might have won that scholarship, but you're never gonna be anything other than a troll. You know that, don't you, Nora?"

"Leave her alone," someone said. It was Sullivan.

"Fuck you," Luke said. He came closer to me and poked me in the chest, hard, even through the down. "You're a troll. You're fat, you're ugly, and everyone hates you. Even your sister."

I flinched. Alcohol made his breath sweet and sickly. I tried to go around him, but he wouldn't let me pass.

"You scared? You should be."

"Luke, knock it off." Sully's voice was harder now.

Luke failed to comply. "You better watch out, Nora. Something shitty might happen to you. You might get fucked-up. Bad things happen when guys get pissed off. I think you know what I'm saying, right?"

I did. Rape. Assault.

Worse.

"Luke, get out of here," Sullivan said, coming up to his brother. "She won fair and square. Leave her alone."

"Where the fuck is your loyalty?"

"What's going on here?" Mr. Abernathy, thank God, was coming in from the parking lot. "Get inside, kids."

"Fuck you," Luke said.

"And you're suspended," Mr. A said. "Nora, you okay? Come on, dear."

"Watch yourself, Nora," Luke called. "You never know what could happen."

Mr. Abernathy stopped dead. "I'm attributing this to your deep disappointment over not winning the scholarship, Luke. Threaten her again, and I'll make sure you're arrested."

And then, horribly, Luke began to cry. "She cheated. I don't know how, but she did. You did, Nora. You know it."

Guilt twisted and flailed inside me, but it didn't get past the hardness. I'd *won*. Luke could've done that assignment, and he chose not to. So *fuck* him. Let him cry. I'd cried plenty, and no one cared about that.

Sully went to his brother, put an arm around his shoulders. "Come on," he said. "Let's take the rest of the day off, go over to Portland, okay?" He looked back at us. "Mr. A, could you tell the office?"

"Sure thing, Sullivan."

Sully's eyes stopped on me for a second, and I thought he was going to say something.

He didn't. Mr. Abernathy walked me inside, clucking about the passions of teenagers.

SULLIVAN AND LUKE FLETCHER did go to Portland that afternoon. They stayed at a hotel and Luke used a fake ID to rent a car.

At three in the morning, driving home from an all-night diner, the boys were in a car accident. It was a weird echo of my English class oral presentation, but in this version, the real version, Luke was the driver. He'd also snorted coke and had an alcohol level twice the legal limit. The boys had been doing more than eighty when they went off the road, bounced along the ditch for fifty yards and then hit a tree.

Luke was fine.

Sullivan sustained a head injury. He was in a coma. We were asked to pray for him.

This was all told to us two days after the Perez Scholarship was announced, the second assembly of the week. Amy Beckman wasn't in school. The Cheetos were sobbing. One fainted. The soccer team was crying, as were several teachers.

Sully was well liked.

I thought about how he'd stuck up for me. How he'd taken his brother out of town for me.

I stared at the floor, feeling the hot, sharp hatred of the student body slicing into me like arrows. This was my fault, they thought. Of course, they did. I stole the scholarship.

I sort of had.

Never had I felt so alone. As the assembly ended, someone spit into my hair. A boy kicked my chair. I got an elbow to the head.

Rather than going back to class, I went outside, not even bothering with my coat or backpack. Walked the four miles home in the raw, damp weather, the wind making my ears burn with pain, pushing tears back into my hair.

The second I walked through the door, I picked up the phone and called Tufts. I had enough credits to graduate; would it be okay with them if I started classes this semester?

It was. The Scupper High guidance counselor, who'd ignored me for three and a half years, said she thought it was a good idea when I called her, too. She contacted Dr. Perez, and that was that.

And so, without a lot of fanfare, I left Scupper Island three weeks later, taking the Boston ferry with a suitcase and two boxes of my belongings. My mother and I stopped at a department store and bought supplies—that white comforter, the throw pillows, the whole lot, putting it all on the credit card Perez scholars were given.

In the dorm room, my mom made my bed and said the right things as students came by to say hello. She watched as I hung up a poster of *Casablanca*, which I'd never seen, her arms folded.

"All set, then, Nora?" she asked.

"I guess so." I looked at her, my sturdy mother, the streaks of gray in her hair. Now it would just be her and Lily. For a second, I felt a flash of sadness.

"Well. See you this summer," she said. "Work hard." She kissed me goodbye, a quick peck on the cheek, and I watched from my dorm-room window as she got into her battered car.

But she wouldn't see me that summer, because I didn't go home to Scupper Island. I got a job at a hospital as an orderly and stayed in Boston. At Thanksgiving, a storm kept me from taking the ferry home (and I was grateful). When Christmas rolled around, I came back for only thirty-six hours, claiming I had to finish a lab report, which was true.

The truth was, I was terrified to be back on the island, afraid someone would see me—especially Luke, or Sullivan (who had "more or less recovered," according to my mom). I felt like a thief, sneaking to my mother's house and back to the ferry, and yes, I wore a hat and a coat and a scarf both ways so no one could see my face.

I didn't go back to the island again.

I couldn't make it back for Lily's graduation, because of finals, though she came to Boston the following September and stayed with me for an overnight before getting on a plane to Seattle. At some point over the summer, she'd gotten a colorful sleeve tattoo and had studs through her nose, lip and eyebrow, and she still was double take beautiful.

I made Mom come visit me, feigning my desire for her to see the city, which she hated, citing my heavy course load and my job as a research assistant as reasons not to go to the island. Once or twice a year, Mom would take the ferry and meet me. She always went home before dark.

Lily got pregnant my junior year and had Poe, and Mom and I flew out to see her. I went out again a year later, then two years after that, and called often, usually getting voice mail. I sent presents for the baby, who was beautiful and smiley in the few pictures Lily sent.

But when Poe was about five, Lily changed her phone number and failed to give it to me. She would occasionally answer an email. I'd ask to come visit, and Lily allowed it once or twice more, the last time when Poe was ten. Lily went out with her friends, leaving me with my niece, and didn't come back till the next day.

I got the message. My sister didn't want anything to do with me. Our magical childhood was a memory and no more.

The truth was, I had done what Dr. Perez told me to do—I made the most of my scholarship. In my first semester at school, I became that girl I'd pretended to be during my English class speech—outgoing, wry, friendly. Maybe it was age, maybe it was being off the island, but I shed thirty pounds in six months, joined the crew team (I'd always been strong) and started running along the Mystic River.

I made friends. I bought them pizza. I was kissed for the first time, dated and eventually lost my virginity to a nice guy. My professors loved me. I did well enough to get into med school right after graduation. Ironically, I did the first year of my residency in Portland, three nautical miles from Scupper Island, until Boston City Hospital poached me with a nice fellowship.

I called my mother every other Sunday, asked after Lily and Poe; my sister had stayed in better touch with our mother than with me. Mom was allowed to visit, and every year I gave her a plane ticket for Christmas. Poe and Lily were fine, from what she could tell.

As for me going back to Scupper Island, no. I managed to stay away for fifteen solid years.

Until now.

9

Dear Lily,
It's rained a lot the past few days. I forgot how loud
it is on the roof of our room. The wind was wild,
and a dead pine tree cracked in half. Sounded like
a gun went off. Poe slept right through it. Did I tell
you I have a big dog named Boomer, who sleeps
in our room? Sometimes he puts his nose on Poe's
bed, like he's tucking her in.
Love,
Nora

THE WALL BETWEEN my mother and me was not going to
be scaled, it seemed. I tried to talk to her a few times,
ask her how she was. I wanted to know if she was lonely
or sad or happy or whatever, but any people skills I'd
developed in Boston had no effect on her. She ignored
my questions on the hug therapy sessions, telling me I
should have better things to do than bother her.

As I'd done in college, the only way I could have a

conversation with her was if I pretended she was someone else…someone who wanted to talk to me. The result was that I ended up doing all the talking, and she
would occasionally grunt or nod or say, "What was that,
Nora? I wasn't paying attention."

The night after my first trip into town, I tried to engage both my mother and my niece, as well as ignore
Tweety, who stood next to my mother's plate, staring
hate at me.

"Have you made any friends on the island, Poe?" I
asked, dragging my eyes off the evil yellow bird, taking a bite of dry chicken. *This could be you, Tweety.*

"No."

"I bet everyone thinks you're really cool. You know.
Coming from Seattle and your—" *piercings* "—style."

She didn't answer or make eye contact.

Okay. Moving on to the other Stuart woman at the
table. "Mom, guess who I saw today?"

She shrugged, chewing.

"Darby Dennings, remember her?"

"Ayuh. I see her all the time."

"Right. I also saw Sullivan Fletcher."

Mom nodded. I wondered if she and Poe ate in silence every night, or if, as I suspected, I was their buzz-
kill. After all, they had more of a bond, since they'd
been allowed to stay in touch.

"Yeah," I said. "So, uh…how's Luke Fletcher? How's
he doing?"

My mother glanced at me. "He's all right."

"Does he still live here? On Scupper?"

"Ayuh." I waited for more. More failed to come.

"You'll never be accused of gossiping, Mom."

"That's a good thing, isn't it?"

"Who's Luke Fletcher?" Poe asked.

Wow, a sentence. "He and I went to school together."

"Was he your boyfriend?"

I snorted, inhaling a piece of chicken, choking a little. "No. We were both up for a scholarship, and I got it. He…he was upset."

"My mom told me about that."

"She did?" Lily knew that Luke hated me? Had yelled at me and threatened me?

"She said you went to college and never came back." Her blue eyes were flat with accusation.

I took another bite of the life-sustaining, flavorless food. "Well, your mom went to Seattle and never came back. I did visit you. Do remember the time—"

"Whatever." And that was the end of the conversation.

"So I got a place to rent, ladies," I said, still pretending we were the type to converse. "It's really cute. A houseboat, actually."

"Is that right?" Mom said. "The one down near the boatyard?"

"Uh…yeah. In Oberon Cove." Which was, now that I thought of it, about a half mile from Scupper Island Boatyard, owned by the Fletchers.

"Then you'll see Luke all the time," my mother said, giving a kernel of corn to Tweety. "He lives there."

Shit. The remembered fear of him and his gang of sycophants made my knees tingle. Not in the good way. Tweety gave a squawk, then flew up to the light fixture.

"When do you move out?" Poe asked.

"A few more days, I thought." Boomer's tail thumped on the floor. "There's a second bedroom, Poe, if you want to sleep over. I would love that."

She glanced at me, the patented incredulous disgust widening her blue eyes. "Sure."

"You, too, Mom. We could have a girls' night. Popcorn, movies." After that, we could fly to Mars, which was just as likely.

"Ayuh. Sounds fun." She took a bite of corn, which squeaked on her teeth as she chewed. "By the by," she added, "the clinic here could use a doctor. If you're stayin' awhile, that is."

"Really? Wow, yeah! That'd be great!" Something to do until Lily got out. "Do you know who's in charge?"

She did, of course, and after dinner, she found the number and handed it to me. The clinic was an extension of the Maine Medical Center, where I'd done a brief stint.

When I was a kid, the clinic hadn't existed. Dr. Locke saw everyone from newborns to those dying of old age. The Ames family put up the money for a clinic about ten years ago (something Mom had never mentioned). Dr. Locke had just retired, and the same hospital in Portland where I'd done a year of residency had been supplying newly minted doctors to cover the clinic.

I still had my Maine medical license, just in case my mom ever needed me in an emergency, though she wasn't the type to have emergencies, and certainly not the type to call me if she did. Say a grizzly bear came down from Canada and bit off her arm. Mom would just shoot the bear, sew her arm back on with the thick black thread she used to sew our buttons back on when we were kids, then butcher the bear, make it into chili and use the skin as a rug.

It would be nice, working a little bit. Living alone

again (which I could totally do, no matter what my hummingbird heart kept saying). Being useful.

For the first time since coming back, I felt a little flush of hope.

A FEW DAYS LATER, Poe drove my belongings and me to the houseboat. I still wasn't driving, though I was pretty sure I could. But Poe had her learner's permit and needed the hours behind the wheel. I figured I'd need a car for the summer; I didn't have one, since I was a big fan of public transportation. So I'd asked my mom to come with me to Portland and rented a dark green MINI Cooper for the duration. Poe was duly impressed, and so we could continue our bonding (ha), I suggested she drive.

Bad idea. She hovered on the brake, stomped on the gas, blew through a stop sign, then screeched to a halt in the middle of the intersection, causing my dog to lose his footing on the back seat.

"It's fine. It's good. You're doing great," I lied, practically stomping through the car floor as I pumped the invisible brakes. "Just ease your foot down the—"

We shot off, nearly clipping a tree. She took the ninety-degree turn onto Spruce Brook Road, which was not paved, at thirty miles an hour, dirt and gravel flying. From the back seat, Boomer let out a doggy moan. "Maybe a teeny bit slower," I suggested tightly.

We were both sweaty when we turned onto the little grassy path road that led to Oberon Cove. "That wasn't bad," I lied.

She threw it into Park before it was quite done moving, and we both jerked forward, the seat belts catching. "Perfect," I said.

Poe got out and stomped around to the back of the car and popped the hatchback to get my two suitcases. She might be grumpy, but she had two good arms. Boomer leaped out that way and trotted off to sniff.

I got out, too, easing my weight onto my healing knee. No more crutches for me, just an ice pack at night.

As ever, memories of my father came with the smell of sea and pine. We'd had a little Boston Whaler back then. Once in a while, we'd come to the boatyard for a part or a repair.

Now Luke lived there. I'd have to see him sooner or later. Maybe time had done its work and gentled his anger. I sure as hell hoped so. At least neither he nor Sullivan had been permanently hurt in that accident. Otherwise, I wasn't sure I'd be on Scupper right now.

But I was here, and I wanted to see my new place.

From what I'd learned about Collier Rhodes, he had money to burn, and based on the look of things, it was true. The cost of running electric and water out here must've been staggering just on its own. He'd even had a septic system put in, Jim the Realtor had told me.

There was a small meadow separating the cove from the road, and my parking area, so to speak, was just a turnoff from the dirt road. A path was cut into the long grass, leading me to the water, which was ringed by pine trees and rocks. Small waves murmured against the shore, and the wind shushed through the trees. The dock itself was made of smooth gray wood, and a rope railing swooped gracefully from post to post. Copper footlights lit the way so I wouldn't fall in the drink at night.

And the houseboat itself was…wow. Even more beautiful than in the photos.

It, too, was made of pale wood, a modern-looking structure of angles and strange curves. Oddly enough, it was well suited to Oberon Cove. Oh, man, there was a deck on the top! Sweet! And was that…a satellite dish? God bless Collier Rhodes. I could still watch *My 600-lb Life*.

I caught up with my niece, who was texting someone, and unlocked the door.

"Whoa," she said before she could help herself.

Whoa indeed.

The door opened to a sleek, modern kitchen. Smoked-glass counters and a stainless steel Viking stove. Big fridge, a banquette that curved around a table and would seat six comfortably. There were windows everywhere, and the place was flooded in golden light. The living room had a *fireplace*. On a boat! A couch, a beautiful leather chair, glass coffee table.

"Wow," I said. "It's beautiful."

My niece said nothing, just clomped in and dropped the suitcases. I winced. "Can you maybe bring those into the bedroom, honey?" I asked.

"I don't know where it is," she said.

"Let's find it, then."

It wasn't far—the whole boat was maybe eight hundred square feet. Poe opened a door and went in, putting the suitcases on my bed…a queen bed across from sleek built-in drawers and closet. The bathroom was nicer than the one in Bobby's apartment—this one was tiled with pebbles. There was even a bathtub.

"It's like a really nice hotel," I said, trying to picture myself here.

"I wouldn't know," Poe said.

"Where's your room?" I asked.

"I don't *have* a room here."

"Yes, you do," I said. "I think it's up those stairs."

I was right; there was a second, smaller bedroom there, bigger than the one at Mom's. Another bathroom, a little loft space with a futon mattress and a ladder up to the deck, which had a stunning view of the cove and ocean beyond. Teak furniture with red-and-orange cushions and a bar. I could grow herbs up here, and have pots of flowers. It was the most fabulous place I'd ever lived. Thank you, Collier Rhodes!

I turned to my niece with a smile. "Isn't this great? I really hope you'll stay with me."

"Whatever."

I hesitated. "The truth is, I… I love company. Sometimes I get a little wigged out being on my own. So I mean it, okay? Come see me whenever you want, honey."

"Will you stop calling me that? I have a name, you know."

Just because she shares 25 percent of your DNA doesn't mean you have to put up with this shit, my wiser self advised.

"Hello? Is this your dog?" came a girl's voice.

Poe and I went downstairs, my knee reminding me that it had recently been separated from the appropriate physiology.

At the kitchen door was a girl with brown hair and a sweet smile. "Hi. Sorry to interrupt. There's a big dog out here. He's really friendly. I guess he's yours?"

She was about Poe's age, maybe younger, and she had a sweet, round face. A chubby girl, much like my teenage self.

"Hi," I said. "He's mine, all right. Boomer, say hello."

I smiled at her, and her smile grew—kind of shocking after two weeks with my niece. "I'm Nora. I'm renting this place, and this my niece, Poe."

"We know each other," the girl said. "Hi, Poe."

Poe grunted.

"I'm Audrey." The girl stuck out her hand, and I shook it, smiling.

"Do you guys go to school together?" I asked.

"Yes." Audrey looked at Poe, who was texting. I suppressed a sigh. To the best of my knowledge and observation, Poe didn't have a single friend here. She came home from school the second it ended and never went out on weekends.

"Come on in," I said. "What's your last name?"

"Fletcher."

"Oh," I said. "I went to school with Luke and Sullivan. Any relation?"

"Sullivan's my dad." She smiled again.

Sully had a kid. Wow. And had her young, apparently.

"He and I used to work together at the Clam Shack," I said.

"Really? That's so cool."

"If you like fried food, it definitely was. And I definitely did." I smiled. "Do you guys, uh, live around here?"

"No, we live in town," she said. "But my dad owns the boatyard, so I'm here a lot."

"And how's your uncle?" So smooth, milking the kid for information.

"He's good, I guess."

"I'd offer you something to drink, but I don't have anything yet. Do you want some water?"

"Oh, no, that's okay! I just wanted to say hi and make sure this great dog had a person. I love dogs."

"Poe, did you hear that? She loves dogs, just like you."

"I hate dogs."

"Except Boomer, of course," I said. On cue, Boomer pushed his nose against her hip.

"Are you gonna stay here, too, Poe?" Audrey asked.

"No. I'm not." Her eyes flickered to me in an unspoken challenge.

"Sometimes she is," I said. "I hope so, anyway. And you can come over anytime, Audrey."

"Thanks," she said, her face lighting up. "This is the coolest place ever, don't you think?"

"I do! I feel so lucky it was for rent."

She smiled again. "Well, it was really nice to meet you. See you at school, Poe."

Poe looked up. "Yeah. See you, Audrey."

I peeked out the door and watched her walk away (and to make sure she didn't fall off the dock and drown). "She's awfully nice."

Nothing from Poe.

"Don't you think so?" I prodded.

"She's fine."

"Maybe you guys could be—"

"Stop. No matchmaking."

"I just think it would be nice if you—"

"Nora. Stop moving your lips."

I felt my eye twitch. "Want to take me to the grocery store, sweetie-pie? I mean Poe?" It occurred to me that I didn't know if my niece had a middle name.

"Do I have a choice?"

"You know, the Sullen but Beautiful Teenager is so

2011. Maybe you could cut me some slack and try not to be such a cliché. I love you, after all. I'm wounded and broken and need help."

"I *said* I'd do it."

Yoga breath, yoga breath. "Thank you. I'll bake brownies when we get back, okay?"

Thus, bribed by the promise of chocolate, my niece and I went to the market to stock up my perfect little kitchen. It was funny, strolling down the small aisles of Sammy's…more people knew Poe than me. Once they said hello to her or nodded—being Sharon Stuart's granddaughter commanded some respect—I caught a couple of them looking at me, recognition dawning, puzzlement coloring their faces. *Nora? Really? That fat little nobody who stole Luke Fletcher's scholarship? The one who put Sully in the hospital?*

Thanks to my psych rotation, I knew all about projection and self-fulfilling prophecies. Ever since the day I left Scupper at eighteen, I'd tried to be someone else.

It was harder back here, where memories never died.

THAT NIGHT, I tried not to let anxiety get the best of me as the sun went down. Boomer was a comfort, sniffing every corner of the houseboat before flopping down in front of the gas fireplace, which I'd turned on. Washed the dishes, which was fun, being in a new place. Read, clicked on the ginormous TV, turned it off again. Then I did a security check, locked the windows—there were so many! Locked the door, then double-checked everything again.

Man, it was *quiet*. At Mom's, there was always the sound of Poe's music, or Mom clicking away on the computer, lost in her spreadsheets. The tapping of the furnace, the place where the floor squeaked in front of the fridge, the hollow sound of the wind in the chimney. Even after fifteen years, I knew those sounds like old friends.

Here, everything was different. The boat moved constantly, a little in every direction, rising with the tide and bigger waves, despite its tight mooring. The water lapped quietly against the hull and rocks of the cove. I caught the distant hum of a boat heading off somewhere… It was lovely, I told myself.

And *quiet*. After the Big Bad Event, I hated that. I'd listened to podcasts every night, afraid to dwell on what had happened. Even lying there with Bobby's arm around me, I needed something to fill my head.

But here, if I did that, I might not hear someone coming.

Boomer would protect me.

Also, I had a pistol. Did I not mention that? Yep. Just in case. And yes, I knew how to use it. It was the first thing I'd unpacked (out of sight of Poe). Just the thought of it, in my night table drawer, made me feel a little bit better.

Pretty soon, I'd have to go to bed. My mouth dried up at the thought.

A knock, and I screamed. Boomer scrambled up, woofing hysterically.

Someone was here. But someone was knocking, so that was… It was probably Mom. Or Poe. Through the window, I could see it was a man, and fear crashed over me, my bladder loosening…but then in the next instant, I saw it was Sullivan Fletcher.

Who was probably not a rapist. Who I'd known all my life. Whose daughter had visited me today.

Heart still flopping and shuddering, I went to the door and opened it. "Hi," I said, my voice squeaking.

"Hey," he said. "My daughter told me you moved in here."

"Yeah. I did. Um…" Should I invite him in? I mean, sure, he had a kid who seemed nice, but a lot of years had passed. Did I really know anything about him anymore? Also, people (maybe himself included) felt like I was responsible for his long hospitalization. Then again, he'd recovered.

We were alone out here. Except for Boomer, no one would hear me if I needed help.

But I was brave and had survived all sorts of creepy, life-threatening shit. I was done being afraid (or so I told myself). New leaf, blah, blah, blah.

"Come on in, Sully," I said.

He did, making the houseboat seem a lot smaller. Boomer, my alleged watchdog, nosed his hand. Sully's mouth tugged, and he scratched my dog's ears, meaning that from that point on, Sullivan Fletcher could've hacked me to pieces with a dull axe and Boomer would watch, wagging his tail, waiting for a belly rub.

"Um, do you want some wine or something? A beer?"

"No, thanks." He glanced at my sling but said nothing. Was he assessing my weakness? My collarbone felt a lot better, but I wasn't up for a fight.

Knock it off, Nora, I told myself. Sullivan had been perfectly pleasant at the bakery last week. I had no reason to be afraid. "Your daughter seems great," I offered.

He smiled, and my fears dissipated by about 50 percent. "She is," he said.

"Do you have other kids?"

"No." He offered nothing more.

"You were pretty young when you had her." *Shit, Nora, none of your business.*

"Ayuh."

He didn't mention who the mother was. I glanced at his left hand. No ring.

"So what brings you here, Sullivan?"

He glanced out the window. "Just wanted to welcome you to the neighborhood, I guess," he said.

"Thank you."

"And give you the heads-up that Luke is staying at the boatyard for the time being."

There was that painful buzz of fear, and my mouth got the best of me. "Yeah. My mom told me. How is he? How's he been doing, I mean? Uh, is he married? Does he have kids, too? Or, I don't know, a dog?"

Sullivan frowned slightly.

"Sorry," I said. "I guess I worry that he still…resents me."

"He does."

Shit.

Boomer lay down at Sully's feet and put his head on his shoe. *Over here, dummy*, I wanted to say. *Mommy needs you. Fight to the death, remember?*

"He never left the island after high school," Sullivan said, rubbing the back of his head—maybe where he'd been injured. He looked out the window. "Well, he did a semester at UMaine, but he flunked out."

I swallowed. "And you, Sully? What happened with you?"

He looked back at me. "Sorry, what did you say?"

"Were you okay? From the accident?"

"Oh. Yeah, more or less."

What did *that* mean? "I was really sorry to hear about…you. Being hurt, I mean," I said.

"It wasn't your fault."

"Kind of felt like it."

He shrugged. "Far as I can remember, my brother was the one who was coked up and driving, not you. Anyway, he heard you're back, and it stirred up some stuff. He'll probably have something ugly to say to you when you run into him."

I stiffened. You know…screw that. I'd had enough ugly things said to me by hostile men. "Well, when you see him, tell him to fuck off for me, will you?"

There. That felt good. That was the brave me. Boomer wagged his tail in approval.

Sullivan gave me a long look. Then the corner of his mouth rose. "Sure thing, Nora," he said. "But he is my brother, and he's sleeping on the couch in the office, so he'll be around."

"Gotcha."

"He's had some drug and alcohol issues, but he's getting clean now."

Oh, fuckety fucking McFuckster. Not bad enough that he still had a chip on his shoulder. He was a drug addict, too. And lived just down the road. "Think he's dangerous?"

"Think I'd let him be near my daughter if I did?"

"I have no idea. I haven't seen you in seventeen years."

"Well, I wouldn't. He's harmless. Pathetic more than dangerous, but he never did like you getting that scholarship."

I nodded. Pathetic, sure. Also, I had a big dog who, despite outward appearances, had been trained to protect me. I also had my Smith & Wesson.

"You have a good night, now," Sully said.

"You, too, Sullivan. Thanks for the warning."

He nodded, turned away to leave, and that's when I saw it.

A hearing aid. The BTE type—behind his left ear, encased in plastic.

"Sully?" I asked before I could stop myself.

He didn't answer. Because he didn't hear me. "Sullivan?" I said more loudly, putting my hand on his arm.

He turned. "Ayuh?"

"You have a hearing aid."

He paused, then nodded.

"How bad is your hearing loss?"

He hesitated a second. "Full loss in the right, losing it in the left."

A loon called, and I instantly wondered if he heard it.

"See you around," he said and then left, closing the door gently behind him.

The second he was gone, I went to my laptop and Googled to confirm what I already knew.

Bilateral hearing loss after traumatic brain injury.

Luke was still mad at me. Big deal (I thought the words with great bravado). More important, Sullivan had been injured to the point where he was partially deaf. If what he said was right—I'd have to consult one of the ENTs I knew at Boston City—he'd be completely deaf eventually. Maybe soon.

While I knew it wasn't technically my fault, I still felt like something that should be scraped off a shoe.

I WOKE UP at 3:15 a.m. Wasn't that the time that Harry Potter had gotten out of bed to sneak into the library in *Harry Potter and the Sorcerer's Stone*? Or was it when the paranormal freak-out started every night in *The Amityville Horror*? Or was it when the twins from the hotel in *The Shining*… Okay, this was not a healthy train of thought.

However, it was not a reassuring time to be awake in a strange place where, just in case a recovering drug addict or rapist or psychopath decided to kill me, no one would hear me screaming.

Why had I taken this houseboat again? What exactly had been wrong with sharing a room with Poe?

Boomer snuggled a little closer, and I stroked his big head. The Dog of Dogs would protect me. Once, a man had approached us on the Boston Common, and Boomer snarled. The first and only time. I had a lot riding on the idea that my dog could sense people's intentions. He liked Sullivan, and Sullivan seemed…well, not harmful.

I picked up my phone and texted Bobby. He'd be on call. Or asleep. Either way, I didn't care. I missed him horribly all of a sudden.

Hey there. Alone in my new place. It's gorgeous. Houseboat, wicked cool. Very quiet here.

A second later, three waving dots appeared. He was awake and answering, thank God. You doing okay?

A little freaked out, I typed.

You're safe, sweetheart. I'm right here at the other end of the line.

Tears of gratitude rushed my eyes. He knew. Of course, he did. There are no lines with cell phones but thanks. ☺

Another message from him popped up. Want to talk a little?

Thx. Anything new at the hospital?

A second later, his message appeared. Had a guy come in carrying his own arm. That was pretty cool.
Me: Did Ortho reattach?
Bobby: No, too much damage. Quite a sight, tho.
Me: I bet.
Him: Everyone misses you.
That was nice. That was good to hear.

Tell them I said hi, Maine is beautiful, I have an extra bedroom and can buy lobster fresh off the boat. Lily gets out August 5, so once I see her, I'll head back to Beantown.

There was a longer pause. Was Jabrielle with him? Were they a couple now? Was she lying in bed next to him, naked and irritable that his ex-girlfriend was disturbing her sleep?
Him: It'll be good to see you when you bring Boomer here.
My heart tugged with sadness and love. We'd had a good thing, Bobby and I. A second later, another text from him. How are your injuries?
Me: Much better. Looks like I'll be filling in at the clinic here. Getting itchy to work again.
A pause, then: That's great, hon.
Hon.
It was time to get out of this conversation before I said something I'd regret.

Thanks for talking, Bobby. I'm gonna make a sandwich
and watch *Naked and Afraid*.

We used to watch that together.

Him: LOL. Sleep tight.

I didn't have any intention of getting out of bed. That
would be too scary.

Instead, I lay there, petting Boomer and wondering if
Bobby and I would be married and expecting our first-
born if the Big Bad Event had never happened.

10

THERE'S A TIME in life when you rewrite your past. First, your teenage years. Just watch a reality-TV show. All those aspiring singers or models or designers or cupcake chefs talk about their tragic childhoods, their sacrifices and struggles. It makes for better TV if you talk about your "homeless" period, rather than the truth. "I was so mad at my mother, I slept over at my friend's house that weekend."

I rewrote my past, too, starting with the minute I walked into my dorm that cold January day. But I did the opposite. I *didn't* want to be known for all the misery I'd been through. I wanted to be seen as the happiest person around.

And I was. God, I was.

With happiness came the end of my stress breakouts, my greasy hair, my nervous sweating. Because I wasn't miserable anymore, I only ate when I was hungry, and my extra forty pounds slipped away. I went to the ridiculously posh athletic center, started running along the Mystic River, took yoga classes, swam, joined crew my sophomore year. In class, I spoke up and found that I was funny. I listened and found that I was a sought-after friend.

No one saw me as stealing a scholarship from the town's golden boy; instead, my peers were filled with admiration that I was this year's Perez Scholar, awe-struck that I'd met him. And because of his generosity, I was able to buy clothes for my changing body, go out for pizza with the gang, take an interim trip to London. The scholarship provided *ten grand* a year in expenses. Because of this, I was practically a rich kid.

I started separating my old self from this new person. My island self from my Perez self.

When I did talk about some of the realities of my life, I stuck to the basic facts and was told I was so well-adjusted, so mature. When I described my childhood home, I said, "It's a beautiful island. And *very* small." I'd laugh ruefully—*it was good to leave that provincial burg behind, let me tell you!*

But I never said anything negative about Scupper Island. I had a little islander pride, at least. And Scupper was still the place of midnight bike rides down Eastman Hill, of tidal caves and pine trees that seemed to whisper secrets.

I referred to Lily as my bohemian sister and not as the sister who was probably dealing drugs, possibly doing them herself. After Poe came into the world, I framed a picture of her and told the truth: I wished I could see my niece more. My mother…well. "She's a classic Mainah," I'd say. "She can fix a boat engine, chop her own wood and shoot a squirrel to fry up for dinner. She's amazing."

I didn't mention that my mother and I hadn't had a meaningful conversation in a decade. That she seemed neither proud nor impressed by me. On Parents Weekend, I acted like a tour guide, chatting about the buildings on campus, the programs they had, the food, my roommate. My mother nodded here and there, said little and left Saturday afternoon, saying she had work to do. Most other parents stayed till Sunday.

I aced the MCATs and got into Tufts School of Medicine, and those years rushed past in a blur. The workload was inhuman, the information endless, and half the time (more than half), I had no idea if I was parroting facts or actually learning. Some nights, I'd wake up from a sketchy sleep, terrified that it was all a mistake, that I'd be outed as an imposter, that I'd be kicked out of med school, denied a residency. I had nightmares that I killed patients, that I was elbow-deep in someone's abdomen before remembering I hadn't taken any math classes, that I was hiding in the hospital so the chief resident couldn't fire me. That he did fire me, and I had to go back to Scupper.

But I held my own. When it came time to declare a specialty, and my peers were positioning themselves for the hardest fields—cardiology, oncology, surgery—I chose internal medicine with an eye toward gastroenterology.

It wasn't as competitive. Most people didn't die. If I made a mistake, chances were high it could be fixed. Despite having come so far, I still felt a little bit like an imposter.

My mother came to graduation. "So you're a doctor now. Imagine that." She smiled. Dr. Perez also came, hugged me and told me he was proud of me, then went off to donate another building.

Fast-forward through my residency, which was nothing like *Grey's Anatomy*, shockingly—no plastic surgeons performing brain surgery, no bombs going off in the hospital. I got a fellowship in my field, and a year later was hired by Boston Gastroenterology Associates, one of the best groups in the state.

I rented a small apartment in a newly constructed building and didn't have a roommate for the first time in my life. I could afford *furniture*...nice stuff, too. My house looked like a model home—the open floor plan with a small but perfect kitchen, a bedroom with windows on two walls. I kept it immaculate, overcome with the thrill of living on my own, being able to afford a painting, a pale green couch, plush white towels. I bought martini glasses with thin, elegant stems, modernistic lamps and a fluffy white rug. I made friends with Tyrese, the security guard, and the Ambersons, the family with two kids in 3F. Avi, who owned the sweet little grocery store two blocks down, knew how I took my coffee and called me Doc. I belonged here.

Heady stuff.

I'd made it off the island, through one of the most competitive colleges in the world, through med school, residency, my fellowship. I was no longer fat, my skin had cleared up, I bought stylish clothes. I was even reasonably attractive. I loved working in a hospital, those little cities rich with drama of every kind. The whole *Lion King* circle of life took place on our floors, and we doctors were at the heart of it all.

The imposter feeling faded. Nora the Troll, Nora whose father had left without even saying goodbye, the ugly sister, the boring sister, the girl who stole Luke Fletcher's scholarship and put his twin in the hospital... She was a creature of the past. Now I woke up every day in my adorable apartment and couldn't wait to get to work, figure out what was ailing my patients, do rounds in the hospital. I was a good doctor, if still new, and the partners in the practice liked me. I got great patient reviews. Some of my Tufts classmates were at Boston City as well, and we'd go out for dinner or drinks, to parties, to the Common or Back Bay.

I dated, went away with my girlfriends, spent the occasional weekend happily alone, reading, cooking, going for a run, ambling through Boston. I was so happy.

Enter Bobby Byrne.

I'd seen him—he was hard to miss. In the immortal words of Derek Zoolander, he was really, really, really ridiculously good-looking. Six-two; muscular build; thick, curly dark hair; aquamarine eyes that are usually only seen after Photoshopping. He was the best-looking guy I'd seen in real life. More beautiful than Luke Fletcher, even.

Once, he would've been so ridiculously out of my league, I would've lowered my eyes to the ground as he passed. Not anymore. Now we were equals. I was thirty-two, secure with my abilities, comfortable in my own skin, someone who enjoyed her own company and loved her friends, too.

Bobby was the head of the ER, a young person's job fit for adrenaline junkies and doctors who didn't love patient interaction. Fix 'Em Up and Ship 'Em Out was the ER's motto, and no one embraced it more than Bobby. Once in a while, I'd be called to the ER for a rectal bleed (usually just hemorrhoids, but everyone always thought they were dying, so it was kind of nice to be able to reassure them). I'd see Bobby, he'd smile at me.

There was a group of us at the hospital who were unmarried; we called ourselves Doctors Without Spouses, and we'd go to Fenway once in a while, or to Durgin Park to get Indian pudding. For the first six months we knew each other, Bobby was dating Mia, a social worker at the hospital. She was quite pretty, if way too thin, and perpetually unhappy. Once in a while, she'd come out with Doctors Without Spouses. Our group clearly irritated her; she wasn't a doctor, kind of missing the joke—the group wasn't just doctors, but somehow, Mia had never heard of Doctors Without Borders, and every time she came, the name of our group had to be explained to her. But more, she was irritated because she clearly would've *loved* to be Bobby's spouse.

She was whiny, constantly drawing attention to herself by being visibly wretched. She didn't like the rest of us, answered questions with one word, sat with a puss on her face. Every time she came with us, she'd have a whisper fight with Bobby and, most of the time, leave, not very surreptitiously wiping away tears. It was all very drama queeny, and I hated it for him…and for me.

She *never* ate, and being a GI doc, I would wince as she asked for water with a slice of lemon, no food. Her fingers were swollen (laxative abuse), her arms dangling like sticks from her shoulders. Because of the habitual vomiting I suspected, her cheeks were puffy, her lips cracked and chapped, and her teeth looked translucent from enamel loss.

I wanted to help her—and like her—but it was hard.

She was obviously troubled and wanted everyone to know it.

One day, I saw her in the hallway, looking harried and on the verge of tears, which was her resting expression. "Mia, got a second?" I asked. We went into an empty waiting room.

"What do you want?" she asked. Not terribly polite.

"Well, to be honest, I'm a little worried about you."

"Why?" she snapped. "Because you want to date my boyfriend?"

I let that sit a beat. "You're very thin, Mia."

"I'm naturally slender." She looked at my size 10 body with clear disdain.

"You have all the signs of an eating disorder. I'm a GI doc. I can tell."

She rolled her eyes in disgust. "I'm fine."

"If you want help, I'm here, okay? I can recommend a bunch of programs and—"

"It's none of your business, Nora." She stomped out, the wounded doe on her toothpick legs. Anorexia was such a horror, the warped sense of self, the bizarre pleasure the person got from self-damage. If she didn't change her ways, she'd face a lifetime of poor health. A short lifetime. I asked Roseline about her, and my friend said everyone had reached out to her, and that she was Bobby's current damsel in distress.

I mulled that over, let me assure you.

I thought about Bobby too much, sitting on my tiny balcony, nursing a glass of wine and looking over at the Zakim Bridge, that architectural stunner. I liked Bobby, but I wasn't about to flirt with a guy in a relationship.

One night, when Doctors Without Spouses was going out (minus Mia), Bobby and I walked side by side. In a low voice, I asked him if he had any concerns about Mia's health.

"You mean her anorexia?" he asked.

"Well…yes."

He sighed. "I'm trying to help, but she's pretty happy being miserable."

"Yeah, that comes across."

"It would be so nice to date a normal person," he said, cutting me a look.

"Who you calling normal?" I asked and he laughed. My stomach tightened with the thrill of it.

Two weeks later, Mia quit the hospital, went back to Minnesota to her parents and enrolled in a treatment program. Bobby texted me with the news. For Mia, I was relieved. For me, I was exhilarated.

Bobby was free, and he wasn't being subtle about his interest.

For the next few months, we kept things at a flirty friendship level—I treated him the same way I treated Dr. Breckenridge, a seventy-something-year-old doctor who was beloved by everyone. But I didn't have the hots for Dr. Breckenridge.

Bobby was fantastic. Funny, smart, snarky. I almost didn't want to start dating, our friendship was such a blast. We went running together along the Charles, saw a great blues singer in an appropriately seedy bar. We grabbed lunch at the hospital cafeteria. We walked the Freedom Trail and got Sam Adams beers afterward.

Then one night as we were walking back from a Doctors Without Spouses pizza outing—the original Regina's in the North End—Bobby took my hand, and it was lovely. Just held my hand, but we knew, and so did everyone else. "How long are you two gonna pretend you're not a thing?" asked Roseline.

"We're not a *thing*," I said. "We're two fascinating, miraculous clusters of cells."

"Throbbing for each other," added Tom from Ortho.

"That, too," Bobby added and everyone laughed. It was a golden moment—the beautiful spring finally here after the long winter, a group of young friends at the start of what would clearly be illustrious careers, love on the horizon. Pizza, just like I'd always imagined back in high school.

Two days later, Bobby kissed me. "You ever gonna sleep with me?" he asked.

"Someday, maybe," I said. "Not today, of course."

I'd had boyfriends before (three…well, two and a half), but I'd never been in love. I was pretty sure that was about to change.

Another month of flirting and kissing and holding hands before we finally went back to my place and proceeded to laugh, undress each other, laugh some more, kiss and finally get it on.

This was it, I thought as we lay there afterward. Fabulous sex, a guy who was funny and popular and smart, and me, who was finally, amazingly, all of those things, too, except for the guy part.

For three months, I had the absolute best time of my life. Life was revving on all cylinders—career, personal, romantic, health. Bobby and I spent at least a few nights a week together, and we laughed and watched old horror movies from the '60s and made love and ate pancakes at 2:00 a.m. and laughed some more.

Bobby was surprisingly thoughtful—surprising to me, because he was brisk and efficient as a doctor,

none of that hand-holding stuff I myself loved doing.
He brought me bubbles one Sunday afternoon, the kind
kids use with the wand, and we sat on my balcony and
we watched the bubbles rise and float. When I sat up all
night in the room of a critical patient who'd had massive
blood loss after a GI bleed, he came up with a dish of
soft-serve ice cream and got me a blanket. One night,
when we were spooning in bed, he said, "If I can't smell
your hair at least once a day for the rest of my life, I
might have to kill myself."

It sounded like a marriage proposal. "Don't kill yourself," I said and squeezed his hand, basking in the glow
of being loved.

At work, I had energy by the bucket load, smiles
for everyone. The urge to burst into song was strong.
When I wasn't with Bobby, I was kind of in love with
myself. One night, as I sat on my balcony, I tried a little
mindfulness, a little *look at you now*. I was a successful
physician who loved her job, lived in a great American
city, had a fabulous apartment with a view. My friends
were wonderful, funny, smart and kind.

And now I had a fantastic boyfriend.

It was a long way from being Scupper Island's most
hated resident. The memory of my last day of high
school made me shiver, but I pushed the thought away.
That was a lifetime ago.

On the street below, a man was walking his dog, a
brown-and-white mutt. The guy looked up, and I waved.
He waved back. "Cute dog," I called, the friendliest person in New England.

"Thanks. Nice view up there?" he called.

"The best," I answered. Yes. Life *was* wonderful.
And then it wasn't.

I left the office one Tuesday, swung by the hospital to check on a couple of patients, popped into the ER and was able to wrangle four minutes of hot kissing in a supply closet with Dr. Byrne. Then I took the T to my neighborhood, came aboveground and stopped at the corner market for some salad fixings, a chat with Avi and a Snickers bar. As I was leaving, a guy held the door for me.

"Thank you!" I said, beams of sunlight practically radiating from my skin, so in love with life was I.

"My pleasure," he answered.

A cloud passed over my sun.

I knew. In that instant, I instinctively *knew* he wasn't a good person. He had on a Red Sox cap, pulled low on his forehead. Wore an oversize jacket. He didn't have any purchases with him, though he was leaving the store.

Nice, Nora, I told myself. *A man holds the door for you, and you think he's a terrorist.*

It turned out, he *was* a terrorist. My own personal terrorist.

Now, I wasn't fresh off the ferry. Granted, I grew up on an island where we didn't even have house keys, because locking up was for the summer people, who had something worth stealing, not for us.

But I'd lived in Boston since I was eighteen. Not once did I have a problem with crime, but I knew how to walk tall, wear my bag diagonally across my body so it couldn't be lifted. I didn't get into elevators with people who gave off a bad vibe. I lived in a building with a guard, the comforting, smiling Tyrese. I always locked my doors. Even the balcony slider, and I lived on the third floor.

I waved to Avi and walked the three blocks home, not too fast, not too slow. Twice, I glanced back, as I'd later tell the police. No one was following me, but I still felt uneasy. I called Bobby; it went to voice mail, but I made it seem as if he'd picked up. "Hey, handsome, how are you? You want to come over later?" He was working second shift, as I well knew, since I'd just been making out with him. "Okay, big guy. See you in a bit." I'd explain it to him later.

I got to my building, grateful for the big and strong Tyrese. I asked about his twin daughters, admired some pictures of them on his phone. Then I got on the elevator, hit 3 and tried to relax. "Stop with your perturbation," my mother used to say when I was nervous, in that strange mix of island dialect where she'd say *ain't* and use an SAT word in the same breath.

My mother wouldn't be afraid. She was never afraid.

Besides, I was home now. I was safe. Maybe the guy *had* been a deviant, but it didn't matter now.

Just in case, I took out my phone and dialed 9-1... and kept my thumb hovering over the 1.

My door didn't look tampered with. I unlocked it, phone still in my hand. The apartment was just as I'd left it—super neat and so pretty, a bouquet of red gerbera daisies on the coffee table, six lemons in a bowl on the counter, just because. The balcony was empty, as it should've been.

It wasn't a huge apartment. The only hiding place would be the bedroom closet or the bathtub with the curtain closed. And I never closed the curtain all the way, because I'd seen the horror movies. I knew about these things. I left it half-open every day, because I liked the pretty pattern of birds and flowers.

I put my groceries down, went into my bedroom and, feeling a bit stupid, looked in the closet. No one. Glanced in the bathroom. No one. The shower curtain was closed halfway, just as I'd left it.

I deleted the 9-1 and set my phone on the bureau, almost laughing at my paranoia. Lowered the shades and figured I'd get into my Gryffindor pajamas (gold-and-red-striped, silk, completely impossible to resist) and watch some TV. Bobby would call later, and we'd laugh like we always did.

But because that creeped-out feeling remained, I decided I'd stay dressed and ask Roseline to hang out. She only lived two blocks away, and I had a nice bottle of fumé blanc in the fridge.

I went into the bathroom to wash up, bending over the sink to splash water on my face.

Something was different.

Run.

It was a command that came from every cell of my body, my lizard brain, that oldest part of the human mind where instinct lives, unfettered by the limbic system of emotion or rationalization. *Run*, it said, telling me my life was at stake, and I obeyed before I fully processed the thought. My brain went into overdrive, the thoughts fast and clear.

I was hyperaware of every muscle in my body—quadriceps femoris, iliopsoas, gluteus maximus pushing forward, deltoids and biceps stretching and contracting in what seemed like the slowest motion—one stride, my foot hitting the carpet, my left arm forward, right arm back, back foot coming forward, leg stretching out in a racer's stride, setting down. I was wearing heels, but my strides were sure and strong, powered by adrenaline.

The shower curtain had been closed all the way.

He was in the bathroom.

I heard the metal rings hiss as he whipped open the shower curtain.

The second stride. I was sprinting and silent. The air seemed to have turned to thick red plasma.

Hurry.

His footsteps were muffled on the hall carpeting. I was in the living room, three strides from the door, and I reached out for the doorknob, hurling myself at it when he tackled me, shoved my face against the floor and sat on my back.

"Hello," he said, and fear unlike anything I'd ever felt flooded me in ice.

I screamed. He punched me on my upturned left cheek, and my scream was cut off, shock and pain and a sense of the surreal blurring my thoughts. I'd never been hit before, and my face throbbed with white pain. I flailed and kicked, accomplishing nothing. Then his weight was gone, and he had me by the ankles, dragging me as I twisted and heaved. There was my shoe. Could I reach my shoe and hit him with it? I reached, but it was too far away.

"No!" I screamed. "Let me go!"

He dragged me down the hall. I grabbed onto the bathroom door frame, but my fingers weren't strong enough to hang on. Down farther, the rug burning my chin, into my bedroom, my pretty bedroom with the soft gray walls, the navy comforter with the pink flowers on it, the red vase, the throw pillows.

I heard myself screaming, again and again and again, with every breath. This was a new building, and the walls were thick so residents wouldn't be bothered with the noise from their neighbors. I tried to fling my body weight away from him, and he lost his grip on one ankle. My leg kicked out, but being facedown, I couldn't see my target, and my foot just flailed in the air. He grabbed it again and twisted my legs so I was abruptly on my back.

"Help!" I screamed, that weakest, saddest word, and he kicked me in the ribs, and Holy Mother, his shoes were still on. Pain blossomed in red, spreading through my whole torso. I couldn't breathe—little squeaks jerked in and out of me.

One part of my brain gave calm instructions; another whimpered in terror. *You're okay, you're still here.*

Oh, Jesus, Jesus, help me.

The wind is knocked out of you. You're okay. Maybe a broken rib.

Please, please, please. What do I— What do I do?

You're going into shock. Stay calm. Stay calm.

The man looked down at me, huge as he towered over me.

He was going to rape me. Kill me, maybe, and the terror won. My brain went white and silent. All I could see was him and how he was going to ruin me.

He looked down at me, a face so ironically banal and forgettable. Voldemort, Harry Potter's nemesis with his evil face and missing nose—at least you could remember that guy.

In the past when I'd considered this situation—because every woman does, every woman sees herself both raped and murdered and also kicking the living shit out of her attacker—I imagined being that fast-thinking warrior who punched in the throat, kneed in the balls, knocked him out cold, the *asshole* who had *dared* to try to violate me, and I'd add another kick for good measure. I'd be triumphant, a hero, a role model for women everywhere.

But now that it was happening, all I wanted was not to die.

My mother would fight. She would win. Lily would, too. No one would dare hurt Lily.

My lungs suddenly worked again, and I sucked in a deep breath, rolled away from him, scrambled to my feet and swung, fist clenched, as hard as I could, catching his head. My fist went instantly numb.

It wasn't a good hit. He punched me back, calmly almost, full fist, square in the face, and my head snapped back, my eyes streaming tears, my nose filling with blood. I fell, tried to kick him, and he leaned over and yanked my hair, wrenching my neck.

I screamed, louder this time, but it was April, and April in Boston can be as cold as winter. The apartment's windows were new and snug and shut tight against the cold snap that was supposed to end tomorrow, it was supposed to be in the sixties tomorrow, typical New England. The walls were made from brick. Bobby had made a joke about it two nights ago after some very athletic sex. "Good thing the neighbors can't hear," he had said afterward, hugging me close.

I had closed the blinds not ten minutes ago. No one would see me being assaulted. No one would see a woman struggling not to be killed. I thought of the Common, so beautiful in the spring, the statue of Paul Revere, the tulips. Of the little brick restaurant where Bobby and I had dinner the other night. Of how it still felt, walking into the hospital in my white coat.

Tonight I was going to die.

Concentrate, Nora. Stay alive. Stay here.

It was my mother's voice.

The man pulled me to my feet by my hair. "I don't want to hurt you," he said, and I almost laughed, because my face was swelling already. I tried to punch him again, in the throat this time, but my head was woozy, and he caught my fist and slapped my burning, aching cheek. I screamed again—no, I whimpered, and the weak sound broke my own heart.

I wasn't going to win, be triumphant, have the cops tell me I was amazing. No one would know how hard I tried.

Try, anyway.

The man, whose name I would never learn, just watched me. I punched once more, arms weak, hitting him on the side of the neck rather than the Adam's apple, because my arm flopped a little at the last second. He slapped me on the side of the head, making my ear ring and my head loll.

"Just do what I say. If you do, I'll leave. If you fight, I'll kill you."

I imagined that he'd kill me anyway, but maybe something miraculous would happen, maybe the Ambersons in 3F would need me to watch Chanelle, the baby, and they'd knock on the door. Maybe I could buy some time.

"What's your name?" he asked.

"Nora," I whispered. I shouldn't have said that. I should've made something up.

"Take off your clothes, Nora."

With hands that shook uncontrollably, I unbuttoned my shirt. Unzipped my skirt and stepped out of it as tears slid off my chin. Off with the bra. *Don't think about it, don't think about being naked.* Off with the panties.

"Get on the bed. On your back."

I obeyed, legs shaking, teeth chattering. "You don't have to do this," I said. "Please. Don't do this. You're not a bad person."

He unzipped his jeans and stuck his hand inside, locking eyes with me.

I started to pray. *Please, let me live. Please, let me live.*

The man started pacing, fondling himself, muttering about what he was going to do to me. He ordered me to tell him I wanted him to hurt me, to rape me, to do all sorts of obscene, unspeakable things.

I said the words.

Apparently, they weren't enough. He couldn't get it up.

A tiny seed of hope poked through the black tar of my fear.

"Maybe we should take a break," I said, and he backhanded me so hard my head slammed to the left. Shock protected me for all of a second, and then my whole face was on fire. I tasted blood, and one of my teeth was loose, maybe.

He shoved his hand back in his pants, muttering horrible words, calling me names. Whore. Slut. Worse.

Think, I commanded. *Think of something.* I should throw up, but lunch was so long ago, my food was way down in my intestinal track, probably in the descending colon by now. Could I pee? Make him disgusted? I tried. Nothing came.

Think.

Bobby and I had watched *The Martian* last weekend,

cuddled up on the couch. What about that, right? Matt Damon, adorable son of Boston, had been stranded on Mars all alone. *He* wasn't terrified all the time, though he had very good reason to be.

I don't think Matt Damon is going to help here, said the calm part of my brain. *Also, that's a work of fiction.*

So not helpful, unless I was trying to make water from hydrazine.

My terrorist kept pacing. He punched himself in the head, and for some reason, that scared me more than the hand in the pants.

I found myself going numb. The pain throbbed, but it was more distant now. There was too much. I was sinking into the mattress. I wanted to go to sleep. It was possible I had a concussion.

Here's the thing about abject terror—you can't stay there. Well, maybe you can. If you're a mother, for example, and your child is the one at risk. And yes, I was abjectly terrified. There was an intruder in my house, and he had beaten me and was trying to maintain an erection long enough to rape me and possibly kill me afterward, and believe me, that was as terrifying as it gets. But here I was, wondering why Matt Damon was so damn appealing.

This morning seemed so long ago. A different life when I had gotten dressed, back when I cared about looking the part of a successful doctor. I loved that white blouse. It was a silk-cotton blend. If blood got on it, would it come out?

Think, Nora. Focus.

I tried to map the man's face. He looked like any ordinary white Bostonian male—not that tall, not that fit, scrawny but with a beer belly, pasty complexion, a few pimples, crooked bottom teeth. Brown hair. Blue eyes.

He looked so *normal.*

"Stop staring!" he said, coming at me with his fist. I curled into the fetal position, to protect myself, but he pounded me on the ribs, and it hurt, God, it hurt, the pain reverberating everywhere, a fierce, fiery throb.

"Roll on your back and open your legs," he said.

Terror surged again, chaotic and churning, and my mind emptied. Again, I obeyed. There was a cobweb in the corner where the wall met the ceiling. I'd clean the apartment this weekend, with the stepladder, really get every nook and cranny.

Or not. I might be a murder case by then.

I glanced at him. He still didn't have an erection, and when he saw that I was looking, he lunged at me, making me flinch, then laughed, a mean, thin sound.

What could I use for a weapon? The red vase from Home Goods? If I smashed that over his head, would it be enough? Could I cut his throat with a shard of broken glass?

Where was my phone? Why had I put it down? I could've pressed that last 1. I *knew* something was wrong, why hadn't I listened to myself? I could've made the call, then thrown it and screamed, and the police could track my number (I thought so, anyway) and they'd come, breaking down the door, and I'd be safe.

His hand was jerking rapidly in his pants.

Think, Nora. Think. Be as smart as Matt Damon. He'd find a way.

"I just have one question," I said. Maybe I could buy some time. My words were slurred, which concerned me. "How did you get in?"

He actually brightened, proud of himself.

He had been planning this, he said. He saw me at the corner market about a month ago. He'd followed me home, trailing well behind, just trying to see where I lived.

Took to walking his dog on my street to learn my schedule, figure out when my boyfriend came over. Saw me on my balcony one night.

He was the man I'd waved to. From three floors above, I hadn't been able to see his face clearly.

He'd been waiting to see me again. Tonight, after he'd held the door for me at the market, he'd run around the block, racing to get home before I did. The apartment below mine was empty. He climbed the magnolia tree, jumped onto the balcony, climbed up onto mine and picked the lock. It was amazing what you could learn on YouTube, he said. He had lain down in the tub, so I wouldn't see him at first glance.

He said he'd just gotten in place when I came in.

If I hadn't stopped to talk to Tyrese, I might've seen him coming in the slider and could've run. Instead, I'd wanted to talk to Tyrese because I hadn't felt safe.

Irony could be such a coldhearted bitch sometimes.

I'd *waved*. I'd waved to my would-be rapist as he was stalking me. Such a nice person, that Nora Stuart.

I looked at the clock. An hour had passed…maybe a little more.

He still didn't have an erection.

Lizard Brain popped in with a new word for me. *Worse.*

"Do you want a drink of water, Nora?" Voldemort asked, and while this night had been completely surreal, that was the strangest moment of all, maybe.

"Yes, please," I said.

"Stay here. Don't move. I'll get you some water, and then I'll leave if you promise not to call the police. Okay?"

"Okay." *Sure, mister. No worries.*

"Stay here," he said again, turning away.

Now, said Lizard Brain. *Go.*

I was off the bed before he even left the room. He didn't notice.

My ribs screamed in pain, and blood flowed from my nose. My left eye was swollen closed, but I followed him down the hall, just a few feet behind him. I could *smell* him, his sweat, his disgusting musk.

He stopped. I stopped, too, just three or four feet behind him, and fear seemed to gather in me and lift me off my feet. I didn't even breathe. Every molecule in my body was focused on him. I could feel my heart beating. Otherwise, not a move.

He started moving again, into the living room, around the pale green couch into the kitchen. I moved silently toward the door, not taking my eyes off him.

He went straight to the end of the counter, because that's where the knife block was, right out in the open, one of my joyful purchases—a Wusthof knife set from Williams-Sonoma. Knives for all occasions—paring, peeling, chopping, slicing. Murdering.

He reached out and his hand closed on the biggest knife handle in the block.

He would kill me.

I saw this out of the corner of my eye, because I was almost there, almost out, so close.

Then my hand felt the cold metal of the doorknob, and I snapped the dead bolt open.

Get out. Go. Go. Go.

Then I *was* out, running down the hall, and I was screaming, my voice unrecognizable, hoarse, hysterical, but spot-on in message.

"Call 911! Call 911! Call 911!"

Jim Amberson, the dad in 3F, opened the door and saw me.

"Help me!" I screamed, staggering toward him.

"Jesus!" he said. "Get in here!"

He slammed the door behind us, threw the dead bolt, yelled for his wife. The kids came running, then halted at the sight of me, bruised, naked, bleeding, swollen. Chanelle started to cry.

My legs gave out, my bladder, too, and I sat in a puddle of urine, my back to their locked door. "Nine-one-one," I sobbed. "Call 911. Call 911."

I WAS TAKEN to the hospital, x-rayed, coddled, given the five-star treatment by my peers. The director of medicine of Boston City came down to see himself, and his eyes filled with tears as he took my bruised hand. My face and chest were x-rayed; I had a cracked rib and a bone contusion on my jaw. My left eye was swollen shut, my face...

Well. We've all seen pictures of women who've been beaten. I also had bruises on my legs, ankles and ribs. No damage to internal organs.

The police told me I was smart and brave and lucky. I told them to check the security video at Avi's grocery store. They took pictures of my injuries and asked repeatedly if I'd been raped. Sent in a female officer to ask the same thing, then a rape-crisis counselor. When they were assured I hadn't been, a sketch artist came in.

So did a social worker to talk about PTSD and shock. I was given a sedative; my teeth wouldn't stop chattering, which made my jaw ache horribly.

"I'll call your mom," Bobby said. He hadn't left my side since I was admitted.

"No."

"She should know, Nora."

"No. It's over. Don't call her."

"You sure?"

"She's not that type of mother. She'll be… Just don't."

Besides, I just wanted to sleep. My mother… There was always that hint of blame or…or something. I was too tired to think about it.

I looked at Bobby. I remembered him wondering aloud what it would be like to date a normal person. And we'd been *so* normal, so happy, so fun…and now look at me. My face was turning all sorts of colors, and I'd just almost been killed. So much for sunshine and bluebirds. "Let's put things on hold," I whispered, squeezing his hand, causing pain to flash in my knuckles from the punch I'd managed to land. "This isn't what you signed up for."

"I'm not going anywhere," he said, his voice fierce and shaking a little. "I'm staying right here. I love you, Nora."

All my friends and colleagues visited the next day, and my room filled with flowers, and Bobby stayed with me. I was in the hospital for two nights, which was more professional courtesy than because I needed to.

It was all over the news—Young Doctor Foils Home Invasion, Survives Rape and Murder Attempt. Suspect At Large. I didn't let them release my name, because I didn't want to be known as *that poor thing*. Bad enough that all my colleagues knew.

The police never did catch him. Apparently, he left the way he came, out my balcony. They canvassed the neighborhood, but he was never found.

I couldn't go back to the apartment.

"You're moving in with me," Bobby said. "Don't even argue about it. It was a matter of time, anyway." I was grateful. I was so, so grateful.

Tyrese, who'd wept at the sight of my face when the ambulance came, oversaw the movers. All my stuff was put in storage.

I had nightmares and awoke drenched in sweat and gabbling with fear. I was afraid to go anywhere alone. Bobby took two weeks off—unprecedented in his career—and was absolutely, utterly wonderful. He let me talk about it. He understood when I didn't want to talk about it. He told me stories from his childhood, and I clung to the love I had for him, trying to let it wash over the ugliness, the fear, the obscenity.

I waited for the bruises to fade and got back to work. Pretended that I'd been brave, that I'd dodged a bullet and was grateful and fine.

I wasn't.

"Did you hear about that home invasion?" my mother asked in our bimonthly phone call. "Saw it on NECN. Wasn't that near you?"

"Yeah," I said. "I actually moved in with Bobby, though. I, um… I don't live there anymore."

"Good thing, I guess. You never can tell." There was a pause. "But you're good, Nora?"

"I'm fine. What do you hear from Lily and Poe?"

"Oh, they're fine, I guess. They moved again, too."

We fake-chatted some more; I told her she should come out and visit, Boston was beautiful in the spring. She reminded me that Scupper was also beautiful in the spring. "Maybe Bobby and I will come out in June," I lied. It was a relief to hang up the phone. My mom couldn't give me what I needed—she never had—but Bobby came through.

He called me during the day if I wasn't at the hospital, making sure our friends were around so I was never alone. He took me to funky restaurants, filled our days with goofy entertainment like the duck boats and trampolining. He made me laugh, cooked dinner, brought me flowers, watched happy movies and home renovation shows, because anything violent, anything about crime made me shake.

When I woke up screaming, he held me close. "I'm here," he'd say. "I've got you, babe. I'm right here."

Somehow, the words never made me feel safe. Roseline, who'd grown up in a rough neighborhood in Port-au-Prince, understood. "When something like this happens," she said, a faraway look in her eyes, "you realize this shit is everywhere, all the time. It's not that the world is different. You just know the ugly side now." She took my hand and held it.

I tried to get better. I saw a counselor who specialized in this kind of thing. She said everything I was feeling was normal, which I already knew. I took a self-defense class, the kind where you got to hit a guy dressed in padding, looking oddly like the Pillsbury Doughboy. I wasn't the only one who'd been attacked, and it helped a little to know other women had gone through this—and worse—and survived.

Bobby and I started having sex again about a month

after the Big Bad Event. I'd started calling it that to lessen its impact, and because the words *assault* and *home invasion* sounded way, way too scary. Whenever thoughts of my attacker came into my head (constantly), I tried to think of him as Voldemort. After all, Voldemort dies. As for the sex, I needed Bobby to take up more space in my brain, to force Voldemort to the side.

I wanted good physical contact, life-affirming sex, normalcy. "You sure?" Bobby asked.

I was. He was kind and gentle, and I was glad when it was over. A hurdle jumped.

But things weren't the same.

My sunshine was gone, and every day seemed a little grayer. We got Boomer, a multicolored ball of fun, and truly, the only time the clouds seemed to lift was with that goofy mutt, who slept with me when I took a nap, his head resting on my hip, a paw on my leg.

Around the ten-month mark, I sensed a hint of... impatience from Bobby. He was getting tired of this. He'd felt that way about Mia the anorexic, too. Being a white knight was fun for a while, but *staying* a white knight...that got old.

The thought of being without him caused rivulets of panic to swirl around my bones. I *would* get back to my old self, that happy, successful woman with great clothes—I'd been wearing scrubs a lot these past few months, which wasn't against any rules except my own. I'd be outgoing and funny again, smart and independent. Bobby would love me with the same ferocity he'd shown at my bedside in the hospital...and even better, with the same sense of eagerness and joy before the Big Bad Event.

So I redoubled my efforts. Forced myself to do the

things I'd done before. I started running along the Charles again, though now with pepper spray and a rape whistle and a big dog—Boomer grew fast. I went out with Doctors Without Spouses, threw Roseline a bridal shower, served as bridesmaid at her wedding. Did some pro bono work at a clinic in Dorchester, though I had a taxi bring me right to the door, and called Bobby as I walked in. I was so scared of seeing *him* or someone of his kind, of being followed, of being attacked, of another Big Bad Event…one that didn't end so well this time.

I did get better. At least, I seemed better from the outside. But those rays of sunshine that used to glow from my skin, that sense of happy wonder with my life… I had to fake that. Everything that had gotten me to where I was seemed gone. The woman who'd won the Perez Scholarship, who'd graduated in the top quarter of her medical school, who'd gotten a fellowship at one of the best hospitals in the world…the woman who'd won Bobby's love was something of a memory now, and in her place was someone who was just going through the motions.

As for Bobby, he still said he loved me. It just didn't seem as heartfelt as it once had.

The grayness stayed, right up until I was hit by the van with the giant bug on the roof.

11

"YOU'RE HIRED, DARLING. And aren't you adorable!"

I blinked. "Uh…thanks. Good. That's great." My interview had lasted four minutes.

Dr. Amelia Ames, medical director emeritus of the Ames Clinic, stood, swaying, and shook my hand. "See you…tomorrow? Did we say tomorrow?"

"Yes, we did. See you tomorrow."

I was fairly sure Dr. Ames's coffee mug did not contain coffee.

Three days after I'd moved into the houseboat, I shed my sling, found my arm to be in working condition with just a little soreness and emailed the director of the Scupper Island Urgent Care Clinic. I attached my CV and necessary paperwork. She called me last night, and here I was now. Hired.

"Ta-ta!" said Dr. Ames now, wobbling to the office door and ushering me out. "Lovely to see you again."

"We've never met be—"

"Ciao!" The door closed.

No tour of the facility, no questions on my experience.

"Hey," said a woman about my age. "I'm Gloria Rodriguez. Are you Dr. Stuart?"

"I am. Nora. Nice to meet you. I'm pretty sure I've just been hired."

Gloria laughed. "You have been. You're a doctor, you're licensed in Maine, and that's good enough. Honestly, the clinic can't get anyone out here except the interns from Portland. No one likes the quiet. Pink eye and sprained ankles aren't exactly sexy medicine, and that's 90 percent of what we do. Come on, I'll give you a tour."

Gloria was a nurse practitioner. There were four nurses on staff, a semiretired doc who took calls at night, the occasional intern and Dr. Ames. "Her family put up the money for the clinic about twelve years ago, so she's the director," Gloria said, making quote marks with her fingers as we walked down the hall. "She doesn't practice."

"Glad to hear that," I said. Gloria was wicked pretty, with sleek, impossibly smooth dark hair and a body like a '40s pinup girl. She was younger than I was—just a year out of her graduate degree, and I liked her already.

The clinic was fairly standard, though nicer than most I'd seen, thanks to the Ames money. There were six rooms for overnight care, six urgent care bays. Once in a while, there'd be a case bad enough to require the LifeFlight helicopter to land and take the patient to Portland.

"Mostly," Gloria said, "it's the basic stuff. Strep throat in the winter, bee stings in the summer, the occasional case of hypothermia when someone stays in the water too long. Once in a while, we get a fisherman who's cut himself pretty bad. Nothing that compares to Boston City, I'm sure."

"It sounds perfect."

"Mind if I ask why you're here?" she said.

The hit-by-the-bug-van story could wait. "My niece is spending the summer with my mom, and I don't get to see them enough. Do you know my mother? Sharon Stuart?"

"Oh, sure, I've met her."

"Yeah. So here I am. I took a leave from Boston City, but I'll be going back in August."

"Nice." Gloria glanced at her watch. "You want to have lunch? It's really quiet this time of year, and if anyone comes in, the receptionist will let us know. We can go to the Red Fox. It's just around the corner."

The receptionist hadn't been in when I'd come in an hour earlier. It was Mrs. Behring, mother of Joey, who'd been in Luke Fletcher's circle of friends.

"Hello, hello," she said warmly. "I'm Ellen Behring, so nice to meet you! I heard a new doctor was interviewing today! What brings you to Scupper Island? Will you be staying here long?"

Another local who didn't recognize me.

"Hi, Mrs. Behring. Nora Stuart. I went to school with Joey."

Her face flickered. "Oh! So you did. I… I didn't recognize you, Nora. You look so…different. Are you a doctor?"

"I am. I'm here for the summer," I said.

"Oh," she said. Confusion was written all over her face.

"We're going to the Red Fox," Gloria said. "Give us

a shout if you need us, okay? Can we bring you something?"

"I brought my lunch from home," she said, still puzzling over me. I was pretty used to it by now.

It was a beautiful day for May—the blackflies were kept at bay by a stiff wind off the water, and the sky was blue and pure. In two more weeks, the summer season would officially begin.

"How did you end up on Scupper, Gloria?" I asked.

"My family's from Boston," she said, "and we used to come to Maine for vacations once in a while. Kennebunkport, Camden, Bar Harbor. I always loved it here. And I had this romantic vision of me coming out and falling in love with a lobsterman—"

"Every woman's dream," I murmured.

"Exactly. Which hasn't happened just yet by the way. But still. It's really pretty, the people are nice, the money's not bad. I've been here for about a year."

"Where do you live?" I asked.

"I rent a house on Rock Ledge Street. A little two-family place, a peek at the water."

The Red Fox was new (to me). We got a seat by the window, since there was hardly anyone else here.

"Welcome to the Red Fox," said the server. "How are you—oh. You. I heard you were back."

It was Amy Beckman, Queen of the Cheetos, once the nemesis to anyone bigger than a size 2, and, all through high school, Sullivan Fletcher's girlfriend.

She looked almost exactly the same—bright blue eyes and sharp cheekbones, athletic build. She seemed to have dropped her addiction to tanning, since her skin was no longer orange. Age had given her some gravitas, too, and *pretty* had become *beautiful*.

Still a little scary, too. How many times had she made me cry? Mocked my clothes? Snickered as I walked past in the cafeteria with a salad, knowing I'd binge-eat cheese when I was home?

"Amy," I said with all the enthusiasm of a dead squirrel on the side of the road. "How are you?"

"So you guys know each other, obviously," Gloria said. "Amy's in my book club. Hey, you should join, Nora! It's more of a drinking club, but we'd love to have you."

"Maybe I will." I wouldn't. "Thank you for the invitation."

Amy was still staring at me. "What can I get you?"

As ever, the old instincts to choose my food based on potential judgment flared up. A salad? No, that would be too much of a throwback. A cheeseburger to prove I could handle calories now (if I did an hour of Pilates back home, which my scapula and knee didn't want me to try just yet)?

"I'll have the lobster salad over arugula," Gloria said with a smile. "Seltzer water with lemon, please. Thanks, Amy."

"Same for me," I said.

"Great," Amy said, snapping her leather-bound notebook shut. "Be right back."

"I'm getting a vibe," Gloria said. "Did you spread typhoid? Are you a serial killer? Sleep with everyone's husband?"

"Have you been reading my diary?" I paused. Gloria seemed great, but...well, I'd known her for half an hour. "Sometimes I think it's hard when a person leaves a close-knit place, you know?"

"Oh, God, yes," she said. "My family? You would've

thought I'd chewed off my baby nephew's leg when I said I was leaving Newton. My mother cried, made a shrine in the living room, lit candles to the Virgin so I'd change my mind, my father didn't talk to me for a month. You'd think I was going to Mars."

"That's kind of sweet, though. That they were so sad to see you go." Unlike my own mother, who'd barely seemed to notice.

"Holy shit, is that you, Nora Stuart?"

Gloria and I turned. "Xiaowen?" I said, my mouth dropping open. It had to be. She looked exactly the same.

"You gotta be kidding me!" she said. "How are you, bitch?" She came over, extended her arms for a hug, smiling from ear to ear.

"I'm good," I said, standing up to hug her back. "It's great to see you! Wow!"

"You look amazing. You're not fat anymore. You're fucking *beautiful*. Okay, not beautiful but, shit, you look great! Look at your hair! I would sell my soul for that shine. Store-bought or what? Spill, or I'll cut you."

"An hour with the hair iron," I said. I gestured to Gloria. "Do you guys know each other?"

"No," Gloria said. "Gloria Rodriguez. I'm a nurse at the clinic where Nora's going to be working. Why don't you join us?"

"Xiaowen Liu. Thanks, I would love to. I usually eat alone when I'm here, which gets pretty fucking boring. I'm on the island for work, but I don't really know anyone here anymore."

Xiaowen's accent had faded a bit, and I sure didn't remember her having such a colorful vocabulary, but it was so *nice* to see someone genuinely enthusiastic about my presence.

"So what brings you here, if you have no friends?" I asked with a smile.

"I'm a marine biologist," she said. "I work out of the Darling Marine Center, but I live in Cape Elizabeth."

"What do you do, specifically?"

"Well, as the saying goes, I am the shit. New England's leading expert in the rejuvenation of the mollusk population. Right now, I'm growing oyster beds about a mile off the coast to replace the overfished areas. Cool, right? Saving the world through shellfish." She looked at me, her eyes smiling. "You always knew I'd be a badass."

"I did," I said. "She had badass written all over her, Gloria. A total Gryffindor."

Xiaowen laughed. "You're still a Harry Potter geek, I see."

"Yes. Of course. I would never betray Hogwarts." I felt it, that flash of my Perez self.

"Are you married, Xiaowen?" Gloria asked. "Did I say that right?"

"You said it fine. Nope, not married. I was engaged, but I dumped him. But that, my friends, is a story best told over martinis. You should come to my house, Stuart. Both of you. Gloria, you're not a serial killer, right? You can come, too. But, Stuart, you have to tell me. What the *hell* are you doing back here? To say you left skid marks on the pavement would not have been an exaggeration."

I gave her the same vague answer I'd given Gloria—family, a minor car accident that left me slightly injured.

Amy brought our food, grunting at Xiaowen before

going back to the kitchen. It was clear Xiaowen and she weren't friends. That made the petty part of me feel good. How many times had Amy and the Cheetos made my life miserable, after all? This time, she was the one left out.

By the end of lunch, Gloria, Xiaowen and I had a date to get together at the houseboat for wine and cheese later this week.

I picked up the tab, telling the other two they could get it the next time, and left Amy a fifteen percent nothing-was-terrible tip. Twenty percent was my standard. Points off for surly attitude.

We parted ways in the parking lot, and because my knee and shoulder weren't killing me, I decided to walk the few blocks downtown to check my post office box.

Maybe Bobby had sent me something.

I squelched the thought. But next week, I'd see him—it was our first trade-off with Boomer.

Daffodils and tulips bobbed in front of most of the stores on Main Street, and a few businesses had already filled their window boxes with pansies, though a hard frost wasn't out of the question. I went past the bookstore, which I would hit on the way back... I needed something to read on the quiet nights on my boat (in addition to Harry Potter, of course). Nothing scary, though. Stephen King would have to woo me back in a few months.

Scupper Island General Store was the jewel of the downtown businesses, the original general store on the island—wooden floors shiny from a hundred years of footsteps, a woodstove in the center, shelves made of oak. It was laden with things a person might actually need, like laundry detergent and dish towels, but also with old-timey goods—blue-and-white tin mugs, hand cream made from goat's milk, homemade cookies, cast-iron frying pans and lots and lots of lobster-eating tools—shell crackers and picks and giant white enamel pots, strainers and serving spoons and little tubs for drawn butter. They also sold plenty of postcards, served ice cream out the back window in the summer and carried T-shirts depicting mosquitoes carrying away children. Business had always been good. For townies, the Fletchers were well-off.

I went to the other half of the building, to the post office, which held a hundred brass boxes with twist combinations.

I got my mail—an envelope addressed in Roseline's pretty handwriting, bless her, and, dear God, a note from Bobby! A handwritten note from my ER physician boyfriend?

Check that. Ex-boyfriend.

Still, it gave me a warm tingle. I'd read it on the deck tonight when I could savor it (hopefully it wasn't just a bill he was forwarding). I'd be a modern-day Lizzie Bennet, with wine instead of tea.

I also had a yellow notice alerting me that there was a package. I went to the counter. Mrs. Fletcher, Luke and Sullivan's mother, was visible at the other end, fussing with some papers.

She ignored me.

"Excuse me," I said. "Hi, Mrs. Fletcher."

Nothing.

I rolled my eyes. "Hello. I have a package?"

Still nothing. There was a bell on the counter, and I dinged it. Hard.

"What do you need?" she snapped.

"How are you, Mrs. Fletcher? I don't know if you remember me, but I went to school with your sons." I smiled, not even trying to make it genuine. "Nora Stuart."

"Oh, I remember you, all right." Insert the sound of evil music—*duh-duh-dunnnn*.

"May I please have my package? Box eighty-eight. Thank you so much."

She snarled, turned and tossed it on the counter. "Such friendly service," I said, glancing at the thick envelope.

It was from Washington State Women's Correctional Facility. My mouth opened.

"Your sistah might be in jail, but she's worth twenny of you," said Mrs. Fletcher.

I blinked, the words stinging. My sister, the drug dealer. The thief.

Then again, Mrs. Fletcher thought I was a thief, too. "Have a nice day, Teeny," I said, deliberately using her ridiculous first name.

I pushed her nastiness out of my head. My sister had sent me something, and that was a first. A complete first. Never once, not at college, med school, afterward, had she sent me anything at all. She only—and very occasionally—answered emails and texts, never initiated them. I hadn't heard from her at all in the past three years.

What would my sister be sending me? It was a small package, the kind lined with bubble wrap. I stared down at it as I walked back to my car.

I'd wait to open this, too.

I stopped at Island Flowers, another new business, and chatted up the owner, a lovely man with dirt on his hands. At my old apartment, I'd had herbs in little pots on the kitchen windowsill. No reason for me not to have them again. I smelled the cilantro and nearly swooned, grabbed some mint, rosemary and oregano. A couple of flowering plants, too. Why not?

"I'll bring my car around," I said.

"Perfect!" said the owner. "I'll box them up for you, so they won't tip."

As I walked down to the clinic, where I'd parked, I looked out at the water, which was dark blue today. Full moon tonight, so the tide would be high. I'd sit on the deck and—

I slammed square into someone. My collarbone twinged. "I'm so sorry!" I said. "I didn't—"

It was Luke Fletcher.

The boy who once—I was almost positive—threatened to rape me because I'd taken something he thought was his.

I straightened up. "Luke," I said.

"Troll."

So, like his brother, he'd recognized me.

He was still *so* beautiful, though I recognized the signs of a hard struggle with alcohol and drugs. He was thinner than I remembered, and a few capillaries were broken in his cheeks. There were a few scars that might've been from skin picking on his face, a classic habit of a junkie.

But drugs and booze hadn't taken away his bone structure or his thick tawny hair or the way he owned the sidewalk.

"Heard we're neighbors," he said, looking over my head. "My brother said he's already been to see you."

"Your niece, too."

"You stay away from my family," he said.

"They visited me," I said. Then, trying to be friendly—new leaf and all that—I added, "Audrey's very nice."

"You think you're hot shit, don't you?" he snapped. "Living in that houseboat, swooping in here with your medical degree—"

"I'm here to spend time with my niece, Luke. That's all."

"I fucked your sister. Did you know that?"

The words hit me like a baseball bat in the chest. I didn't say anything.

"Then again, most guys did," he added. "She was hot. Not like you."

I swallowed. "Are you done reliving high school? Because last I checked, we graduated seventeen years ago." A good line, but he knew he'd hurt me.

"Some things never change," he said.

"And some things do. Well, I have work to do. You should try it. Might be good for you."

"See you around, *neighbor*," he said.

"You probably will." My voice was casual, almost bored.

I went around him, walking back toward my little car, wishing now I'd rented a huge Range Rover or Escalade. My legs were shaking, but hopefully he couldn't see that.

I'd dealt with far, far worse than Luke Fletcher.

But my legs shook just the same.

WHEN I GOT back to the cove, I unloaded my things, brought the plants up to the deck and told Boomer not to eat the mint.

Then I sat there for a few minutes, practicing my yoga breaths.

Luke was all talk. A classic story—the golden boy turned bitter man.

Jim the Realtor had assured me the houseboat was as secure as any regular building. It sure didn't feel that way now. But I had a big dog who worshipped me and a pistol.

I killed the rest of the afternoon by cleaning, which always made me feel better. After dinner and a few chapters of *Harry Potter and the Prisoner of Azkaban*, I went up to the deck. The plants and flowers had been just what I needed. It was heaven up here. Also, I had a great view in case anyone approached.

Time to read my mail. I wasn't going to let Luke Fletcher ruin my night. He'd ruined too many already.

Roseline had sent me a card of two old women obscenely eating sausages with a cute note just to say she was thinking of me and wanted to ditch her husband of four months and come live with me on the houseboat, so I should stock up on good vodka. I knew it was all for my sake—she and Amir were crazy happy—but I appreciated it.

Next envelope—Bobby's or Lily's?

I chose Lily's.

Inside the thick envelope was a single piece of notepaper, the words written in pencil, the handwriting heartbreakingly familiar even after all these years.

Don't write to me anymore.

The words razored through my heart like a knife through an overripe plum. For a second I couldn't breathe, then I sucked in a ratcheting lungful of the piney air. My lips trembled with the effort of keeping in the…the curse words. Or the sob.

I guess she didn't like my notes about the cormorant or the rain.

Nothing about how she was doing. Nothing about how I was doing. No questions about Poe or Mom or anything.

"Boomer!" I called, my voice cracking, and my dog came running, his ears flopping, his big goofy face smiling. He leaped the ten feet from dock to boat, then scrabbled up the narrow stairs onto the top deck, right into my arms.

I didn't know what I'd do without my dog, and I didn't want to know. I couldn't handle the thought right now. I hugged his furry neck and let my tears drip into his ruff while he panted in my ear, his big tail wagging.

I wasn't sure I could ever accept the fact that my sister didn't love me anymore. That she hadn't for years. Decades.

I had Roseline, who was more like a sister than Lily had been in two decades. I had other friends back home, back in Boston, that crooked, twisted little city. I had Bobby, even if we weren't together anymore. And here on Scupper, I had…well, Gloria and Xiaowen, new but full of potential. I had my mother, sort of. I had Poe—

Best to stop while I was ahead.

I let go of my dog and opened the envelope from Bobby, not as uplifted by his attention as I'd been before. The stationery had been a gift from his mother—Crane's, embossed with his initials, RKB. Robert Kennedy Byrne. If you were Irish and lived in Boston, at least one family member was named after the Kennedys.

Hey, Nora, the note said. *Hope you're on the mend. I wanted to let you know that Jabrielle and I aren't together. It was stupid and impulsive and a mistake, too.*

Besides, she isn't you.

I'll see you next week. Let me know if you need anything.

Bobby.

Well. That was something to mull over.

She isn't you.

It sure was nice to hear, especially after my sister, alone in prison a continent away from her family, had no room in her cell—or her heart—for me.

12

SOMETHING SHOCKING HAPPENED.

My mother came to visit me *and* asked for advice.

One of the nice things about the houseboat was that I could see a person approaching, since they had to walk down the dock to get to me. And sure enough, Wednesday evening, as I was slicing vegetables for a stir-fry, my mother pulled off the road and came striding briskly down the dock to my door and into my kitchen. No knock.

"I'm worried about Poe," she announced. Boomer hauled his bulk from the rug and went over to greet her, wagging his tail and knocking a coaster off the coffee table.

"Hey, Mom," I said. "Have a seat. Do you want some wine or a beer or anything?"

"Water," she said. "Thanks." She eyed my new digs. "Pretty fancy, aren't you?" There it was, the little stab of disapproval.

"It's a special place," I said calmly. I got her a glass

of water (God forbid she take something that was more than just life sustaining). "So what's going on with Poe?"

My mother sat at the counter, stiffly, as if she'd never sat on a stool before. "Welp, her grades are abominable, and though she was a little more talkative before you got here—" pause so the guilt could sink in "—she's clammed up. Gawt no friends that I can see. Sits there with that phone glued to the end of her nose and barely leaves her room."

"Sounds like a typical teenager," I said.

"Well, her mother's in jail, Nora, in case you forgot. Hahdly typical."

I hadn't told my mother about Lily's note. Nor would I.

"So maybe Poe can sleep over here Friday night," I suggested.

"What good would that do?"

Talking to my mother was like being pecked to death by chickens.

"Change of scenery, maybe we could watch a movie, talk, eat something chocolate, do things that usually bond women."

My mother frowned. "If you think that would help, go ahead and try. Though I don't see how it would."

"Is Lily still scheduled to get out in August?" I asked.

"Ayuh."

"Then I guess the best we can do is make Poe feel loved and safe until then. Even if she doesn't react to it, it matters, hearing someone say they love you or they're glad to see you or that they want to spend time with you."

"Is that what they taught you in college?"

"Yes. And in medical school and residency. I did a psych rotation. I *am* a doctor, let's not forget. So how about if we practice? I'll say something nice to you, and you can tell me if it makes you feel better."

"I'm fine."

"Humor me."

"Fine." She took a slurp of water and rolled her eyes.

"Mom," I said, "I have always admired how calm and capable you are."

"Well, how else am I supposed to be? Like a chicken with its head cut off?"

"Great job, Mom. And now you say something nice to me." Sneaky of me, I know. Fishing for maternal approval.

She sighed. "Well, I think you looked better with a little meat on your bones, frankly."

"Nope, you've got it wrong, Mom. Something nice."

"That was nice."

"So you're saying I look too thin."

"I'm sayin' you were always a decent-looking girl and you didn't have to lose weight and wear fancy clothes for a person to see it."

She gaveth with one hand, tooketh away with the other. "Thank you, Mom. That's very sweet of you. Now, for Poe, maybe you could say something like 'Even though these aren't the best circumstances, I'm so glad we get to spend this time together.'"

"Well, I'm nawt glad, Nora! My daughter's in jail!"

"We're lying here, Mom. Okay? Personally, I'm dead inside, but I'm faking it till I make it. See this smile? See me going through the motions of making a nutritious, pleasant dinner for one? See me enjoying life through one glass of wine per day? This is what humans do."

She frowned. "Why are you dead inside?"

"I'm not. I'm just exaggerating." I resumed cutting

carrots. Collier Rhodes had fantastic knives, and I had to watch carefully that I didn't slice off the tip of my finger, because I was still nervous around knives.

"You've been different this past year."

"Really, Mom? How would you know?" I took a hostile drink of wine, if one could do that. "I'll text Poe, and you make sure she gets here. Okay? Great. Thanks for stopping by."

"You ought to be eating more meat," my mother said. "You look pale."

"Okay. Bye."

It was only when she was off the dock and in her car that I chugged the rest of my wine. "I'm a gastro-enterologist, Mom. How many colons have *you* cleaned out, huh? You think I might know a little bit more about healthy eating than you do, huh? That maybe med school wasn't just to kill time?"

There was a knock on the door. Whoopsy. *Must keep the rants to myself.*

It was Audrey Fletcher, Sullivan's daughter.

"Hi, Audrey!" I said.

"Is it okay if I come in?" she asked shyly.

"Sure! I'd love that. I'm just making dinner. Have a seat. Can I get you a drink?"

"Do you have any Coke?"

"I don't, honey. How about seltzer water with a slice of… Let's see here…" I opened the fridge. "How about with a few blackberries thrown in for flavor?"

"That'd be great. Hi, Boomer! Hi, buddy!" She knelt down on the floor and loved up the dog.

"Do you have a dog?" I asked, getting her drink.

"No. A cat. He's nice. Sooty. He's pretty old, and a dog would be kind of hard for him to deal with."

"Sure. So what's new? How's school going?"

"It's fine." She smiled uncertainly, and I felt a rush of kinship with her.

"I hated high school," I said, handing her the drink, which looked sophisticated and fun, the berries bobbing around with the ice, dancing on the bubbles.

"Why did you hate it?" she asked.

I put a few carrot sticks in a bowl, sprinkled them with pepper and put them on the counter between us, taking one to chomp on. Then I resumed my chopping, moving on to the cilantro, the clean, fresh smell filling the air. "Well, I wasn't real popular. Too smart, too much of an oddball, too clumsy. And my sister was ridiculously beautiful, so self-esteem was kind of hard to come by."

"My mom's really pretty," she said wistfully. She took a sip of her water. "And my dad is super handsome."

"That's true," I said, though Luke's face was the one that flashed before me—not in the best way. "Your dad was really nice in high school."

She brightened. "I bet. He's the greatest."

"Are you an only child?"

"I have a half brother. Rocco. He's seven." She paused. "My parents got divorced when I was three."

"Would I know your mom?"

"Amy Beckman? She was in your class, too, I guess."

I looked up sharply. "Huh. So they stayed together."

"Not for very long. They were twenty when I was born, twenty-three when they divorced."

I felt the bite of satisfaction. I'd always thought Sullivan could've done better than the clichéd Amy.

Then again, I also remembered seeing her skip up

to the Clam Shack with a bouquet of lupines for Sully one summer afternoon, all smiles and sweetness, and I pretended not to look as he kissed her.

Everyone had two sides. Or three. Or seven.

"Do you get along with your brother?" I asked.

"Oh, yeah. I love him. I mean, he lives with my mom, and I live with my dad, so he doesn't mess up my stuff or anything. But he's great. A real cutie." She beamed, and I smiled back. "I make him shirts once in a while, and I stencil dinosaurs on them and stuff."

"Wow, you can sew?"

"I'm in the fashion club in school. We make clothes and stuff, and at the end of the year, we have a show. Like on *Project Runway.*"

"I love that show! Do you make your own clothes, too?"

She looked down at her T-shirt and too-tight, unflattering jeans. "No. Call me Michael Kors. I create better than I dress."

I laughed. "Poe loves fashion, too," I said. At least, I thought she did. She looked at magazines a lot, and many of those magazines showed celebrities on the red carpet. And Poe certainly had her own look going on with the blue hair and all.

"I thought she might join the club, but..." Audrey shrugged, her cheeks coloring. Poe had turned her down, clearly.

My niece could use a nice girl as a friend. And maybe Audrey could use a badass as a friend.

"Hey, Audrey, any chance you want to sleep over on Friday? Poe is coming, and it'd be great to have you here, too."

"Really?" Her face brightened so fast that I knew

she didn't get many invitations. Crap, it was like looking at a version of my teenage self.

Except her father was here and loved her. And her brother. And hopefully, Amy did, too.

"Yeah. Only if you're interested, though. And obviously, I'd have to ask your parents."

"I'll call my dad right now!" she said, whipping out her phone. "Dad? Hi! I'm at Nora's... Uh-huh!... No, I rode my bike here... I don't know, I didn't see him. Listen, can I sleep over here on Friday? Poe's gonna be here... Her niece... Okay, hold on."

She passed the phone to me. "Hi, Sullivan," I said.

"Nora?"

"The one and only." I winced. "How are you?" I tried to speak clearly without overdoing it.

"I'm fine. How are you?"

"Great. Uh, my niece is sleeping over, and I thought it would be fun if Audrey was here, too. Would that be okay?"

There was a pause, and in it, all my insecurities opened their eyes and stretched. *Why would I let my kid come to your house, Troll? Why would I want her being friends with your mean-ass little niece? Are you some kind of sexual predator, asking my daughter to sleep over?*

"Sure," he said. "Thank you."

"Great! She can come over before dinner, how's that?"

"That's great. Can she bring anything?"

"No, but thank you."

"Thank *you*," he said. "I'll drop her off around five, then."

I handed the phone back to Audrey, who said she'd be home soon. She hung up and beamed at me.

"Listen," I said, "Poe isn't the… Well, she's having a hard time these days. I really appreciate you saying yes to this."

"Are you kidding? I'm never invited anywhere." She cringed, then clamped her mouth shut, her face going red.

"I was the same way, Audrey. So let's be outcasts together, us three," I said, smiling, and relief blossomed over her face. Someday, though she'd never believe me now, Audrey Fletcher was going to be striking. Not pretty—she looked too much like her dad for pretty—but the kind of looks that lasted for decades, not just senior year of high school.

ON FRIDAY NIGHT, I was ready. I had a marathon of *Project Runway* on the DVR, some healthy food, some not terribly unhealthy food, four shades of nail polish and a mud mask allegedly made with products from the Dead Sea (or La Mer Morte, as the package said). I'd taken the ferry to Portland and hit Target to stock up, bought the latest teen apocalypse movie and a few board games (old-school, I knew, but it was going to be hard to get Poe to engage in actual conversation).

I'd also gone to some effort to make her room welcoming. I picked flowers and put them in the bathroom and on her night table along with my own copy of *Harry Potter and the Sorcerer's Stone* (read so many times I couldn't count).

Audrey would sleep in the loft under the peaked roof. I put flowers up there, too.

At five o'clock, my niece came through the door.

"Hey, honey!" I said, going to hug her. She turned her shoulder away.

"Why am I here? Am I being punished?" she asked.

"Rewarded, actually, by spending time with your fun and adoring aunt," I said.

"I'd rather be home."

"With Gran?"

"Anywhere but here."

I was twenty years older than Poe, I reminded myself, but the urge to ask "Why are you so mean to me?" and burst into tears was strong.

"Why are you so mean to me?" I asked (not bursting into tears, yay for me).

"Why are you pretending to care?" she said. "I know you're only here for the summer."

"So should I ignore you for the entire summer, then?"

"Yeah." She made it into a three-syllable rejection, and I sighed. Boomer, blissfully ignorant to teenagers and their leaden moods, nudged Poe's skinny thigh with his nose.

"Well," I said, "just another thought…maybe we could hang out, do things together, get to know each other, act like relatives." I shrugged, eyes wide.

"From what I've heard, our relatives just up and leave and you never see them again," she said. "Dog, get away from me."

"I take it you're referring to my father." Good! Finally! We could talk about it. "What did Lily tell you?"

"Can I have some wine?" Poe asked, sliding onto the counter stool, her posture shrimp-like.

"No. What do you know?"

Poe sighed. "Like, he was great, and Gran was a total bitch all the time, and he had this book, but she totally resented his talent, and she kicked him out, and life got even shittier after that."

"It did get shitty, but that's not quite the whole story." Not that I knew the whole story. "Life was pretty fantastic before he left." Stupid of me, still defending my absentee father.

Poe's eyes flickered, not quite meeting mine. Aha. Interest. "That's not what my mother says."

"Really. Well, maybe I could show you some of the things we did, and you can decide for yourself."

Her eyes went back to the counter. "Maybe," she muttered.

"Excuse me?"

"Maybe."

"As in, yes, why not, there's nothing else to do here?" I swear, she almost smiled. "Maybe," she repeated.

"Hi! Am I too early? Or late?" Audrey was here, standing at the half door. Her father stood behind her, one hand on her shoulder.

"Hey, Audrey! No, this is perfect." I kicked my niece's leg.

"Hi, Audrey. Wanna play Barbies?" she said.

Audrey smiled uncertainly.

"Come on in," I said. "Hey, Sully."

He nodded.

"Any food allergies, medication, anything I should know about?" I asked him. I tried not to look at his hearing aid.

"No," he said. "You'll be alone here tonight?"

"Do you mean, is she entertaining gentlemen callers?" Poe said.

"Ayuh. That's what I meant." One corner of his mouth pulled up.

"It'll just be us girls," I said. "Hey, got a second?"

He was looking at Audrey, who was petting Boomer.

"Sullivan?" I said, laying a hand on his arm. His eyes jerked back to mine. Brown eyes, calm and deep. "Can I talk to you for a minute?"

We went out on the deck, able to see Poe not talking to Audrey, and Audrey pretending not to care by rubbing Boomer's belly.

"What's up?" he asked.

"I saw Luke the other day," I said.

He waited.

"He wouldn't do anything, right?"

"No. He's just…" Sullivan shrugged. "He's just a little bitter. Especially now, with you back, living here—" he jerked his chin at the boat "—making friends with Audrey and such."

"Is he still using?"

"No. He drinks too much once in a while, but he doesn't drive anymore. Lost his license."

I nodded.

"Heard you ran into Amy," Sullivan said.

"Yep."

"She doesn't know Audrey's here tonight. I have custody."

"So Audrey said." There was a story there, I was sure.

"If Amy knew," Sully said in a softer voice, "she would've asked Audrey to stay over at her place, and Audrey would've said yes, because she loves her mother and Amy doesn't spend a lot of…well. Audrey would've said yes."

"Ah."

"So I didn't mention it, because I think it'd be nice if my kid had a friend, and Poe seems like a good kid."

"She does?"

He shrugged. "She doesn't seem horrible."

"No. Not horrible."

He smiled a little, and something pulled in my chest. "Thank you for having Audrey over. Call if you need anything." He handed me a piece of paper. "My cell."

We went back inside, and Sullivan said, "I'm leaving, sweetheart. You have fun, okay?"

She hauled herself to her feet—fifty or so pounds overweight, and I remembered that difficulty, that envy at the girls who could stand from a cross-legged position as gracefully as an egret. "Bye, Daddy," she said, hugging him and kissing his cheek.

Another tug in my chest.

"Bye, honey. Love you." He jerked his chin at Poe. "Have fun, Poe."

"Thanks," she said, not looking at him.

Sullivan left, and a momentary silence fell over the three of us. "Well, I thought we'd make homemade pizza for dinner. I have some games, and *Project Runway* is booted up, and, uh…we could go for a canoe ride, if you want."

"A canoe ride?" Poe said. "Are you serious? I'll pass."

"Um, me, too," Audrey said. "Maybe another time. The mosquitoes are fierce this time of day."

"Good point," I said. "Well, who likes what on pizza?"

"Pizza's too fattening," Poe said, dropping her eyes to her phone to text her mysterious friends from Seattle.

Great. There was no way Audrey would eat pizza if Poe the Gazelle had just deemed it fattening. My jaw tightened with anger at my niece.

"I like tomatoes and sausage," Audrey said, and my head whipped around at her.

"Great!" I said. "Me, too. How do you feel about mushrooms?"

"Love them."

"Poe, why don't you make a salad?"

"No, thanks."

"Let me rephrase. Poe, please make the salad. Everything's in the fridge."

With a martyred sigh and a long, long pause, Poe stood up, shrugged out of her leather jacket to reveal her tank top and delicate shoulder blades. There was a fresh tattoo on her back—angel wings, the perfect skin still red from the needle.

I wanted to hug her, wash her face and send her to bed.

"What can I do?" Audrey asked, and I gave her plates to set the table.

She chattered sweetly as we worked, talking about her job at the boatyard, how she loved to fish, what she might do this summer. "My dad said we could go somewhere for a long weekend," she said. "I kind of want to go to a big city, since I've only been to Boston a few times. Maybe New York. Or, um, Seattle? I've heard it's cool out there."

We both waited for Poe to respond. She didn't, just cut up scallions as if the knife weighed forty pounds.

"Seattle's beautiful," I said.

"Oh, are you an expert because you've been there three times?" Poe asked.

"Five, and yes. Audrey, the Space Needle is—"

"For idiot tourists," Poe said.

"—weird looking from the outside, but you can eat up in the high part, and the view is fantastic. The food there is great. I mean, I've never had a bad meal in Seattle. Salmon and crab in everything, fresh seafood, I mean, not that we don't have that here. But—"

"Can we change the subject?" Poe asked.

"Sure," Audrey said. "What would you like to talk about?" She smiled at my niece, who returned with a pained look.

"I don't know, Audrey," Poe said. "How about Girl Scouts? You must be a Girl Scout, right?"

"Not anymore," Audrey said. "But it was pretty fun while it lasted."

Touché, Poe. Audrey would not let her good mood fade, and God bless her for it.

So the evening went. Audrey, lovely but a little nervous, as if I'd send her home if she were anything but Little Miss Perky. Poe, on the other hand, stayed determinedly miserable. We played Apples to Apples, watched *Project Runway*, ate food. Well, Audrey and I did, though I noticed Audrey kept looking at the pizza after eating her one slice. Poe chewed a piece of spinach from the salad and left everything else on her plate.

By the time I announced it was bedtime (11:30 p.m., a respectably late enough hour, I thought), I was exhausted. I showed them to their rooms and told them to sleep well. Poe closed her door immediately.

"Sorry about her," I whispered.

"I heard that," Poe said.

"She speaks!" I said. "Sleep well, honey." No response. "You, too, Audrey."

"Thank you so much for having me," she said. "I've never slept on a houseboat before." She gave me an impulsive hug, then, blushing, went up to her loft.

I felt guilty for liking her a hundred times more than

I liked Poe. "Come on, Boomerang," I said to my dog. "One more pee, and you can come to bed."

I let my dog out and walked down the dock a few paces as Boomer loped into the woods to sniff and do his business.

The stars were a glittering swipe over the cove tonight. No wind, the slight, almost-unnoticeable bob of the dock as the tide slipped in. The pine trees were silhouetted in black against the dark plum of the sky, and I breathed in deeply, imagining the island air scrubbing my city lungs clean. Though I loved Boston, it did have some pretty nasty smells—the exhaust of belching trucks on the Mass Pike and the swampy, human-excrement smell from the Back Bay; the Orange Line, which always smelled like urine; the sulfuric smell of North Station in winter.

Here, the air was so pure you could feel your lungs turning pink.

"Come on, Boomer," I called softly, in case the girls were already sleeping. My dog loped obediently onto the dock. "Good boy," I said, scratching his head. "Thank you, good boy."

Just as I turned to open the door, I saw something.

A tiny light from the woods glowed orange, then faded.

Someone was out there, smoking a cigarette. As soon as I thought it, I could smell the smoke. The orange glowed again as the person took another drag.

Boomer growled.

I didn't own this land. This wasn't my property, so I couldn't call for trespassing. I did, however, go inside, then locked the doors and closed all the windows and pulled all the shades. Checked on the girls, who were both asleep.

I texted Sullivan. Someone is smoking in the woods on the north side of my dock.

The phone screen showed three dots waving reassuringly. He was awake and he was answering.

Lock the doors.

Me: Already done.
Sullivan: I'll call my brother right now.

Then I went to my room and took out my Smith & Wesson 1911, went back to the living room and waited, staring at the door.

If someone came in—if Luke Fletcher came in— would I shoot him? Kill him with his niece upstairs? Could I actually pull the trigger? Would it be enough that I was here with a big dog and a gun, or would I have to fire? I could shoot him in the leg. I didn't want to kill him.

The *other* guy—my personal terrorist—yeah. I might kill him. But he didn't know I was here. There was no public record that had me moving here to Scupper. Was there? My rental agreement? Was that public information?

A second later, my phone rang, and I jumped like I'd been stabbed. "Hello?"

"It's Sullivan."

"Hi."

"Luke said he was taking a walk in the woods. Didn't mean to scare you."

I took a breath, aware that my heart was thudding. "Right."

"I told him to leave you alone and go back to the boatyard."

My shoulders dropped four inches with relief. "Thanks, Sully."

"Excuse me?"

"Thank you."

There was a pause. "You want me to swing by?"

I did.

But I also remembered lying on the street, the Beantown Bug Killers mascot looming over me, thinking I wasn't the person I wanted to be, and now my chance was over.

I cleared my throat. "No, I'm fine. I'll see you tomorrow. Hey, I have to take the ferry to Boston…why don't I drop Audrey home on my way?"

Another pause that made me wonder if he heard me clearly. "No, she can walk to the boatyard," he said. "She's working there tomorrow."

"Oh. Okay." I bit my lip. "Well. Sorry to wake you."

"I wasn't asleep."

I pictured him, home alone (or maybe not alone), sitting on the edge of his bed.

He had a good face, Sullivan Fletcher did. A calm, reassuring face. Just thinking of it made me feel safer.

"Good night," he said.

"Good night," I echoed.

And I went to bed. Me, my dog and my pistol, just in case.

13

Dear Lily,
I know you said not to write to you, but who cares
what you think?
So guess what? I'm working at the clinic on
Scupper for the summer. Yesterday, a lady came
in with a brand-new baby, and the smell of his
head made me think of Poe when she was tiny.
She was the most beautiful baby I've ever seen.
Still is. She misses you. I do, too.
Love,
Nora

THERE WAS THE bowl of six lemons on the counter. The
red gerbera daisies on the coffee table. My pretty little apartment, just as tidy and lovely as I'd left it. My
perfect home.

But this time, the glass slider was open, and I already
knew he was here. I pretended not to know, thinking that
if I could pretend hard enough, he'd disappear. I could

hear him in the bathroom, getting into the shower, the hiss of the rings as he slid back the curtain. But I was sure, I was so sure that if he thought I didn't believe he was here, he'd somehow disappear.

Then the shower curtain opened, and this time he already had the knife.

I jolted awake from the nightmare, drenched in sweat, panting like Boomer after a run.

Speaking of, where was my dog? What about the guy in the woods last night? Was it really Luke, or had Voldemort found me?

Holy shit, where were the girls?

I burst out of my room, and there they were, at the kitchen table, Poe sprawled out, Audrey sitting across from her. They both looked up at me.

"Are you all right?" I blurted.

"Shockingly, yes," Poe said.

"Want some coffee?" Audrey asked.

My heart clattered and banged in my chest. "Um… sure. Thank you."

Audrey brought me a mug. She'd set the table with the sugar bowl and creamer already.

"Bad dream?" Poe suggested, eyes flicking up and down my form.

I nodded.

"You talked in your sleep all the time at Gran's."

"Sorry," I muttered. I wondered if I'd said anything that would make her worry. Then again, worry for her aunt didn't seem to be one of Poe's problems, and that was good. I wanted to help her, not add to her burdens.

"Want me to make waffles?" I asked. Collier Rhodes's houseboat was equipped with every appliance known to Williams-Sonoma.

"I have to work," Audrey said. "I'm gonna walk down to the boatyard. But thank you so much for having me over," she said to me. "And, Poe, it was nice hanging out."

"Yeah. Same here." She gave an awkward smile, and my heart tugged. I was almost positive that under her tough-girl act was a lonely kid.

I hugged Audrey. "Thanks for coming, honey. Drop by anytime."

"I will! Thanks. This was really fun. Bye, Boomer." She ruffled my dog's fur, then grabbed her backpack and left.

"She's so nice," I said, sitting down.

"Bet you wish she was your niece instead of me."

I took a sip of coffee. "Nah. She doesn't have blue hair, and I love blue hair."

Poe rolled her eyes, practically dislocating them, reached for the coffee and winced. There was a damp mark on the shoulder of her T-shirt.

"How's that tattoo?" I asked.

"Fine."

"Mind if I look at it?"

"Yes, I do mind. Too pervy."

"I'm thinking it might be infected. I'm a doctor, re-member?"

She hesitated, then pulled her shirt up.

Yep. Those angel wings were oozing. "I'll get some bacitracin. Hang on."

Once, when I visited and Poe was about four, she had loved pretending to be sick so I could fuss over her. She'd hold up her little hand and I'd put a Band-Aid on her finger and give her a Hershey's Kiss to make it better, then take her temperature and prop her up with pillows. "You just rest," I'd say, "and Auntie will rub your feet."

That had been the best visit. I'd really thought Lily and I would be close after that one. She even hugged me when I left.

When I'd called a week later, she didn't answer or return my call or answer the subsequent email.

I went to the bathroom and got the first-aid kit and a clean facecloth, then ran it under hot water and wrung it out. Poe sat at the table, her back to me. Her shoulder blades were those of a little girl's, it seemed, thin and fragile.

"Is it gross?" Poe asked, and for once, there wasn't any snark in her tone.

"Not to me," I said, gently pressing the cloth against her tattoo. "I've seen gross, and this doesn't even come close."

"What are some gross things you've seen?" she asked. Gasp! Interest in her aunt's profession!

"Well, there was this woman who came into the office because she had bad breath. And I'm not talking onions-at-lunch bad breath." I eased the hot compress off and put on some bacitracin, covered it with gauze and taped it in place, then held an ice pack against it to help with the swelling. "Her breath smelled like feces. Actual sewage."

"Gross."

"Yes. It was hard not to gag."

"So what was wrong with her."

"Fetor hepaticus. Breath of the dead, they call it. Late-stage liver failure that basically meant her liver enzymes were oozing into her lungs."

"Oh, God!" Poe made a gacking sound. "Did she make it?"

"No. She died a few hours later." Beatrice LaPonte of Dorchester. My second fatality.

"Is it hard, seeing someone…you know?"

I took off the ice pack and pulled Poe's shirt back down. "Yes."

She was quiet for a minute. Her neck was slender, the blue hair oddly complementary to her fair skin. I couldn't resist and reached out to touch the back of her head.

She jumped up. "What are you *doing*? Don't get weird, okay? Jesus."

I closed my eyes briefly. "You want to come to Boston with me today?" I said.

"Why?"

"I'm bringing Boomer to see Bobby. My ex-boyfriend. We could go shopping, maybe? Or see a movie?"

"I'll pass." The sullen teenager was back.

"Okay, but before I take you back to Gran's, I want to show you something, okay?"

"Do I have a choice?"

"You do not. I was just being polite."

FIFTEEN MINUTES LATER, we were in the car, Boomer in the back seat, crooning his joy, his enormous head out the window. Poe had turned down the chance to drive, so I did the honors. Down the bumpy, sandy road till we hit pavement, then into town. Already, traffic was starting to pick up a bit with weekend visitors. The line was out the door at Lala's, I was glad to see.

We went west of Penniman State Forest and up East-

man Hill, where Dad had brought Lily and me so many
times. The Hill of Thrills, Dad had called it.

It was steeper than I remembered.

My little car automatically downshifted to a lower
gear, lumbering up the hill, which was a good half mile
long. At the top, there was the huge granite rock, surrounded by pine and oak trees. The oaks were just starting to bud out, and though the air was cool, the sun
was warm.

"You brought me to see a rock?" Poe said, hauling
herself out of the car, Boomer on her heels.

"This is a place your mom and I used to come. Our
father would put our bikes in the back, and we'd come
up here at night. We'd sit on this rock for a few minutes,
and our father would give us a pep talk."

She glanced at me, interested against her will. "About
what?"

"About not being afraid. Having adventures. Living
life to the fullest." Had I done that? Fulfilled his hopes
and expectations? Would my father approve of me as
an adult? Or would Lily's lifestyle be more what he'd
had in mind?

Not that he was a great role model, ditching his
daughters the way he had. But love for him had been
carved into my heart at a young age, and erasing that
was easier said than done.

Well. The point of this little trip was to show Poe
that her mother and I had been close once upon a time,
maybe give her a sense of a time when Lily had been…
different. Boomer licked my shoe encouragingly. "It'd
be so dark," I said, "and we'd sit here and look down at
the town and see the lights, and nothing ever looked co-
zier. But to get back home, we had to conquer the hill."

Silence from Poe.

"So we'd get on our bikes—well, Lily would have to go with my dad, because she was too small—and we'd go down this hill as fast as we could."

More silence, then. "Did you ever crash?"

"Almost." But I'd been afraid every time, pep talk or no pep talk.

Looking down the hill, I remembered how each time, I'd be terrified I'd lose control of the handlebars, hit a bump and go flying. Each time, the horrible flash of fear shot through me, the noise of the gravel scraping as I swerved, the sting of sand and rocks hitting my shins.

The euphoria—and relief—when we reached the bottom.

"Your mom loved it," I said. "She would sit on our dad's handlebars with her arms out, like she was flying."

"She likes speed, all right."

I wasn't sure if the double entendre was intentional or not.

"Is she a good mother?" I asked.

"She's in jail, Nora. What do you think?" But even as she said the words, her lips trembled.

I wanted to put my arm around her. "Still, you must miss her."

"I need to do homework. Can you please end this journey down memory lane?"

"Sure." I sighed, and we got back in the car. The rest of the short trip was in silence. Poe got out the second I pulled into Mom's dirt driveway.

"Poe?" I said, getting out after her.

"What?"

"Wash that tattoo three times a day with warm water,

and put bacitracin on it every time. You don't want it to get worse."

She didn't look back.

FOUR HOURS LATER, the Boston skyline came into view, and my heart leaped. Boomer, too, seemed to know we were back home; of course, he could smell Boston well before I could. His big tail wagged, and I smiled at him and rubbed his head.

I'd miss him like I'd miss my right arm. But I'd be okay on my own. I had to be. As my father had said so many years ago, life was about taking on fear.

As the ferry pulled up to the dock, I saw Bobby, his hair needing a trim, razor stubble on his jaw, looking like an ad for J. Crew. The guy won by Cute Nora, successful GI doc, the Perez Scholar and McElroy Fellow of Gastroenterology.

He smiled when he saw me. "Hey, stranger," he said. "You look a *lot* better."

Boomer leaped over to him, wagging, slobbering, molesting—the usual Bernese mountain dog greeting.

I went over, too, and Bobby opened his arms for a hug.

A long hug.

He smelled so good. I could feel his ribs, and my cheek pressed against his shoulder.

"Hey," I said, and my voice was husky.

"I hope you don't have to go home right away," he said, taking Boomer's leash. "I thought we could have lunch."

"Sure," I said.

"You really look fantastic." He palpated my collarbone gently, and a ripple of attraction flowed down my side. "All healed?"

"Pretty much," I said.

"No lifting over twenty pounds, okay?"

I smiled. "Yes, Dr. Byrne."

"Where would you like to go?" he asked. "I have the whole day off."

Now, that was odd. He never took the whole day off. "I have dinner plans with Roseline, but…well, how about a walk? It's a lot warmer here than it is on Scupper."

"Is your knee up for it?"

"It is for now."

"Great." He took my hand, and a warm, slightly nervous feeling wrapped around me. I was glad I'd worn a nice outfit—jeans and low-heeled suede boots, a bottle green cashmere sweater, brown leather jacket and the vintage Hermès scarf I'd found at a consignment shop for a fraction of its worth.

"How are things at the hospital?" I asked, and he told me stories of patients and staffers and the kid who'd disappeared for twelve minutes because he hadn't wanted a tetanus shot, causing a Code Adam and complete hospital shutdown. We wove through Boston's crowds, dodging the ubiquitous Red Sox fans heading for Fenway, the clusters of students talking too loudly, horsing around.

It was nice to be back.

We stopped at a little café near the Contemporary Art Institute and just sat for a little while, watching the people, the wind ruffling my hair. The waitress came over and admired the Dog of Dogs, and we ordered lunch and wine.

It felt so romantic, the sun shining, a breeze off the

bay, Bobby smiling his flirty smile at me. Just like old times.

"Tell me how things are on Scupper," he said after our meals arrived, and I launched into a cleaned-up version of events. Told him about my houseboat and how beautiful it was, how my niece had slept over the night before, seeing old schoolmates, hanging out with my mom.

And as I talked, events began to shape themselves to my words. My mom seemed friendlier, not distant; the noises of the Maine night beautiful, not a reminder of how exposed I felt on the houseboat. Poe was colorful, not angry.

After all, I had never really let Bobby know the truth about my family. There was no reason to start now.

The server brought us the check, and Bobby paid. I glanced at my watch. "You want to come back to my place?" he asked suddenly, reaching forward and tucking a strand of hair behind my ear. That gesture that had always irritated me. I could manage my own hair, thank you. "Our place, I mean?" he added.

"We broke up, Bobby."

"I know. But I'm not with Jabrielle."

"You're not with me, either." I raised an eyebrow and smiled a little to take the edge off.

"I miss you."

Good. You deserve to miss me.

He leaned back in his chair, petting Boomer, who was attempting to climb onto his lap. "I mean, of course, I miss you. We were together for a long time. Friends for longer than that. But I guess I didn't realize how empty life would feel without you."

He was always so good with words. My wine was gone, but I pretended to sip it, needing a shield.

"Okay," he said. "No answer is an answer, too. I'm sorry."

"I appreciate the sentiment. But I think…well. I think at the very least, we need more time apart." I put down my glass. "I'm gonna go. Take good care of my boy here." I bent down, wincing as my knee reminded me that I'd been dumb enough to get hit by a van, and kissed my dog. "I'll talk to you soon, okay?"

"Text me when you get back to the island, so I know you made it safe and sound." Bobby stood up and hugged me again, kissed me on the cheek.

Then kissed me on the mouth. A quick kiss, but warm and firm. A reminder of life before the Big Bad Event.

"Take care," I said and walked away as fast as I could manage.

For the first time, it occurred to me that maybe taking a break was exactly what Bobby and I had needed.

14

A FEW DAYS after the Boomer swap, I was at the clinic, doing computer work. As Gloria had said, most of our cases were really basic stuff—I'd seen a girl for a sprained ankle, a teenager who'd been stung four times by bees and was hysterical (though not allergic) and now an elderly woman with severe stomach pains due to constipation.

"I haven't pooped for eleven days," she growled. I suppressed a wince. It wasn't uncommon in elderly people, but jeezum crow! No wonder she was snarling.

"I'll let *you* handle this, Dr. Stuart," Dr. Ames said, beaming at the patient. Gloria and I strongly suspected her coffee was laced with alcohol, though I had to give it to her. Her lipstick was perfect. "I once had a patient with such severe impaction, she was *seven* pounds lighter when we discharged her! I have never seen so much stool in my life!" She smiled, pleased with the memory.

"Thanks for sharing," I said.

"You're welcome!" She raised her voice. "Mrs. Constantine, Nora is *excellent* at *disimpaction*. Aren't you, darling? Very *gentle* hands! Well, I have calls to make. Let me know if you need me, Nora, dear!" She wobbled off to her office.

"Why is she yelling at me?" the patient asked.

"She's a unique personality," I said. "But she's right, I'm good at this."

"Good," she said. "The last time I had this done, it felt like the doctor used an elephant tusk."

"We got rid of all our tusks last year," I said, smiling.

I'll spare you the details, but one gently administered enema later, and armed with some glycerine suppositories, Mrs. Constantine left, a happier woman.

"Busy day," Gloria commented as I finished the report and sent it to the insurance company. "Are you dying of boredom?"

"Not at all. It's kind of fun, seeing all different types of cases."

"Do you miss Boston?"

"A little. Do you?"

"Well, I'm not from the city proper, you know?" she said.

"What brought you out here, anyway? Aside from the lobsterman fantasy, that is?"

"I wanted a change. I like the slower pace on the island, and I like running this place. No offense." She smiled. "My family's pretty intense. Like every other day, someone's having a first Communion or a christening or a baby. My mother calls me four times a day just to 'catch up.' I have to pretend the cell service sucks out here just to get some peace and quiet. I love them, but too much of a good thing, you know?"

"Not really. Maybe we could trade families."

"You're not close with yours, I take it?"

I shrugged. "You've met my mom."

"She's an impressive woman."

I felt an unexpected flash of pride. "She is. Not warm and cuddly, though."

The bell buzzed, letting us know we had another patient. "Four in one day," Gloria said, pulling a face. "Grand Central Station here. I'll go see what's up."

A few minutes later, Gloria called me to the exam room. It was Mr. Carver, the man who'd occasionally given my father work. First name Henry, according to his chart. "Hi, Mr. Carver," I said. "Nice to see you again."

"Oh, Nora," he said, blushing. "Ah... I didn't expect you."

"BP is normal, heart rate's perfect, O_2 sat 98 percent," Gloria said. "Call if you need me." She left the room.

"What can I do for you today?" I asked.

"Well... Is there another doctor I can see?" he asked. "A man?"

"I'm afraid not."

He sighed.

"Everything you say will be confidential, Mr. Carver."

"You don't seem old enough to be a doctor."

I always loved that comment. "Well, I'm thirty-five. Tufts undergrad, Tufts Medical School, fellowship at Boston City, partner at Boston Gastroenterology Associates, board certified in family practice and gastroenterology... Shall I go on?"

"It's just...personal."

"I assure you, I've heard everything."

He blushed.

"Erectile dysfunction?" I guessed.

He looked away, his face getting redder. "Bingo."

He'd been put on blood pressure medication, a classic cause of ED. I asked him some questions and did an exam. He was basically the guy for whom Viagra had been invented. I wrote him a prescription, went over the side effects and warning signs and recommended a pharmacy in Portland if he didn't want it filled here.

"This is great," he said, clearly relieved. "Thanks, Nora. I mean Dr. Stuart."

"Nora's just fine," I said.

"Your mom must be very proud of you."

"I hope so. Hey, I was wondering…do you know anyone who might be interested in…well, in dating my mother? I worry about her being too lonely."

His face colored again. "She's… Well, I, ah, I'd have to give that some thought."

"I know, I know, I'm matchmaking, but what can I say?" I smiled. "Everyone deserves love, right? Let me know if you have any questions about the medication."

He left, still blushing. Too bad he was married. I wouldn't have minded him for a stepfather.

I hadn't seen my mom for a few days, though I'd left a message on her landline; she didn't usually respond to texts. Poe had come over for supper on hug therapy night and made a few grunts as I tried to ask her questions. Progress.

I stuck my head in Gloria's office. "I'm off to see my mom," I told her. "Want me to bring you any lunch?"

"I'm eating a salad," she said, pulling a face. "Kale."

"Your digestive track will thank you. Okay, see you in a bit."

The Excelsior Pines, where Mom had long worked, was a beautiful white, three-story hotel on the water with unrivaled views. It was a popular place for weddings in the summer and ran special fall and winter packages in the off-seasons to lure the mainlanders here.

Mrs. Krazinski worked at the front desk—mother of Lizzy Krizzy. "Hi, Mrs. K," I said as I came in. Her name tag said "Donna." Funny, how when you're a kid, you never know the names of the adults.

"Hello there, Nora," she said. "Your mother told me you were back for the summer! How are you?"

"I'm good. How are you? How's Lizzy?"

"Oh, she's fine. Lives in Connecticut now, works on Wall Street. Her husband stays home with their kids. Three of them now." She whipped out her phone and flashed a picture of a smiling family at me. Lizzy looked just the same.

"Aw, that's great. Tell her I said hi, will you?" I remembered that their house has been listed as a rental. "So where are you and Mr. K living these days?" I asked. "I saw your house listed as a rental."

"Well, we got a divorce about five years ago."

"Shoot. I'm sorry. You know my mom. She's not one to gossip."

"Ayuh. I've got a little place here in town just around the corner from the Clam Shack. You here to see your mom, I'm guessing?"

"I am. Is she free?"

"Well, you know her. Always working. Go on in, honey."

Mrs. K. She'd always been nice. I paused. "Mrs. Krazinski," I said in a low voice, "I hope this doesn't put you in an uncomfortable spot, since you work with Mom, but I was wondering if you ever heard anything about my father. Where he went after he left the island."

Her brows drew together. "No, honey, I'm sorry. I never did. I used to ask your mom about it way back when, but she didn't know much, either, and after a while, I just stopped asking. Figured if she wanted me to know, she'd have told me."

Sounded like Mom, all right. "Well, I sure would love to know what happened, so if you think of anyone I could talk to..."

"Sure, honey. Now, go see your mom."

I obeyed. My mother was sitting at her desk, a container of yogurt next to her on top of a pile of folders.

"Hey, Mom."

"Hi, Nora. What's the matter?"

"Nothing. Just wanted to say hello."

"Oh. Well. Hello."

My two burning questions—*You getting any these days?* and *Whatever happened to Dad?*—were too freaky to include in the same conversation. I decided to go with Operation Find Mom a Honey.

"I was wondering if you might want to come by the houseboat for dinner on Friday," I said. "I'm having a little dinner party." Not that I'd planned on it, but why not? Time to show off my new digs.

"I'm not much for parties, Nora."

"Please come, Mother." I stared at her.

"Well, what about Poe?"

"Poe can come, or she can stay by herself. She's almost sixteen."

"I have work to do." She turned back to her computer.

"You always have work to do."

"That's right. So thanks all the same."

"Mom. Come to my house for dinner. Please. For me."

She sighed.

"Otherwise, I'll be forced to show up at hug therapy and—"

"Fine, fine. I'll come. What time? Don't make it too late. I like to be in bed before nine-thirty."

Victory. "Seven?"

"Are we in France or somethin'? Fine."

Yoga breath, yoga breath. "Thanks, Mom. It'll be nice."

"Who else is coming?"

"Just a few friends." Every unmarried man under the age of eighty I could find. I'd ask Mr. Dobbins (Bawb), our hug-hungry first selectman, and, uh…well, I'd find one or two more. I could think of three. I'd ask Xiaowen to come, and Gloria, too. My place could fit ten, I thought—Collier Rhodes hadn't skimped on size.

A party would be fun. I did like to cook, and let's face it, without Boomer, I was lonely.

Mission accomplished for the moment, I left the hotel and walked back to the clinic. The dogwoods along Main Street were blooming, their flowers seeming to float on the air in a way that never failed to charm me. I stopped in The Cracked Spine, bought the latest Stephen King novel (against my will, but the man had a hold on me). I added a few postcards of scenic Scupper Island to send to my Boston buddies.

"Where are you from?" the woman behind the desk

asked as she rang me up. She looked familiar. Penny, that was her name. Penny Walters. She'd gone to the same church as we did. No kids, if I recalled.

"I'm from here, actually," I said. "I'm Sharon Stuart's daughter."

"Oh, sure! I just love your daughter," she said. "So nice to see a teenager who reads."

"Poe is my niece," I said. "I'm Nora, the other daughter." At her blank stare, I added, "The doctor who lives in Boston. My mother has two daughters."

"No, I remember. It's just that you look very... young."

"Thank you."

It wasn't that I looked young, I knew. It was that I wasn't a fat kid with acne and bad hair anymore.

And I hadn't been back in fifteen years. And my mother didn't talk about me much, apparently.

Penny busied herself behind the counter.

The door opened, and in came Xiaowen. "Hey!" I said, brightening.

"Hey yourself. What did you buy? Oh, Stephen King. I hate that man."

"I know. He's crack. What are you looking for?"

"I made the sad mistake of loaning out *Harry Potter and the Chamber of Secrets* to my nephew, and guess who dropped it in the bathtub? He's out of the will, let me tell you."

"You loan out your Harry Potters?" I asked in horror.

"Not anymore. The little bastard owes me twenty-five bucks. Do you have it in stock?" she asked Penny. "Hardcover, of course."

"I'll order it for you," Penny said.

Xiaowen sighed. "Well, there goes my weekend."

"Listen," I said, "just this once, I'll loan you mine. But I expect you to treat it like the Book of Kells, okay?"

"I'll wear gloves when reading it."

"No food, water or fire near it."

"I understand." She smiled.

"What are you doing Friday night?" I asked. "I'm having a dinner party."

"Like a real grown-up?"

"Exactly. Want to come?"

"Shit, yes! What time? And are you inviting men? Because I do have to warn you, I am *not* on the market, but they'll all make a pass. My cross to bear—all straight men and half the gays want me."

"Who can blame them?" I said, smiling.

"Are you girl-crushing on me? Who can blame *you*? I'd love to come! Any old classmates we can torture with how well we've aged?"

"Do you have anyone specific in mind?"

"Georgie Frank. God, I had the worst crush on him in high school. He still lives here, right?"

I grimaced. "Um… I don't know. I can't say I remember him."

"You're kidding! He was so hot. Receding hairline? Those big teeth? Come on! He was basically Neville Longbottom! Wouldn't give me the time of day back then."

"Oh, him! Yes, of course. I'll give him a call."

"Maybe the Fletcher boys, too. Who was the hot one? He was my lab partner. Mike?"

"Luke. I probably won't ask him." Nope, one doesn't invite an asshole to one's home.

"Oh, wait. You beat him out for something… What

was it? A scholarship! You were the Perez Scholar! I forgot about that!"

"You did? I mean, weren't you up for it, too?"

She snorted. "I'm sorry to say I didn't have a tiger mom, Nora. She's more like a kitten. My GPA was no-where near yours. I was only good in math and science. I barely passed English and social studies, and not because I'm from China. Because I hated reading until J.K. Rowling showed me the light."

"I'm closing for lunch," Penny said. "If you ladies are finished…?"

"Fine, we're leaving. Order me that book, okay? I'll come get it next week." She gave me a quick hug. "The oyster beds await. I'll see you Friday. Want me to come early and lie around and drink wine and watch you do all the work?"

"I do!" I said. "I'm so glad you can come. This party just got much better."

"It really did." She grinned.

We left the shop, and Xiaowen got into her car, a sporty silver Porsche, and pulled away from the curb.

My phone buzzed. Bobby, texting me a few pictures—Boomer lying in the middle of what was once our bed, his head on the pillow; Boomer at the Commons, sniffing a Chihuahua and looking very handsome. We miss you, read the text. Hope you're having a good day.

I did not want to get back together with Bobby Byrne, I reminded myself.

Except we'd only had three normal months. If we could go back to how things had been…

But we couldn't. He'd gotten tired of my woes after the home invasion. He'd fondled Jabrielle's hair and flirted with her as I lay unconscious and bruised. He wasn't worthy of me.

Still, it was disturbingly *fantastic* to know he wanted me back.

THAT NIGHT, I lay on the couch, nursing a glass of red wine for health, smugly satisfied with my dinner party plans. Guess who wasn't married, even though he still wore a ring? Mr. Carver, he of the Viagra prescription (may Mrs. Carver rest in peace, but clearly he was ready to get back in the game, so…). And yes, he was free on Friday, if a little confused by my invitation.

Bob Dobbins said yes the second the words *my mother* left my lips. Also coming was Jake the grumpy ferryman, because he was also single (twice divorced, but I wasn't judging). Hopefully, he would shower first, because based on the smell of him, it wasn't a daily—or weekly—habit. So three eligible-ish men for my mother, plus Gloria, Xiaowen and myself.

Georgie Frank owned the hotel where my mother worked. Who knew? And according to his LinkedIn profile, he had grown into his looks, just like the actor who'd played Neville Longbottom. Unfortunately, he had another commitment that night, so I told him we'd have to get together with Xiaowen and catch up on old times. He sounded so nice.

It was funny how my memories were shifting now that I was back home. In high school, I'd felt like the loneliest girl in the world. But Georgie had sounded so happy to hear from me, I wondered if maybe I'd missed out on potential friends, too busy being miserable.

The birds were singing; Lily used to call them their pajama songs. How cute was that? On impulse, I got up and found one of the postcards I'd bought today. It was the gratuitous-sunset-over-the-harbor shot, the sailboats (all belonging to summer folk) reflected in the calm waters, the golden rocks and pine trees of the island behind them like a distant fortress.

Dear Lily,
The birds are singing their pajama songs, and the bats are out. The other day, I brought Poe to East-man Hill. It was steeper than I remembered. You used to hold your arms out like you were flying, but you never fell. Dad never let you.
Love,
Nora

So what if she hadn't written back? Or told Poe to say hi to me? Or contacted me in any way in the last five years? My sister was going to hear from me, damn it. I scrawled on the prison's address, peeled off a stamp and shoved it in my purse so I could mail it tomorrow at Teeny Fletcher's stupid little post office. I took a defiant sip of my wine. Nobody puts Nora in the corner.

Then, all of a sudden, the lights went out. I jumped and felt wine slosh on my shirt. Shit.

When I say it was dark, it was more than just the absence of light. It was as if the darkness had a texture and a sinister presence.

Also, I'd had a glass and a half of wine, started a Stephen King book and was slightly buzzed.

Without the hum of the fridge and water heater, without the little lights I took for granted—the laptop charger, the microwave clock, the smoke detector—I felt completely lost. I felt the houseboat move on the water in a way it didn't seem to when I could see.

There was a thump on the dock. But that was normal, right? The dock and houseboat made noise all the time, thunking, squeaking, creaking. Maybe once in a while, thumping, too.

If only Boomer was here, I'd feel much, much safer.

My heart stuttered and sped. Not quite V-fib, but close.

The power is out, Nora. Get a grip. The electricity went out on a little island like this all the time. Sure it did. Practically everyone had a generator for storms—hurricanes and nor'easters in the fall, blizzards in the winter.

Except there was no storm now.

Had someone cut my power?

Luke Fletcher. Or…or *him.* Voldemort, he who could not be caught, thanks for nothing, Boston Police Department.

Could he have found me?

It was possible. He could've followed me here. If he was really obsessed with me, he could've figured it out. This time, there *had* been something public: the *Scupper Island Weekly*, which had an online version, had a snippet about me two weeks ago. *Dr. Nora Stuart, a graduate of Scupper High, will be practicing medicine at the Ames Medical Clinic four days a week.*

I whirled to look for my phone—it had a flashlight feature, God bless Apple—and slammed into the table, which was bolted to the floor. My breath hissed out of me. That'd leave a bruise for sure, but I couldn't yelp, because if someone was out there, I didn't want him to know where I was.

Crawl. Yes. That was a great idea. I wasn't sure why, but everyone crawled in the movies, right? And maybe I wouldn't crash into the table if I was on the floor.

I dropped to my knees and groped around. Where the hell had I left my phone? Table? Nope. Uh…couch? I crawled, my knee burning with pain. Right, right, I'd dislocated that sucker, hadn't I? This made me try to crawl without using that knee, kind of humped up but still technically crawling, which made me feel like a werewolf in the throes of changing.

I groped. Groped some more. Nothing.

Shit! I banged my head on the coffee table. Must all the furniture be bolted to the floor? I mean, yes, I guess it did, since this was a houseboat, but it sure was inconvenient when crawling from a potential killer, wasn't it?

I couldn't find my phone.

But I knew exactly where my Smith & Wesson was, yessiree.

I crawl-hobbled to the hallway, hit my head on the wall—just call me Audrey Hepburn—and groped my way toward my bedroom, feeling for the door frame.

He dragged me by the legs down the hall. I grabbed onto the bathroom door frame, but my fingers weren't strong enough.

Shit. Now was not the time for a flashback.

"You're in Maine," I whispered. "You're okay. Get your gun and find your phone."

There was another thump on the dock. Oh, God, oh, God. Now I was in my room, my knee on fire. I groped for the night table drawer, found it.

I stood up. I knew where I was now; my eyes had adjusted to the darkness. Like a ninja (with a bad knee and an intense case of the shakes and smelling of a plummy merlot with tobacco overtones), I shuffled back down the hall and crouched behind the kitchen counter. *You're a very brave, strong woman, Nora*, I told myself. Myself didn't believe me.

A man was coming down the dock, flashlight aimed at his feet.

Could I shoot a person? Someone who might be trying to kill me? What was the law in Maine about killing trespassers? Was it okay? Probably not. I mean, there were laws about killing moose. People were probably protected, too.

Also, there was that "first, do no harm" thing I'd sworn to. Shooting someone with a gun seemed like harm.

Calm down, Nora. Take a breath.

Before I let myself become Dirty Harry, I should probably know who was there.

"Nora?"

He knew my name, whoever he was. Luke knew my name.

So did the man who tried to kill me.

"Nora? It's Sullivan Fletcher."

"Oh, Jesus," I said, slumping to the floor and letting the gun slide from my limp fingers.

"Nora, you home?" he called.

I hauled myself up and hobbled to the door. "Hi," I said. He was silhouetted against the starry sky, but it was Sullivan, all right.

"Thought I'd check on you. I was at the boatyard." Just then, the lights came back on, and I blinked. Sully frowned. "You okay?" he asked.

"Sure," I said.

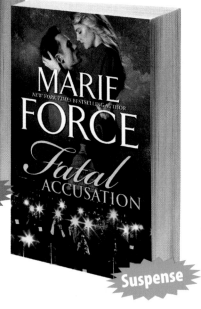

Get up to 4
FREE FABULOUS BOOKS
You Love!

To thank you for being a loyal reader we'd like to send you up to 4 FREE BOOKS, absolutely free.

Just write "YES" on the Loyal Reader Voucher and we'll send you up to 4 Free Books and Free Mystery Gifts, altogether worth over $20, as a way of saying thank you for being a loyal reader.

Try **Essential Suspense** featuring spine-tingling suspense and psychological thrillers with many written by today's best-selling authors.

Try **Essential Romance** featuring compelling romance stories with many written by today's best-selling authors.

Or **TRY BOTH!**

We are so glad you love the books as much as we do and can't wait to send you great new books.

So don't miss out, return your Loyal Reader Voucher Today!

Pam Powers

LOYAL READER
FREE BOOKS VOUCHER

YES! I Love Reading, please send me up to 4 FREE BOOKS and Free Mystery Gifts from the series I select.

Just write in "YES" on the dotted line below then return this card today and we'll send your free books & gifts asap!

➡ _ _ YES _ _ ⬅

Which do you prefer?

☐ **Essential Suspense**
191/391 MDL GNR4

☐ **Essential Romance**
194/394 MDL GNR4

☐ **BOTH**
191/391 & 194/394
MDL GNSG

FIRST NAME

LAST NAME

ADDRESS

APT.#

CITY

STATE/PROV.

ZIP/POSTAL CODE

ST-220-OMLR20

BUSINESS REPLY MAIL

FIRST-CLASS MAIL   PERMIT NO. 717   BUFFALO, NY

POSTAGE WILL BE PAID BY ADDRESSEE

READER SERVICE
PO BOX 1341
BUFFALO NY 14240-8571

NO POSTAGE
NECESSARY
IF MAILED
IN THE
UNITED STATES

His gaze went to the kitchen floor. "That's a very impressive gun there."

"Yes. Yep."

"You sure you're okay? You look...out of sorts."

Did I? I glanced at the mirror that hung to the left of the door. Oh, shit, yes, *out of sorts* was accurate. And generous. My hair had taken on the proportions of an unchecked tumbleweed, and my mascara was smeared under my eyes. My shirt had a splotch of red wine right over the boob. "I'm fine!" I said. "Just a little... Hi! How are you? Come in."

He did, a bit warily.

"Can you give me a second? I, uh, I have to change."

"Sure."

I reached for the gun.

"Why don't I get that?" he said, neatly intercepting me. He picked it up, took out the magazine, opened the chamber and removed that bullet, too. "I wasn't planning on being shot today."

"No. Me, neither." I drew in a shuddering breath. "Right. Back in a flash."

I went back into the bedroom and closed the door. Pulled off my clothes and hastily tugged on some yoga pants and a loose T-shirt, then grabbed my hair and gathered it into a ponytail. Ran some moisturizer under my eyes and wiped them clean with a tissue. My hands were still shaking a little.

Sully was sitting on the couch when I came out. Mr. Smith & Wesson was on the counter.

"So," he said.

"Want a drink, Sully?"

"Sure."

I grabbed him a beer—he seemed like a beer kind

of guy—and got myself a glass of water and sat down in the chair opposite him.

We eyed each other for a minute. He took a sip of beer, then set it on the coffee table where I'd whacked my head. "You always answer the door with a gun?"

"Not always."

"That thing would do some damage."

"That's why I have it."

He was looking at me intently; right, he had hearing loss, so he probably needed to watch my mouth when I talked.

It was a little unsettling.

"How are your ears?" I asked, then closed my eyes. "I mean your hearing. How is it?" I looked at him, feeling my cheeks blaze.

He didn't answer. I hoped he hadn't heard me, then felt guilty for hoping that.

"How's Audrey? I mean, is she alone? With the power out?"

"She's with her mother."

"Oh, good! That's great, I mean, because you said they didn't spend a lot of…well! That's nice! That they're hanging out." I took a deep breath, held it and let it out slowly.

There was no threat to me. I could relax. I was fun. I was brave and smart.

"How are you, Sully?"

His eyes crinkled the slightest bit. "I'm fine."

"Good."

His smile grew. Not by much, but by enough. That was a good face, especially with the smile. A calm face. A nice face.

"Do you want to have dinner here on Friday?" I asked on impulse. "I'm having a little party."

"Sure."

"You don't have to come, but—oh. Great. Um, seven o'clock." He said yes. That was… That was really nice.

He looked at me steadily. I guess he had to, what with the hearing loss. I took a breath, trying for normal. "Can I ask you some questions, Sully?"

"Go for it."

"What's it like? Not hearing?"

He looked at his beer. "Well, I *can* hear, obviously. Just…not that well. Not at all on the right. It's getting worse on the left." He took a pull of beer. "Some words cut out or get fuzzy. I have to string things together. Sometimes I get it wrong, especially when I'm tired."

So he had auditory processing disorder in addition to true deafness on the right. Very common for a traumatic brain injury. "Do you lip-read?"

"Ayuh."

"What about sign language?"

"I'm starting that. Audrey, too."

The picture of them learning sign language together made my heart swell painfully. "Sullivan, I'm so sorry about that accident."

"Already told you it wasn't your fault."

"But I was…involved."

"No, you weren't."

Again, he was being generous. "Well. It feels like I was."

"Can I ask *you* something now?" he said.

"Sure."

"Why are you afraid of the dark? Power goes out all the time here. You know that."

I hesitated. "Don't tell anyone, okay?" He nodded and I trusted him. Audrey's dad, after all. Good old Sullivan, the quiet one. "I, uh… I had an experience last year. A bad one."

"What kind of experience?"

"The not-good kind." I pulled a face, trying to make light of it. The less said, the better as far as I was concerned.

He didn't say anything for a second, and I wondered if he'd heard me.

"Were you hurt?" he asked.

A memory of my face, purple and blue, the cut on my jaw, my left eye swollen shut, came back to me. Those days when only my schizophrenic hair made me believe it was me in the mirror. "A little bit."

He didn't ask any more, and I loved him for that. "But here you are," he said.

It wasn't a lot, those words, but somehow, they steadied me.

Bobby used to hold me close and murmur that he was here, I was safe, he'd never let anyone hurt me. At the time I'd been so, so grateful to have him there, feeling like a broken bird, needing him to a degree that made me feel weak.

Sully and his calm brown eyes…they said something different. I wasn't sure what, but it was something better.

"You all set here?" he asked rather abruptly. "Now that the lights are back on?"

"Yes. Thank you. Thank you so much, Sullivan. For checking on me."

He pulled out his wallet and took out a card. "That's my landline and the boatyard phone. You have my cell," he said. "If you ever need anything, call me." He put the card on the counter, then looked at me again. "Good night."

With that he left, his work boots thunking on the dock. After a second, I heard his truck start up. The sound faded into the distance, and all was quiet again.

A half an hour before, I'd been so scared I'd almost shot my old classmate. Now, however, I was just fine.

15

I WOKE UP late on Friday. Because I had the day off, I didn't have to rush the party prep.

I had ended up inviting Amelia to the party, too; Gloria told me she didn't have much of a social life, and my innate sense of Lutheran duty flared. Also, she signed my paychecks. There was that, too.

School was out today because of professional development, so I decided to take Poe for an outing and drove to my mom's house. After only twenty minutes of cajoling, ordering, begging and bribing, I convinced my precious niece to finally shove her arms into a denim jacket and slump outside with me.

The road that led to our house continued a few hundred feet past it, into the state forest, marked by a sign that lectured on littering and swimming at your own risk. I went around the chain slung across the path, Poe a few paces behind me.

"Where are we even going?" Poe asked.

"It's a place where your mom and I used to play," I said.

"Yay," she muttered.

We walked through the woods on a path springy with pine needles. The wind was gentle today, the sky achingly blue. Seagulls squawked overhead, and a crow fluttered from tree to tree, clicking occasionally, as if it wanted to be part of the conversation.

Poe almost walked into a tree, so busy looking at her phone. "There's no cell service out here," she said.

"Oh, well."

"Stupid," she muttered, shoving her phone back into her pocket.

"How have things been at school?" I asked.

"Fine."

"Do you and Audrey ever hang out?"

"Not really."

"Any other friends?"

"Is there a reason to make friends, when I'm going back to Seattle in a couple months?" she asked with exaggerated patience.

"You have a point," I said. "But it might be nice to have a friend back here. For when you come to visit Gran." I pushed a tree branch away from my face and held it for Poe. The smell of the sea was stronger now. "By the way, I'd love if you came to visit me, too. Anytime. Maybe you'll want to go to college out here. Boston has a lot of great schools, and so many great restaurants and things to do." I sounded like a tourism brochure.

"Do you have an apartment?" she asked.

"Not at the moment. My boyfriend and I were liv-

ing together. But before that, I had a really great place."
Best not to think about that. "Okay, we're almost there."

We came out of the woods onto the great golden slabs
of rock that made up the shore. The tide was low, and
the rocks were dark brown where the water had been
just an hour before.

My feet hadn't forgotten a thing. The cracks where I
had to jump, the slanted rock that was perfect for pushing off, the little plateau with the best tide pool. Sure
enough, two fiddler crabs were inside, skittering around
each other in their own little world. I knew the way as
if I'd never left the island.

There was the rock that looked like an old lady in
profile, then the rock Lily called the Tooth, because it
had little ridges and bumps, like a molar.

And here we were. I jumped down onto the rocky
little beach. "Ta-da," I said, waving my arm like Vanna
White, pretending it didn't hurt my heart, seeing this
place again. "Come on in."

To access the entrance to the cave, you had to go out
a bit. Unless the tide was dead low, as it was now, your
feet would get wet. At high tide, the cave was underwater. I led the way, my shoes crunching on the pebbles
that made up the shallow beach.

Inside, it was damp and briny, and memories flooded
in like a storm surge.

I could almost see Lily, her unexpected, booming
laugh as she crouched next to me. Her sweet smile, the
dimple in her left cheek, her shiny black hair.

Poe followed me inside. Even she couldn't look dis-
interested in this. "Cool," she said, her mouth opening a little.

"We used to pretend this was our house," I said,

more to myself than Poe. "We'd drape seaweed over the opening to make a door, so none of the fishermen could see us from the ocean." I pointed to a spot in the back, where the cave narrowed and a piece of rock jutted from the shore, making a surface that was more or less flat. "That was our bed." I'd hold my sister against me, since it wasn't quite wide enough for two, her skinny little body snug against my side.

I swallowed. "We'd set up rocks here and pretend to have a fire. Sometimes Gran would make us peanut-butter-and-apple sandwiches, and we'd eat them here. The seagulls would follow us in to get a bite."

And then later, when Dad was in charge of us, we'd do what he called the Cave Challenge—who could stay in the longest as the cave filled up with water? It was a survivalist skill, he said, and I remembered the fear as the water came up to our knees, our waists, our shoulders.

I was always the first one out, waiting anxiously on the Tooth for their heads to pop up in the water. Dad and Lily would stay in there till I was terrified they'd drowned, and just as I was about to go get help, there they'd be, laughing, gasping, triumphant.

I wouldn't tell Poe about that.

The cave was big enough for us to stand, but not much else. Like so many things from childhood, it seemed to have shrunk. But it smelled the same—the wet, cold rocks, the salt water that slushed and slapped.

"Your mom and I thought we were the only ones who knew about this place," I said. "Our Dad, too. But we made a pact never to show anyone else."

"Did you ever?" Poe asked. "Bring someone here, I mean?"

"Not until today."

"Did she?"

Maybe she had. Maybe she'd come here with the boys she'd slept with, or with Amy Beckman to smoke weed. The thought stabbed like a dull spear. If Lily had made fun of me here, if she'd mocked our little games, if this place wasn't as sacred to her as it was to me...

"I don't know," I said, my voice husky.

It didn't matter. She'd given me up a long time ago.

A little wave sloshed over my shoe. "We better go," I said. "The tide has turned, and it fills up fast. It wouldn't be hard to drown in here."

"Yikes," Poe said. "Nora..."

Funny, I couldn't remember her saying my name before.

"Yes, honey?"

"Thanks for showing me."

"You bet." I smiled at her, and she almost smiled back.

When we got back to the house, my mother was home. I glanced at my watch; lunchtime. Mom often came back home to eat or, more often, brown-bagged it. Never bought something from town, never went out. That would be wasteful.

"Hello, you two," she said.

"I'm going to my room," Poe said. She gave me a look, then, shockingly, a shy hug, fleeting and all the sweeter because of it. My throat tightened.

"Are you coming over for dinner?" I asked.

"With all the old people? Uh, no. Thanks." She rolled her eyes, but it wasn't with the usual disgust, then went upstairs.

Mom was in the kitchen, glancing through the mail.

I sat down at the table. Like everything in the house, it was sturdy and worn, just like my mother. Last weekend had been Mother's Day. I'd given her a gift certificate to a spa in Portland—manicure, pedicure, facial, same as I did every year. But this year, I saw her tuck it in the spice rack, and when she was out of the room, I went to check. Sure enough, there were all the other gift certificates from all the other years. She never used them.

Then again, she always said what a nice gift it was. She was an enigma, my mother.

"How was your day, Mom?"

"Fine. Yours?"

"Lovely. I can't wait for our little dinner party later on."

"About that, Nora. I really don't want to come."

"But you will, and you might even have fun."

She snorted, then opened the fridge to make herself a sandwich. Same sandwich she always ate—two slices of chicken, one slice of American cheese, mustard and butter, whole wheat bread. She saw me watching. "You want one?"

"No, thanks. Hey, American cheese is all fat, you know. It's not really even cheese."

"I like it."

So did I. Who didn't? "Just watching out for your cholesterol."

She plated the sandwich, poured herself a glass of milk and sat down at the table. Took a bite of her sandwich and chewed placidly, like a cow.

It was as intimate a moment as we were going to have. "Mom, I have a question for you."

"You always do."

"Yes, well…it's about Dad."

The chewing didn't stop. "What about him?"

"Did you ever hear from him? Ever?"

She swallowed, took a drink of milk. "Nora, we've been over this a thousand times."

"No, we haven't."

A sigh. "I haven't heard from your father in more than twenty years."

"But did you *ever* hear from him? I mean, he must be somewhere."

"I'm sure that's true."

"I just want to know what happened to him. If he's alive, even. Do you know that?"

"You think I murdered him?"

"That did cross my mind, but no, I don't."

She took another bite of sandwich. "There were days I wanted to."

"Yes, I'm sure. But come on, Mom. I've Googled him a thousand times. Maybe he had a friend I didn't know about?"

"I don't know, Nora. I don't see what the point is after all these years."

"He was a great father. It never made any sense."

She didn't say anything for a minute. "If he was a great father, he wouldn't have left you girls."

I nodded. "It's hard to reconcile those things."

"Well, you've had twenty years to do just that, dahlin'. Twenty-four, but who's counting? I have to get back to work. I'll see you tonight. What time?"

"Seven."

"Guess I won't be home for *Wheel of Fortune.*" Another sigh. She got up and started to wash her plate and glass.

"I'll do that, Mom."

"I got it," she said, not looking at me. She was irritated, both by the dinner party and the conversation.

"Okay," I said. "See you later."

XIAOWEN MADE GOOD on her offer to come early, drink wine and shuck the oysters she'd brought, harvested from beds she'd planted herself. We slurped down a couple with a glass of wine, the fresh taste of ocean with a little bit of sweetness, thanks to the mouth of the riverbed where she'd planted them, she told me. Also, she'd put on her wet suit and dived for them herself, because she was just that cool.

It was so nice, having her here. "Did you hate high school as much as I did?" I asked, chopping the ends off the asparagus I was serving.

"Oh, God, yes," she said. "Those mean girls were brutal to me. I always appreciated when you said hi to me in the halls."

"Same here." I paused. "I wish we'd been closer back then."

"Yeah, me, too. I was shy back then, and you…you seemed so sad all the time."

"I was." I chopped some parsley, not looking at my friend. "My father left us when I was in fifth grade, and my sister and I weren't really close after that."

"I remember her as quite a bitch," Xiaowen said. "She threw a used tampon at me in the bathroom one time."

My head jerked up. "Are you kidding?"

"Nope."

"I'm so sorry! God, that's… That really is horrible." I'd always suspected Lily was like that… I just didn't want it to be true.

My phone buzzed—Gloria, with an apologetic text saying she couldn't make it; her brother had a crisis and she'd taken the last ferry to Boston and would see me Monday. I texted back that I hoped all was well.

"Gloria can't come, I'm afraid," I said.

"Too bad," Xiaowen said. "You guys close?"

"Not yet. But she's a great nurse, and we get along really well at work. Hey, speaking of work, I've seen at least three girls this week with eating disorders. Two overeaters, one anorexic. Maybe you remember, I had a problem with food myself."

"You Americans." Xiaowen sighed.

"I know. But I was thinking of doing something to raise public awareness." I thought of sweet Audrey. "Some kind of fun run. All shapes, all sizes, that kind of thing."

"Want help? Since I'm not getting married this summer, I have plenty of time on my hands."

"That would be great!" I handed her another oyster. "You want to talk about the fiancé?"

"If by *talk about*, you mean *murder*, the answer is yes." She sucked down the oyster. "In all seriousness, no. The classic story of I saw what I wanted to see, and then got bitch-slapped by reality. He cheated on me."

"I hate him."

"Thank you."

A knock came on the door, and there they all were, lined up on the dock like I was about to shoot them: Mom; Bob Dobbins; Henry Carver; Jake Ferriman, holding a twelve-pack of beer; Amelia with a bottle of her own; and just coming down the dock now, Sullivan. It was exactly seven o'clock.

"Sullivan Fletcher," Xiaowen murmured appreciatively. "If my heart wasn't encased in iron, I'd climb him like a tree." She cut her eyes to me. "You could do worse."

"His daughter's been hanging out here," I said. "And he did me a favor the other night." But, hey, she had a point. I opened the door. "Hi, everyone! You're so punctual! Come on in."

"After you, Sharon," Bob said. My mother gave him an irritated glance; I guess if Bob wasn't paying for hugs, she had no use for him.

Then again, Bob was wearing a brilliant yellow, uh, blouse, complete with ruffles, and, if I wasn't mistaken, had marinated himself in a barrel of Polo by Ralph Lauren. "Bob." I wheezed as he kissed my cheek. "So glad you could come. Mr. Carver! How are you?"

"Call me Henry," he said. "I brought you some wine."

"Thank you!" I said, taking it. Boone's Farm Strawberry Hill. "We'll have to open this for dessert." Or regift it to a wino on the streets of Boston.

"What a charming place!" Amelia cooed. "Isn't! This! Lovely! I'm Amelia Ames," she said to Jake. "Wonderful to meet you."

"We've met," he said, clutching his twelve-pack a little closer.

"Have we? I don't remember. Nora, darling, I brought you some vodka." She set it on the counter with a thump. "Be a good girl and pour me some, won't you?"

"Not her first, I'm guessing," Xiaowen murmured. "Come on, people! Move along, you're crowding the kitchen."

Sullivan was last in. "Hi," I said.

"Hi." He handed me a pie.

A *pie*.

It was still warm. "Strawberry rhubarb," he said.

"Did you make this?" Because of the chatter from the living room, I made sure to look right at him so he could hear me.

"Ayuh."

"Do you mind if I go in the bedroom and eat it right now?"

He smiled, just a little. My girl parts also smiled. I cleared my throat. "Would you like a drink?"

"Sure."

I poured my guests wine (vodka for Amelia) and offered Jake a glass, which he refused, already downing his second can of beer, his eyes on Xiaowen's chest.

"When's supper?" Mom asked.

"Soon," I said. "We have cheese and crackers and shrimp, and Xiaowen brought us some beautiful oysters."

"What's your name again?" Bob asked.

"Xiaowen," she said.

"Sh—what? That's quite a mouthful," he said. "Do you have a nickname that's easier to say?"

"I *do* have a nickname! It's fuck off. Can you say that?" She slurped an oyster down and raised her middle finger. Bob blinked, then looked at his shoes.

I smothered a laugh. "*She-ao-wen*, Bob," I said. "Just three little syllables. Mom, would you like a glass of wine?"

"Water, please."

Of course. Far be it for her to loosen up with a drink. Her expression said she'd be happier on death row.

"Speaking of names, I was named for Amelia Earhart," Amelia said, gazing up at the ceiling. "She was a great-aunt of mine."

"Really?" Mr. Carver said. "I always admired her. My wife…" His voice thickened. "My wife went to a Halloween party dressed like her once."

Jake popped another beer. "You like older men?" he asked Xiaowen.

"I like older men who bathe," she said. "When was the last time you hit the showers?"

"Let me help you with things, Nora," Mom said, getting up. "So we can get this show on the road."

Sullivan, meanwhile, watched. I hoped he was catching the conversation. He saw me looking and gave me a little nod.

"Why are all these men here?" my mother hissed at me in the kitchen.

"Uh… I don't know. I just ran into them," I lied. "Xiaowen isn't a man. I'm not a man. You're not a man."

"Are you matchmaking, Nora Louise?"

Ruh-roh. The middle name. "No! I ran into Mr. Carver at the bakery and remembered that he used to hire Dad for some work, and, of course, Bob from hug therapy knew Dad. I thought maybe they might know something."

My mother sighed. "You're obsessed with your father."

I was lying, actually, but she wasn't wrong.

"You like everyone here, though, right?" I asked. "I mean, you're not on the outs with anyone?"

"No, Nora. Everyone here is fine," she snapped, irritation thickening her accent. "It's just an awd group for a thehty-five-year-old to have ovah for suppah."

I tried to look innocent. Busied myself with dinner.

We were having lamb and scallops, mashed potatoes with bacon, asparagus, and crème brûlée for dessert. I thought I'd save Sully's pie for just me. Maybe Poe and me. And Audrey. And Xiaowen, of course.

I checked the lamb, took the asparagus out of the fridge, herded my mother back into the living room and snagged some cheese. "How's Audrey?" I asked Sullivan.

"Excuse me?"

I finished chewing. "How's your daughter?" I said more clearly.

"Oh. She's good."

"She's getting chubby," my mother said.

I flinched. "Mom!"

"She is." She shrugged. "You should put her on a diet. No fun bein' fat."

It was like a slap in the face, to me and to Sullivan.

Sullivan looked at my mother. "Thanks for your input," he said.

"I'm so sorry," I murmured. He didn't hear me.

"Diet is so important to good health," Amelia said. "And of course, Nora agrees with me! She's a gastro-enterologist, after all. Who wants another drink? Can I top anyone off?" She got up and went to the freezer, where she'd put her vodka.

"Livers are also important to good health," Xiaowen said. "Jake, if you don't stop looking at my boobs, I will stab you in the eyes."

"So, Sharon," Bob Dobbins began. "That hug therapy is really helping me. I was wondering if maybe I could book a private appointment."

"Bawb, we've talked about this. The answer is no."

"Are those ostrich-skin shoes you're wearing?" Xiaowen asked him.

"They are!" he said, pleased.

"You have quite a sense of style."

"I *love* a man who can wear jewelry!" Amelia said. "Those bracelets are copper, aren't they?"

Bob held out his arms. "Yes," he said. "They help with my arthritis. See these rings? Also copper." He wore one on every finger except his thumbs. God help him around meth addicts looking to score a quick buck.

My mother glanced at her watch. "How about that suppah, Nora?"

"Ten more minutes, Mom. Hang in there. Have an oyster."

"No, thank you. Does anyone mind if I turn on *Wheel of Fortune*?"

Damn it. No one said no. "Where's your clickah?" Mom asked.

"On the bookcase next to the globe," I muttered. She got the remote, pushed the button, and there were Vanna and Pat in high-definition splendor.

"I don't know how they do it, all these years," Mom said. "That Vanner is still a *stunning* woman."

"My wife loved this show," Mr. Carver said. This time, his eyes filled with tears. I sat down next to him and patted his shoulder.

"How long has it been?" I asked.

"The enchanted forest!" my mother barked. "Christly, how could she miss that?"

"Three years," Mr. Carver said. "Seems like yesterday, though."

He started to cry.

Oh, God. I handed him a cocktail napkin and psychically begged Xiaowen for help. Alas, as was so often the case, all eyes were now on the TV, including hers.

"Clear and present danger!" she said gleefully. "Got you, Mrs. Stuart."

"Nawt bad," Mom said.

"I was once a contestant on *Who Wants to Be a Millionaire*," Amelia said.

"Are you a millionaire?" Jake asked, popping another beer. Another guest with a drinking problem. I wondered if Scupper had Uber.

"Yes," said Amelia, "but not because of that show. My grandfather was a robber baron! Isn't that fun?"

I patted Mr. Carver some more, then went into the kitchen and tossed the asparagus in the same frying pan I'd use to cook up the bacon.

"Need help?" Sullivan asked, joining me.

"Oh, no, I'm fine. Sully, I'm so sorry for what my mother said. Audrey is a lovely, wonderful girl."

"I know," he said. "And she's overweight. Amy likes to…" He rubbed the back of his head. "She likes to buy Audrey junk food, and when I tell her not to, she gets mad at me. Says I'm trying to keep them from having fun."

"That's tough." I nudged the asparagus spears, which were turning bright green.

"I just don't want Audrey to have any troubles. Healthwise or at school. Kids can be such shits at that age." Then he seemed to remember who he was talking to. "Uh, by the way… I'm sorry for the way my brother teased you."

Teased wasn't the word I'd have chosen. And not just his brother. His ex-wife, too, and most of his friends. "No. That wasn't pleasant." We looked at each other for a minute.

The weather had etched lines around his eyes, and

he was already tan. Working at the boatyard meant a lot of time outside, I imagined. There was nothing particularly special about his face—brown eyes, straight nose, normal everything else, but when you put them together, the porno music started playing distantly in my brain.

He was a man who said a lot with his eyes. They looked slightly amused with my ogling.

The porno music got louder.

"Right," I said. "Here, want to take this to the table?" I handed him the bowl of steaming mashed potatoes.

"Adopting a puppy!" my mother shouted. Xiaowen gave her a high five.

"Dinnertime," I said.

"Program's over, anyway," Mom said, clicking off the TV. "Speaking of dogs, where's Boomer?"

"He's with Bobby. Have a seat, everyone."

"Who's Bobby?" Amelia asked, weaving to the table and nearly missing her chair.

"Her boyfriend," Mom said.

"My former boyfriend," I corrected.

"Don't sit next to me, Jake. I don't trust you," Xiaowen said. "Sully, sit between us, okay? Good man." She steered him to where she wanted him. Not next to me.

I wondered what it would be like, not to hear everything, to perhaps be wondering why someone was moving you, to try to piece together the words you did hear.

I hoped he'd heard me say *former boyfriend*. His face was hard to read.

Bob slid past me, his cologne like a green fog. "This smells wonderful!" he said.

Maybe it did. My sinuses were clogged with Polo by Ralph Lauren.

"Where's Jake?" I asked. Could've sworn he'd just been here.

He answered by opening the bathroom door. "Got any Febreze?" he asked.

"I told you this was a bad idea," my mother said.

"Is this lamb?" Mr. Carver said. "My wife made the best lamb." More tears. Jesus.

"Did I mention I'm vegan?" Amelia said merrily. "I told you that, didn't I, Nora?"

"No, you did not," I said.

"Is your vodka vegan?" Xiaowen asked.

"It is," she said smugly. "Don't worry, Nora, I'll just have this beautiful asparagus." Before I could stop her, she took a bite. "Oh! Delicious! You'll have to tell me how you cooked it!"

In pig fat, I thought. Ah, well, what she didn't know wouldn't hurt her.

Jake sat down next to my mother. When the potatoes were passed to him, he took a bite from the serving spoon. "I'll get another spoon," I said, hopping up. I went to the kitchen, came back, replaced the tainted spoon, then sat down. "I'm so glad you could all come."

"Uh-oh. I better hit the head again," Jake said. "I musta eaten somethin' for lunch that didn't agree with me, if you know what I'm sayin'." He bolted from the table, knocking over his chair, which Sully righted.

I hoped I had enough bleach.

"Sharon, you look very beautiful tonight," Bob said, leaning forward and folding his copper-clad fingers together with a faint clinking sound.

"Knock it off, Bawb."

He turned his attention to Xiaowen. "You know, I've developed an interest in the Korean War recently."

"And why are you telling me this?" she asked.

"Because you're Korean?"

"I'm Chinese."

"Do you like Chinese food?" Bob asked. "I'm a big fan of General Tso's chicken."

Xiaowen sighed. At least she and my mother were getting along like a house on fire—I even heard my mother laugh, which was a rare occurrence. Jake returned from the bathroom, then went again five minutes later. Amelia drank her vodka. Mr. Carver got it together enough for me to ask him how he liked retirement, but he just kept talking about his wife. One wondered why he wanted the little blue miracle pill.

"What was her name?" Sullivan asked him.

"Beatrice," he said, tearing up again. "She was a wonderful woman." He began to sob.

"Nora," my mother said, "why don't you get on with it so we can all get home?" She fixed me with her turtle stare—implacable and steady.

"Uh…get on with what, Mom?"

"You asked us here to see if we knew what happened to your father."

Oh, right! My lie, back to bite me in the ass. Well, half lie. I did want to know about my father, of course. "Yes. Well, as many of you know, my father left the island when I was eleven. That was twenty-four years ago. I hoped one of you might remember where he went."

"Kind of late to be asking now, isn't it?" Jake said, coming out of the bathroom. "You need more toilet paper, by the way." He grabbed a roll of paper towels from the kitchen counter and went back to the head. I smothered a scream.

"I remember your father," Bob Dobbins mused. "A good man."

"Jake's right," I said. "It was a long time ago, but I was wondering if anyone had heard anything. I've Googled him a thousand times, but he has a common name, and…well. I never found anything."

Sullivan was looking at me intently. He didn't say anything, though.

"No one's got anything, then?" Mom said, clarifying for me.

"So many people gone," Mr. Carver mused. "Your father. My Beatrice. My dog, Licorice, isn't getting any younger, either."

"Well, if my father's…uh, passed away, I'd like to know that, too," I said.

No one said anything for a second.

"So there you go," Mom said. "Welp, thanks for dinner, Nora." She pushed back her seat. "Can I help you clear? We don't want to overstay our welcome."

"I, um…" I'd managed to get one bite of lamb so far, but looking around the table, I saw that, yes, everyone's plate was clean.

"There's no hurry," I started to say, then stopped myself. Jake was violating my bathroom, Bob was not a candidate for stepfather, and Mr. Carver was currently weeping into his napkin.

"I drove Amelia and Jake here," said Bob. "Can't have any DUIs under my watch," he added. "Since I'm the first selectman and all. Can't have that! Sharon, would you also—"

"No," she said.

Fine. Everyone could leave. Maybe Xiaowen and Sullivan would stay.

Where *was* Amelia, by the way? I was terrified of going into the bathroom after Jake had been there. I knocked on the door. "Gimme a minute!" Jake called from inside. There were sounds that every gastroenterologist recognized. I flinched, then suppressed the urge to cry. Maybe I would just burn the houseboat.

Amelia must've gone onto the deck. Alternatively, she'd fallen in the water and drowned, which wouldn't be great.

Nope. As I passed my bedroom door, I spotted her. On my bed. Fast asleep. Drooling on my pillow, in fact.

"Hey, Amelia. Amelia? Time to go." I shook her shoulder gently. She didn't stir. I shook harder.

"I'm very tired," she said. "I worked so much this week." She sat up, lipstick still perfect. "I don't feel so well." She put her hand on her stomach.

"Let's get you home," I said. "Bob's ready to go."

"Can I help?" It was Sullivan.

"Would you give me a hand, darling?" Amelia said, extending an elegant arm in his direction.

"Sure thing." He went over to her and put his arm around her, helping her up.

"You're *quite* a charmer," she said, then puked on him.

I mean right *onto* him. It hit him in the throat and slid right down his shirt. I felt my own gorge rise.

"Whoopsy," she said. "I'm terribly sorry. But I feel *much* better now." She puked again, just in case Sullivan missed the point. "Did I eat butter, perhaps? Was there butter in that asparagus? I've been a vegan for so long, any animal product upsets my stomach."

"No butter," I said. "Uh, Sully, my bathroom's right there. Towels and stuff. I'll be right back."

He gave me a look and went in, and I ushered Amelia down the hall to the other bathroom—Poe's, not the powder room Jake had been using, and handed her a washcloth.

"What a beautiful boat!" she said, cleaning up. "Do you know who the architect was?"

"I don't. But thanks for coming, Amelia. Let's get you home, okay? It's getting late." It wasn't even eight-thirty. I steered her down the hall to the dock, where the others waited.

"Well, safe home, guys," I said. "Where's Mr. Carver? I didn't get to say goodbye."

"He left already," my mom said, pointing to a set of taillights heading down the road. "Uh-oh." She cupped her hands around her mouth. "Watch out for the deer, Henry!" she called. "Henry! The deer! Oh, for Christ's sake!"

The rest of us watched in horror as Mr. Carver ran smack into one of the wild residents of Scupper Island.

Xiaowen made a noise that sounded suspiciously like a laugh.

I ran down the dock. Mr. Carver's car was only about fifteen yards from where he'd parked it, but apparently he'd been going fast enough.

The deer was panting, lying on its side. Oh, God, the poor thing! We'd have to call the police chief to shoot it, and God knew how long it would take him to get here.

Its eyes were wide. Should I pet it? Then again, that might scare the poor critter. Also, ticks. But if it was in the throes of dying, maybe I should comfort it? Her? It was a doe.

"Is it dead?" Mr. Carver sobbed. "Is it hurt?"

"Um…it's not dead yet," I said. I pulled out my phone

and called 911. No signal, of course. Shit. I got on the hood of Mr. Carver's car, held my phone up. Aha. Two bars. That was enough.

"Nine-one-one, please state your emergency."

"Hi, this is Nora Stuart on Spruce Brook Road. A deer was just hit by a car."

"Hi, Nora, it's Mrs. Krazinski! How are you, honey?"

"Well…not that great. And you?"

"I'm fine. Your mother said you were having a dinner party tonight."

"I am, and well, I'm afraid Henry Carver hit a deer, and—" I lowered my voice "—I think it needs to be put down."

"Damn. And the chief's away. His daughter, you remember her? Caroline? Well, she had a baby! A boy. Her third."

"That's great. But what about the dying deer?"

"Can't your mom take care of it?"

"Probably, yeah." Chances were high my mom could do one of those Jason Bourne neck twists and Bambi would be on the way to heaven.

The entire dinner party had made its way down the dock.

"With a little physical therapy, you never know," Xiaowen said. "Could be eating hostas by next week."

"I'll put it outta its misery," my mother said. "Nora, run home and get my butchering knives."

"What?"

"It's a *fresh deer*," she said, as if I was the stupidest person on earth. "I'm not gonna let it go to waste."

"Mind if I take a haunch?" Jake asked, popping another beer.

"Oh, God," wailed Mr. Carver. "Beatrice... She loved animals."

"When I was a child at our camp in the Adirondacks," Amelia said, "a fawn walked into our house and lay down next to the dog. It was utterly adorable. Until our Irish setter killed it, that is. Whiskey, that was his name. A beautiful dog."

"You don't mind if I stay to watch, do you?" Xiaowen asked. "I'm kind of crushing on your mom."

"You're a horrible friend," I said.

My mother came back down the dock, knife in hand.

He reached out and his hand closed on the biggest knife handle in the block.

Ice-cold fear slithered down my back, and for a second, the dark Maine sky and heavy half-moon were gone, and I was in my apartment, the door so close. Would I make it? Would he grab me again? The door handle, smooth and hard under my aching fingers, me out, running, screaming...

Nope, nope. Not gonna go there. That was my mother, the world's most capable woman. Not a killer, not a rapist. And behind her, Sullivan Fletcher, shirtless in the waning light, his puked-on shirt in his hand. *Focus on that. Focus on him. You're safe. You're safe. You made it.*

My heart rate slowed. There was a calm about Sullivan Fletcher that tugged at me. Maybe because he was a father. Maybe because he was spared from some of the chatter and buzz of this world. Maybe because he'd been hurt, too, and recovered.

I guess I should've offered him a T-shirt. Then again, I'd had a spewing boss and a dying deer to contend with.

Also, shirtless Sully was a very nice view.

Suddenly, the deer gave a lunge. I jumped back as it scrambled to its feet and ran off crookedly into the woods.

No one said anything for a minute.

"Okay!" I said. "What a fun night! Take care! Mr. Carver, are you okay to drive?"

"It didn't die," he said, wiping his eyes. "Maybe it was Beatrice, working a little miracle."

"I was thinking the same thing," I lied. "Bye. Thank you for coming."

They all got into their cars. Xiaowen hugged me, shaking with laughter. "I'll call you tomorrow," she managed before sliding into her silver Porsche. Then she was gone, and I was alone with Sully.

"Come on in, and I'll get you a T-shirt," I said, starting down the dock. He followed.

"I was kind of hoping to see your mother skin that deer," he said, and suddenly, I was staggering with laughter. Sully's smile flashed in the darkness, and he took my arm so I didn't fall into the water.

I laughed all the way inside.

My place was a disaster—plates still on the table, the coffee table, the floor. A thousand glasses, it seemed. Food everywhere. I went into my room and got the biggest T-shirt I had—Blackbeards Bait & Tackle, a leftover from a long-ago trip to Cape Cod with Doctors Without Spouses, back when Bobby and I were just friends.

"Here you go," I said, handing the shirt to Sullivan. He pulled it over his head in a quick movement, the muscles on his rib cage flowing, his shoulders rolling in a perfect example of male anatomy.

Xiaowen was right. I could do far worse than Sullivan Fletcher.

But a summer fling was not what I was looking for. In August, I'd be back in Boston. Sullivan would never leave this island. And he had a kid, besides. Also, there was the fact that I had no idea if Sullivan was looking for a fling himself. He had a daughter, an ex-wife, a business and a troubled brother to contend with.

"Let me help you clean up," he said.

"No way," I said. "You get on home."

"I'm not leaving you with this mess." Those eyes were caramel deliciousness, warm and tempting.

"Oh, but you are," I said. "Being puked on by a dinner guest gets you a free pass."

A faint frown settled between his eyebrows. "I'm more than happy to help."

"I'm good, Bobby." Ah, shit! Where did that come from? "I mean, jeesh, Sullivan. Anyway, I'm kind of anal about cleaning up, and I have to make a few calls, besides."

Without moving a muscle, his face changed. "Got it. See you around, then. Thanks for a nice dinner."

He started out the door, and I closed my eyes. A perfectly nice man, and I was kicking him out.

I went to the doorway. He was about halfway down the dock. "Sully? Sullivan? Thank you for the pie."

He either didn't hear me or didn't want to answer.

16

Dear Lily,
I forgot how pretty May is on the island. All the
leaves have popped, and the birds are awake at
4:47 a.m. every morning. I saw three baby rabbits
this morning, and they were so cute. The other
night, Poe came over to do homework, and I made
her grilled cheese and tomato. We always used
to eat that on the first day of winter, remember?
Love,
Nora

THE WEEKEND BEFORE Memorial Day, I took the ferry to
Boston to retrieve my dog. I was ridiculously excited
to have him back, to tug his silky ears, gaze into his
pretty brown eyes and feel his reassuring bulk on the
bottom of my bed. Bobby loved Boomer, sure, but the
Dog of Dogs was mine. My soul mate.

It had been my decision to get a dog two months
after the Big Bad Event. Bobby and I went to the ani-

mal shelter, and there he was, twelve weeks old, the result of a Bernese mountain dog and a Rottweiler love affair. He'd grow too big for most Bostonians and their apartments. One look in his worried eyes and the deal was done. And you know what they say about adopted pets—they never forget that they were rescued.

Turns out, Boomer rescued me. He got me outside (armed with pepper spray and rape whistle). If a stranger approached, Boomer's tail let me know if the person was okay, because I was scared of everyone.

At home, when my heart turned on me in a panic attack, fluttering like that damn hummingbird, and I couldn't breathe or remember where I was, Boomer would sense it and nudge my hand with his velvety snout, whining his love and concern. When Bobby worked nights, the dog stayed glued to me, and the truth was, he made me feel safer than Bobby.

So yes, I was glad to have him back. That was an understatement.

And I was eager to see Bobby again, too. He'd been perfectly lovely over these two weeks, sending me pictures, checking up on me via text and even a nice long phone call one night, when I sat on the top deck of my houseboat and watched the sunset. I almost felt like my Perez self.

I wondered what would happen in August, after Lily and Poe reunited and left for Seattle again, as was the plan. When I'd go back to Boston—hopefully with Mom dating someone, because for all her independence, she had to be lonely—what would be in store? I'd need a new apartment. Maybe I'd love it as much as I'd loved my old place. Maybe I'd feel safe there.

Maybe I should give Bobby another chance. I

shouldn't have been indulging in thoughts about Sully—
I was only temporary here.

And Bobby *wanted* to get back together. If I was past
the grayness, maybe it would be like old times. I almost
couldn't blame him for fondling Jabrielle's hair. She *was*
beautiful, if bitchy, condescending and without morals.

Those three months of perfection when Bobby and I
were new together…maybe they were worth another try.

So that morning, while I didn't go crazy with makeup
and staring into my closet, I did take a little time to
look put together. Traded in the jean jacket for a light
brocade coat, and instead of the L.L.Bean muck boots
that were required wearing in springtime up here, put
on some cowboy boots instead. Added a scarf and dan-
gly earrings.

On the ferry ride over, I decided to quiz Jake on
my father. I was the only one on the boat, which was
skipping and dipping across the swells, the salt spray
undoing my hair ironing. Frizz it would be. I'd come
prepared with a hair elastic.

I went into the pilothouse. "Jake, remember I was
asking about my dad the other night?"

"Huh? I think I was in the bathroom, maybe."

"Yeah, and speaking of that, if you want a free GI
consult, I'm here for you. Or you could just try some
Imodium next time."

"What about your father?"

I tugged my coat closer. "Well, you've been the ferry
captain since forever. Do you remember him leaving
the island that time? He would've had a suitcase or two.
Might've been upset."

Jake lit his pipe, and a sweet, smoky smell filled the
air. "Ayuh, I remember."

My heart leaped. "You do? So…can you tell me about it?"

He drew on the pipe, clenching it between his yellow teeth. "Well, you're right. He had a suitcase or two. He was aflutter. Talking to himself. Talking to me, talking to what's-his-name…the Fletcher boy and his mother."

"Which Fletcher boy? Sullivan?"

"The one who played all the sports."

"Luke?"

"I guess so. The one who wasn't at your party the other night. Anyway, your father was a regular rig that day." Mainespeak for *over-the-top*. "Guess your mother kicked him out. He wasn't happy about it. Said she'd get what she wanted, kept yappin' on and on about what was fair and what wasn't and how no one could tell him what to do."

So they *had* been fighting. Mom never copped to it, but Lily had known somehow.

"Do you remember if you were going to Portland or Boston?"

"Portland."

I looked out at the gray sea, the lobster buoys bouncing on the whitecaps. "Anything else, Jake? Anything else you remember?"

Jake looked at me, his craggy face unexpectedly kind. "Yep. He had a picture of you two girls in his hand. Kept starin' at it. Might've been cryin' just a dite."

My throat clamped tight. "Thanks, Jake," I whispered.

"Nawt a bothah."

I went back onto the deck and sat in the hard-molded plastic chair.

The image of my father, distressed and angry, holding a hastily packed suitcase and a photo of Lily and me…that made me want to put my head down and cry.

It seemed I'd have to talk to Teeny and Luke if I wanted to find out any more.

WHEN WE PULLED into the landing an hour later, Bobby was already there waiting for me, checking his phone. Boomer went nuts the second he saw me.

"Boomer!" I said, kneeling down and hugging my wriggling dog. "My buddy! I missed you!" He whined with joy and licked my face, then tried to hug me, putting his big paws on my shoulders. "Who's a good boy? You are, Boomer! Everyone says so!" I smooched his head, then stood up, still petting my doggy. "Hi, Bobby."

"Hey," he said, pocketing his phone and handing me the leash. "How's it going?"

"Great. How are you?"

"Good. Listen, I can't stay. I'm really sorry. Work stuff."

Oh. My heart dropped a few inches. "No problem. Everything good with you?"

"Yeah. Excellent. I'm gonna miss the big guy, but I guess I can deal with it." He bent down and rubbed Boomer's head. "See you in two weeks, Boomer. Love you."

Those last two words were definitely for the dog. Bobby lifted his hand and, just like that, strode away.

Okay.

So. Cross *lunch with Bobby* off my mental list of things to do today. It sure was different from two weeks ago, when he had the whole day for me.

This was good. This was reinforcement that our

breakup had been for the best. This was exactly the kind of classic Bobby nonchalance that I'd grown to hate.

Even so, it threw me a little.

Still, it was a beautiful day in Boston. I called Roseline, told her I was free earlier than I expected, and she said she'd be on Newbury Street in ten minutes so we could power-shop and eat.

"Oh, my God, I miss you so much!" she said when she saw me, throwing her arms around me. "And you, too, Boomer!" she added, bending down to get a sloppy kiss. "I actually miss you more, puppy. Don't tell Nora." She held me at arm's length. "You, my friend, look fantastic." We hugged again and started walking, arm in arm.

The brownstones of Newbury Street were beautiful, and Roseline chattered nonstop, giving me all the gossip about our friends and acquaintances. She and Amir were going to Haiti for a delayed honeymoon to see the family, most of whom I'd met over the years. We went in and out of shops, tying Boomer's leash around a signpost so he could woo the sun-deprived Bostonians, and did our usual thing—fondled purses and tried on shoes. It was great to be together again.

But had Boston always been so loud? Did every driver have to scream curse words out their window? (Yes, of course, it was Boston.) The f-bombs rained down in a nearly benign fashion, so common in this city that the impact was almost nil.

"You should hear how quiet it is on the island," I told her as we ate lunch, Boomer at our feet, the sunshine warming our hair. "At night, I sit on the deck and watch the sunset and swat the blackflies, and it's beautiful. Please tell me you'll come visit."

"Do you love it there?" she asked.

I didn't answer right away, taking a slurp of my clam chowder. "Sometimes, I do," I said. "On the one hand, everyone knows me there and…" I shrugged. "It's like I'm the same person I was at fifteen, rather than an actual adult."

"It's the same for me when I go back to Haiti," she said. "Harvard, Yale, they mean nothing. I'm still the little girl who peed in church on Easter Sunday."

"Exactly. This week at the clinic, I was called 'the fat one' and 'Sharon's other daughter, not the pretty one.'"

"That's so sweet," Rosie said, rolling her eyes. "First of all, you're very pretty. And *fat*? Come on! Don't they have eyes?" She took a bite of her burger. "How's your sister, by the way?"

Roseline knew Lily was in prison; I'd told her when it happened, and now I felt a wave of shame at how I'd done it, making it seem like no big deal. After all, Lily's sentence wasn't long, and her crimes weren't terrible, but she was in prison nonetheless. Then again, a few months ago, I'd been desperate to talk about *anything* that made me feel better, and somehow my sister going to State did that. I mean, I might've been beaten within an inch of death, but at least I wasn't Lily.

Yes. Shame.

"She's okay, I guess," I said, not that I knew. "I've been spending a lot of time with Poe and this other girl, my old classmate's daughter. It's nice. I forgot I liked teenagers." Audrey had stopped by this week. Twice, as a matter of fact. We talked about movies, and on Thursday, she was going to come over to watch *Project Runway*. I wanted to have another sleepover for both girls, but I wasn't sure Sullivan would welcome that, since I'd kind of blown him off the night of my party.

"So what's going on with Dr. Bobby Byrne?" Roseline asked.

"I don't know," I said. "He *was* being really...attentive. Lots of texts and emails, a few phone calls. Today, though, he pretty much tossed me the leash and left."

"Are you thinking about getting back together?" Her voice was suspiciously neutral.

"I don't know," I said. "We got off to such a great start, and then..."

"Then you got beat up and almost killed and after the thrill of being noble faded, he got bored," she finished.

"Thanks for reminding me. But I *was* pretty pathetic. I'd get bored of me, too."

"Nora! You weren't pathetic! You were almost murdered!"

The elderly women at the table next to us looked over with obvious interest. "True story," I said. "How's your lobster?" They turned back to their meals.

Rosie lowered her voice. "So getting bored because your girlfriend was on shaky ground...that's kind of shitty."

"I know, but I didn't like myself, either. I hate shaky ground."

"Well, we all have to walk it, girlfriend. Best to have someone who'll hold your hand while you're doing it, not run ahead and start flirting with some slutty-ass resident."

I smiled. "You're so good for me."

"I know, I know. And you're such a slob of a friend to me."

"Come out next weekend," I suggested. "It's Memorial Day, we have a boat parade, and *rugged charm* is our middle name. Please? You can meet my other friend and everything."

"You have another friend? I'm devastated!" She grinned. "Okay, I'll leave Amir home. You know how he is about boats. *Titanic* ruined him forever."

"It ruined us all. There was room for two on that door."

"Preach it, sister. But those last two minutes are worth everything," she said.

She picked up the tab, and we spent the rest of the afternoon like our old selves, before she got married, before I was attacked.

On Monday night, after a day at the clinic that consisted of me removing a hook from Jeb Coffin's palm and closing it with one entire stitch, I went home, changed into jeans and a cute little shirt with cunning little buttons up the back. I fed my beloved, then threw him the tennis ball in the little meadow that spread between the cove and the road.

Then I put my dog inside. Tonight, I was hitting the townie bar to see if I could talk to Luke Fletcher about my dad.

Red's was the local hangout for serious drinkers and those who hated tourists. The parking lot was full of rusting, dented pickup trucks—beatahs, they were called—and a few cars from the 1970s, not in the classic sense, but in the held-together-with-wire-and-duct-tape sense.

I'd never been here, too young to go to bars when I left the island. Time to see if it was all I'd heard in my youth.

I parked my MINI Cooper at the edge and went in. It was a seedy, dark little place with sticky floors, a few grubby-looking tables and a bar where the serious drunks of Scupper Island sat propped up in a row. This was not a place sought out by flatlanders, that was for sure—it was locals only, and the air itself had a bitter, angry tint to it.

There at the bar was Luke Fletcher, leaning heavily on his elbows. And though he'd been horrible to me, I couldn't help the pity that ran through my heart. This was a man whose life had not gone as planned, who couldn't find his way out. There was no victory here for me.

The seat next to him was empty. I slid onto it. Luke didn't notice.

"Whatcha want, deah?" asked the bartender, a woman who must've weighed three hundred pounds, body mass index of at least forty. Hypertension, judging from her weight and flushed face, and diabetes on the horizon if she didn't have it already.

"Uh…a beer?" I was not about to order a pomegranate martini in this place, that was for sure.

"What kind? Bud, Bud Light, Miller, Miller Light, Genesee, Old Mil."

"Old Mil," I said, not that I'd ever had it. I didn't even like beer.

Luke turned his head toward me, then did a double take. "It's you."

"Hey, Luke, how's it going?"

He seemed pretty wasted; bleary eyes and slow to answer. "Just great."

"I'm glad you're here. I was wondering if I could talk to you."

"You already are."

The bartender put a beer in front of me. It was the color of urine from a severely dehydrated person—dark yellow and, well, disgusting.

"Luke, I know we have a little history between us about the Perez Scholarship, but I'd like it if we could be friends."

"A little history? Why don't you tell me how you got it? You did something, I know that. Some fat little trick up your fat sleeve."

What a prince. "I worked really hard, Luke. I'm sorry you didn't get the scholarship, but I'm not sorry I did."

"Well, that doesn't make any sense."

"Anyway, maybe I can buy you a drink." I paused. "Are you driving home?"

"No," he said sullenly. "I lost my license."

Good. "Well, I wanted to talk to you about something." I gestured to the bartender. "Another one for my old classmate, please?"

The bartender squinted at me. "Holy crap. I'm Luke's classmate, too. Who are you?"

"Nora Stuart."

Her mouth dropped. "Whoa! So you lost all your fat, and I found it and then some." She laughed. "I'm Carmella Hurley. Long time no see."

One of the Cheetos back in the day, along with Darby Dennings and Amy Beckman. Except she didn't seem mean anymore.

"Is it true you're a doctor?" she asked, pulling a beer for Luke.

"I am," I said. "I'm working at the clinic this summer."

"Cool! Good for you! You always were smart. Maybe

I'll stop by. Do you do gastric bypass?" She laughed again. "Just kidding. But seriously, maybe you can put me on a diet. I keep meaning to drop a few pounds, you know? Oops, Froggy there needs another drink. I'm coming, Froggy. Jesus. Don't wet yourself." She looked back at me. "Beer's on the house. I was kind of a bitch to you back in school. In fact, I probably owe you a keg."

And just like that, a wound closed up. People *did* change. The thing about mean teenage girls—they were never happy. There was pressure and darkness in being a Popular Girl—I knew, because I'd watched Lily peel away her soul in exchange for hanging with the in crowd.

But from here, it looked like Carmella found her way to happiness, even if it did entail gaining 150 extra pounds.

"So what do you want?" Luke said.

I turned to look at him.

He was still ridiculously handsome, even now, even drunk. The irony was, he had what seemed to be a kind, happy face, always verging on a smile. Even when his eyes were bloodshot and his eyebrows drawn, it was impossible not to want to like him, to see a better version of himself hiding in there somewhere.

Poor Luke. He'd had so much potential.

"I don't know if you remember," I said, "but my father left Scupper Island a long time ago. When you and I were in fifth grade."

He frowned. "Oh, yeah?"

"Yeah. Jake Ferriman said you and your mom were on the boat to Portland that day. The day he left."

"I don't remember."

I nodded. "It was a long shot."

"My mom might, though. Ma! Come here!"

I blinked. I hadn't seen Teeny Fletcher when I came in, and the truth was, she scared me more than Luke.

When she saw who was sitting with her baby boy, her eyes narrowed. "What do you want?" she asked. "Why are you botherin' my boy? Rubbin' your fancy job in his face?"

Lee Harvey Oswald also had had a shitty, overprotective mother, they said.

"Hi, Teeny," I said. "No, I just had a question about my father."

Her overplucked eyebrows rose. "What would Luke know about that?"

"I understand you were both on the ferry the day he left. Jake Ferriman said you were going to Portland. My dad talked to you both. He was upset."

Her lips narrowed in a hateful smile. "Oh, yeah. Ayuh. We were there."

"We were? I don't remember," Luke said, finishing his drink.

"I'm hoping to find out what happened to him," I said to Teeny.

"And what's in it for me?"

Sweet woman. "What would you like?" Damn. That was a mistake. I should've offered her twenty bucks.

"What would I *like*?" she screeched. "I'd *like* my son to go to Tufts University, that's what I'd *like*. But you killed his chance, didn't you? And now you want something from me? I doubt it, flatlander."

Ooh. The ultimate insult, calling a Mainer a flatlander.

The bar had gone more or less quiet.

"Mrs. Fletcher, I'm sorry you're still under the delusion that I stole anything from Luke. As you well know, the Perez Scholarship goes to the student with the highest GPA. I was that student. I understand, however, that Luke got a nice scholarship to the University of Maine, which is another fantastic school. Xiaowen Liu got her doctorate there, and look at her now. So whatever happened to Luke since high school isn't any of my doing, and all of his."

"Fuck you," Luke said, draining his drink.

"You're a snotty little thing, aren't you?" She rubbed her son's back in a way that was quite icky, given that he was thirty-five. He didn't seem to notice.

"Thanks for your time," I said. "Carmella, nice seeing you again." That, at least, I meant.

And I went to my car, more angry than shaken.

Teeny Fletcher had said not a damn thing about her *other* son. The one who was completely innocent. She could've said *My son had a TBI because of you, and he's losing more of his hearing every day.* While not completely accurate, that sentiment would at least be understandable, a mother grieving her child's injury and difficulties.

Instead, she was still fixated on a stupid scholarship.

Nope. She hadn't mentioned Sullivan at all.

17

ON THE FRIDAY of Memorial Day Weekend, Roseline came to Scupper, just about fainted with glee at seeing the houseboat and said she was never leaving. We killed a bottle of rosé, ate coconut cake and watched movies till 2:00 a.m.

In the morning, we got dressed, guzzled some coffee and took Boomer downtown to see the boat parade. It was one of Scupper Island's biggest deals. More than a parade, it was our way of welcoming back the summer people, letting them show off their pretty wooden sailboats and Chris-Crafts, their small yachts.

Main Street was decked out in red, white and blue, and Lala's had a sign out front that said Show You Love America: Eat a Donut. Roseline and I had proven our patriotism and now made our way through the crowds of people to sit on the rough wooden town dock.

The dock was edged with a thick wooden beam, so little kids and people on bikes wouldn't fall into the drink. We sat on the lip now, as did half the town, our legs dangling over the edge, sugar on our fingertips, the donuts still steaming hot and soft.

"This is so bad for your digestive track," I said, taking another bite.

"Shut up," she said, taking her second out of the bag. "Who cares what you think? You some kind of expert?"

"Oh, there's my friend," I said. "Xiaowen! Over here! We have donuts for you!"

"I thought those were all for me," Roseline muttered, but she smiled and said hi and scootched over to make room as I made the introductions.

"You're so beautiful, Roseline," Xiaowen said. "Nora, you have the most gorgeous friends, don't you?"

"I do," I acknowledged. "People often compliment me on my taste in women."

"Hi," said a voice behind us, and I jumped up.

"Poe! Hi, honey! Hi, Mom! You guys remember Roseline, right?"

"Hello," my mom said stiffly, never comfortable with people she hadn't known her entire life.

Roseline stood up. "Wow, Poe, you probably don't remember me, but I came to visit you with Nora one time."

"I remember," she said shyly. "You bought me a scarf and wrapped my hair up in it."

"That's right! You looked so cute." Rosie smiled and sat back down. "Sit next to me. I love your hair! How long does the color last before it starts to fade?"

Mrs. Krazinski walked over, a donut in her hand, a bag from Lala's in the other. She handed the bag to my mom. "For you, Shar," she said. "One for you, too, Poe, honey." Such a nice lady.

"Hi, Mrs. K.," I said.

"Dahlin,' don't you think it's time you started using my first name?"

I laughed. "I don't know if I can."

"Try. It's Donna." Or *Donner*, if you pronounced it her way. "Mind if I join you ladies?"

"Of course not! Have a seat."

My mom and Mrs. K sat down next to Xiaowen, leaving me square in the middle, Boomer drooling in between the bites of donut I gave him.

This was nice. This was kind of perfect, really—me and my girls. The foghorn sounded, a long, mournful blast, and the parade began. Mr. Brogan, who was an elderly Navy veteran, was the parade master, and tradition had him in the *Miss Magalloway*, the old tugboat used during the First and Second World Wars.

A cheer went up, and a lump formed in my throat at the sight of the old man in uniform. We all stood and waved the little American flags the Exchange Club has passed out earlier, and Mr. Brogan saluted.

And there on the deck was Audrey. That's right—the tugboat was owned by the Fletcher family.

"Looking good, Audrey!" I called, and her head turned. A smile lit up her face at the sight of me.

"Hey, Audrey," Poe yelled. "Nice work if you can get it!"

"That's my little pal," I told Roseline. "The one who comes by to visit."

Sullivan was behind the wheel. He looked over at us and pulled the horn three short times, eliciting a cheer.

And, if I wasn't mistaken, smiled at me.

I waved, a chunk of donut still in my hand, and he gave me the Yankee nod—a chin jerk of recognition.

It was enough that I blushed.

The tugboat slipped around the curve of the cove, followed by the lobster boats, which got more calls of recognition from the crowd. Then came the summer nuisance boats, the kind that were for fun only. Being hospitable Yankees, we waved and cheered as they went by, too, but our enthusiasm was a little pale compared to the reception Mr. Brogan got. Obviously.

When the boat parade wound down, we got to our feet. "You guys want to come over tonight?" I asked Mom and Poe. "We're having a nice dinner. Gloria will be there, too. From the clinic? You, too, Mrs. K. Donna, I mean." At my mother's glare, I added, "Women only."

"Sure!" Poe said. Enthusiasm! So thrilling. I'd have to text Audrey, too. And her dad, to make sure it was okay. Maybe he and I would get to talk a little. The idea caused a little tingle in my stomach.

"What we got here?" came a thin, nasty voice. "The United Nations or some such?"

It was Teeny Fletcher, commenting on the shocking fact that there were two nonwhite people in town. She scowled down at Xiaowen. "Aren't you that Oriental who went to school with my sons?"

"I don't know. Am I?" Xiaowen said.

"You all look alike."

"My God," Roseline said. "She did not just say that." Teeny sneered. "And who are you?"

"This is my best friend in Boston," I said. "Teeny, meet Dr. Roseline Baptiste. Roseline, our postmistress, Teeny Fletcher."

"I always thought you had the prettiest name, Roseline," my mother said. Unusual for her to compliment someone. Maybe she was mellowing, after all.

"Thanks, Mrs. Stuart," Rosie said. "I'll tell my mom you said so."

"Gettin' pretty snooty over here," Teeny observed. "All these doctors."

"Lucky for you, in case you get sick," I said.

"Like I'd go see you," she said. "I'd go to Portland, thank you very much."

She turned hard, and her elbow hit me in the stomach. I stumbled back, and something was behind my heels—shit, it was the lip of the dock! Then I was in the air, falling, and I could see Roseline's horrified face. The hard water smacked my back, and then I was under and freezing. My scalp ached instantly. The cold would be good for inflammation and bruises, I thought, still sinking. My eyes stung, my arms floated at the side of my head.

Then I touched bottom, pushed off and rose through the greenish, frigid water to the air and noise.

"Are you okay? Nora! Are you all right?" people were shouting.

"I'm fine!" I called, spitting out salt water, gagging a little. Gah. I could taste diesel fuel from the boats, too. Lovely.

Well. Best get out of the water. I started a feeble breaststroke to the shore. My brain did a quick assessment. Head, eyes, ears, nose and throat: normal. Neck: supple (if cold). Heart and lungs: so far, so good. Abdomen: full of donut. Extremities: in working order, though pretty damn cold right about now. Neurologic: I seemed normal to me. I'd have Rosie check me out when I got on shore. My back stung from the slap of the water, but otherwise, I was pretty sure I was okay.

Teeny Fletcher was a bitch. Lucky it was high tide, or the fall would've been ten or twelve feet farther.

Poe ran down to meet me, and my heart squeezed at the sight of her perfect face etched with concern. "Are you okay?" she asked.

"I think so. That water is *freezing*, though." I smiled to reassure her.

She took off her jacket and gave it to me. "Come on. Lean on me."

I did, if only because…well, because she wanted me to.

My mom and friends swarmed me in a concerned little knot. Xiaowen pulled a bit of seaweed from my hair, and Roseline began asking the typical doctor questions—what day it was and so on. I rolled my eyes and answered as she palpated my head, neck and spine.

"No pain anywhere?" she asked.

"Nah," I said, my teeth starting to chatter. "I'm fine."

My mother, who'd been silent until now, whirled on Teeny Fletcher. "You better get an attitude adjustment, and fast, Louanne Peckins," she snarled. Uh-oh. Using Teeny's original name. I couldn't help a smile.

"It was an accid—"

"Shut it," Mom said. "I've had enough of your snipin' and whinin' all these years. Touch my daughter again, and I'll punch you in the gawddamn throat."

My mouth dropped open.

"And I'll kick you," added Poe. "Come on, Nora. You need a hot shower and clean clothes."

And thus, surrounded by women I loved, I was escorted to my car.

Who knew falling off a dock would be, in some ways, the happiest moment of my life?

SEVEN HOURS LATER, we were having a rollicking good time up on the top deck of the houseboat. Roseline, Mom, Poe, Donna Krazinski, Xiaowen and Gloria—our little United Nations of womanhood, all of us eating and laughing and talking. I told them about the fun run—Xiaowen and I had come up with a name, Go Far, Be Strong, and Bob Dobbins had signed off on it. Donna thought it was a great idea. Even Mom said she'd help, and Poe only grumbled a little when I asked if she'd run.

"I'm not an exercise freak like you," she said.

"I run four times a week. I'm hardly a freak."

"No, you are," Xiaowen said. "You're right, Poe, but I need someone to run with, so you have to do it, or Serena Williams here will leave us in the dust."

"Serena's a tennis player," Poe said.

"Do you think she can't also run?"

"Good point."

I was on call tonight, so Poe and I were drinking seltzer and cranberry juice—everyone else was having mojitos, made with my very own mint.

Mrs. K was a hoot, something I hadn't known, and she got my mom to tell stories of horrible hotel guests—the man who got locked out of his room with a sock on his penis, the couple who insisted on doing it with the door propped open, the lady who got so drunk she threw up in the bathtub, then climbed in there to sleep.

Rosie and Poe were hitting it off—Rosie was telling Poe about a birth where the baby's hand popped out first, like a little victory fist, and how she had to reach into the mother's vagina with both hands to turn the baby's head so he'd come out without breaking his shoulder. Poe looked suitably awestruck (and nauseous).

Good old Roseline—there was no better birth control than gruesome tales from Labor and Delivery.

Audrey had replied to my text earlier—she was doing something with her mom, and she was so sorry not to be able to make it. I just about could hear the wistfulness in her words. She'd have had a great time with us, I thought, trying to squash my not-so-sweet thoughts about her mother and Teeny. But yeah, it might serve her to be around women who were a little nicer than those two.

"So I met someone," Gloria announced as we sat down to eat. "A man who has a job, doesn't live with his grandmother, is good-looking, age appropriate and wants children."

"A unicorn?" I asked, and we all laughed.

"Where'd you meet?" Xiaowen asked.

"When I went back to Boston to see my family last time. He was wearing a green-and-gray rugby shirt—"

"No!" Xiaowen said.

"Dump him," I said.

The rest of them looked confused. "What are you guys talking about?" Poe asked.

"He's a Slytherin," I explained. "Green and silver are the Slytherin colors."

"You're such a dork," Poe said.

"That didn't occur to me," Gloria said, "since I've only read Harry Potter twice, like a normal person. Anyway, we were standing in line at Starbucks, the one by the ferries, you know? And the line was like, fifteen people long, so we got to talking, and he was really cute, and maybe I gave him my number."

"Invite him out here," I said. "So we can observe, advise and pass judgment."

"No way," Gloria said. "He doesn't get to know where I live for at least a month. I didn't even tell him my last name."

"Why's that, dear?" Donna asked.

"The last guy I dated ended up stalking me," she said, waving her hand. "Nothing too bad, but you know, getting up to pee at 3:00 a.m. and seeing him standing on the sidewalk, looking up at my window? No, thank you."

There was that cold, strong snake of fear sliding down my spine again. I cleared my throat. "What happened? I mean, how'd you get rid of him?"

"I called the police, my four brothers and my dad. You don't want to mess around with that shit. Sorry for my language."

"Totally justified," Donna said. "Men are pigs. Well, many men are pigs. I've heard some aren't."

"So will you see Slytherin again?" Poe asked.

Just then, my cell phone buzzed. It was the clinic.

"Hey, Doc," said Timmy, the nurse on duty (one of the men who wasn't a pig). "Come on down! We've got a teenage girl with acute abdominal pain."

"I'm on my way," I said. "Ladies, I'm so sorry. I have to go to the clinic. Don't wait for me. Mom, can you handle grilling the fish?"

"Your mother is an expert griller," Donna said. "And I'll help just in case."

"Let us know when you'll be back," Gloria said, pouring herself more wine.

"We'll try not to burn this place to the ground," Xiaowen added. "No promises."

I pulled out onto Spruce Brook Road, a little sorry to be leaving, a little excited to practice emergency medicine. The strep throat swabs on the Robinson twins yesterday didn't really get the heart pumping, though the kids were super cute. And this would be right up my alley—abdominal pain. Given her age, appendicitis was possible. We'd have to ship her to Portland for that, and if I suspected an abscess or a rupture, I'd be going with her. Could also be pelvic inflammatory disease.

I got to the clinic in under ten minutes, went in and started washing my hands. Timmy came through the swinging doors from the exam area. "Sorry to call you in on a Saturday night," he said.

"No worries," I said. "What have we got?"

"The patient says she knows you. Audrey Fletcher? She's here with her father and her grandmother, too."

Audrey? Shit. I frowned and rinsed my hands, then pulled on my white doctor's coat and went through the door.

Audrey was the only patient here, lying on the hospital bed in a little ball, changed into a johnny coat. Sullivan sat by her side, looking ten years older, rubbing her back. Teeny was fluttering about like an irritable moth. "When will the doctor get here?" she demanded just as I came in.

"I'm here," I said, going to Audrey's side. "Hey, kiddo. Not feeling so hot?"

"Pretty bad," she whispered. Her knees were drawn up, and her eyes were wet. I patted her leg.

"Oh, wonderful. Isn't there another doctor?" Teeny said.

"Mom, be quiet." Sullivan looked at me, lines slashing his face with worry. "She started having a stomachache about an hour ago."

I glanced at the computer screen where Tim had entered her vitals and chief complaint. Everything was normal except for a slightly elevated BP and pulse, which was normal for someone in pain.

"Do an X-ray or something," Teeny said. "Maybe she needs to go to the mainland. I'd be more comfortable if she was in Portland."

"Mom, please," Sullivan said.

"Does Grandma need to be here?" Audrey whispered.

"Nope," I said. "Teeny, would you mind waiting out front, please?"

"I'm staying." She folded her arms.

"Go, Mom," Sully said. "There's no need for you to be here."

She didn't move. "Tim, would you escort Mrs. Fletcher to the waiting room?" I said, not looking away from Audrey. Her face was a little flushed.

There was a hiss behind me, Timmy's low voice. Good.

"Is it her appendix?" Sullivan asked.

"Let's find out. Okay if I feel your belly?" I asked Audrey, pulling on exam gloves.

"Sure." She rolled onto her back, grimacing.

"Any vomiting or diarrhea?" She shook her head. "When did you first start feeling this?"

"Um…this afternoon. And then it got really bad after Mom dropped me off at Dad's."

"Did you eat anything unusual?" I pressed on Mc-Burney's point. No flinch, so it wasn't her appendix.

"No. Not really."

"Have you ever had pain like this before?" I asked.

She glanced at her father. "Um…maybe? Once or twice."

"Any blood in your stool?"

"Stool?"

"Poop."

"Oh." She blushed. "No. I don't think so."

"Have you lost any weight recently?"

"I wish." Her face got even more red.

She winced as I felt her left lower quadrant. "When was the last time you pooped?"

"Dad, can you go or something? This is so embarrassing."

"Yeah, and I changed your diapers. I'm not leaving."

I looked at him and smiled. "I don't think it's appendicitis, Sully. But maybe Audrey would be more comfortable talking without you here."

"I definitely would be," she said.

"I'll stay."

"I need to be Audrey's doctor right now," I told him. "She's still a minor, so you can stay if you really want to, but you're making her uncomfortable."

"Indeed you are, Dad." Snark. Always a good sign.

He frowned, twin lines appearing between his eyebrows. "Okay," he grumbled. "I'll be right outside, angel." He kissed her forehead, sucker punching me in the heart.

"I'll take good care of her," I said.

He nodded and walked out, wiping his eyes with the heels of his hands, and for that, I fell in love with him a little bit.

"Nothing like an overprotective father," I said.

"I don't really like talking about my bodily functions with him here, that's all."

"Understandable. Okay, some of these questions *are*

a little embarrassing, but I can't treat you for the right thing if I don't have honest answers. Okay?"

She nodded.

"Last time you pooped?"

"This morning."

"And it was normal?"

"Yes."

"Good. Next question—are you sexually active?"

"No! God, no. I probably won't be for another thirty years. Or I'll die a virgin."

I squeezed her hand. "How would you describe the pain?"

"It's like there's a knot in my stomach. Down lower, actually."

I felt where she pointed. She was significantly overweight, so it was a little tough to get a read on her organs. "Turn on your side, honey."

She did, and I saw that she had two purple stripes on her skin. "Have you always had these?" I said. They looked like stretch marks and could've been—lots of kids got them during sudden growth spurts or weight gain.

"I'm not sure," she said. There was a pause. "I try not to look in the mirror too much."

My heart twisted. I knew that feeling. She grimaced again.

"Is the pain right here?" I asked, pointing to her left side. She nodded. "I'm going to press on your stomach, sweetheart. If you have to pass gas, go for it. You'll feel a lot better."

"I can't fart in front of you!" she said.

"Honey, people have vomited on me, pooped on me, peed on me, bled on me." I pushed gently with the palm of my hand. "Once, I was doing a rectal exam, and the second I took my finger out, the patient pretty much exploded with diarrhea."

She laughed…and passed gas. A lot of gas.

"Oh, man, I'm so sorry," she said, her sweet round face turning scarlet.

"But you feel better," I said.

"I do." She sounded amazed.

I palpated her abdomen again, but she seemed cured. "What did you have to eat today?"

"I didn't want to tell my dad," she admitted, "because he hates when Mom and I do this, but we ate Oreos and drank a lot of soda. We pig out and watch movies. It's… Well, it's fun. Kind of. I *do* try to eat right most of the time." She looked chagrined. "It's just that Mom and my little brother are skinny, so they don't think about that."

I ran my hand along her spine. It curved at the base of the neck. Dowager's hump, as it was unkindly called. "Are your periods regular, Audrey?"

"Not really. Every few months."

"How old are you again?"

"Fifteen."

I looked at her chart on the laptop. She was five-one and weighed 195 pounds. "How about backaches?" I asked. "Do you get those a lot?"

"Yeah. How did you know?"

"Another way-too-personal question—are you a little hairier than you'd expect?"

She covered her mouth with her hand. "Yes. It's so embarrassing."

She had Cushing's disease. I was almost sure of it.

"Okay, here's the deal," I said, sitting on the bed with her. "Your stomach pain was probably just gas from the

Oreos and soda, which is a pretty horrible combination for your gut. But I think you might have something else going on. Something treatable that would explain some of the other things we've talked about. Is it okay to get your dad?"

She nodded, and I went to the waiting room, where Sullivan was pacing and Teeny was whispering into her phone.

"She's feeling much better," I said. Sully sagged with relief, then ran his hand through his hair. "Come on in, Sullivan." Teeny stood up.

"Stay here, Ma," he said, not looking at her.

"I'm coming in."

"Stay!" he barked. I liked him even more, knowing he took no shit from that harridan.

In Audrey's exam room, I gestured for Sullivan to sit down. Timmy came in, too. I made sure Sully could see me and spoke carefully so he'd catch every word.

"The pain seems to have been just gas, which can cause really bad abdominal cramps. That's resolved now, so she can go home tonight. But Audrey also has some markers for Cushing's disease, and I'd like her to get tested."

I explained what the disease was—a possible tumor on her pituitary gland, which then produced too much cortisol, resulting in just about everything Audrey had going on. The obesity in her stomach, her much thinner arms and legs, the extra hair, the full, round face, the curve in her spine.

Sullivan didn't look away from my face, the furrows between his eyes deepening. "What causes this?" he asked. "Did we do something wrong?"

"No, not at all," I said. "If she does have it, surgery will take care of the tumor."

"Surgery?" Sully asked.

"It's not bad, though it sounds kind of gross. They'll probably go in through your nose, Audrey. It's a very treatable problem."

Audrey was staring at me with a mixture of fear and relief. "So there's a reason I'm like this?" she said.

"Like what?" Sullivan asked.

She started to cry. "I'm fat and ugly and short, Dad. I'm tired all the time and have backaches like I'm an old lady! I have hair on my back! I hate myself!"

He wrapped his arms around her and pulled her close. "Hush," he said. "You're beautiful. You're the best thing in the world. And if you have this Cushing's thing, we'll get it taken care of. But don't you ever say you hate yourself. That's my best girl you're talking about. My favorite person in the whole world. I love you, and Mom loves you, and we think you're perfect."

She tightened her grip and had a good cry. Sully murmured to her, stroked her hair, and I turned away so they could have a little privacy. Timmy and I looked at each other and smiled damply.

Grabbing a box of tissues, I went back to Audrey's bedside and handed them to her. Took one for myself and one for Timmy, too.

"I think you should go to Boston for this," I said. "I know a couple of great doctors at Boston City who specialize in this. I'll call them tomorrow, okay? In the meantime, Audrey, just go home and enjoy the rest of the weekend."

She pulled back from her dad and gave me a dazzling smile. "Thank you so much, Nora," she said. "My stupid pediatrician never said anything about this. Just told me to eat more vegetables and stuff."

"Well, Cushing's disease is rare. I'm still not positive you have it, but we'll know pretty soon." I *was* sure, but doctors didn't get to say those things.

"I can't believe I can get fixed! This is probably the best day of my life." She got off the bed, grabbed her clothes and bounced into the bathroom to change.

"I'll be up front," Timmy said, leaving the room. We could hear Teeny's indignant squawking. Well. I could hear it. In this case, Sully might be lucky not to catch everything.

Sullivan stood up. "Thank you," he said gruffly.

"Just doing my job."

"You're good at it." He let out a shaky breath. "What would've happened if this hadn't been caught? Is it… you know. Fatal?"

I hesitated. "It can be."

"Jesus H. Christ."

"If you have any questions, and I'm sure you will, just ask me, okay? Don't be—"

My words were cut off by his hug. A hard, long hug.

Sullivan Fletcher was lean and strong, and his neck smelled like the sun. He held me tight for a long moment. "Thank you," he said again, quietly, and his voice caused a ripple down my side.

Then he let me go, and the bathroom door opened. I got another Fletcher hug, from Audrey this time. "I can't believe all this," she said.

"Well, let's get it confirmed," I said. We doctors, always covering our butts in the face of too much hope or too much darkness.

"I want to be you when I grow up," Audrey said,

beaming at me. She slid her arm around her father's waist and tucked her head against his arm.

Sullivan glanced at me. He put his fingers to his chin and then moved them away and down, almost like he was blowing me a kiss, but not quite.

I knew that gesture. It was sign language for *thank you*.

Yeah. Not falling in love with Sullivan Fletcher was going to be quite a challenge.

18

WHEN I WAS a junior and Lily was a sophomore, we both went to the prom.

I went with another girl—Emily Case, who, like me, was on the fringe of high school, another invisible girl with bluish-white skin and hair the color of dirty dishwater. We weren't friends; we were simply united in the knowledge that no one would ask us, we wanted to go, and there was safety in numbers, even if that number was two.

I honestly don't remember where I got the guts to go through with it. I remember that I simultaneously didn't want to go and couldn't *not* go. I had no delusions of a *Carrie*-like turn of events where, even if for a little while, the freaky girl got to be popular. So what if she was drenched with a bucket of pig's blood? Small price to pay.

No, I knew how it would be. Emily and I would barely exist at the prom unless someone took it upon herself (because it would be a girl) to mock us. But even

at the age of seventeen, I knew that on prom night, the
Cheetos would be too obsessed with themselves to notice people like Emily and me.

Without telling anyone, I took the ferry to Portland,
went to the Goodwill store and bought the first dress
that didn't pinch too much, an utterly unremarkable royal
blue halter-top dress with sequins along the neckline.
There was a tear along the zipper, but I could fix that.

On the Saturday of the prom, my sister announced
that she'd be going to Darby's house to get ready.

"I'd like to see you all dressed up," Mom said.

"Then come to Darby's," Lily said. "If you have to."
The disgust in her voice was so thick you could cut it
with a dull knife.

"Are you goin' to Darby's, too?" Mom asked me.

Lily's head nearly spun off her shoulders. "You're
going to *prom*?"

"Yes," I said, feigning calm. "Emily and I thought it
would be fun." Things that were also on par with prom
fun would be performing a limb amputation on oneself
or eating a live rat. Still. Had to do it.

"Emily who?" Lily asked.

"Case."

"Who's that?"

I sighed. "She's someone in my class, Lily."

"Why do you even want to go?"

Excellent question. I started to answer, but Lily cut
me off. "Just try not to talk to me." Even after all this
time, her cruelty slashed like a razor.

"Lily, apologize," our mother said, her voice harsh.

"Sorry," she sang.

"Who's your date?" I asked. I knew, of course. Everyone knew.

"Luke Fletcher." She looked at me and smiled evilly, her pure blue eyes narrowing like a cat's.

That's why I was going, of course. To see them together. To see what it would be like to be as effortlessly beautiful and confident as my sixteen-year-old sister, to have the attention of the best-looking, most popular boy on the island. To torture myself with unrequited love for both of them.

I didn't go to Darby's, of course. I stayed home and tried to flat-iron my hair, which was having none of it. I ended up putting it in a puritanical bun. Emily's father picked me up, Em sitting in front, me in the back of their minivan, which smelled like dog. There was a bag of pretzels on the floor, reminding me that I was hungry.

Back then, Scupper Island couldn't afford a big prom at a banquet facility or hotel, so it was held at the gym each year, the decorations comprised of tired crepe ribbons in yellow and black—our school colors—with clusters of black and yellow balloons tied to a weight for centerpieces.

Aware of our status as Invisibles, Emily and I clung to the edges of the gym and took a seat at the table farthest from the entrance. I tried to talk to her (maybe we'd become real friends!) and asked all the questions I could think of—*What bands do you like? Have you seen any good movies? Do you like math?* I was treated to monosyllabic answers and gave up. Emily chugged Hawaiian Punch and manically nibbled Chex Mix, one piece after another, like a starving mouse. I occasionally offered a comment, no matter how banal, just for the sake of making it look as if we were talking. Not that anyone was checking.

"Check out Mr. Severy's tie!" I said, laughing, though his tie was perfectly normal. Emily didn't respond.

Chances were, we both looked unstable. Neither of us cared.

The Cheetos hadn't arrived yet. Prom had already been going on for more than an hour, and they'd probably spent that time getting drunk or high. Until then, everyone (except the freaks like Em and me) had been having a pretty good time, dancing, talking, the girls a little nervous in their finery, the boys awkward and sweaty.

Then the doors opened, and in they came—Amy, Darby, Carmella, all so hatefully beautiful, so fake-tanned, their teeth bleached too white. I'd have sold my soul to look like any of them. They were like beautiful, exotic birds in their bright dresses and sparkling sequins. Sullivan, Brett, Lars and Luke trailed in after them, aware that prom was really for girls.

And then I saw Lily—oh, Lily, she was the most beautiful girl in the world. She was Snow White—pure and lovely and perfect, and I couldn't help the surge of pride and love that flooded through me at the sight of her.

My sister, though she belonged to the group, was not technically a Cheeto—her skin was ivory, her hair black and shiny, its natural color, cropped short and chic when all the other girls in our school, including me, kept theirs long. Her dress was a one-shouldered black gown, full skirt with some kind of silky, sheer fabric over the skirt, so it looked as if she were floating. I didn't know when or where she got the dress; she well may have stolen it, but no matter the case, it was *ethereal*, making my royal blue dress seem as cheap and common as it was.

For once, Lily's makeup wasn't overdone, making the Cheetos look like RuPaul on performance night. No, my sister was simply stunning. She was Audrey Hepburn. She was Anne Hathaway. She was Lily Stuart, the most beautiful girl in Maine. In the world.

And she was with Luke, who already looked sloppy, his tie askew, his gait crooked.

"That's your sister," Emily said flatly.

"Yes."

"You don't look anything alike."

I didn't dignify that with a response. The truth was, I couldn't take my eyes off Lily. Everything about her was flawless. She seemed both to absorb the light and reflect it, and I felt such a rush of tenderness for her, the same as when we were little and she'd fall asleep, and I'd just stare at her and stroke her hair until Mom told me to stop.

Then Lily bumped into a chair and burst into wild laughter, and the spell was broken.

My sister was high. That probably wasn't new, but it was the first time I'd seen it so blatantly. I stood up, the metal chair screeching behind me. Lily was lost in the crowd of Cheetos and their dates. Sullivan and Amy were dancing, I noted, their foreheads touching. He could do better, I'd always thought.

I made my way to the dance floor, alone, moving like a silent hippo through the crowd, who parted reluctantly for me, a few castigating looks from girls at my dress, my hair, which was coming out of its bun, my ordinary sandals. I didn't care. I wanted to get my sister home.

Her pupils were dilated, her voice shrill. "Shut up, Brett!" she said, giggling wildly. "I did not. Not yet, anyway."

This caused a roar of laughter and some jostling among the boys. Whatever Lily hadn't done yet was sexual. I wasn't stupid.

"That's not what Conrad says," someone said.

"So what? It's no big deal," said Darby, trying to steal the attention from Lily. "I already did it."

"So did I," said Carmella.

"Yeah, no kidding," Brett said. "Come on, Lil. Have some more." He offered her a flask.

"Lily," I said. "Hey."

Silence fell over the little group. "Hey, Nora," Luke said. After all, this was junior year, before he realized I might threaten his future.

"What are you doing here?" Lily asked. "Oh, right! You came with that girl! Are you a lesbian, Nora?"

Another roar of laughter. "Lily, come with me a second, okay?" I said. I took her arm and started dragging her to the bathroom. She struggled for a second, but, hey, I outweighed her by at least seventy pounds.

"Everything okay?" Luke asked, trailing after us, blinking too much. Stoned, I guessed.

In my instant fantasy, he'd be sober. I would tell him someone gave Lily drugs, and he would be furious. It would be Brett, and Luke would whirl around and punch Brett in the face and take Lily and me to Stony Point Lookout (I had no idea why). Lily would fall asleep in the back seat, and Luke and I would talk and talk, remembering good times at the Math Olympics and Robotics Club in seventh grade. He'd say something like "Nora, you're so funny."

And that would be enough. That would be the world to me.

But in reality, I knew better. "We're fine," I said.

I got Lily into the bathroom. "What did you take?" I asked, future doctor that I was.

"Don't worry about me," she said. "I'm *great*. Where the *hell* did you get that dress, by the way?"

"Lily. Do you know what you took? What it looked like?"

"Nora. Do you know how you look in that dress? Like a fifty-year-old housewife crashing the prom, that's how."

Anger and hate and love wadded in a ball in my throat. "You are such a *bitch*, Lily," I hissed.

It was the first mean thing I'd said to her...ever. She looked at me for a second with those clear blue eyes, shocked.

Then she heaved forward into a stall and started puking.

Oh, God. And yet, good. She'd get it out of her system, whatever it was. Ecstasy or a roofie or painkillers.

I crouched next to her and put my hand on the back of her neck, the way Mom used to when we had a stomach virus.

"Nora," she said, glancing up at me. Her eyes were streaming, and I was undone.

"It's okay, baby," I said. "Get it all out."

She vomited again, and then again, and then there was nothing but dry heaves. I stroked her cropped hair until she stilled, her sleek little otter-like head resting on that skinny arm.

"Come home with me, honey," I whispered. "Let's go home and watch TV, okay?"

She turned her head and looked at me. "You don't understand, Nora," she said, closing her eyes, and her voice was so weary and old my eyes filled with tears. "You just don't get it."

"No, and I don't want to. Not if it means being with them. They're so hateful, Lily. They'll use you up."

"I don't have any other choices, do I?"

"You do. You can come home with me."

She almost laughed. Didn't open her eyes. "Yeah, right. If I'm not with them, then what am I? How do you think I'd survive if I wasn't popular?"

The same way I do, but we could be together again. "Let me take you home and take care of you. Please, Blueberry." My old name for her.

"I miss Daddy."

The words punched me in the heart. "I know," I whispered, petting her head again, savoring the sleek curve of her skull. "Come on, sweetie. Let's go."

Lily opened her eyes and looked at me for a second, and I saw how tired she was, how empty, and all I wanted was to save her.

But then the bathroom door squeaked, and in came Amy. "Um…are you two okay?" she asked.

For one second, I thought Lily might choose me. For one second, her eyes said something other than disgust.

Then she looked at Amy. "I had the pukes," she said brightly, struggling to stand up. "I feel better now. Do you have any gum?"

"Yeah. You sure you're all right?"

"Totally. Just not used to that, you know?" She rinsed her mouth out and spit into the sink, somehow making it not look gross.

Amy glanced at me, then back at my sister. "Lily… um, watch out for Luke, okay? He gets around."

"I know."

Amy looked at me again.

"Why don't you come home with me?" I said. "Lily? I think it's best if we go home."

She glanced at me in the mirror. "I'm staying, Nora," she said, her voice full of contempt. Whatever moment we'd had was dead.

The tears gathered in my throat. "Okay," I whispered. I kept my eyes on the floor, the ugly beige-tiled floor, and stood there as Amy gave my sister the gum and they chattered and laughed and then, finally, left.

You wonder how much abuse you can take and still love someone. You wonder how long they can treat you like nothing but still want them back. You wonder how many years it will take to forget how things used to be, how long you'll burn yourself with that tiny ember of hope before the deluge of their neglect drowns it.

A long time, in my case. A long, lonely time.

ON THURSDAY ABOUT an hour after I got home from work, Sullivan Fletcher called and asked if he could take me out to dinner. "To thank you for everything you've done for Audrey," he said.

"Um…sure!" I said. I'd been sitting on my couch in a tank top and pajama bottoms, watching the news (always a bad idea), eating sunflower seeds and fantasizing about cheese.

"How about Stone Cellar?" he suggested, naming the chic restaurant I hadn't yet graced with my presence. "Pick you up in an hour?"

"Sure!" I chirped again. "See you then!"

I hung up, then ran to my room. It wasn't a date, per se. I shouldn't treat it like a date. It was a parent who wanted to thank me for being (cough) a brilliant doctor, because yes, Audrey's diagnosis had been confirmed in Boston. Sullivan probably wanted to ask me a bunch of questions about treatment and such.

Which didn't mean I couldn't dress up a little.

I'd given up on my hair here in Maine. My flatiron was no match for life on a windy island where it rained a lot. I pulled it back into a ponytail, though, and put on a pair of cropped jeans, a cute pink peasant blouse and a suede jacket. Sandals with a stacked heel, a little blush, a little mascara, and voilà. I was date ready, even if it wasn't a date.

"How do I look?" I asked the Dog of Dogs.

"Beautiful," he said. Well, his eyes said it. I fondled his silky ears and gazed into his loving eyes. Dogs. The best work God had ever done.

Sullivan arrived five minutes early. He looked like he'd come right from the boatyard—faded jeans and a T-shirt, making me glad I hadn't tried too hard (pause for laughter). Despite it being June, a chilly wind gusted. It would be in the forties tonight, for crying out loud.

"Hey," he said. "You ready?"

It was Maine. Conversation wasn't really our thing. "You bet." I turned on the porch light, and off we went.

"So this is unexpected," I said as we bounced down Spruce Brook Road in his pickup.

Sully didn't answer. Right. He was deaf in that ear, and unless he turned his head, he wouldn't be able to hear me. He glanced at me, didn't smile and glanced back at the road.

It was a little odd. Something I'd have to get used to, no car chatting. Or no, I wouldn't have to get used to it. I was only here for the summer. Riding with Sullivan Fletcher wasn't going to be a regular thing.

Fifteen silent minutes later, we were seated at a table

in the restaurant, a newer place, a perfect mix of comfortable and posh. "Your server will be right with you," said the maître d', handing us the menus.

"Thank you," Sully said, looking at his.

The restaurant was fairly full with the pleasant rattle and hum of food preparation. "Thank you for asking me out," I said.

No answer.

Right. I touched his hand. He looked up. "Hey. This is nice. Thank you."

He looked at me a long minute. "This is really nice," I repeated.

"Well. The least I could do."

"Audrey stopped by yesterday. She's pretty excited."

"Yeah. Weird for a kid to be psyched about surgery." But he smiled, and if he was nervous the way I was, it cracked for a minute.

"Hi, I'm Amy, and I'll be your—oh."

We looked up. There was his ex-wife, pad in hand. Her face was frozen. Sullivan stood up. "When did you start working here?" he asked.

"Yesterday."

"You should've told me."

"What I do is none of your business."

"Of course, it is. We've had this conversation, Amy."

"Well, you're not exactly falling over yourself to fill me in on things, are you?" she said, gesturing with her elbow at me. "If you have a girlfriend, don't you think I should know?"

No, this wasn't awkward at all.

"Hey," I said. "How are you, Amy? I'm not his girlfriend."

"Right," she said. "So. Listen. Thank you for Audrey.

We went to Boston on Monday, and she's good to go for surgery. Me and Sully, we owe you big-time."

They were still both standing. "Why don't you sit down for a second?" I asked. "Pull up a chair. Sully asked me out so he could pump me for information. Do you have any questions about the procedure or recovery or anything?"

Sullivan sat back down. I was fairly sure he'd missed everything I just said.

Amy hesitated. "I gotta work."

"Here." I fished a pen and gas receipt out of my purse and wrote down my cell number. "Call me for anything. Audrey's a sweet kid, and I really like her. You've done a great job raising her."

Amy's face softened. "Thanks," she said quietly. "Okay. Drinks, you two? Sully, you want a Sam's Summer?"

"Sure," he said. "Thank you."

"I'll have a mojito," I said. "Supposedly, it's summertime, no matter what the weather says."

"Be right back." She snapped her pad shut and walked away.

Sullivan and I looked at each other. "My ex-wife is our server tonight," he said, and we both laughed.

"It's okay. She's still very…" *Think of something nice to say, Nora.* I glanced at the menu. *Succulent? No.* "So pretty."

"Excuse me?"

I looked right at him. "She's still so pretty."

"Ah. Ayuh."

Amy came back a minute later with our drinks. "On me," she said, setting down my drink.

"Thank you so much," I said.

She smiled—*Amy Beckman, smiling at me!* squealed my inner dorky adolescent—and put down Sully's beer. "What would you like for dinner? Want to hear the specials?"

Sully would have to work that much harder to hear over the crowd, looking up at Amy.

"No, that's fine," I said. "I mean, unless you do, Sullivan."

"No, I'm good."

I ordered the lobster roll (I would go for a run to-morrow, I swore it) and a salad to counteract the butter (ha). Sully ordered scallops.

When Amy had taken our order, I leaned forward. This kind of intense conversing was a little unnerving. "Do you have any questions about Audrey?" I asked.

"No," he said. "The doctor you recommended—Patel?" I nodded. "He covered everything. She goes in next week."

"It's a great hospital, and Raj is the best. I'm sure everything will go smoothly."

"Amy and I, we…we really can't ever thank you enough."

I shrugged, a little embarrassed (and secretly thrilled). "Just doing my job. You know, like a firefighter, run-ning into a burning building and saving lives and stuff."

"I'm sorry. I missed everything you just said."

Just as well, since I was babbling.

"Hey, you two." Amy again. "I got you another table where it's quieter. He's deaf as a stump, you know," she said to me.

"I heard that," he said.

And so we moved to a back room where there were only three tables, all empty. "Thanks, Ame," he said.

"Yeah, whatever," she said. "Brian will be your waiter back here. Give a shout if you need anything." She started to leave, then turned back. "How's your sister?" she asked.

"She's…she's doing okay," I said.

"Tell her I said hi."

"I will. Thanks."

She left, and the relative quiet settled around us.

"How *is* your sister?" Sullivan asked.

"I don't know," I answered. "She doesn't speak to me."

"Why is that?" His brown eyes were steady on mine, and there was something about the intent way he looked at me, the gentle calmness of his face. All of a sudden, there was a lump in my throat. I shrugged.

"You and me, we both have problem siblings," he said.

"How's your brother?"

Sully glanced out the window, a rueful look on his face. "Well, he stole about a thousand dollars from the boatyard last week."

"I'm sorry."

"Yeah, whatcha gonna do?"

"Call the police?"

"Not an option."

"Why not?"

He sighed. "Well, you should know. He's lost a lot in life."

"Are we still talking about that fucking scholarship?"

Sully laughed out loud. "Listen to you! Dr. Stuart dropping the f-bomb." I felt my cheeks warm and took a sip of my drink. "No," he continued. "Not the scholarship. Not just the scholarship, I should say. He lost the chance to do something with his life."

I rolled my eyes. "Yeah, well, he's not quite dead, is he? There are a lot of choices he could make that would serve him better than being a druggie and a drunk. And as for loss, I have to ask you—what about you? I mean, you're the one who got hurt in that accident, Sullivan. Because of your brother being coked up that night. And you're the one who was in the hospital and a nursing home for six months. You're the one who's losing his hearing because of it. If anyone's lost something, I'd say it's you."

He looked at me for a long minute. "Some people can handle things better than others."

"So it's your job to look out for him?"

"Ayuh. Don't you look out for your sister?"

"No. She's in jail, currently refusing to answer any letters I send her."

"But you're looking out for her daughter."

He had me there. "Yes."

"And I'm guessing that you've had some losses, too. But you've handled them better, that's all."

I mulled that over. "Is that a compliment or a chastisement?" I asked.

"Both?" He grinned, and his face went from ordinary to wicked in a flash.

Sullivan Fletcher was…yeah. He was. My knees tingled with all that he was.

"You got a boyfriend?" he asked. Not terribly subtle, but again, we were in Maine.

"Not really," I said.

"You sure?"

"We broke up just before I came back here."

Our waiter chose that moment to place our food down. "Hi, I'm *Brian*!" he said, as if he'd just been named and couldn't get over the wonder of it. "We have the delicious lobster roll for the beautiful lady, excellent choice, I might add, sweet potato fries, a personal favorite, and coleslaw that our chef makes with just a little bit of radish to really bring out the flavor. And for the gentleman, the scallops, which I totally adore, by the way, the mashed potatoes with scallions and a little bit of sour cream, hey, we all have to live life, am I right, and the brussels sprouts, my favorite veggie, let me tell you. All our produce is locally sourced and organic, of course. Can I get you anything else? Fresh ground pepper, grated cheese, extra bread, ketchup, more butter, sea salt, pink salt, Himalayan salt, a foot massage?"

That last one may have been merely implied. "I think we're all set," I said.

"Fantastic! Enjoy!" Brian cooed. "I'll check on you in a few! *Mangia!*"

"Sometimes being hard of hearing is a blessing," Sully said.

"I stopped listening ten seconds in," I said, and he grinned.

For a few minutes, Sullivan and I just ate. I was starving, I realized. And lobster that was swimming at the bottom of the icy Atlantic a few hours ago, now drenched in butter and served on a soft Portuguese roll…yes, yes, I would run tomorrow. But today, I'd just eat lobster. Eat and ask prying questions, that was.

"How are things going with your sign language and all?" I asked, licking butter off my fingers in that classy way.

"It's okay. Kind of hard to learn on your own, so it's good of Audrey to help me. She picks up on it faster than I do."

I smiled. "She seems really smart."

"She is."

I took a sip of my drink and watched him a second. When he looked up from his plate, he said, "Sorry, did I miss something?"

I shook my head. "But on the subject of what you can't hear…are you okay with that? Are you sad or angry or…depressed?"

He smiled a little. "Not really. I mean, I've known this was happening for a long time now." His smile faded. "I try to listen to things more, try to store them up. The birds in the morning. Favorite music. Audrey's laugh. Trying to fill up my head with the best sounds. Been watching a lot of home movies lately." He gave a half shrug and looked back at his plate.

Le sigh. I hoped I wasn't visibly swooning, but I couldn't be sure.

"What's your favorite music?" I asked.

"Bach's cello suites," he said. "Well, that and 'Purple Rain.'"

"God, I love that song! And I used to listen to Bach's cello suites when I was pulling an all-nighter in med school," I said, smiling. "It was supposed to help with studying."

"I guess it worked," he said.

When he smiled, I could see that his incisors were just a little more pointed than average, giving him a vampiric look. I pictured those teeth on my neck, and my girl parts gave a mighty throb.

"So why did you come back here, Nora Stuart? You, who haven't been back in all this time?"

It was his voice. His soft, deep voice, and I hoped he could hear it, because it was so delicious, that voice, the timbre and hint of roughness in it, like the stones on the shore tumbling over each other after a hard ocean wave.

I cleared my throat. "What was the question again?"

Another wicked smile. A dastardly, bad-boy smile on this ultimate dad. "Why'd you come back to Scupper?"

"Oh. Yeah. I was hit by a pest control van. Beantown Bug Killers. My life flashed before my eyes."

"Did it?"

"No, actually. But I... I wanted to spend some time with my mom. And my niece."

"Scared you good, did it?"

I nodded.

"And that thing...that not-good thing that happened to you. The thing you mentioned the night you almost shot me. Was that being hit by pest control?"

I picked up a sweet potato fry and broke it in half. "No."

He waited.

"A man broke into my house and beat me up and tried to rape me, and then when that didn't work out, he, uh, he tried to kill me. With a knife. But I got away, and they never caught him, and that was last year, and please don't tell my mother."

I sucked in a breath and grabbed my mojito and drained it. Didn't *quite* mean to dump the worst night of my life in his lap, but there it was.

"How is everything?" Brian asked, appearing with a huge smile. "Gotta love that lobster, am I right? We buy it right off the—"

"Not now," Sullivan said.

"Got it!" Brian said. "Call when you need me!"

He left, and the quiet floated down around us again. Sullivan didn't say anything.

"Freaky story, huh?" I said. I wished I'd ordered another drink.

"How'd you get away?"

I sighed. "I just…went. I was lucky. I ran. I didn't… I didn't even know what he was planning."

"Yes, you did. You knew."

He was right. I *had* known. Lizard Brain hadn't said the word *knife* or *killed*, but it had said the word *now*.

"You were more than lucky. Jesus." He took a deep breath. "Good for you, Nora. Good for you."

I looked down at the table. "Thank you."

Sully reached across and tilted my chin up so he could see my face.

"Thank you," I repeated.

This time, his smile was gentle. "You're an impressive person," he said, and I laughed. "You want dessert? Seems like you earned it."

I suddenly wanted to be naked and in bed with the man in front of me.

"How we doing, kids?" Brian sang.

Not *that* man. Sullivan.

"We'll take the check," I said.

"You *got* it," Brian said. "Back in a flash, you two!"

"I hate that guy," Sullivan said, and I laughed so long and hard tears ran down my face.

Sully just sat back, watching me and smiling.

UNFORTUNATELY, BY THE time we got back to the houseboat, I was all nerves and idiocy.

Why? Because it was Sullivan Fletcher, a boy I'd known my entire life. A man now, a man whose daughter looked up to me, a man who'd been married to one of the girls who'd left scars on my adolescent soul, a man whose brother and mother hated me, etc.

Also, there was Bobby. Not Bobby, not really, but… he'd confused me again, this time by sending a very romantic email, this time detailing all the stuff we used to do before the Big Bad Event. My old life, my Perez self.

I wasn't staying on Scupper Island forever. I wasn't sure I should start something with Sully, no matter how many pheromones were clogging the air, and yeah, it was childish and dopey, but I wasn't sure I could be my Perez self when Sully had known my island self. I realized that was stupid and dopey and childish, but I also knew Sully deserved me to mull that over before anything happened between us.

He was far, far too good to be someone's summer fling.

He turned off the engine. "I'll walk you in," he said.

Shit. How would I tell him no? He was too delicious, too nice, that voice, those eyes, that sense of calm and granite reliability, and also, remember that hug after Audrey's diagnosis? That. Yes.

Boomer barked sharply. "It's me, buddy," I said. He barked again, not happy about Sullivan (or not happy that he wasn't being allowed to leg-hump Sullivan, more likely).

Sully and I stood outside the door, moths fluttering around the light.

I would have to reject him now. Damn. That would not feel good.

"Thank you for dinner," I said. "I had a really nice time."

"Me, too," he said. "Thanks for coming out on such short notice."

Maybe I'd let him kiss me. That would be okay, wouldn't it? And then, once he kissed me, I was pretty sure sexy time would be inevitable.

"Good night," he said at the same second I said, "Want to come in?"

"Excuse me?" he said, and yeah, yeah, I was glad he was hearing impaired. Sue me.

"Nothing," I said. "Good night. Yeah. Have a safe trip home. Back to your house, I mean. Where do you live, anyway?"

"Oak Street."

"Bon voyage, then." *Jesus, Nora. Shut up.*

He looked at me another minute. Maybe the kissing idea wasn't dead yet.

Nope, it was. He gave me the Yankee nod and walked back down the dock.

Date over.

Then again, I guess it hadn't been a date.

Except it had felt so *stinkin'* romantic.

"Sure, Nora, it was," I said as I got the key out. "Who doesn't want to hear about jail and home invasions? Totally romantic."

"What was?" came a voice, and I nearly wet myself.

Luke Fletcher stood on the deck of the houseboat. My heart leaped into my throat.

"Wh-what are you doing here?" I asked. Boomer barked from inside. Shit. My one-hundred-pound dog was inside. My hands started to shake.

"Just thought I'd stop by for a drink. You know. Because we're neighbors."

"Your brother just left."

"So I saw." His voice was friendly. That scared me more, for some reason. Oh, right. Because the other guy's voice had been friendly, too, sometimes. When he wasn't beating the shit out of me.

I swallowed. "Well, I'm tired, Luke. Maybe another time."

"Don't fuck with my brother."

"I wouldn't. Don't worry."

"I wouldn't. Don't worry," he mocked in a falsetto. Boomer barked again.

Then Luke jumped off the boat onto the dock next to me, and I flinched. I hated myself for it, but I did. Inside, Boomer went crazy.

But Luke just brushed past me, close enough that I had to move. He followed his brother's path down the dock, heading left down Spruce Brook Road toward the boatyard.

My legs were shaking. I opened the door and let Boomer go out. My dog ran after Luke, barking. Good. Let my dog maul him and eat him.

"Boomer!" I called after a minute (not really the dog-mauling type), and my good dog turned back. Besides, what if Boomer just licked Luke? Best keep up the pretense that I had a ferocious watchdog before he could prove me wrong.

As I locked up a few minutes later, I wondered if Sully *had* come in, after all, would Luke have stayed up on the deck.

Stayed and watched.

19

Dear Lily,

I'm staying in Oberon Cove this summer. At night, I can hear the riptide on the other side of the island. Do you remember when we came to this cove to fish, and you caught a striped bass bigger than you were? It flipped off the line, and Dad caught it like it was a pop fly.

I took Poe fishing Friday afternoon, but when she caught a whiting, we threw it back. She wants to be a vegetarian now. Sorry about that. Her hair is growing out black now, but I told her I'd help her keep it blue if she wants.

Love,
Nora

ON SUNDAY, I stopped by my mother's place before heading for the long trip to Boston on the ferry. It was Bobby's turn with the dog.

She was splitting wood in the back, something she

did with an axe, not a log splitter. Tweety, whose devotion to my mother kept him close to her, even outside, dived at me, making Boomer leap behind my legs. I swatted at the bird, not hitting it (alas). Mom looked up briefly, then resumed chopping.

"Maybe Poe should be doing this," I suggested.

"She'd cut off her thumb," Mom answered. "Also, she's still in bed."

"Well, wood chopping is a good life skill. Everyone should be able to use an axe."

"It's a maul."

"Maul, then. Maybe there's a kid you could hire to do this? One of the Bitterman kids? Don't they have four boys?"

She swung the axe, and another log split neatly in two. "You got a problem with me cuttin' wood, Nora?"

"Not really, no." My mother was just past sixty and stronger than most NFL players.

But someday she'd be too old for this. And I'd be going back to Boston in two months. Mom was still alone, despite my feeble attempt at the dinner party. I had, however, registered her on LivelySeniors.com and was presently fielding a few offers.

She was getting older. The gray streak that had run through her thick hair as long as I could remember was white now, and wider every year.

I sat on a log and watched for a minute or two as Boomer got in his last sniffs of pine needles before we left. "Mom, I might have a problem with Luke Fletcher," I said.

She placed another log on the chopping block and thwacked it in half, then in quarters. "Why do you say that?"

"He was on my houseboat the other night. Uninvited."

"Tell him to leave you alone."

"I have."

"Want me to talk to him?"

The image of my mom cleaving Luke in half *was* rather beautiful. Then again, I was terribly brave and strong myself. "No, I can handle it. I just… I don't know. Can you tell me a little more about him, what he's been doing since I left?"

"Well, if we have to talk, stack those logs and be useful," she said. I obeyed, not mentioning that I wasn't really dressed for physical labor. Mom wouldn't want me to be a pussy about clothes.

I stacked, she chopped, and after a few minutes, she said, "Welp, he flunked outta UMaine. Came back here and helped his father at the boatyard, but then Allan Fletcher died all of a sudden, so the other one, Sullivan, he took over. Did a fair job from what I heard. Luke, though, he wasn't much for it. Always was a drinker and a druggie."

I picked up some of the logs she'd halved. Tweety screeched at me for getting too close to his beloved. I mentally flipped off the bird. "What drugs? Do you know?"

"Nothin' more than what I heard. Heroin, cocaine, cough syrup, you name it."

"How did Mr. Fletcher die?" I asked, dumping my armload of logs on the woodpile. Since I hadn't asked Mom directly about Mr. Fletcher over the years, she hadn't told me.

"Bad heart, I think. Or a brain bleed. One of those. Sully found him dead out by his truck. Anyways,

Luke... Teeny gave him some money, and he headed off to the big city or some such."

"New York?"

"Portland."

"When did he come back?"

Mom's axe—maul—swung again. "Oh, he comes back every now and again, usually when he needs money. Teeny used to put him up, but Sullivan had a problem with that. I guess Luke stole her engagement ring and pawned it. So Sully has him stay at the boatyard." She paused and wiped her brow. "That Teeny always favored the bad seed. Made me feel bad for Sullivan."

Ah, irony. My own mother always favored her bad seed, too. "Mothers aren't supposed to have favorites?" I couldn't help saying. Lily, for all her drama, bitchery and crime, had been and remained Mom's little darling. Still was.

She didn't answer.

"Has Luke ever gotten clean and sober?" I asked, going back to the subject at hand.

"Oh, sure. Plenty a' times. Same with your sister." She slammed the axe into the chopping block and looked at me directly for the first time today. "Speaking of Lily, she said you've been writing to her."

"Ayuh."

"She wishes you wouldn't."

"Why? Too busy making license plates?"

"Don't put your sister down, missy."

"Why wouldn't she want mail?"

"I don't know, Nora." That was Mom. Never one to take sides, at least, not overtly.

I sighed. "I have to go to Boston. I was kind of hoping Poe would come with me."

"Ask her."

I went inside, but Poe was back to being Queen of the Damned. "Why are you waking me up? It's only ten-thirty! Go away!"

"Want to go to Boston?"

"Why would *anyone* want to go to Boston?"

"Change of scenery? Shopping? Clam chowder? Freedom Trail? Red Sox game? Jewel of New England? Nothing? No?"

"I'm *tired*!"

I took a breath. "Okay, sweetie. I'll see you in a day or so."

She pulled her pillow over her head. I sensed our conversation was over.

So it was just Boomer and me, his raccoon toy, his Nylabone and his long leash climbing onto the ferry.

I took a seat on deck, pulled my Red Sox hat down firmly to keep the wind from molesting my hair and put on my sunglasses. Boomer lay at my feet, gnawing on his bone. I hated bringing him to Boston, hated being without him. What if Luke came over now, huh? It'd just be me and my gun, and the last time I'd needed it, I'd almost shot Sullivan.

Maybe I needed hug therapy. Xiaowen was somewhere off the coast of Oregon, saving the mollusks there, and wouldn't be back for days. Roseline couldn't meet me this time; she had a thing with her in-laws. Gloria was visiting her family and her Slytherin beau, but we were supposed to take the last ferry back together.

I heard the sound of feet and looked up. Sullivan,

Audrey and Amy were coming down the dock, a suitcase in tow.

"Hey!" I said.

"Hi!" Audrey said, jumping onto the boat and giving me a hug. "Tomorrow's the big day, so we're staying overnight. At a hotel!"

"Wow. Exciting. No little brother?" I had yet to meet Rocco. Since he wasn't Sullivan's son, he wasn't at the boatyard the way Audrey was.

"No," she said. "He's staying with my grandmother. Not happy about it, either, but I'll bring him the shampoo from the hotel."

"Nice," I said. Damn, she was such a good kid.

Sully nodded at me and handed Amy aboard, then got on himself. Both parents looked a little drawn and worried, unlike the patient herself, who was practically dancing in place.

"Any questions? Anything I can do?" I asked.

"You've been great already," Audrey said.

Amy and Sullivan were talking in low voices, their body language indicating an argument. Alas, the ferry motor prevented (and saved) me from eavesdropping. "Where are you staying, Audrey?" I asked.

"The Copley Square Plaza. Mom and Dad let me pick."

"You picked the best one," I said, because clearly this was what she wanted to focus on. "They have a tea, I hear."

"We're going. Hey, do you want to come?"

I didn't even glance at Amy and Sullivan. "No, but thank you. I'm meeting friends."

"Drat." She bent down and rubbed Boomer's ears. My dog looked up at her and smiled and wagged, then went back to destroying the bone. Jake turned the ferry to open water, and we picked up speed.

Sullivan was staring out over the ocean. Amy was texting.

"Well, you guys have my number if anything comes up, or if you have any questions," I said to Audrey.

"Thank you," she said.

"Yeah. Thanks," Amy added. Sully's back was to us, so he didn't hear…or just had bigger things on his mind.

"Well, if you don't mind, I'm going in. I have some reading to do," I lied. This was their time together, and they didn't need me hanging around.

At least I had a dog. "Come on, Boomerang," I said, and my faithful beastie followed me into the small cabin.

WHEN WE DOCKED in Boston, I hugged Audrey and wished everyone the best. Amy and Sullivan were preoccupied, and who wouldn't be? Their kid was going to have medical instruments stuck up her nose and into her head. No matter how great the odds for Audrey were, they were both scared.

I watched as they walked away, then slung my bag over my shoulder and headed for Bobby's apartment. He was working and asked if I could drop the dog off. And being a schmuck, I said yes.

It was sunny and warm, a lot warmer than on the island. I took off my denim jacket and tied it around my waist. Boomer and I were stopped a lot by people who wanted to worship him, and I allowed it. Didn't have any other plans, after all. Maybe I'd go shopping. A little retail therapy might lift my blues.

I read the signs on the second and third floors of

buildings as I walked, always curious what other people did for a living. Piano lessons. Yoga studio. Attorney. A knife sharpening place—*Est. 1938*. Amazing that it hadn't gone out of business. A ballet school. A private investigator.

I stopped.

James Gillespie, Private Investigator, Licensed, Bonded, Insured.

"What do you think, Boomer?" I said.

"I think it's a great idea," he said. Well, he *implied*.

We went up the stairs and knocked, and a second later, an older gentleman answered the door. "Hello," he said in a lovely, Morgan Freeman kind of voice.

"Hi," I said. "I might have a case for you."

"Do you, now? And who's this?" He bent over and scratched Boomer's ears, getting a croon of approval.

It only took seven minutes. There wasn't a lot I knew about my father, after all.

"If he can be found, I'll find him," Mr. Gillespie said. "There are a lot of things I can try." Coming from that voice, I believed him.

I paid the retainer, signed a paper, and that was that. Mr. Gillespie said goodbye, and I went back out into the sunshine and humidity, feeling considerably better.

At least it was something. I could tell Lily about it when she came to get Poe. I could tell her I'd tried, and even though Mr. Gillespie was the third private investigator I'd hired, it felt better to be doing something.

I headed for the Commons. The Dog of Dogs would appreciate that. Plus, more hearts and minds for him to win over.

Boston's little park was full of people. Kids tugged on adult hands, begged for ice cream, splashed in the

Frog Pond. There were at least six Frisbees flying through the air, making Boomer cock his head in wonder as his fellow canines chased these flying things. Two twentysomethings lay on a blanket in the grass, turned toward each other, just gazing into each other's eyes. I smiled and looked away. Young love. What could be sweeter?

Then I saw him.

Him. Voldemort.

My heart froze, and my knees turned to water. I sank to the grass and slid my arm around Boomer without taking my eyes off the man who'd terrorized me.

I'd thought I'd seen him a couple dozen times in the past year, and each time, I'd been jolted with fear. Each time, I'd been wrong.

This time, Lizard Brain was sure.

He was just sitting on a bench, eating something—ice cream. Khaki pants, blue T-shirt, that completely unremarkable face, occasionally glancing at people walking past. People who had no idea what he could do. What he liked doing.

I had to find a cop. Or call one. I pulled out my phone and, trying not to take my eyes off him, dialed 911.

"Nine-one-one, please state your emergency."

"Hi, I was attacked last year, and they never found the guy, and I see him right now. I'm at the Commons, right across from Frog Pond, you know? Uh, I mean, north? North of the pond? And he's sitting on a bench on the path."

"Okay, calm down, ma'am. You say he attacked you?"

"Yes. I filed a report. I was in the hospital. I… It was bad."

"What's your name, ma'am?"

For a second, I couldn't remember. I honestly drew a blank. "Um… Nora? Stuart? Nora Stuart. With a *u*. Shit, he's getting up! He's getting up and walking, uh, east. Toward Park Street. He's leaving! He's past the frog statues! Hurry up!"

"Ma'am, I've found your record. I have police on the way. Can you describe the man?"

"Five-nine, five-ten, about 170 pounds. Sandy blond hair, blue eyes. He's wearing khaki pants, a blue T-shirt, a Red Sox hat." Like every freakin' male in Boston. I got up, grabbed Boomer's leash and started walking. Fast. "I'm following him."

"Please, don't do that, ma'am."

Shit. Shit, shit, shit, there was a throng of people approaching, all with name badges on lanyards around their necks, a guide loudly describing the wonders of the Freedom Trail. Tourists, damn them, and he was swallowed by them, all those people, their iPads and phones held high. I darted around.

"Oh, I just love your dog," said a woman in a thick Southern drawl.

"Not now," I said, bolting past, the epitome of rude Yankee. Where was he? Where was he?

There. I started running.

And maybe he had a lizard brain, too, because he began to trot past the hot dog vendors and the guy juggling balls, which made Boomer want to stop and play, and I had to yank hard, but this was important. There. There he was, yes, *him*, at the T stop, damn it all to hell.

"He's getting on the T!" I said to the dispatcher. "Where the hell are the cops?"

I ran down the stairs, the dispatcher yelling at me,

Boomer chuffing with excitement. The train was right there, people getting on and off, and I couldn't see him anymore. If I dropped Boomer's leash and left him, I could jump the turnstile.

The train pulled out of the station. Tears of fury and frustration burned my eyes.

Gone. He was gone.

WHEN I UNLOCKED the door of Bobby's (formerly our) apartment later that afternoon, I was shocked to find he was home.

"I thought you were working," I said.

"Hey!" he said, coming out of the kitchen to hug me. "How are you, Nora? Boomer! Who's my boy?" He crouched down and let Boomer put his paws on his shoulders, then looked up at me. "You look fantastic. It's great to see you."

I was still nauseous with adrenaline, clammy with sweat and fear and could feel my hair expanding with Boston's humidity. I couldn't look *fantastic*, and it irritated me that stupid Bobby couldn't see that.

The police had shown up a minute after the train pulled away. They took notes, but we all knew the guy wouldn't be found. It had taken an hour of walking before my heart rate dropped to normal.

"Have a seat," Bobby said, standing up. "Make yourself at home. I mean, it's still your home, isn't it?"

"Not really," I said. "But I appreciate the thought."

"Wine?" he asked.

"Water, please?"

For the next half hour, Bobby talked, and I sort of listened and stroked Boomer's head.

This was the place I'd come to recover. Bobby's

apartment had never really felt like home to me any more than my office downtown did. It was pleasant and comfortable and familiar, and yes, there were still touches of my personality here and there—the throw pillows for the couch, the umbrella rack, because everyone in Boston should have an umbrella rack. The cheerful yellow kettle in the kitchen.

Today, having seen my attacker, it felt like a sanctuary once again, and I didn't like that. I didn't *want* Bobby's sanctuary. I wanted to make my own.

I wished I was back in Maine. With Boomer, who was really my dog, not *ours*. The deal was that we were supposed to alternate taking the ferry. So far, I'd been the one doing it because of my easier schedule. No more.

"What's wrong, babe?" he said. Babe. Blick.

"I'm a little distracted, that's all. I should go."

"But you haven't told me how you're doing," he said, stepping a little closer. "And you know, obviously, I still care about you."

Just then, my phone chimed with a text from Jake Ferriman. Ferry canceled because of weather. Check back at 7 a.m. for next available.

"Shit," I muttered.

"What is it?"

"My ferry got canceled."

"Yeah, a big rain's coming in." He tilted his head. "Let's have dinner. You can stay over if you want." He reached out and touched my cheek, and no, thank you, it was a little too reminiscent of last year, when my face had been swollen and bruised and throbbed with every beat of my heart, when Bobby had taken care of me. Good care, mind you. Until he got tired of it.

"No, thanks." I bent down and kissed my dog's head.

"Be a good boy, Boomer. I'll miss you." I looked at Bobby. "See you soon."

"You sure you don't want to stay?" He gave me a soulful look.

"I'm sure. Thank you, though."

Out on Beacon Street—because Bobby had really, really wanted a Beacon Street address, even though it cost the earth and my old apartment had been bigger and nicer and cheaper—I texted Roseline and told her I was in town for the night.

Get your ass over here! she wrote back. This is the best news ever!

I sighed with relief. Thank God for female friends.

ROSELINE DID EVERYTHING for me that I would've done for her—she fed me, gave me wine, loaned me soft, clean pajamas and urged me to take a bath in the enormous tub in the guest bathroom. Her husband was a sweetheart, the kind of guy who was great at chatting but also who knew when to leave.

I didn't tell her about seeing Voldemort. There didn't seem to be any point.

I called the clinic and told them I was stuck in Boston; a few minutes later, Gloria called and told me she'd left via Portland, driving up the coast so she could see another sibling's new baby. "Dr. Larsen will cover," she said, referring to our on-call night doctor. "He loves being needed. Don't worry."

"Did you have fun with Slytherin?" I asked.

"I did," she said. "Gave him three guesses as to where I lived, and he got them all wrong. And we had a little fight, which was kind of fun."

"I take it you made up."

"Yep. He texted me an hour ago, begging forgiveness."

"A great quality in a man." That was one of the things about Bobby—getting him to apologize was akin to extracting bone marrow.

"You have fun with Roseline," she said. "Tell her I said hi."

I didn't sleep well. Then again, I didn't have a panic attack, either, or a nightmare. I just thought.

In the morning, the rain whipped against the windows. "Want me to call in?" Roseline offered. She was already dressed for work, and Amir had left. "We can go to a museum, get a pedicure, whatever you want."

"No, that's okay," I said. "Actually, I want to swing by the hospital. My friend's daughter is having surgery today. Pituitary tumor. Cushing's disease."

"Well, let's go, then, *chouchoute*." Rosie's office was just down the block from Boston City.

On the way there, I got a text from Jake Ferriman that he was running, rain or no rain. I wrote back and told him I'd catch the later boat, or go to Portland and to Scupper from there.

The differences between New England's biggest hospital and the island clinic were vast. The clinic could be as tranquil as a yoga studio. In fact, I'd found Amelia in lotus position in her office, sound asleep, last week.

But I did love working there more than I expected. At my Boston practice, I'd see upward of a dozen patients a day. On procedures days, it might be six or seven. I loved my field, but the clinic gave me more variety. Jimmy McNulty, who needed eight stitches when he fell off the monkey bars in the park. Aaron James had had food poisoning (those expiration dates mean something, people!). He was so dehydrated from vomiting and diarrhea that I had him stay overnight. I'd stayed, too, just because he was a widower (gay, though, so not a contender for stepfather, unfortunately). Since he had no family on the island, I slept in another bay, checking on him every two hours, chatting when he started feeling better.

And I loved my coworkers. Gloria and Timmy were rock-solid nurses, unfazed by anything we'd seen so far, even the patient with the foreign body in her va-jay-jay—a perfume bottle—that she most assuredly did *not* sit on, despite her claims. (Nice try. I'd seen at least half a dozen of those cases during my residency.) Gloria and I had gone to a movie the other night at the island's tiny theater and giggled inappropriately through the previews.

Here at Boston City, there were more employees than residents of Scupper Island. I smiled and waved to the folks I knew, stopped to talk to Del, my favorite CNA, then made my way to the surgical floor. Checked in with the nurse on duty, flashed my hospital badge and asked after Audrey. She'd gone into the OR about an hour ago. Dr. Einstein, who'd been recommended by Raj, was the best surgeon for the job. Such a reassuring name, Einstein, and a wicked nice guy.

"Mind if I check in?" I asked.

"Be my guest," said the nurse.

I went to the OR, the thrill of getting the behind-the-scenes pass still with me. For obvious reasons, I couldn't just burst in, no matter what they showed on *Grey's Anatomy*. There was, however, a window and an intercom. I couldn't see Audrey—she was surrounded by three surgeons, the anesthesiologist, two OR nurses and a PA.

I pushed the button. "Hi, Dr. Einstein, it's Nora Stuart, Audrey's referring physician. Just wanted to see how she was doing."

"She's doing beautifully," he said. "Vitals strong and steady, and a beautiful siting of the tumor." Doctorspeak for *I won't have to muck around in her brain all that much.* It was fantastic news.

"I'll tell her parents. Thank you so much." I said a quick prayer that the rest of the surgery would go smoothly, then went back down the hall.

There in the waiting room sat Sullivan, arms folded over his chest, scowling at the floor, clenched tight as a fist.

He was alone.

"Hey," I said. He didn't look up.

I went over and sat next to him. "Hey," I repeated.

He jumped. "Is she okay?" he asked.

"She's great," I said. "I just checked in with the surgeon. It's going really well."

He swallowed, nodded, then ran a hand across his eyes. "I thought you were about to say…something else. What are you doing here?"

"Ferry was canceled last night. I stayed with a friend." He gave a nod. "Sully, I know it sucks to have a kid in the OR, but this is not a complicated surgery." It wasn't a cakewalk, either, but it had a very high success rate.

"Say that when it's your kid."

I smiled. "I can't even imagine." I looked around the waiting room. There was an elderly woman with her middle-aged daughter and a woman sleeping on the couch, her mouth slack. "Where's Amy?"

Sullivan shook his head a fraction. "She had to go back home. Rocco's got a cold." He looked at his hands, and his jaw grew tight.

"I see."

"Hospitals freak her out, anyway. She wasn't doing much good here, so she took the ferry this morning."

"Why do hospitals freak her out?" I asked.

"Because I was in one for so long," he said.

Oh, God. Of course.

But still. Her *daughter* was in the OR under general anesthesia with a metal cannula scraping a tumor off a gland in her brain. And Sully was by himself.

I touched his arm again. "I'll stay with you, if you want."

He looked at me with those dark, lovely eyes, which grew wet again. He gave the Yankee nod and looked back at the floor.

What the heck. I slid my hand into his and gave it a squeeze. He squeezed back, his hand big and rough and calloused.

He didn't let go.

20

I STAYED WITH Sullivan the entire three hours of the operation, and when Dr. Einstein came in to say she was in Recovery and things had gone "perfectly," Sully turned and gave me a long hug.

"Can I see her?" he asked, wiping his eyes with the heels of his hands. All this weepiness over his daughter…it was damn hard to resist. The doctor said absolutely, though she'd be groggy.

"I'll check back with you in a few hours," I said. "Give her my love."

"Thank you," Sullivan said. He started to say something else, then changed his mind and left the waiting room.

"Nice catch, by the way," Dr. Einstein said to me, holding the door for Sully. "A lot of doctors might've missed the diagnosis." He winked and then guided Sullivan down the hall.

Einstein told me I was smart. Maybe I'd get a tattoo of those words.

I checked my phone—three texts. One from Rosie

urging me to stay over again, another from Bobby with a picture of Boomer on our—his—bed and the last one from Poe. is today audrey's surgery? tell her i said good luck & see her when she gets home.

Good girl, Poe. I texted her back, said Audrey was doing well and asked if she'd come for dinner tomorrow night.

She wrote back immediately. okay. thx.

Underneath her bad attitude was a good kid waiting to come out, I was sure of it.

Then again, I'd thought the same thing about Lily, hadn't I?

No. Maybe it was my cynical age back then, but I never did believe there was a better version of my sister. It died when our father left us.

The next ferry wasn't till six this evening. I called my office, told them I was in town and asked if they needed me. "Want to take two colonoscopies?" Angela asked. "Waterman had an emergency, and you'd save my ass. And the patients'!" She laughed merrily.

So I went down the street to our offices and chatted with the other docs and nurses and Angela, who ran the practice, and did the colonoscopies, which aren't as horrible as you might think, especially because of the first-rate drugs we used. Snipped a couple of polyps, sent them to Pathology, did paperwork.

Around three, my phone rang. It was Sullivan.

"Audrey's kicking me out for a couple hours," he said. "I don't know why, since I'm father of the year here." I heard a voice in the background. "She wants to talk to you," he said.

"Hi," said Audrey, her voice sounding like she had a bad cold.

"Hi, Audrey!"

"God, Dad, the volume on this phone is killer! A little warning next time? Hi, Nora."

"How are you feeling, sweetheart?"

"Kind of gross, but super happy this is over with. Do you know when I'll start…you know? Improving?" I knew what she meant. When she'd start losing weight, maybe getting a little taller, losing the extra hair and purple marks. After all, I'd been an overweight teenager, too.

"Well, your endocrinologist can tell you better than I can, but in a couple of months, I think you'll start to see and feel a difference."

"I can't wait."

I smiled. "I hear you."

"So the nurse needs to help me in the shower, and my dad won't leave. He's like the world's most irritating dog." She said this last part very clearly, obviously wanting her father to hear.

"I'm at my office right down the street. Want me to drag him out for a little while?"

"Oh, my God, yes! That would be fantastic. Dad, Nora's coming to take you for a walk. Wanna go for a walk, boy? A walk?"

"You can stop that now," he said in the background. I could hear the smile in his voice.

"Tell him I'll be there in fifteen minutes," I said. "Do you need anything?"

"I'm all set. Thanks, Nora. You're the best!"

THE WEATHER HAD CLEARED, the sun was shining, the rain now out to sea. "We can just go around the block," Sully said after I'd led him outside. He glanced up at the hospital as if he could see into Audrey's room.

"I told her I'd keep you out for two hours," I said. "Don't make me lie to a child." I took his arm and dragged him down the block. It wasn't easy. He was like a truculent four-year-old, going all stiff on me.

"Two hours is way, way too long."

"Sully, she's fifteen. She wants to pee and poop without her father in the next room, listening. She wants to take a shower and get into her own pajamas and text her friends. She'll be fine."

"Well, I don't agree. I think I should be there. She's sick."

"No, she's *been* sick, and now she's recovering. And, man, how happy is she, right?"

This got a smile. Then his eyes got shiny again. "I never really knew how unhappy she was with...you know. Being a little chubby."

From my limited knowledge of Audrey, I bet she was protecting her dad from her own misery. My admiration for her shot up a notch. Me, I'd bled misery all over the place. It never occurred to me to hide it.

"She adores you," I said. "The best thing in a girl's life is a father she can count on."

Well. Didn't I sound like a Facebook meme. I felt my face get hot and looked down the street. But Sully nudged my shoulder with his. "Thanks," he said, a slight smile on his face. "Any luck finding yours, by the way?"

I shook my head.

"How long has it been?" he asked.

"More than twenty years."

"Jeezum crow."

The legendary Boston traffic was picking up, so talking wasn't really an option for people with hearing issues. We walked in silence for a little while. When we hit Thoreau Path, I realized I was heading for home.

My old home. My apartment in the North End.

"Where are we going, anyway?" Sully asked, studying my face so he wouldn't miss my answer.

"Um… I don't know. I was on autopilot, I guess." I flexed my hands, which were tingling. "Want to see where I used to live?"

"Sure. If you want to show me."

"I haven't been back there since…since I left."

Sully took my hand in his. Didn't say anything.

"Okay," I said. "Let's go, then." Brave. Strong. And this time, with a guy who'd spent the morning being brave and strong as well. I could do this.

It wasn't the most scenic walk—the ubiquitous Boston construction, the rude drivers, the blaring of horns, the hulking gray Boston Garden. But once we got into the North End, things improved.

I turned onto my street, not quite sure what I was feeling. Nostalgic for the happiness I once had, the simplicity of my life back then, when work and friends were just about all I thought of. Tyrese, the sweet security guard who used to carry spiders out on a piece of paper rather than step on them.

"This is it," I said, stopping in front of the modern building.

"Nice."

"It was. It is."

"You want to go inside?" he asked.

"Sure."

Now my heart started kicking. The last time I'd walked into this lobby was *that day*, and breathing was suddenly hard. Sully squeezed my hand. We went in, through the glass doors into the cool lobby with its tiled floors and tasteful lounge.

Tyrese sat behind the desk. He did a double take when he saw me. "Dr. Nora! My God! It's so good to see you!" He came out and gave me a hug, practically crushing me. When he let me go, his eyes were wet. "Look at you. Aren't you a sight for sore eyes!"

The last time he'd seen me, I'd been wearing Jim Amberson's bathrobe and smelled like urine and was being carried out by paramedics. "Hey, Tyrese," I said, and my voice was husky. "This is my friend, Sullivan Fletcher."

"Great to meet you, man, great to meet you." Tyrese pumped Sully's hand. "This lady here, she's the best."

Sullivan smiled.

"We were just in the neighborhood, Tyrese," I said. "Figured I'd stop in and say hi. How are your kids?"

"They're great. Growing so fast." He smiled. "It's so good to see you, Doc."

"It's good to see you, too." I hesitated. "Is anyone in my apartment?"

He gave a half nod. "They repainted it and put in new cameras on the exterior, so nothing like that would ever happen again. A couple lives there now. Nice enough."

"Good. I loved that place." I took a breath. "Well, tell the Ambersons hi for me, okay?"

"I will. You take care, Doc. Take good care." He hugged me again, and Sully and I left.

"Let's get you back to the hospital," I said.

He looked at me a long minute, then nodded. Took my hand again, and graciously didn't say anything as the tears slipped out of my eyes.

When we got back to the hospital lobby, I walked over to the elevator with him. "I'm gonna try to catch the six o'clock ferry," I said. It was just five now.

"Okay."

A man of few words. We got off on the surgical floor and went to Audrey's room.

"Hi, Daddy!" she said. She looked refreshed—no one looks great immediately after having surgery. Now her hair was pulled back into a ponytail, and she had a dinner tray in front of her.

"Hi, baby," he said, leaning over to kiss her forehead.

"How do you feel, Audrey?" I asked.

"Fine. Excellent." She beamed.

"Poe said to say hi, and she'll see you back home."

Audrey beamed even more. "I know! She texted me."

"Maybe we can have another sleepover when you feel up to it."

"Sure! That'd be great!" My heart squeezed at her enthusiasm. I loved this kid, no doubt.

"Okay, I should get going," I said. "Call me if you need me, okay? You, too, Sullivan."

He gave a nod and followed me out into the hallway. "You want to go out with me when we get back and Audrey's feeling better?"

"On a date?"

"On a date." The corner of his mouth pulled up.

All the reasons I had for not dating Sullivan Fletcher seemed to evaporate. My mouth was suddenly dry. "Okay. Yes. Sure. Yeah." I took a breath and told myself to calm down. "Now that I've given you four affirmative answers, I think I can go."

His smile widened.

"Bye, Sully. Thanks for today."

"Bye, Nora. Thank *you* for today."

I smiled all the way back to the ferry. And halfway to Maine, too.

21

ON THE FOLLOWING THURSDAY, I convinced Gloria and Xiaowen to come to hug therapy with me. I'd seen a flyer at Lala's that morning and almost choked on my coffee. *Hug Therapy from Hug Therapist Sharon Stuart, HT* (for Hug Therapist, I presumed). *All Are Welcome. Hugging Only, No Groping. 7 p.m.* It must be serious if it cut into *Wheel of Fortune* time.

Mom's little project, which she wouldn't discuss with me, had mushroomed, apparently. She had to relocate to the basement of St. Mary's of the Sea Catholic Church, where we all now stood, waiting for the recovering addicts—Luke not among them—to trickle out.

Poe was here as well, suffering mightily as demonstrated by heaving sighs and the gnawing of her fingernails. "Why are you here?" she asked. "I *had* to come to collect money, but you're free and adults. You should be drinking cocktails somewhere."

"Hear, hear," murmured Xiaowen. "Then again, the pageantry, the splendor that is hug therapy."

"Your mom is clearly onto something," Gloria said. "There must be thirty people here."

It was true. Not just Bob Dobbins looking for thrills, but Mrs. Krazinski, Mrs. Downs of the resting bitch face and a bunch of summer nuisance, looking for quaint thrills.

And also Amy (a regular, it seemed), who gave me a little wave but stayed on her side of the basement. I knew Audrey was back on the island; Sully had brought her in for a checkup today. He'd left with that half smile that did things to my girl parts and a call-you-soon parting message.

I liked him. I liked him a *lot*.

Mom walked past and scowled at me. "What are you doin' here?" she hissed.

"I need a hug," I said. "Also, hug therapist is not a real thing, and you should stop putting initials after your name."

"Twenty-five bucks."

"I see someone raised her prices."

"Every hug lasts twenty seconds, so I earn it. And pipe down, by the way."

"Love you, too."

She rolled her eyes and clapped her hands. "All right, everyone, stop drinking AA's coffee and have a seat. Let's get stahted. Who wants to go first?"

"Me," Xiaowen said instantly.

"Did you pay Poe there?"

"I did." She went over to my mom and stood like a penitent.

I fished out my wallet and took out a twenty and a ten and shoved it at Poe. "The family rate," I whispered. "We get charged extra." She snorted.

"All right, sweethaht," my mother said to Xiaowen. "Come here." She opened her arms and hugged my friend—a long, firm hug. A hair stroke. Then she pulled back and said, "You're a good person, Xiaowen."

To my shock, Xiaowen wiped her eyes. "Thanks, Mrs. Stuart." She came back to me. "Your mother has some serious fucking Hogwarts magic going on there. Damn." She pulled a tissue from her bag and blew her nose.

Bob Dobbins was getting his fix, I saw. "You're a good man, Bawb," my mom said, extricating herself after the requisite twenty seconds had passed. Mrs. K was next, and my mom smiled. That hug seemed more natural. They were old friends, after all, and Mrs. K wasn't trying to rub herself against my mother the way Bob did.

Amy was next. "It's been a hard time for you, dah-lin'," Mom said. "Things are gettin' better, though. You hang in there. You're a good person."

A summer person, clad in pink shorts printed with whales and a white polo shirt, was next. Mom worked her magic on him, and he asked if he could have a selfie with her. "For five more dollars," my mother said.

I popped into the line. Mom sighed when she saw me. "I'm a paying customer," I said.

"What are you, foolish in the head? Fine. Come here."

She wrapped me in her arms and held me tight.

Xiaowen was right.

It had been a long time since I'd had anything other than a hard peck on the cheek. She felt so familiar—her strong shoulders, the smell of Head & Shoulders shampoo. My throat was tight, and I hugged her back tentatively. "You're a good person, Nora. Now, get outta here and let me work."

Ah, mothers. All sentimental mush, I went back to my pals. "Gloria? Are you getting one?"

"I'm good. My own mother wants me to move back into her uterus, and I have to pry her off me every time I leave."

"Then let's go back to my place. Our cocktails await."

"I wish I was a grown-up," Poe muttered.

"Tell you what," I said. "Come over afterward, and I'll make you a virgin drink, and you can hang out with us."

Her face brightened, which she must've realized, because she immediately rearranged her expression back to ennui. "Maybe. Okay."

Twenty minutes later, the three coolest babes on Scupper Island were slurping mojitos made with my homegrown mint and sitting on the top deck, cheese, crackers and grapes on the table. I'd picked flowers and added a few sprigs of rosemary for fragrance. The sun was still shining, and the air was clean and clear.

"Big news, ladies," I said. "I have a date with Sullivan Fletcher at an undetermined time and place in the future."

"Which one is he again?" Xiaowen asked.

"Not your lab partner. The other one."

"He's nice," Gloria said. "I like his vampire teeth."

Xiaowen laughed. "My thoughts are so dirty right now. So, Nora, you gonna do him?"

I felt my cheeks warm. "It's just a date. He's really sweet."

"But his brother is lava hot," Xiaowen said.

"Except for being a dick and all," I added.

"Yeah, I hate when they speak and ruin the fantasy," she said. "My ex-fiancé was the same way." Sadness flickered across her face. "Whatcha gonna do?"

"Why did you guys break up?" Gloria asked.

"He cheated on me. On me, can you believe it? On this." She gestured to herself.

"What an idiot," I said. But I reached over and squeezed her hand, anyway. She shot me a grateful look. "Do you want to talk about it?"

"Shit, no. Gloria, how's Slytherin?"

"I think Slytherin and I are taking it to the next level," Gloria said.

"Does he want to Slytherin to your chamber of secrets?" I asked.

"Was that a wand in his pocket, or was he just happy to see you?" Xiaowen added.

"Come on over here, sweetheart, and I'll show you my patronus."

"You two are funny," Gloria said, "in a juvenile, idiotic way." She sipped her drink. "Actually, we did play a little Quidditch, if you know what I mean. God. I can't believe I'm sinking to your level."

"Did he capture your Golden Snitch?" Xiaowen and I said at the same time. We high-fived each other, giggling like the tweens we were channeling.

"Not exactly. Still early days, you know? But I told him my last name, and I'm thinking of letting him know where I live."

"Is that first base these days?" Xiaowen asked.

Gloria smiled. "Well, after my old boyfriend turned out to be a stalker, yeah. But Slytherin's nice. I even told him we called him Slytherin, and he thought it was great."

"So he's read Harry Potter," I said. "Thank God we can check that box. What does he do for work?"

"He's a doctor at Boston City," Gloria said.

"That's where I worked!" I said. "What's his name? Maybe I know him!"

"Robert Byrne."

I sucked in a breath—and a bit of mint leaf, which my airway most assuredly didn't like. I choked and coughed and coughed and wheezed.

"Heimlich her," Xiaowen ordered.

"If she can cough, she can breathe," Gloria said, and rightly so, but it was hard to care, as tears were streaming down my face.

Also, she was dating my ex-boyfriend.

I managed to get the leaf up (so genteel, so classy) and wiped it on my jeans. "Robert Byrne," I said, wheezing. I took a napkin and blotted my eyes. It could be Robert Burn. Or Burns, like the poet. "Is he an emergency room doctor? Blue eyes, tall, lives on Beacon Street?"

"That's the one! So you *do* know him!"

I took a breath. "I dated him. Uh…he and I broke up just before I came out here."

There was silence. Xiaowen's eyes darted back and forth between us as she sucked on her straw.

"Well, shit," Gloria said.

"I mean, it's okay, but…how did you not know? How did *he* not know that you and I work together?" Had *I* told Bobby I worked with a nurse named Gloria? I didn't think I had.

Gloria closed her eyes. "I've been really vague with him. I mean, seriously, I didn't tell him my last name until Friday. He knows I'm a nurse and I live near Portland and my family's from outside Boston."

"I take it he never mentioned me. Or Boomer." Not so long ago, there'd been a picture of Boomer and me on the fridge.

"He said…" She broke off. "He said his ex-girlfriend took their dog, and he was thinking about getting a new one. We went to the pound together on Saturday to look at puppies."

"We share Boomer," I said. "That's where he is right now. With Bobby."

"He goes by Robert now."

"Does he?" I was pissed, all right. Not because Gloria was dating him…but because he clearly hadn't told her about me.

What about asking me to stay over the other night when my ferry was canceled? I was pretty sure that wasn't an I'll-take-the-couch offer. What about how he still cared about me? The hints that he wanted to get back together?

He hadn't told Gloria a thing about me, that was clear. And not for nothing, but I was a pretty damn good story. Home invasion. Hit by Beantown Bug Killers.

"I should go," Gloria said.

"No, no," I said automatically, aware that I'd been silent. "It's just a surprise, that's all."

"I… I think I'll go, anyway. This is a lot for us both to wrap our brains around, so…yeah. I'm sorry."

"You haven't done anything wrong," I said. "I'll see you at work."

"You bet." Her face was troubled. "Okay. Thanks. Bye, Xiaowen."

"Bye."

Xiaowen waited till we heard Gloria's car start, then poured me another drink from the pitcher. "Small world?"

"He didn't tell her about me," I said.

"Yeah, I got that."

What was I, invisible? First, high school. No, first, my father. Then high school, then when I was allowed to visit Lily in Seattle and more than one person said, "I didn't know Lily had a sister!" Then I came here, and half the town thought I *was* my sister, since apparently she was the only daughter my mother talked about.

Now Bobby had erased me. *And* said I took the dog, when I'd been bending over backward, taking Boomer back and forth since I'd been here.

Xiaowen fumbled in her bag and pulled out an iPad. "What's his middle name?" she asked.

"Kennedy," I said automatically.

"Of course," she murmured. "So original." She tapped a few keys. "Whoomp, there it is. He posted a picture of him and Gloria."

She held out the iPad, and there they were, smiling, wearing sunglasses, right there on Instagram, which I still didn't belong to.

"Thanks," I muttered.

"So who are you mad at? Him or her?"

"Well, this sure would've been easier if she'd used his actual name like a grown-up," I said, taking a sip of my drink.

"I think we're the ones who called him Slytherin."

"Shit. You're right." I took a deep breath and looked out over the cove. "Xiaowen, he was kind of hitting on me this past weekend. Asked me to stay over."

"Are you fucking kidding me?"

"Nope." I closed my eyes. "Do I tell her?"

"Oh, I think he'll have some explaining to do. Bet she's on the phone with him right now and not real happy, either." She stood up. "Come on. Let's go swimming."

"Why?"

"To wash off the stink of your ex-boyfriend polluting your mind."

"The water's probably about fifty-three degrees."

"You grew up here. I'm a marine biologist. We can handle it."

"Do you have a bathing suit?"

"No. Can I borrow one?"

"One that will fit you? No. One that *maybe* won't fall off if I tie it on with string? Yes."

Xiaowen was right. Ten minutes later, we were laughing as we made our way down the rocky shore to the edge of the cove to a rock that jutted out. The tide was in, and the water looked black and deep. "On the count of three," she said, taking my hand. "One... two...three!"

We jumped, and the water bit us with icy teeth. I popped up immediately, my skin burning with cold. Xiaowen swam a ways out, then popped up, her dark head like a seal's. "Holy Christmas, it's cold without a wet suit!" she said, and I laughed. Our voices bounced against the rocks and the reddening sky. I ducked under the water again, the cold clamping my head, but it was a clean hurt, cooling off my angry heart. I was over Bobby. The fact that he was an eel...well, I knew that already. I'd just put it aside, hadn't I?

There was Poe, standing like Lily's ghost on the rock Xiaowen and I had just jumped off. "Nora? Are you guys *swimming*? Are you crazy?"

"Come on in, Poe!" I said.

"Not gonna happen," she called.

"Don't be a pussy!" Xiaowen yelled, though her teeth were starting to chatter.

I swam to the edge and climbed out carefully, not wanting to slip and end up in the hospital for the third time in a year.

Poe reached down and helped me up. "You're freezing!" she said.

"Give Auntie Nora a hug," I said, wrapping my arms around her. She shrieked and pulled away.

She was wearing shorts and a tank top and little flip-flops. "Come on in, chickadee," I said. "The water's beautiful. I'm a doctor. I won't let you die."

"Super reassuring."

"Come on. Live a little."

She looked at me for a second. "That's what my mom says."

It was the first time she'd mentioned my sister without my prodding. She took her phone out of her pocket and set it down.

"Count of three," I said, echoing Xiaowen, and we jumped, holding hands. My niece clutched me tight when we surfaced. "Holy crap, that's cold!" she said, then pushed my head underwater. I tickled her and popped up, completely numb now. Poe's smeared eyeliner made her look like a ghoul, but she was laughing.

The sound hugged my heart, and I seized the moment and smooched her on the cheek, then dunked her. Xiaowen swam over, and the three of us laughed and splashed and shivered and laughed some more.

It was almost completely dark when we got out, shaking with cold.

"Hot showers and food at my place," I said. "And you can both sleep over. In fact, I insist."

"Like I was going back to Cape Elizabeth soaking wet," Xiaowen said, linking her arm through mine.

"I'll call Gran," Poe said. "She probably could use the alone time after giving out all those hugs."

Just as we got onto the dock, something made me glance into the woods.

There among the dark of the pines, a tiny dot of orange glowed as Luke Fletcher took a drag on his cigarette.

If he thought he was scaring me, he was wrong.

"Go home, Luke!" I yelled. "And get a life, how about that?"

But the orange glow stayed put.

22

Dear Lily,
You'd be surprised how cute Scupper has become.
I can't wait to see you in August. Mom and Poe
are doing great. Poe really likes my dog, too. I bet
you will, too. He's a sweetheart.
Love,
Nora

I WENT TO work the next day with a happy heart, thanks
to Xiaowen and Poe and the frigid, cleansing Maine
water. Yes, I was still furious with Bobby—or *Robert*.
He'd be getting a phone call from me once I cooled
down a little. And I would also be taking Boomer back
forevermore. Fuck that joint custody shit, yo.

Ironically, I was more angry that he hadn't mentioned Boomer. Forget the my-ex-was-crazy-but-I-
loved-her-so lie. Boomer was pure love. Boomer was
perfect. If Bobby wanted to date Gloria, well, he had
great taste in women. She was smart, gorgeous, funny.

And let's not forget—he did love a good chase, so her unwillingness to tell all would definitely have grabbed his interest. Same as how I wouldn't sleep with him the first few months we dated.

But Boomer… What kind of a dick doesn't mention his faithful dog by name?

I said hello to Mrs. Behring, who'd gotten over her shock that I'd turned out okay and even liked me a little bit now, especially since I brought in homemade, delicious yet nutritious oatmeal cookies every Wednesday. Amelia poked her head out of her office. "Hello, my dear!" she said. I had to give it to her—she was always so happy. And that matte lipstick…something I could never pull off.

"How are you, Amelia?"

"Wonderful! Darling, come in a minute, won't you?" I went into her office, which was beautifully furnished with sleek, comfortable furniture and a cool oil painting that was just splashes and swirls of color.

"What can I do for you?" I asked, taking a seat.

"Darling, you're planning to stay how long on our fair island? September?"

"Mid-August. I'm staying until my sister gets back."

"She's in prison, yes?"

I flinched. I hadn't realized Amelia knew. "Yes."

"Is there any way I could convince you to stay till Christmas? The doctor who was supposed to come in this fall has abandoned us, leaving our little ship uncaptained through what is sure to be a stormy season."

Since the off-season months were morgue quiet, I was pretty sure she might be exaggerating just a touch. "I'm sorry, Amelia. My leave of absence is only until August 30."

"Very well. Of course, you have a fabulous career back in Boston! And wonderful for you. All right, then, carry on!"

"Thank you for asking, though," I said.

"Let me know if you change your mind. You're a lovely addition to Team Ames!"

"Amelia," I began, then paused.

"What is it, dear?"

"Well, if you'll let me get a little personal..."

"Go right ahead, darling!"

"Have you thought about getting treatment?"

"For what, dear?"

"For your drinking."

Her smile froze, and a flicker of sadness crossed her face. She looked down at her desk, then back up at me. "I've been in treatment many times. This is about the best I've been able to manage." She paused. "I'm so sorry about my behavior at your dinner party. I was mortified to throw up on that young man."

"Oh, don't worry about that. I think I may have goofed with the, uh, butter. But I worry about you, Amelia."

She smiled. "Thank you. You're so kind."

"If I can ever help..."

"Thank you," she said again, her voice quiet, and I felt both sorry for her and full of respect. It wasn't easy, God knew, being an alcoholic. Especially if you were once brilliant and smart enough to realize what you'd lost. It took guts for her to show up here every day, full of good cheer, knowing she couldn't practice anymore.

"I'd better get to work," I said.

"Wonderful!" she said, smiling firmly again. "Just call if you need anything."

"Thanks," I said. "Let's have lunch one day this week."

"I would love that," she said.

I went into the main part of the clinic to see what was up.

"Explosive diarrhea in Room One," Gloria said, handing me a folder.

"And good morning to you," I said with a smile.

"Morning." She didn't smile back.

My smile slid away. "Gloria, we should probably talk, don't you think? About Bobby?"

"*Robert* and I talked last night," she said. "I think I'm all set."

Wow. I closed my mouth. "Okay, then. Actually, not okay. I think I should tell you a few things."

"Not necessary. Thanks, anyway." She turned and walked away.

Message received. Just not expected.

I went into Room One and got to work. It was explosive, all right. The poor woman had eaten undercooked lobster, and that lobster had wanted out and fast.

Because Gloria had been here longer and because I was essentially a temp, she'd always triaged the cases. If she could do the job—say, a throat swab for strep—she'd do it and let me know. If the day was quiet, I'd pop in and have a chat. If the patient's presentation was more complicated, she'd assign the case to me, or we'd do it together.

Today, however, I got them all. And it was a very busy day.

Sun poisoning on a teenager who didn't like sunscreen, a sprained ankle on a seven-year-old, a vitamin B shot for an elderly woman, a mono diagnosis and a birth control prescription for a young waitress, accompanied by a firm lecture on the necessity of condoms, too. Two stitches in the chin for a boy who'd fallen off his bike.

"Trouble walking," Gloria snapped. "Room Four."

"Got it." I went into the exam room, where a rather shabby old man sat in a chair. Ernest Banks, his chart said. The name wasn't familiar. He had the unmistakable odor of a person who didn't wash regularly, and his hair and beard were gray with grease.

"Hi, Mr. Banks, I'm Nora Stuart." I offered my hand, and he took it. His blue eyes were a little confused. "What seems to be the problem today?"

"It hurts when I walk."

I washed my hands and asked him a few questions about his home situation—did he live alone (yes), did he eat regularly (yes, he said, but his skinniness told the truth), was he healthy otherwise (yes…but again, a lie)?

His shoes were worn, his socks gray and damp. I took them off slowly and carefully, noticing his wince.

It wasn't uncommon for elderly people to neglect their feet. It could be hard to reach their toes, and taking a shower or bath might be a risk they didn't want to take.

But my God. Mr. Banks's feet were the worst I'd seen. His toenails were so long they'd curled over his toes and dug into the soles of his swollen feet.

And the smell. There was infection here, oozing and green.

"We'll take good care of you, sir," I said, looking up at him with a smile. "I think we can definitely make you feel better. Hang on one second while I get some supplies."

Gloria wasn't around. What Mr. Banks needed was a

shower, a medical pedicure, some oral antibiotics and a topical antibiotic for his feet. "Where's Gloria?" I asked Mrs. Behring.

"She taking a late lunch."

"Super." I knocked on Amelia's door. "Can you give me a hand, Amelia? We have an elderly gentleman who needs some help."

For the next hour, Amelia and I did the work that I'd never do in a big-city hospital. We soaked Mr. Banks's feet in warm water and hydrogen peroxide, and I cut his toenails bit by bit. They were thick and hard, more like barnacles than something that grew on a human. The clinic had a shower, and we took him there, undressed him gently, layer by layer, and lathered him up a few times. He had a few more cuts and bruises, and he was seriously underweight.

We put him in a pair of scrubs, gave him a shot of B12 and antibiotics, then wrapped his feet in gauze and put him in bed.

"Mr. Banks," Amelia said, "I'm going to ask that you stay here for a few days."

"I don't have any money," he said.

"You don't need any," Amelia said. "You're our guest. There's no charge."

"I guess that would be all right," he said, relief painted over his face.

"Are you hungry?" I asked.

"A little," he said, but his eyes lit up.

"I'll take care of this," Amelia said. "It's the least I can do, Nora, and you have more patients. Mr. Banks and I will get to know each other." She smiled at him kindly.

"All right," I said. "I'll check back with you in a little while, Mr. Banks. Make yourself comfortable."

He smiled at me, looking so much better than he had when he came in.

My heart felt too big for my chest. The poor man! We'd have to call Social Services to check his home and see how bad his conditions really were.

The warm fuzzies were short-lived. "Perineal abscess in Room Two," Gloria said, back from her break. "Hugely inflamed."

Okay. She was definitely sending me a message. With a sigh, I went to see my next patient and got ready to drain pus.

I managed not to say anything else on the topic of one Robert Kennedy Byrne for the rest of the day. He hadn't texted, emailed or called me, the coward.

If Gloria didn't want to talk, that was up to her.

She changed her mind.

At 5:07 p.m., she came into my office and shut the door. "Hey," I said.

"So I know the whole story," she said, sitting down.

"Before we get started," I said, "let me just say this. I really like you and don't want this to be an issue. Bobby didn't mention he was seeing someone, so it came as a surprise. Small world and all that. But you and I are coworkers *and* friends. I really wouldn't want that to change."

"Well, it *has* changed," she said. "He told me everything."

"Is that right?" I had my doubts already.

"We talked a lot about our exes," she said. "That was one of the things we really bonded over. Robert told me all about you, even if he didn't use your name."

Really? He never uttered my name? And that never tipped her off to anything strange? Also, this *Robert* thing was pissing me off, as was her raised, know-it-all eyebrow. "It's funny," I said. "I've never heard him called Robert, even by his mom." She didn't respond. "So, what would you like to talk about, Gloria?"

"I'm kind of shocked at how dishonest you've been with me."

"Me? I haven't been dishonest."

"You never mentioned how you left him, just like that, breaking his heart."

I snorted. "Is that what he said?"

"You dumped him when he was going through a really hard time and moved back in with your mother."

"Okay, well, first of all, I'm pretty sure *I* was the one going through a hard time, which I define by being hit by a van and knocked unconscious, breaking bones and dislocating joints. It was also hard when I woke up in the ER and he was flirting with—"

"He talked about how you took his dog—"

"Boomer is *my* dog."

"—and even before that, how you totally changed after you started dating and were so needy and depressed that he had to do a suicide watch on you, and then when *he* was going through *his* stress, you dumped him."

I took a long, slow breath. "I was never suicidal. Good God. I don't know where he got that. As for his stress—" I raised my hands in a helpless gesture "—that's news to me. Would you like to hear another version of our relationship? Because Bobby has left a lot out, it seems."

"No," she said. "I'm good." She folded her arms and

sat back in her chair, daring me to contradict anything she wanted to believe.

"Okay, then," I said. "Believe what you want, and good luck with him."

"I don't need luck. Robert and I might've only known each other a month, but I can tell he's the one. He already said he loves me."

"Even though he still doesn't know your last name or where you live."

"He knows now." She tilted her head.

Shit. I had to try. The Female Solidarity Commandment said so. "Gloria, he asked me to spend the night on Sunday. I didn't get the impression he meant sleeping on the couch."

"Yeah, right. Sure he did. He told me what happened, how you showed up and asked if you could stay and said you still loved him…"

The cowardly, lying *shit*. "Okay, we're done here."

"I hope you and I can continue working together," she said. "It'd be a shame if you had to leave. Then again, I may be moving back to Boston soon."

With that, she got up and left.

I sat there, my ears hot with anger, taking back every generous thought I'd had about Gloria. If she wanted to be obtuse—if she *insisted* on being obtuse—then let her.

I picked up the phone to call Xiaowen, then decided not to. After all, they were friends, too. Instead, I went to Gloria's Facebook page.

Uploaded just last night were fifteen pictures of her and Bobby. Her relationship status had just changed from *Single* to *In a relationship with Robert K. Byrne, MD*.

Only Bobby would be asshole enough to register on Facebook with MD after his name.

Time to call him. It went to voice mail. Coward.

"Hi, it's the pathetic ex-girlfriend who broke your heart and was on suicide watch and begged you to take me back. I'm calling to say I'll be picking up Boomer on Friday, and this joint custody thing is over. Also, you're a lying piece of scum."

Then I hung up the phone and called Poe and asked if she was free for dinner, and if she'd mind if Audrey joined us. *When you're feeling sorry for yourself*, my mother used to say, *do something nice for someone else*.

Speaking of that, I went down the hall into Mr. Banks's room. Amelia had left for the day, so he was alone, asleep, looking very peaceful. I checked his chart—Amelia had already put in a call to Social Services, it said on the chart, and he'd had a good meal.

I went over to his bedside and pulled up the blanket to cover his shoulders.

This man might be my father, for all I knew. Alone, barely scraping by, sick, dirty.

Tears flooded my eyes. If my father was still out there, I'd take him in. I'd let him live with me, and I'd make sure he knew someone loved him.

If only I could know for sure. If only I could find him.

AUDREY WALKED DOWN from the boatyard, and Poe rode her bike to the houseboat. I made us a beautiful salad with scallops and pecans and let the girls tell me about their days. Audrey had power-washed three boats; Poe had slept till noon.

"Do you have a job for the summer, honey?" I asked.

"No," she said. "Gran said I should get something,

and I did apply to four places, but no one called me back."

"You can work at the boatyard," Audrey offered.

"Doing what?"

"Whatever needs doing. Clean the boats, varnish decks, pump the head—"

"What's that?"

"You know. Emptying the crapper."

"Gross."

"You're telling me." She smiled.

It had been ten days since her surgery, and she already looked better, healthier, less tired. She had a light tan from working outside.

"You really think I could?" Poe said. "I'd love to get out of the house."

"I'll ask my dad, but yeah." She took another bite of dinner. "I love your shirt, by the way. What does that mean, anyway?"

Poe's shirt was a little crop top that had some French words written in cursive on it.

"Head full of stars," she said.

"It's so cute. Did you make it?"

Poe nodded.

"You did?" I asked.

"Gran's been teaching me to sew."

"You have to join the fashion club in the fall," Audrey said. "It's really fun, and we have these great sewing machines and everything."

"I don't know that much," Poe said.

"That's okay. That's what it's for. I'm pretty good. I can show you. My mom is great at sewing."

"Why don't you live with her?" Poe asked, and I cringed inwardly. Then again, I also wanted to know.

"She got married and had another kid," Audrey said. "Her husband didn't like me much."

"What an asshole," Poe said.

"Who couldn't like you?" I said, outraged. "I have to agree with Poe. Asshole."

She shrugged, blushing a little. "Well, anyway, I moved in with Dad full-time. But I spend a lot of time with my mom, too. Rocco's great. I mean, he's disgusting, too. He's a boy, after all. He makes fart jokes all day, every day, and still can't pee without half of it going on the floor. I'm happy not to have to share a bathroom. And my mom divorced the asshole."

"You're so cool, Audrey," Poe said. "I mean, nothing fazes you."

"It's all a front," she said, taking a bite of salad. "Sometimes I just pretend to be okay with everything because you know how it is. You show weakness, the mean girls attack."

"Anyone gives you a problem, you come to me. I'm terrifying," Poe said.

Audrey laughed. "So terrifying." Both girls laughed, some inside joke I didn't quite get. After all, I still thought Poe was pretty scary sometimes.

I got up to make coffee...well, really to give the girls some time to talk without the dorky aunt hanging out with them. Allegedly, I had a social life of my own.

I checked my phone, and lo and behold, my social life was right there. Sullivan Fletcher. Free for dinner Saturday?

My face flushed. I'd had my phone muted, so the requisite half hour of not appearing too eager had passed. Sure. Where did you have in mind?

The three dots of anticipation waved. My place. Audrey will be w/ Amy. 7:00 p.m.?

I counted to sixty (honestly, dating in this day and age was ridiculous) and then texted back. Sounds good. Thank you.

I had a date with Sullivan Fletcher.

I would definitely have to catch up on my shaving.

23

THE DATE WITH Sullivan began to spiral into disaster before it even started.

A word to the wise: don't attempt sexual relations to salvage what is clearly a FEMA-level catastrophe.

The first thing that went wrong was that my mother insisted that I'd told her I was going to dinner at her house that night. This, of course, was completely freakish, because she hadn't once invited me to dinner (nor had I wanted to go, given her culinary craftsmanship or lack thereof).

"Nora, you *said* you'd come, and Poe is looking forward to it." Her voice was hard as nails. Tweety screeched his support of his beloved.

"I have plans, Mom."

"Yes. With us. I made ham."

Ooh, ham. All that delicious sodium and cholesterol. Of course, Mom would cook it till it was jerky. "I'm really sorry," I lied.

"I didn't spend my day off cookin' for you, only to

have you decide you've got something better goin' on, Nora Louise."

Shit. My middle name. "Okay, okay, let me make a call." I paused. "Can I invite someone?"

"Fine." She hung up, mad at me for not remembering an invitation that hadn't been offered. If Sully was willing, he and I could eat at Mom's—dinner never lasted more than seventeen minutes, after all—leave, take a lovely walk, maybe have a drink back at his place and then see where things led. Maybe to bed, even. Hey. We weren't kids.

And now that any shred of thought about giving Bobby another chance was dead, why not?

Bobby. I hissed at the thought. Or *Robert*, I should say, still hadn't called me, and yesterday, when I'd taken the ferry to Boston, he'd conveniently been at work. My dog had been waiting there, wagging at me. A note on the table said only *Please leave your key*.

Which I happily did. I also took my kettle, thank you very much, looking slightly insane; my purse, my dog and a yellow Le Creuset kettle banging my leg with every angry stride.

Gloria was welcome to him.

In fact, *she* was the big disappointment here. One expected guys to be shallow and self-serving and all that, but when a woman behaved like an idiot, it always came as a shock. Even though I'd only known Xiaowen a couple of months now, I was positive this would never happen with her. And Roseline, forget it. She'd never dream of dumping me, not with a gun to the back of her head.

Well, whatever. I called Sullivan. "Hi," I said. "My mother has this notion that I'm supposed to come over tonight for dinner, and she's annoyed that I forgot, even though she never invited me. Would you mind if we went there?"

"That's fine," he said. "I haven't even started cooking."

"Okay, great. Thank you."

"What time should I pick you up?"

"Five," I said. "You know the elderly. They like to eat early." My mother would kick me if she knew I'd called her *elderly*. "Hey, why don't I just walk down to the boatyard? I can see Poe in action that way."

Because yes, he'd given her a job. Audrey had texted him the other night when the girls were here, and Poe had started her first ever job this morning.

So Mom swooping in with an imaginary dinner invitation, that was strike one.

Strike two was Luke Fletcher, or Luke Fucking Fletcher, as I was coming to call him.

I dressed in a cute little summer frock in bright yellow and wedge cork heels, which turned out not to be the best choice for taking a mile-long stroll on a dirt road. My ankle kept trying to roll, and it was hotter than I thought. Sweat dripped down my back, and all of a sudden, it felt like every mosquito in Maine had gotten a text as to my whereabouts.

I swatted and slapped and tried to walk faster, feeling my heel start to itch and burn where a blister was emerging. I could take off the shoes, I supposed, but the sand was hot.

Damn it! A bug flew into my hair, which was on high frizz, and got stuck there. A big bug. I tried to extricate it—it felt like a dragonfly—and, oh, crap, pulled it right in half.

"Lovely," I said, disentangling the rest of it. "Just

lovely. Sorry, dragonfly." Of course, it had to be a beautiful insect, not these evil bloodsuckers.

By the time I got to the boatyard, I was damp, frizzier, itchy and limping. I took a few breaths and tried to exude serenity and grace. Failing that, I pasted a smile on my face and went with *fake it till you make it*.

There was Audrey, sanding the deck of a sailboat in dry dock about twenty feet over my head. "Hey!" I called.

"Hi!"

"You taking it easy enough, missy?" I asked. "Don't forget you just had surgery."

"I'm barely even here," she said. "Dad said I could work for half an hour."

Another head popped over the deck. "Hi, Nora," said Poe, smiling.

Smiling. "Hi, honey," I said. "How's your first day been?"

"Great. Audrey can drive a boat, did you know that?"

"I suspected. I hear we're having dinner tonight at Gran's."

"Ayuh," she said in an exaggerated accent, and Audrey and I laughed.

"What are you doing here?" came a low voice behind me.

I turned around. "Hey, Luke," I said. "I'm here because I'm having dinner with Sully. And my niece."

The sun had streaked his hair white blond in places, and he looked good. Tan and lean.

"Right. Your niece is working here now." He scratched his arm idly. "She's a pretty girl."

"She's a minor," I said, just to be clear.

"Age of consent in Maine is sixteen."

My forefinger jabbed him in the Adam's apple before

I even knew I'd moved. He made a satisfying gagging sound and stepped back. "If you lay one finger on her, I will rip you apart, Luke Fletcher," I hissed.

"I was kidding," he said, wheezing.

"I'm not. Don't you even look at her."

"Hey. What's going on?" It was Sullivan.

I turned to be sure he'd catch everything I said. "Your brother just made an alleged joke about the age of consent in Maine regarding my niece."

Sully grabbed him by the front of his shirt and shook him. "I will kill you, Luke. I mean it."

Luke held his hands up. "Come on, bro! You think I'd do something like that? I was just trying to piss off Dr. Superior here. It was a joke. Jesus."

"You don't joke about sex with a teenager, asshole." Sully shoved him back. "Pack your stuff. You're leaving."

"Sully, come on. It was tasteless, okay? I'm sorry. I'm sorry, Nora. I would never do that. Okay? I'm really sorry." He gave me a penitent look.

"Are you guys fighting?" Audrey asked.

"We're discussing in a heated manner," Luke called up to her, grinning.

"Don't be a loser, Uncle Luke," she said, a frown crossing her face.

"I'm trying not to be. I've got you as a role model."

She smiled, then murmured something to Poe.

"Can I stay, Sully?" Luke asked. "I swear to God, I'd never lay a hand on someone under twenty-five. Twenty-three at the very youngest." He paused. "I don't have anywhere to go. You won't let me stay with Mom, and I'm working for free here."

"To pay off what you stole."

"Right. My point is, it's good for me to be around you, doing all this hard work, and it's helping me stay clean. Come on, bro. It was a stupid thing to say, and I really am sorry."

I almost believed him.

Sully took a deep breath. "We'll talk tomorrow."

"Okay. Thanks, bud. You guys have a good night." He smiled, but there was a hardness in his eyes I didn't like. He held my gaze a minute longer, dipped his chin, then walked off into one of the buildings.

"Is he stable?" I asked bluntly. "Sober? No drug use?"

"As far as I can tell," Sullivan said. "I'm so sorry, Nora. He likes to piss people off, and he's good at it."

"Is Poe going to have a problem here?"

"Excuse me?"

My words came out more sharply than I intended, given the subject matter. "Is *Poe* going to have any *problems* here?"

"No. I'll make sure of it. You don't have to yell. Just speak clearly, okay?"

"Yes. Okay. Sorry."

Sullivan ran a hand through his dark hair, and I caught a glimpse of his hearing aid. "I honestly don't think he'd ever cross that line. Luke just has this…problem where you're concerned. Resentment."

"Yeah, well, he needs to get over it."

"Yes. He does. Especially if we're gonna be a thing."

The words took me by surprise, slamming my heart in an almost-painful rush. "We'll see about being a *thing*, Mr. Fletcher, you wordsmith, you. First, you have to endure dinner at my mom's."

MOM GREETED US with "You're late" and sent Poe up to take a shower. "What have you been up to today, Nora? You're sweatier than a racehorse."

"Thanks, Mom. Glad we got that out in the open." Tweety squawked, then dived at my head. "Sullivan, this is my mother's pet, Tweety."

"Cute," he said.

"I hope you like ham," my mother said.

The bird took another swoop at me. I ducked. "God, Mom. Can't you put him in a cage?"

"He's a good boy. Aren't you, sweetie-Tweety? Come here, now." She held out her finger, and the bird flew onto it. "Got a kiss for mama?"

"Mom, please. Avian flu. Histoplasmosis. Crypto-coccosis."

"What are you babbling about? He's not sick. Are you, baby?" She kissed his beak. He squawked, then flew off her finger to parts unknown, probably to wor-ship Satan.

I looked at Sullivan. "Sorry," I mouthed.

"So you datin' my daughter?" Mom asked.

"Not quite yet," he said.

"And you're deaf, is that right?"

"More or less."

"You make a good living at the boatyard?"

"Ayuh," Sully said. Mom may have met her match in the art of conversation.

"Mom, please," I said. "Can we just eat ham?"

"Go check it," she said. "I think it needs a few more minutes."

"It comes cooked, you know. You just have to heat it up."

"Just do what I say, Nora. I want a few minutes with Sullivan here."

"This is fun, isn't it?" I said, squeezing his arm. He smiled down at me, and I felt a surge of attraction.

Maybe we could salvage this night. I scratched a mosquito bite and did as I was told. Opened the oven door—the ham smelled good, all right, and Mom had put pineapple slices on it with maraschino cherries in the middle, making it look like the ham had strange nipples popping out all over it. Baked potatoes sat, hardening on the lower shelf—Mom never wrapped them in foil or rubbed them with olive oil the way I did. There would be no butter, either.

Ah, well. I closed the oven door.

In her odd way, Mom was trying for something here. She usually only made ham on Christmas.

"I'm starving," Poe said, coming into the kitchen, her blue hair wet.

"Hey, I wanted to tell you something, honey. I'm so glad you have a job at the boatyard. But Luke Fletcher… keep your distance, okay?"

"'Cause he's a druggie and might corrupt my pure soul?"

"Exactly. He also might be a dirty old man."

"Gross."

"Yep."

"I'll just knee him in the nuts if I have to." She demonstrated the move. "Take that, motherfucker!"

"Language, language. We're at Gran's. But yes. That's my girl. You make me proud."

To my surprise, her eyes filled with tears. She looked away, embarrassed, and started to leave the kitchen. I grabbed her arm and turned her to face me.

"You do," I said. "You definitely do."

She hugged me, hard and long.

It was a beautiful moment—my skinny niece, all arms and legs, her skin soft and sweet smelling, and my heart overflowed with love. *This* was why I was here. This was why I'd come back.

Then I smelled something other than Poe's shampoo.

Something bad. Something unmistakable.

Feathers.

"Oh, dear baby Jesus, no. No, no," I whispered, letting go of my niece.

"What?" she asked.

"Shh! Uh…um…" I opened the oven door.

There was Tweety. And he was dead, his little talons curled up against his chest, right next to the last baked potato on the right.

I slammed the oven door closed.

"Holy shit, is that Tweety?" Poe said, covering her mouth. Horribly, she started to laugh. "I hate that bird."

"What should I do?" I hissed.

"Mouth to beak?"

"Too late for that. Get Sully, okay? And don't let Gran in here!"

"Nora," Mom called. "What are you doing in there? What's that smell?"

"Nothing! I just, uh, dropped something on the burner," I called. "Go," I whispered, shoving Poe a little.

"Gran," she said, "I got a B on my paper. You want to have a look? Mr. Fletcher, why don't you help… Nora? Help *Nora*. She…needs *help*." She was wheezing with laughter now, the evil child.

"Why?" my mother asked. "Has she ruined my ham?"

No, I killed your pet. "Just thought Sully could help set the table," I said.

There she was, in the kitchen doorway. I threw my back against the oven like I was hiding Edward Snowden in there. "Hi!" I said brightly. "What's up?"

"Sullivan's a guest, Nora. We don't ask him to help."

"Mom, just go upstairs and read Poe's paper. Okay?"

She frowned at me but, mercifully, went upstairs.

The smell was stronger now. "What do you need help with?" Sully asked.

I opened the door to the oven so he could see.

"That's... Oh, boy."

"He must've flown in when I checked the ham."

From upstairs, my mother yelled, "That smell is god-awful, Nora! What are you doing down there?"

"Uh, my sleeve got a little singed. Not a big problem!"

"What do you want me to do?" Sully asked.

"Take him out," I hissed, shoving two oven mitts at him. "I hated him in life, and I'm totally freaked out by him in death."

Sully reached in. Oh, poor Tweety! He was browning, his yellow feathers the color of toasted marshmallow now. If this was *Naked and Afraid*, they'd eat him. I closed my eyes.

"We gonna tell your mother?"

"Are you kidding me? No! Can you just...toss it in the woods or something?"

He frowned at me. "Nora. Doesn't Tweety deserve a Christian burial?"

"This is not funny."

"It's pretty funny."

"Just get him out of here." I was grateful Sully could read lips—sound traveled in this house.

"Got a box or something? Tupperware?"

"No! Just…just throw him in the woods."

"Then the foxes will eat him."

I thought of all the times Tweety had pecked me or dive-bombed my dog. "Circle of life, Sullivan. Go." I glanced down at Tweety. "Sorry again."

"I'll say a prayer as I'm tossing him," Sully said.

"Don't bother. Satan's already got him." But Sully had already turned, so he didn't hear.

I went to the sink and washed my hands, not that I'd touched the bird or anything, but… Gah! Sullivan came back and did the same, and I buried the oven mitts in the trash, then scrubbed again. I sprinkled some nutmeg on the rug in front of the sink to mask the smell.

"This ham doesn't smell normal," my mother said, thumping down the stairs.

Oh, God. We were going to have to eat that ham. What if Tweety had touched it? Why did my mother teach the damn bird to eat human food?

I subtly jacked up the heat to 450. That would kill just about any bacteria in the world.

"All right, then, what are you waiting for? Sit down, Nora, Poe. Sullivan, go ahead now." We obeyed. Sully sat across from me, smiling, and I tried to smile back.

"Where's Tweety?" Mom asked, and Poe began laughing, which she covered by pretending to choke. I narrowed my eyes at her.

"Tweety!" called Mom. "Suppahtime! Come on, sweetie-Tweety. Where'd he go?"

"Hell?" Poe suggested quietly.

Sullivan smothered a smile, his shoulders shaking with laughter. "Stop it," I whispered as my mother searched the den.

"Tweety boy!"

"He can't hear you," sang Poe softly, and Sullivan took a napkin to blot his eyes, he was laughing so hard. Poe grinned at her audience's reaction.

"Mom," I said, my voice strained, "Tweety's probably just resting."

"The eternal sleep of the dead," Poe whispered. "Slipped this mortal coil, free from strife and pain."

"Shush, Poe," I hissed. "Mom! Come on. We have company."

"He loves eating with me," Mom called. "You know that."

"Well, it's not healthy." *Especially since decomposition has already begun.* "Let's just eat."

"Fine," muttered Mom. "Ah, Jesus, Nora, you're cookin' the hell out of this ham. All the pineapple's black now. What did you do?"

"Sorry! You know what?" I said, standing up. "Let's go out instead!"

"I'm not gonna waste a perfectly good ham. Sully, do me a favor and just carve off the black parts, all right?"

"I'm a vegetarian," Poe announced. "I forgot to mention it." My mother set down the bowl of potatoes. "And I don't eat carbs anymore."

"What is wrong with you tonight?" Mom asked her. "Eat your dinner and none of this dieting foolishness."

And so it was that we ate leathery ham and potatoes the texture of rock, green beans boiled until they were dull gray and squeaked on our teeth. "Nora, since you brought him here for dinner, think you can find some time for me this week? So we can talk?"

"Oh! Uh, sure," I said. My mind was on Tweety and the foxes. Scupper Island had a ton of that kind of wildlife, so Sully had a point. Though I hated the bird, I shuddered at the thought of his little head being gnawed on. "Excuse me a second," I said. "I have a phone call. Might be an emergency. Sully, could you, um, come with me?"

"Why? He's not a doctor," Poe said.

"He… Right."

"Make your call, Nora, but come back. You've barely eaten a thing. Tweety! Tweety, we got green beans here. Where the hell is that bird?"

God. I got up from the table and went out the back. I didn't know where Sully had put Tweety, but there was a shovel against the back of the house. I took it and scanned for brownish yellow. Looked under a few trees. Nothing. No Tweety here, no Tweety there.

Fine. This would have to wait till after dinner. The woods were too big, and I really had no idea where Sully had put the body. I'd ask, he'd tell, and maybe Poe would bury old Tweety if I paid her. A lot.

Just as I was coming back to the house, I saw something coming right at my head, and instinctively, I swung the shovel and hit the thing square on, like Big Papi sending one over the Green Monster at Fenway.

It was Tweety.

Fuckety fucking McFuckster.

I'd killed Tweety twice in one night. He lay on the ground, burnt yellow wings spread. One flap. I swore he turned his head to accuse me with his eyes. Maybe I could splint him if he was just hurt, make a tiny neck bracc… No. He was dead. His ickle chest rose no more.

Shit.

"Nora?" My mother stood in the doorway. "Is that…
Aw, Tweety!"

"Mom, I'm so sorry." Guilt caused sweat to break out
over my whole body. "I'm really, really sorry."

"What happened?" she asked.

"He dive-bombed me and, uh…"

"And he hit the window," Poe said loudly. "I saw it,
too. So sad, Gran."

Mom stood there, her face blank. Then she shrugged.
"Ah, well. He was old. Glad he didn't suffer. Thanks for
burying him for me, Nora. That's real sweet of you."

With that, she went back inside. Poe patted her shoulder as she passed, then widened her eyes at me. "Bird
killer," she whispered.

"Not funny," I said. I mean, yeah, someday it might
be funny. In three or four decades.

Sully came out. "I think I missed something," he said.

"Lazarus here tried to attack me."

"Can't say I blame him."

"And I hit him with the shovel."

"So we shouldn't get a bird, is that what you're saying?" He took the shovel from me and scooped up the
poor little bird. "You want to check his pulse or anything?"

"No. He's a goner for real this time. Sorry, Tweety,"
I said.

"Go back inside," Sullivan said. "I'll take care of this."

THERE WAS NO DESSERT, of course. Mom reminded me to
come over some night this week, refused my offer to
help clean up and told me to go on my way.

"Sorry again about Tweety, Mom. I know you loved him."

"Well. Pets die. Whatcha gonna do?"

I tried to give her a hug, the kind she'd given me that night at St. Mary's of the Sea. "Yeah, okay, Nora, let's not get hysterical," she said, pulling back. "See you, Sullivan. Be good to my girl."

And that was that. We said goodbye to Poe, who was in far too good of a mood, and got into Sully's truck and, since he had to watch the road and not my face, drove in silence the ten minutes into town.

I kept seeing Tweety's sad, not-quite-yellow body on the ground.

"So that was fun," Sully said as we pulled up into a narrow driveway. His house was small but charming— a modified bungalow, two stories, the requisite gray shingles, white shutters and trim. A little grass, some tiger lilies by the white picket fence. There was a porch with two planters filled with purple flowers.

Teeny Fletcher stood on the top step, her arms crossed.

"Hello, Ma," he said.

"Oh, no, you don't," she said. "Don't *hello, Ma* me. Lukie told me you were out with this one." *Lukie.* He was doomed if he was thirty-five years old and his mother still called him that.

"I was out with this one," Sullivan said. "I still am."

"Hi, Teeny," I said.

"You're *nawt* dating my son," she said.

"I actually seem to be," I said. "Go figure."

"You're so high and mighty, aren't you? Little miss doctor, think you're too good for us."

"Beautiful night, isn't it?" I asked.

Sullivan sighed. "Mom, go home. Okay? I'm old enough to pick my own—"

"What about Amy? What does she think about all this?"

Sullivan walked up to his mother, put his arm around her shoulders and walked her down the steps. "Have a good night, Ma. Talk to you soon."

"You're not good enough for my son!" she said as she passed.

"See you around town," I said.

She gave me the finger as she got into her car.

"What a sweet lady," I said as Sullivan came back toward me.

"Sorry about that. Come on in and make yourself at home. I'll get us something to drink."

"Make it strong," I said, but his back was turned. I'd have to get used to this way of talking. Or not. I wasn't here for that long.

Maybe we could have a long-distance relationship. I guess we'd see.

I liked Sully's house immediately. The front door opened into a great room with a comfortably worn couch in front of the TV cabinet. I could picture him and Audrey here, watching a ball game or movie. There was a big armchair and a red-and-cream rug, a bookcase with paperbacks and DVDs. At least a dozen pictures of Audrey, Audrey and him, Audrey and Amy and him, even.

And one of Audrey and Luke, taken in the not-too-recent past. Last summer, maybe? Audrey looked about the same size as now and was wearing shorts and a sleeveless shirt. They were squirting each other with water guns, both of them laughing, the sunshine making little rainbows on the water.

So Luke loved his niece. And she loved him, too. It was reassuring.

Sully came in holding two glasses of white wine. "Kind of a shitty date so far," he said, sitting next to me.

I nodded. "I can't disagree." Took a big sip of wine. "I like your house."

"Thank you."

"How's Audrey? Is she feeling good? Any problems?"

"She's great. You saw for yourself."

I nodded. Tried to think of something to say. Came up empty.

So did he. We glanced at each other at the same time, offered each other a pained smile and averted our eyes.

Bird killing seemed to put a damper on things.

He took a deep breath. "Well."

"Yeah."

"I heard that nurse is dating your old boyfriend."

I jerked, slopping wine onto my dress because why not, right? "Wow. Did you? It's true. They met at a Starbucks near the ferry station in Boston."

"I'm sorry, I can't hear you if you don't look at me."

"Shit. Sorry." I faced him square on and repeated what I said.

"Small world," he said. "You okay with that?"

"Oh, sure," I lied. "I mean… I guess. I don't think he's being completely honest with her. I know he's not, in fact. He lied about me, and she doesn't care and this is when you really hate being a woman, because guys seem to handle this stuff much better."

He nodded.

I nodded, too. "You wanna make out?" I asked, because conversation was just not going to be our thing tonight.

He laughed, and then I felt something stir in my belly, a lovely warm squeeze of attraction. At the same time, we both leaned forward to put our wine on the coffee table and bumped heads. Hard.

"Ow," he said. Just what the guy needed. Another brain injury courtesy of yours truly.

"No, it's just part of my sexy dance," I said. "You could be my next Tweety."

"What happened with that bird, anyway?"

"I hit him with the shovel. Anyway, back to the kissing. What do you say?"

This was not how things usually went with me. Not to brag, but I used to be kind of adorable.

Great, great, he was leaning forward. He cupped my face in his hands and looked at my mouth for a second, studying it. My heart sputtered and flapped like...well, like a dying Tweety.

A laugh popped out of my lips just as Sully kissed me. I pulled back. "Sorry, sorry. Try again."

He did. And he wasn't a bad kisser, and I didn't think I was a bad kisser, either, but nothing was happening. His mouth was gentle, his hands slid into my hair—a mistake, because my hair immediately curled around his fingers like malevolent thorn bushes in a fairy tale. "Ow," I said when he tried to move his hand.

"Sorry."

"No, it's my hair. It's alive and evil. Here." I pulled back a little and helped free his hand.

We did, eventually, make it to the bedroom through force of sheer will. I'll spare you the details. Technically, we did have sex. And it wasn't awful. There were a few moments where we...connected. It just wasn't... Yeah.

It was hard to make eye contact after, and unfortunately, eye contact was necessary for conversation with this guy. I propped myself up on an elbow and did the brave thing.

"Did I hurt you?" I asked.

He laughed. At least there was that. I ran my hand through his hair and knocked out his hearing aid.

I sighed, handed him back the earpiece and said, "Maybe we should just be friends. I mean, I'm leaving in August and...well."

He touched the tip of my nose with one finger. "You weren't awful," he said.

"And neither were you. Maybe we should quit our jobs and write Valentine cards." I kissed him on the cheek. "Friends?"

"Sure."

"You're a good sport, Sullivan Fletcher."

Half an hour later, I was back in my houseboat. I took a shower and got into my jammies and cuddled up with Boomer on the couch. Texted Sully to thank him again for bird disposal, eating my mother's food and doing me.

He texted back, thanking me for putting up with his mother and apologizing for his brother. *See you around* were his parting words.

So not what I'd hoped for or expected. Not exactly an enchanted evening.

Nonetheless, it was hard to get to sleep that night. There had been a couple moments in bed with Sully where...well, where it felt like something special was about to happen.

"You're leaving in six weeks," I reminded myself. "It's better this way."

It just didn't feel like it.

24

A FEW DAYS after the Date That Wasn't, Poe came over after work to have dinner.

She'd only been employed for a week, but she'd already gotten a little color, despite slathering on the sixty-factor sunscreen she wore to protect her bluish-white skin. Tonight, she was full of talk about how cool Audrey was, all the things Audrey knew—dropping lobster pots, tides, storms, all the things island kids knew. "She wants me to sleep over sometime this week," Poe said. "So we can make posters and stuff for the Go Far, Be Strong thing."

I thought of that cute little house, the stability Audrey had. Even if her parents had divorced, it was clear Amy had a huge role in the girl's life, and while I didn't think too highly of Luke or Teeny, they loved Audrey. As for Sullivan, I'd bet a lung that there was no better father on earth.

I wondered if he ever did things like my father had done with Lily and me. The midnight bike rides down

Eastman Hill, the springtime swims, the Cave Challenge.

I hoped not. A father's job was to make his children feel safe.

Poe never knew her father. She only had Lily and a grandmother who visited dutifully once a year...and an aunt who'd accepted *no* a little too easily.

"That sounds like fun," I said, snapping out of my funk. "I mean...do you want to sleep over?"

Poe shrugged. "I guess. Yeah, I do. She's so positive all the time. I mean, nothing gets her down, but it's not like she's oblivious, either." She paused. "By the way, I'm not a lesbian in case you were about to ask."

"I wasn't, but it would be fine if you were," I said.

"Everyone thinks I am because of my hair and tattoos and stuff. But I think I like guys. Just...not yet."

"You're not even sixteen. 'Not yet' is a really mature answer."

"Did you have a lot of boyfriends?" she asked, spearing some asparagus. I'd cooked extra healthy tonight—quinoa salad with asparagus, chickpeas, red peppers, cucumbers and salmon. There was pie waiting on the counter as our reward.

"I didn't date at all in high school. Back then, I had all the appeal and energy of a pile of sweaty gym clothes."

Poe snorted.

"But in college and med school, sure."

"Were the guys nice?"

"They were." I took a drink of water. "Does your mom date a lot?"

Poe didn't answer for a minute. "Yeah. A new guy all the time, even if she pretended they were just friends."

"How was that for you?" I asked.

She shrugged. "It was fine. I mean, there were always people around. We almost always had someone staying with us, or we were staying at someone's place. Usually one of Mom's guys." She poked a chickpea with her fork. "I've been living at Gran's longer than I ever lived in one place before."

My heart twisted. I wanted so much to tell her she could stay here on Scupper as long as she wanted. I wanted to grab my sister and shake her and tell her kids needed stability and constancy and to be able to rely on the adults in their lives, and what the hell was she thinking, having all those men parade through Poe's life?

In the past, I'd made some gentle suggestions. When Poe was just a little thing, I'd suggested that maybe she needed more sleep and less fast food. "And how many kids have you raised?" Lily had asked, her eyes going cold and hard. She didn't let me visit them the next day, and I'd been forced to wander around Seattle alone, feeling angry and useless.

I'd offered to give my sister money, loan her money, cover her rent, buy things for Poe. The only answer I ever got was "We're fine."

In other words, I had no say in Poe's life. All I could do was spend this summer with her, and hopefully it would be at least a small positive in her life.

"Want to help me find Gran a boyfriend?" I asked, and she grimaced and brightened at the same time.

"Seriously? That's so gross. Why would you?"

"I worry about her. She's been on her own for a long time." And both Poe and I would be leaving soon. "Come on," I said, standing and gathering our plates. "I registered on a dating website. I'm screening her men before I introduce her."

"She told me she thought you were matchmaking," Poe said, putting her glass in the dishwasher. "When you had that dinner?"

"I was. It didn't go so well. Someone hit a deer, though."

"What is it with you and animals? Boomer, watch your back, boy." She bent and rubbed him behind the ears. First time she'd called him something other than *dog*.

I wiped down the table, then got my computer. Poe helped herself to a slice of blueberry pie (no sugar, very nutritious, minus the lard I used to make the crust) and sat down next to me.

A sudden lump filled my throat. I was going to miss her. Lily was due out in a little more than a month. The countdown on my time with Poe had begun, and the summer, which had seemed so long at first, was slipping past like a fast-moving stream.

But Poe was older now, and now that she knew me, she'd keep in touch.

At least, I hoped she would.

"Okay," I said, clearing my throat. "Here we go." I clicked on the dating website and went to the profile I'd set up for my mom. I'd called her SuperMainah in her profile.

"'Divorced woman,'" Poe said, reading out loud, "'sixties, enjoys animals'—well, she used to, until you killed hers—'reading, the satisfaction of a hard day's work. I'm a no-nonsense kind of person, honest and straightforward. Attractive and fit. Great sense of humor.'" Poe looked at me. "Sense of humor? Gran?"

"You pretty much have to say that," I said.

"So who took the bait?" she asked.

"Let's see! Three people. Wicked pissah." I clicked on the first guy—Servus.

"'Hello, Supermainah!'" I read. "'You sound very in control of life and you could be in control of me.' Oh, God, here we go. 'I am a very submisive betta male—' look at this spelling, Poe '—seeking a strong, dominent alpha female. I acsept my inferiorty and know my place. I live with my mother, who is 103 years old and instilled my love of obedience. If you don't mind helping with her diapers and baths, let's hook up!'"

"He sounds perfect," Poe said.

"She does like to boss people around," I murmured. "Moving on." I clicked on GotLove2Offer.

"My turn to read," Poe said, turning the laptop toward her. "'Hello, SuperMainah, I'm glad you are so capable. I'm going to be blunt, I'm poor. I don't have a car, my financial situation is horrible, and I still live at home with my five sisters, who are nasty bitches, all of them. I'm not the greatest-looking guy, either. I am looking for someone to give me financial support, likes to cook (for my sisters, too) and enjoys long walks but doesn't necessarily want sex.'" She started snickering. "'I will make your heart full again. My interests include pro wrestling, military-grade guns and…and…and cuddling.'" She shrieked with laughter.

"Oh, God," I said. "See what you have to look forward to? Okay, next one." I clicked on Musical-Fisherman. "'Hello there! You sound very nice and uncomplicated.'" I looked at Poe. "I'd give her *uncomplicated*, wouldn't you?"

"Absolutely."

"'I'm a widower, a retired music teacher, no kids. I enjoy fishing and watching documentaries on the History Channel. I moved to Maine from Florida four years ago and really love it here. If you'd like to meet for coffee, I can come to your neck of the woods. I live in Kennebunkport and don't mind driving.'"

We looked at each other, a little surprised at his normalcy. "Let's set it up," I said.

"You gonna pretend to be Gran?" Poe asked.

"No, I'll come clean. Here." I read aloud as I typed. "'Dear Fisherman, this is actually SuperMainah's daughter. I've been helping my mom with online dating. You sound really nice. Anything else we should know about you before we set up a date to meet?'"

"Oh, you're good."

"Once I get his name, I'll do a background check."

"See? This is why you're the adult."

Speaking of background checks... "How's Luke Fletcher been toward you?" I asked.

She shrugged. "He's okay. He doesn't talk to me much. He works on engines, and I do grunt work, so I don't really see him."

That's what Sullivan had told me, too, when I texted him two days ago.

The computer beeped. "It's our suitor!" I said. "He likes us."

"Poor Gran," Poe said. "You know she won't be happy about this."

"Yeah, yeah," I said. "But maybe once she meets him, she'll get swept off her feet."

"Can you really picture that happening?"

"No. But let's pretend."

Two days later, Richard Hemmings, aka MusicalFisherman, met me at Jitters, the new coffee shop that had just opened. It was cute inside; whereas Lala's was a true bakery, this was a coffeehouse, with a tin ceiling and black-and-white-tiled floor and lovely old oak door. There was a bean roaster in the back, and the smell was dark and rich. They sold baked goods (bought from Lala's so as not to antagonize the locals, a smart business move). They also had tables on the sidewalk where extremely beautiful dogs could recline and drink water (or iced decaf, in Boomer's case).

Xiaowen arrived about five minutes after Boomer and I did and went to the counter to order a drink. She'd wanted to check out my mother's possible beau, and we also had some work to do on Go Far, Be Strong, which was turning into a real pain in the ass, great cause aside.

It was full tourist season, and Jitters was filling up.

Xiaowen came over, coffee in hand. "I just got these guys to sponsor us," she said smugly, taking a pull of her drink, which was topped with a mountain of whipped cream.

"Yay!" I said. "And my practice in Boston is kicking in some money, too."

She pulled her iPad out of her bag and showed me the bottom line.

Just about every business in town was sponsoring Go Far, Be Strong, so in addition to covering the cost of the permit, insurance, public safety and all that, we had plenty of money left over. We ordered T-shirts, and I was working on a brochure that talked about the new food pyramid and how to read nutrition labels, and a website that would link to other websites full of great information regarding health, exercise and nutrition.

The biggest message I wanted to send was our slogan—Healthy Looks Different on Everyone.

I'd gained a little weight this summer. The truth was, I needed to. Maybe it was the stress after the Big Bad Event, maybe it was just trying to be perfect all the time, at work, with Bobby, at the hospital. Here, I'd let my standards loosen a little. I had pie. Sometimes I had pie with ice cream. Not every night, but not never, either. I still ran and rode my bike whenever possible, the Dog of Dogs galloping majestically at my side.

"We should have a different tagline every year," Xiaowen said. "Next year, it can be something like You'll Be Amazed What You Can Do."

"I love that," I said.

But next year, would I be able to do this? I'd be in Boston. This was a pretty big commitment.

Well. We could get a committee, I supposed.

"Do I actually have to run in this thing?" Xiaowen asked for the forty-sixth time.

"Yes. To inspire the troops."

"Like Lady Godiva. Should I run naked?"

"No. We don't want a riot on our hands. Oh, look, he's here. Hi, Richard!"

He'd sent a picture—he was tall with glasses, a fairly good head of hair, on the rangy side. He'd been quite nice about me running interference. He was a bit younger than Mom, but I thought that was okay.

He wore a polo shirt and khakis, boat shoes. No baseball cap, thank God. What was it about men in baseball caps that halved their sex appeal?

"Hello," he said, blushing. "Very nice to meet you, Nora." He shook my hand, then Xiaowen's.

"Xiaowen Liu," she said. "A great admirer of Sharon Stuart."

"Nice to meet you both," he said.

"This is my dog, Boomer," I said, and though he was power napping, Boomer wagged at the mention of his name.

"He's very beautiful." Boomer's tail thumped harder. "Can I get you more coffee?"

Manners, very nice looking, a little shy. "I'm all set," I said.

"I wouldn't say no to a slab of chocolate cake," Xiaowen said.

"Be right back," he said with a smile and went to the counter.

"It's a test," Xiaowen told me. "If he doesn't make me pay, he passes."

A minute later, Richard came back and set the plate in front of my friend. "On me," he said.

My friend and I exchanged a smug look.

"Xiaowen," Richard said thoughtfully. "How do you spell that in Chinese?"

She jotted her name on our spreadsheet, the characters so complex and lovely.

"That means color of the morning clouds, doesn't it?" Richard asked.

Xiaowen's fork froze halfway to her mouth. "Uh… yes. More or less."

"I lived in China for a few years. It's a beautiful name."

"Thank you." She glanced at me. "And what does Richard mean?"

He laughed. "Powerful leader. I think my parents missed the mark on that one. I'm a music teacher. Well,

I retired after a back injury. I sure miss the students, but I'm doing a little pro bono work in Portland."

"How nice," Xiaowen murmured, taking a bite of her cake.

"So!" I said brightly. "Richard, I just wanted to warn you again that my mom is... She's a wonderful person. She doesn't like the idea of being fixed up, so..."

"Got it. We're just friends, and she happens to run into us."

"Bingo. We met... Where do you think we should say?"

"In a rose garden under a full moon," Xiaowen said, and Richard laughed.

"How about on the ferry?" he suggested.

"Perfect."

I texted my mother, hoping she'd answer for once, while Richard and Xiaowen chatted about Portland, oysters and sailing. *Mom, pop into Jitters for your break. I'm here right now, and the coffee is fantastic.* Should she resist (and she would), I would play the someone-I-want-you-to-meet card.

A second later, the unexpected answer popped into my screen. *Sure. Be there in five. The Excelsior Pines was just down the street.*

I showed Xiaowen the phone. "Unlike her to be so spontaneous," I murmured.

"She must smell the coffee."

"It's excellent," Richard said, taking a sip of his. "Xiaowen, have you been to Bard for coffee? It's my favorite."

"No, no, no. You have to try the Speckled Axe. Bard is for beginners."

"Sounds like a coffee throw down," he said, smiling.

A few minutes later, Mom came in, wearing the hotel uniform of white shirt, black pants. "Hi, Mom!" I said.

"Hello. How are you, Xiaowen, deah?" She looked at Richard. "I'm Nora's mother. And you are?"

"Richard Hemmings." He stood up and offered his hand, which she took suspiciously. "So nice to meet you, Sharon."

"That's Mrs. Stuart to you." She scowled. "How do you know my daughter here?"

"We met on the ferry," he said with a wink to me. "She invited me to have coffee with her and her lovely friend. Would you like something to drink?"

"I'm fine," she said, sitting down.

"Xiaowen and I were just arguing about where to find the best coffee," Richard said. "Do you have a favorite place to go?"

"I make my own."

"That's always the best."

"Ayuh." Mom folded her arms and looked at me. She was not pleased.

"Nora tells me you like animals, Sharon. Do you have any pets?"

"My bird just died," she said.

Xiaowen choked on a laugh, having been far, far too amused of my tales of Tweety. "Excuse me a second," she said, heading for the bathroom to let the not-so-young lovers get to know each other.

"I'm gonna get a refill," I said. "Anyone need anything?" My mother looked ready to bite me, but Richard smiled and said he was all set.

I stood in the line, which was about six people deep, and watched my mother. *Open up*, I pleaded silently. *Don't be so cutoff from everyone.*

Then again, maybe it was just me. Everyone else seemed to like her tremendously. Look at her hug therapy group.

"Nora Stuart? Is that you, dear?"

I looked up, and there was Mr. Abernathy, my old English teacher, holding a cup of coffee to go. "Mr. A!" I exclaimed, hugging him. "How are you?"

He beamed. "I'm doing very well. Look at you! It's wonderful to see you!"

"Do you have a minute to chat?" I asked.

"Sure!" he said, his voice so familiar. We took a table near the counter.

"Do you still live here?" I asked. "I haven't seen you around."

"No," he said, "but we kept the house here and come back a few weeks every year. Rent it the rest of the time. How are you? I always hoped to see you back here at reunions and whatnot."

I nodded, feeling a prickle of shame. "Well, I went to Tufts, as you know, and then went on to medical school."

"How wonderful! Your mother must be so proud!"

"Well, yes. When did you retire?"

"About eight years after you left. Ten, maybe." He took a sip of his coffee. "You know, you remained the only student ever to do that Great Works project."

And there it was. "Yeah. About that, Mr. Abernathy," I said. My hands twisted in my lap. "I have a question you might be able to answer. Was that... Is that how I got the Perez Scholarship?"

He tilted his head. "What do you mean?"

"Is that what put me over the edge? Because I..." I

closed my eyes. "I smeared the assignment on the black-board so Luke Fletcher wouldn't see it."

"All of you had four months to see that assignment."

"I know, but… I wanted to make sure."

Mr. A nodded. "Well, from what I know, you moved heaven and earth to get that paper done, during finals, no less. I doubt very much young Mr. Fletcher would've been able to pull that off. But it really doesn't matter, dear. You already had an A+ in my class, so the paper didn't change your grade at all. That's why I was so surprised that you did it."

"If Luke had done it and gotten an A, too…"

"Ah, I see the root of your guilt. Feel guilty no more, my dear. Luke ended the term with a B−. His grades had been sinking all semester, and not just in my class. We all talked about it. The night of the car accident… That wasn't his first experience with drugs, apparently."

I blinked. Blinked again. "Oh," I said. "I didn't know that."

Mr. A reached across the table and patted my hand. "You won that scholarship fair and square, Nora. No one else was even close." He pulled his phone out of his pocket. "Ah, there's Mrs. Abernathy, wondering where I am. I have to go, dear. It was wonderful to see you. Congratulations on everything."

With that, he left.

I hadn't stolen the scholarship, after all.

In a bit of a fog, I stood up and got back into line, and there was Sullivan, smelling like sunshine and salt air and motor oil. His skin was brown, making his eyes look like hot fudge.

I didn't steal the scholarship. I wasn't responsible for that accident.

Sully had never blamed me…and now I could stop blaming myself.

"Hiya, handsome," I said.

The corner of his mouth rose, and so did my entire reproductive system, reminding me that I'd had *sex* with this guy. Mediocre sex, sure, but there'd been a few flashes of greatness.

Maybe we should revisit that effort.

He stood very close to me, close enough that I could feel the heat of his skin beneath. *Meow.* He wasn't wearing a baseball cap, either, God bless him.

"Can I buy you a coffee?" he asked.

"What? Excuse me? Say again?"

His smile widened. He said some words—*let's have sex on this table.* Or no, I think that was just my brain.

"Sorry, what?" I said, clearing my throat.

He laughed. "I'm usually the one who can't hear things."

"I'm… I'm dazed with lust, it seems."

His eyes wandered over me. "Is that right?"

"Mm-hm." God. My legs were getting weak. I swayed and put my hand against his chest, feeling the sun-warmed T-shirt, the solid thump of his heart.

"Hey, hot stuff," Xiaowen said, coming up to us.

"Hey, Xiaowen."

"We're fixing up Nora's mom with that guy over there."

"I see."

"You can tell it's going well by the way she's glaring at her child," Xiaowen said.

I snapped out of my fog. "Right. I better… I better go back."

"You free this weekend?" he asked.

"Yes."

"Good."

"God, you two," Xiaowen said. "You need to work on your pillow talk. Sully, see you around. You're doing Go Far, right?"

"Wouldn't miss it." His eyes came back to me. "See you soon."

"Okay."

"Close your mouth, Nora. Bye, Sully." Xiaowen took me by the arm and pulled me back to the table. "You'd better be tapping that, or I will," she said.

"Yeah, yeah." I could barely formulate a thought.

"Nora," said my mother, her tone somewhere between *You're grounded, young lady* and *I've just put you up for adoption.* "This poor man thinks I'm looking for a boyfriend. Came all the way out here to meet me." She turned back to him. "Sorry you wasted your time, mister. Make my daughter pay for your ferry ride." She stood, jammed her hands on her hips and said, "Get your butt home for dinner tonight."

"Sounds fun," I said. She glared. "Yes, ma'am," I amended.

"Sorry again, pal," she said to Richard. "Xiaowen, always nice to see you."

My phone dinged—it was the clinic. I wasn't on duty today, it being Friday, but this usually meant something big. "I have to go," I said. "I'm so sorry, Richard."

"Not at all," he said graciously. "I've always meant to come out to Scupper Island."

"I'll walk you to the ferry," Xiaowen said. "Don't get any ideas. I talk a good game, but I've sworn off men."

"At least tell me why over a drink."

They left, flirting and chatting. My mother glared some more. "What the hell was that?"

"I have to get to the clinic."

"Nice try. They'll either die or get better, no matter what you do."

"I have a slightly different attitude, being a doctor. Walk and talk, okay?" She stomped out in front of me; I'd walked here, and it was only five minutes to the clinic. "I confess, Mom. I want you to have someone in your life. Lily will be out soon, Poe will go back to Seattle, I'll be back in Boston, and life on this island isn't easy! Is it so wrong for me to worry about you?"

"Worry all you want!" she snapped. "Stop fixing me up! I'm fine the way I am. And don't be late for dinner."

I STASHED BOOMER with Amelia, who loved him, and saw the patient—a summer kid who'd scratched his cornea. Piece of cake, definitely something that could've been handled by Gloria, but she was all about making my life harder these days. I gave the mom the gel antibiotic, told the little guy to take it easy and went to the counter where Gloria sat, staring straight at the computer monitor, pretending I wasn't there.

"Paperwork on the last patient. I'm surprised you needed to call, but I'm glad you did. Whenever you feel over your head, just give me a shout." *And take a bite, missy*, I added mentally. It was the end of a long day, and I was itchy and scratchy from her shitty attitude.

I'd ridden my bike to work today, and it had been a great choice. There was something intimate and exhilarating about riding a bike through a town, even one I knew as well as mine. The pace was fast enough not to get into a conversation, slow enough to smell the good smells of burgers and some kind of dessert and someone's pipe smoke, all made more intense by the salt air. Boomer loved it, too, since I was too slow for him on our runs, forcing him to trot. With the bike, he could canter alongside.

I stopped at the package store, once a dive with yellowing windows where serious alcoholics got their booze, now a rather lovely wine shop, and bought a bottle of pinot noir to bring to my mom's, put the bottle in my basket and continued on.

I turned on Oak Street, where Sullivan lived. Hey, it was a legitimate through road. I slowed a little past his house. His truck wasn't there (which was good, since I was stalking), but I didn't know if Audrey was home or at the boatyard or maybe at Amy's.

You could tell a lot about a person by where they choose to live. Sully's house was quietly charming, well kept and fairly unadorned, just like the man himself.

It made me smile.

I kept riding, intending to go home, maybe (maybe) take a quick swim and then shower. It was getting warmer, and the sky, which had been pure blue two hours ago, was now filling with towering gray clouds. Thunderstorms were coming. I hoped I'd be home for them. I'd gotten to the point where I loved the rocking of my little houseboat, the flashes that lit up the cove and sky, the bolts that made me squeak and jump in my chair.

About forty feet from the top of the hill, where the road curved and steepened, my cell phone rang. "Dang it," I said. I'd wanted to make it to the top without stopping, get my cardio and burn off that creamy iced coffee I'd had. Cholesterol, yo.

I pulled over under a pine tree and pulled my phone from my purse.

"Dr. Stuart, it's James Gillespie."

For a minute, I couldn't remember who that was, but the Morgan Freeman voice clued me in. The private investigator I'd hired that day in Boston, the day I'd seen Voldemort.

"Hi! How are you?" I said.

"I'm fine. And yourself?"

"I'm good. Do you… Do you have anything?"

There was a pause. Never a good sign. "Well, yes and no. As you said in my office that day, your father's name is extremely common. Without his Social Security number, it's a bit of a crapshoot."

"Right."

"I did find two notices of death of men named William Stuart, however. Both with your father's date of birth, both born in New York City."

Panic flashed across me, finding every injury I'd ever had—my clavicle, my knee, my shin from where I'd whacked it so hard in college on the steps of the library, every place Voldemort had hurt me. *Don't be dead, Daddy. Don't be dead.*

"One is from seventeen years ago. Cause of death was a car accident, El Paso, Texas." There was a pause. "The other, I'm sorry to say, was a suicide. Buffalo, New York, eleven years ago."

A chickadee lit on the branch next to me. So pretty, those little birds, so industrious and smart. I felt a little faint suddenly, gray spots hiding the bird, and sucked in a breath.

"Dr. Stuart?"

"Still here," I said. My voice was odd. Another breath. The gray spots faded.

"Neither had obituaries, and there were no next of kin or spouses listed." He paused. "Would either of those locations have made sense?"

"Um…no. Not really. I mean, he could've gone anywhere."

"If you had his Social Security number…"

"Right."

"It would be on your parents' marriage certificate, if you have access to that. Without it, I'm afraid I'm at the end of the road."

"Thanks, Mr. Gillespie. I'll let you know if I find anything else." I hung up and got back on my bike.

I didn't realize I was crying till the wind blew its breath against my tears.

RATHER THAN GO HOME, I went to my mother's, propping my bike near the back door, a leftover habit from childhood. Poe was at work and so was Mom, which meant I could snoop all the way up till dinnertime.

If my father was dead, I wanted to know. I couldn't imagine my mother throwing away a document like her marriage certificate—or divorce papers.

God. I didn't even know if my parents were legally divorced.

I hadn't thought about snooping when I first got here, and given my injuries, it would've been tough. Man, that seemed like an age ago, when I had the crutch and the sling.

The house smelled like meat loaf. Mom made hers in the Crock-Pot, one of her few not-horrible dinners. At least I wouldn't have to contend with Tweety, I thought, then felt immediately guilty.

Boomer lay down in front of the woodstove, panting happily. I got him some water and took a breath. The den would be the place to start, I guessed.

Unsurprisingly, my mom's desk was tidy and organized. Feeling another kick of guilt (*twinge* just wouldn't cover it), I opened her file drawers. Neatly labeled files of bills, receipts, the local businesses who hired her as a bookkeeper. Health—God, did I even dare? I did. It contained a copy of her lab work, all perfectly normal, and a prescription for glasses.

There was one for Poe—school records from Seattle, a report from the Greater Seattle Department of Children and Families. "No evidence of abuse or neglect," it said. Seemed like my sister had been investigated after her run-ins with the law.

Oh, Lily.

There was nothing here about my father.

I went upstairs into Mom's room, just across the little hall from mine. A memory drifted down—me, scared of something at night, coming across the way in a nightgown, wanting my parents but not wanting to wake them up. My father's hand on my head, getting a glass of water, waiting for the water to be cold, then tucking me back in bed, telling me Mr. Bowie, my teddy bear, would protect me.

No. That had been *Mom*. I remember her talking in a growling voice, pretending to be Mr. Bowie. "No one will get past me!" And we'd laughed there in the moonlight, Lily fast asleep in the other twin bed.

Her bedroom hadn't changed much.

I opened the night table drawer and closed it fast.

Okay, then. Mom still had womanly needs. Good for her. I'd get some eye bleach and erase that memory, stat.

The other night table drawer had a Stephen King novel in it. Funny. I didn't know my mother liked him. She didn't used to—she'd ask me why on earth I'd read something scary before bed. Guess she'd fallen into the trap.

Her bureau contained the normal things—socks, underwear, turtlenecks, jeans. In her closet, not much of interest. Winter coat, boots, sweaters, her one dress.

Hang on a second.

There, behind her bulky winter coat, was a box. I pulled it out.

It contained pictures. Pictures of my dad. Of *us*. Our family.

Seeing his face after all these years hit me square in the chest.

He was so young! How had so much time passed without him? How had we survived the loss of him?

Here he was, laughing in the canoe, his hair black and big smile. Maybe when they were dating? The two of them on a hiking trail, both wearing jackets and hats, the foliage brilliant around them.

Dad holding me in the hospital after I was born. I knew, because my mother had written on the back—*Bill with Nora, 2 days old.*

There were dozens. Some were in frames, and I remembered them sitting on the shelf over the couch in the living room. Some had faded, some were better quality, but all a treasure chest of memories. Lily, about three, sitting on a pony, Dad holding the halter. Daddy and me sitting in his chair, reading a book. The four of us squinting into the sun. Mom and Dad eating cotton candy. When the heck had that happened? Dad flipping burgers on the little round grill we'd had as kids. Lily sitting on his shoulders, reaching out for snowflakes.

The pictures were mostly from our golden years—the first seven or eight years of my life. They tapered off after that.

Why had Mom kept these from us?

When was she supposed to give them to you, Nora? said a voice in my head. *You've been away from home for half your life.*

And so had Lily.

Boomer nudged my head, and I turned. He licked my cheeks—I was crying again, for the second time this day.

The love my father had for us—for all three us—radiated out of these pictures like sunshine.

How could he have borne life without us?

I leaned against my dog's solid neck and let the tears seep into his fur.

25

I was so lost in memories and sadness, I didn't hear my mother's car. I had no idea how long she'd been home when I heard laughter. Boomer whined to see his grandmother, but I held his collar.

Mom wasn't alone. Was Poe home? No, this was her sleepover with Audrey. Or maybe it *was* Poe, home to grab some things.

Nope. That definitely wasn't Poe's voice. And Mom didn't laugh very often...at least, not when I was around.

I stood up, my knee crackling. My legs were stiff—I'd been on the closet floor awhile.

I wanted to talk to my mother about this box. About Dad. She had to have some answers. She had to. Maybe that was the point of this dinner, why she'd been so insistent that I come over.

I went to the top of the stairs. Boomer, wrongly thinking it was nap time, went into my old room and climbed onto Poe's bed.

"All right, I'll get out of your hair," came a woman's voice. "Good luck tonight."

"Yeah, I'll need it," answered my mother. "Call you later."

"You better." There was another laugh. Donna Krazinski, that's who it was. I wondered why she'd wish my mother luck.

I went down the stairs, turned into the kitchen, and saw my mother and Donna kissing.

Let me repeat. My mother and Donna were kissing.

"Holy shit," I said, and they broke apart.

"Aw, damn it," Mom said. Her neck and face turned bright red.

"Donna," I said. "How are you?"

She smiled. "Fine, sweethaht. Have a seat. There's something your mother wants to tell you."

"I think I might know what it is." The chair was good, though, because my legs were a little wobbly. "There's a bottle of wine in my bike basket," I said. "I highly suggest we open it. Right now. I parked in the back."

Donna went outside.

My mother leaned against the counter, not looking at me, arms across her chest. The clock ticked. In the distance, a crow screamed (not really, but it felt that way).

"Here we go," Donna said, bustling back in. When we all three had glasses, I chugged mine, then held it up for a refill. Donna obliged.

"To love," I said.

Mom glanced at Donna, who smiled. "To love," she echoed. My mother had apparently been struck mute.

"How long have you been together?" I asked.

"Coming up on five years," Mom said, causing me to sputter up wine.

I blotted my mouth with a napkin. "And you never said anything because…"

Mom shrugged. "Wasn't any of your business."

"I practically have a stepmother. That's sort of my business."

She sighed.

"Are you guys out, or is this a secret?"

"We're mostly out," Donna said when Mom failed to answer. "I think just about everyone knows."

"Bob Dobbins doesn't," I said.

"Yeah, well, just about every smaht person knows," Mom said.

"I take offense at that."

Mom straightened out the napkins, still held in the plastic fruit holder from my youth. "We, uh, cooled things off a little when Poe came. Didn't want her to feel… I don't know."

"Like she wasn't wanted," Donna supplied. "She needed to be your mother's first priority."

I nodded. "So my mother is gay. Go figure. Well, Mom, you couldn't have picked anyone nicer than Mrs. Krazinski. Well done."

Donna beamed and squeezed my shoulder. Mom just blinked. "Is that all you got?" she asked.

"Um…should there be more?"

She thought for a minute. "No."

"Good. Let's eat. I'm starving."

DINNER LASTED LONGER than our usual seventeen-minute eat-to-survive mode. With Donna here, it was almost like a party.

I could see that they were an established couple (sure, I could see it *now*). Donna got Mom water without ice, the way she liked it, and Mom got out a container of sour cream for Donna's baked potato, a pleasantry denied to me my entire life. Love and sour cream. Might make a good song.

Donna's house was up for rent because they'd been planning to move in together. I asked Mom when she'd realized Donna was the one for her, and Mom blushed and said it was when she'd had to give Donna a ride home in a snowstorm, and they got stuck and had to wait in the car for an hour until Jake Ferriman came to tow them out.

I couldn't fault her for not telling me. I really couldn't. "You should tell Poe," I said.

"Ayuh. Just wanted to tell you first. Been tryin' like crazy to get you alone."

Ah. The dinner when I killed Tweety, her readiness to accept my invitation at Jitters today.

"I guess I have to stop fixing you up," I said.

"Thank the Christ," she answered and told Donna about meeting Richard today, making Donna laugh till tears flowed down her cheeks.

"You have a good heart, Nora," she said, squeezing my hand, and suddenly, my eyes overflowed.

"I'm glad you have someone, Mom," I said into a paper napkin. "I'm really glad."

But those pictures… God, here I was, thirty-five years old, trying to accept the fact that my parents weren't going to get back together, even if they'd been apart for twenty-four of those years.

"Donner, I need some time with my daughter," Mom said, because yes, I was weeping it up good now.

"I'll see you tomorrow. Thank you for being so wonderful about this, Nora," she said, bending down to hug me.

"I'm really thrilled. Don't let these tears fool you. Hey, does Lizzy know?"

"Oh, sure. She's known since forever."

Right. Because they were a normal family.

Donna left, and Mom and I cleaned up the kitchen without talking. She made her sludgy coffee, and we sat back down at the kitchen table, where all really important conversations took place.

"Why the tears?" Mom asked.

I took a deep breath. "I found the pictures of Dad today."

She nodded, not even bothering to chastise me for rooting around in her closet.

"What happened, Mom? What happened with Daddy?"

"I guess it's time you knew," she said, her tone weary. No, not weary.

Sad.

Ever since she first met him, my mother said, Bill Stuart was the most wonderful man she knew. Life of the party. Full of energy. "He could charm the pants off anyone," she said. "Charmed them right off me, that's for sure."

"Skip that part," I said.

"We were married five years before you came along, and Lily right on your heels," she said. "Those were five good years. I mean, they weren't perfect, but they were just fine." She took a deep breath. "But your father, he had these dark moods once in a while. He'd just sit there and…and do nothing. Wouldn't talk to me, wouldn't get outta the chair, wouldn't even take a shower. I'd leave a sandwich next to him and go to bed, and the next

NOW THAT YOU MENTION IT 403

morning, it'd still be there, him sittin' like a statue in the chair like he hadn't even moved."

I pictured that, how confusing it would be to a pragmatic person like my mother.

"Then he'd just be done," she continued. "Back to normal, and if I asked what the hell that had been, he'd just say he was having one of his moods. And the flip side of that was he'd get wound up. That's how I thought of it. He'd be wound up, talkin' nonstop, laughin', makin' me laugh. At first, I thought it was fun—he'd stay up for two days, paintin' the living room—two days straight, no sleep. Guess I thought he just had a lot of energy."

"Bipolar disorder," I said.

"Ayuh. He wouldn't go see a doctor, though." She took a deep breath. "Most of the time, he was fantastic, Nora. You remember, don't you?"

I swallowed the lump in my throat. "I do."

"Having you girls was the best thing evah. God, he loved you! He was good for a long time after you were born. Maybe he was takin' medication. He never would tell me. Then when you were about five or six, the moods came back. He quit his job, wanted to write that novel. And I was all right with that, more or less. But then he started all that with you girls, takin' you with him at all hours, doin' all sorts of nonsense..." She shook her head.

All that adventuring. The wild bike rides, the swims in the icy ocean, the dares and thrills, the lack of rules and order.

More memories began flooding back in—my father's grandiose ideas about how successful he would be as an author, how we'd have servants and live in a mansion. The time he took Lily and me to Portland and bought us brand-new clothes until the credit card was denied. Mom took all those clothes back the next day, and Lily and I had cried and cried. Dad would get so annoyed at Mom for not going along with his ideas—tear down the house and build a tree house we could live in, sell the house and move to Africa.

And on those adventures... God. It was a miracle we hadn't ended up in the hospital or dead.

I remembered the time when we swam out to a little island about half a mile away from Scupper, so small it was just a pile of rocks and a pine tree. I was so tired and cold, my limbs stiff, my head sinking underwater, my little dog paddle not doing much to propel me forward. And there were Lily and Dad on the rocks, yelling at me, irritated that I wasn't there already. My teeth chattered and my head ached, and suddenly, there was my mother in our little Boston whaler, the engine the best sound I'd ever heard. My father had yelled at her, saying I'd never learn if she kept coddling me, that his daughters were exceptional, that she would ruin us.

Except she hadn't. She'd saved us.

Well.

She'd saved me.

"Lily has it, too, doesn't she?" I asked. It wasn't really a question.

My mother nodded, and her eyes filled with tears. Maybe if I'd seen my sister more than five times in the past fifteen years, I would have known sooner.

"So what happened to make him leave?" My voice was just a whisper now.

Mom tapped her fingernail against her cup, not looking at me. "I gave him an ultimatum. A doctor and medication or a divorce. That was the day he left." She took a deep breath. "When a few weeks had passed, I tracked him down in Portsmouth. He'd been using our credit cards, taking out new ones, too, so Visa and I found him. I begged him not to do this to you girls, to call you, to get into treatment. But he wouldn't. He was wound too tight. I couldn't reach him. He hated me by then."

A tear dropped on the table. My mother's tear, something I'd never seen before. "Before you girls came into the world, it was different. We loved each other. But you both loved him so much, thought he was the whole world, and my opinion just didn't matter anymore. It was always three against one."

"Oh, Mom," I whispered. I grabbed us each a napkin so we could wipe our eyes. "Why didn't you ever tell us?"

She waved her hand. "Maybe I should have. I kept hoping he'd come home. After a year, I figured he wouldn't, and by then, both you girls were hurtin' so bad. You were so sad, and Lily was just furious. I was afraid to let you know your father was…mentally ill. I was afraid it'd crush you both. I thought it'd be better if you thought it was about him and me."

"I didn't think that. I mean, I did, but I knew if Dad wanted to see us, he would have."

She nodded. "I admit, Nora, I was outta my league. I should've gotten you girls into counseling. I figured the more steady home life was, the better you'd be. You were doing so well in school, and Lily had her friends… I guess I wanted to think you were both all right."

"I was. I am, Mom. I'm fine."

"Yes. You are. Your sister, though…" Her voice broke off.

"You can only do what you can do, Mom."

She nodded and blotted her eyes again.

I got up and refilled her coffee cup, set it down next to her. Boomer, whose sleep had been interrupted by all this human distress, came over and put his head in her lap, and she stroked his ears.

"Do you know if Dad's still alive?" I asked.

She looked down.

I guess I had my answer. "Was it suicide?"

She shook her head. "Car crash during a hard rain down in Texas somewhere. Tractor trailer crossed over the line and hit him head-on. He was the only one in the car."

Mr. Gillespie had found him, after all. A car accident in El Paso, Texas, seventeen years ago.

Seventeen years.

My *dad*. He was really gone, my daddy, and even though it had been so, so long since I'd seen him, the pain was like my heart had just been ripped from my chest.

My father, who had made life so special—and so dangerous—had died all alone.

Oh, Daddy.

I put my head on the table and sobbed.

"I'm so sorry I didn't tell you," my mother whispered, stroking the back of my head. "I didn't want to break your heart all over again."

Her hand kept petting my head, and Boomer wormed his snout under my arms, unwilling to have his beloved in such distress, and I sputtered with a laugh.

"This dog is very attached to you," Mom said, and I looked up at her, her mouth wobbling with all those years of secret pain.

The rain that had been flirting with the island all afternoon opened up, and for a few minutes, my mother and I just listened to the ceaseless rush of it.

"Does Lily know she's bipolar?"

"Oh, ayuh, she does. I got her on medication, but once she got pregnant, she went off it. I don't think she was real steady after that."

It wasn't uncommon. Treated, bipolar disorder could be managed quite well in most cases. Two of my med school professors had talked openly about having it. But for some people, the medication made them feel flat. Gray. The mood swings and mania were the price they paid for a life full of color.

Maybe I could help my sister yet. I was a doctor, after all.

Mom twisted her napkin into a hard little knot. "Do you think Poe's got the same thing?"

"No," I said. "I think Poe's just gone through a long, hard time."

"I tried to help. I went out every year, sometimes more."

"You're a good mother. And a good grandmother, too."

Mom snorted, then blew her nose. "I don't know about that," she said.

"Well, I do." I reached across the table and gripped her hand, and after a second, she squeezed back, and we just sat there for a minute, looking at each other, our eyes teary, our hands linked.

"You killed Tweety, didn't you?" she asked.

"Oof. Yes. I'm so sorry. I really didn't mean to."

She smiled. "At least he didn't suffer."

I didn't disabuse her of that notion. My mother had been through enough. For a long time, we just held hands and listened to the rain.

26

Sullivan called me Saturday afternoon at two. "You free tonight?" he asked.

"You know," I said, stroking Boomer's ears, "you should probably call earlier. I'm a very busy person with many friends and responsibilities." The truth was, I'd spent yesterday weeping on the couch, the bed and the lounge chair on the deck. Hopefully, I had it out of my system now.

"So you're free?"

"Yes."

"Pick you up at eight?"

"Sounds great."

I'd be glad to see him. Knowing my father was gone was like a stone on my heart. I told myself it didn't really change anything, except of course, it did.

There was no upside to it. My mind kept saying *At least he didn't suffer* and *Now you know* and *This is better than having him out there, still not caring enough about you and Lily, maybe homeless or a junkie.*

But the little girl in me was so, so sad.

Sully would be a balm.

At eight o'clock sharp as the sun was a red ball sinking in the clear, pink sky, I heard the sound of a motor. A boat motor. Sure enough, there was a good-looking guy coming toward my dock in a little outboard boat. Boomer wagged his tail.

"Ahoy," I said as Sully tossed me the rope. "Fancy meeting you here." I wrapped the rope around the cleat.

"Figured I'd take you for a ride," he said.

"Will you also feed me?"

He nodded at a picnic basket.

Pretty stinkin' romantic.

I put Boomer inside, apologized for not bringing him, grabbed a bottle of wine from the fridge and two glasses, and went back out. Sully handed me in, untied the boat and came aboard.

"Nice boat," I said. It was—varnished wood, two seats behind the wheel, a bench in the stern and two outboard motors. Enough space between the wheel and the back bench for more people, fishing gear or, maybe, to stretch out and look at the stars and smooch a cute guy, if one were prone to that kind of thing. And yes, there was a blanket sitting under the picnic basket.

I sat in the passenger's seat, and Sully got behind the wheel. "This is my grandfather's boat," he said. "A 1959 Penn Yan angler. He used to take us out on it to fish or to tie in Portland or Bar Harbor for the day. It's not much in bad weather, but she'll do just fine for tonight." He glanced at me, and I smiled.

We purred out of the cove and headed east. The sky was raspberry pink now, deepening with every minute. There was the boatyard with its docks and moorings. I touched Sully's arm. "Does Audrey know we're on a date?" I asked.

"Ayuh. Her idea to go out on the boat. Away from the mosquitoes, she said."

"Tell her thanks for me."

A light went on in one of the boatyard buildings. I touched Sullivan's arm again so he'd look at me. "Does Luke know we're on a date?"

He nodded and offered no more.

We rounded the western side of the island and passed Osprey Point. I could see Deerkill Rock, where Dad, Lily and I used to jump into the water. My heart curled in on itself, picturing Poe jumping from that height. But we'd never gotten hurt. I had to give him that, even if it had only been a matter of time.

The sky was violently red now, and from the water, the island looked so beautiful, the golden slabs of rock, the pine trees silhouetted against the sky. Scupper *was* beautiful.

Funny how I'd never missed the island. Now I couldn't imagine being away from it, the smell of sun-warmed pine needles and salt, the pure air and cold water, the call of the loons at night.

I hope you're at peace, Daddy.

We headed out to sea. As the color seeped into the horizon, stars started to emerge like magic—first the North Star, then the Big Dipper, then so many at once the sky went from navy to purple. The Milky Way in all its endless, mysterious glory.

Sully cut the engines, got out of his seat and dropped the anchor. Then he spread out the blanket and ran a hand through his hair.

He didn't say anything. He might've been feeling shy.

I got up, too, uncapped the wine (a screw top, always thinking) and poured us each a glass.

"Have a seat," he said.

We sat on the blanket opposite each other, our legs stretched out on the floor of the boat. Audrey was right. There were no mosquitoes.

"You hungry?" he asked. I shook my head.

"There's a light I can put on if you want."

"No, this is fine. This is beautiful."

There was a pause. "It'll be hard for me to know what you're saying if I can't see your face."

I got up and moved to his left side, where his hearing was better. "How's this?" I asked, taking his hand.

"This is just fine." He cleared his throat. "What's new with you?"

"Oh, let's see. My mom's in love with Donna Krazinski, and my father died seventeen years ago."

He looked at me a second, then kissed my temple and pulled me a little closer, so my head rested on his hard shoulder. "I'm sorry to hear that. The second thing, that is. I already knew about the first thing."

I smiled, even though tears seemed to be leaking out of my eyes.

For a while, we just sat there, the rocking of the boat familiar, thanks to my houseboat, but more pronounced at sea than in the cove. My tears stopped, and my hand rested over Sullivan's heart, feeling the steady, slow thud. The boat bobbed up and down, little waves slapping against the hull. The stars were blazing now.

When my wine was gone, and Sully's was, too, I took our glasses, put them on the bench, climbed onto his lap and kissed him.

His hands slid into my hair, and he angled my head

a little. The kiss was warm and long and perfect, his mouth moving gently against mine. He tasted like wine, and I slid my arms around his neck and deepened the kiss, a heavy, wonderful shiver moving through my bones, making me hold on a little tighter.

When we broke the kiss, we just looked at each other for a minute. Then he smiled, that irresistible half smile, and I found myself smiling back. "I'm glad we're not just friends," he said.

"Now that you mention it, me, too."

He touched the tip of my nose with one finger.

We lay back, just holding hands for the moment, and stared up at the sky. The bottom of the boat was hard under my back, but I didn't care. In this moment, I was completely, utterly happy, and moments like that don't come around too often.

"You all done with your old boyfriend?" Sullivan asked.

"Ayuh."

"You sure?"

"Very sure. He's a bit…" I paused.

"Of a dick?"

I snorted. "Well, that, too." I paused. "Arrogant. I think there was a part of him that really liked charging in after the home invasion. The whole white-knight thing, being so needed, having everyone tell him how wonderful he was. But he got bored with it." I paused. "And me. I can't blame him, though. I got bored with me, too."

"So what changed?"

"I got hit by a van."

"Jesus." He laughed. I did, too.

"Yeah. Beantown Bug Killers. Such a metaphor."

I didn't need to tell him about the grayness, making amends, being closer to my mom. I had the idea he already knew. "So I came back here."

"Good."

"You're a man of few words, Sullivan Fletcher."

"It helps with that air of mystery and sex appeal."

"It's working. What about you? You must've dated after Amy."

He linked his fingers through mine and ran a finger up and down my arm, making my girl parts hum. One finger, ladies and gentlemen. I *knew* our mediocre sex had been a fluke. "Yeah, I dated a little. But once Audrey came to live with me full-time, not so much."

"Can I ask you something I've wondered about since we were fifteen?"

His smile flashed in the darkness. "Sure."

"Why her?"

His finger continued trailing up and down my arm. "She's not exactly how she seems," he said. "There's a lot of sweetness there." He paused. "You weren't exactly how you seemed back then, either."

"No, I was. I was miserable and lonely and an outcast."

"Okay, yeah. I remember. But you were also smart and funny and good with people."

"Good with people... You mean, like getting shoved in the hallway or having spitballs in my hair or getting picked last for gym every fucking class?"

He squeezed my hand. "You were great with teachers. And at the Clam Shack with the tourists. We worked together. I got to see you in action."

"Ah, the Clam Shack. Nothing like smelling like grease on top of everything else I had going for me."

"You barely remember me, do you?" he said, and he was smiling. Flirting, even. "Too busy being in love with my brother."

I put my free hand over my eyes. "I'd like to invoke my right to the fifth amendment. And I certainly do remember you."

He laughed again, and it was such a turn-on, low and dirty, like he knew all my secrets. Which he probably did.

"Sometimes," I said, tracing a finger along his cheek, "sometimes it takes a few years before you understand what you're worth. And who's worth your time."

We were kissing again, lips and tongue, and his hand wandered down my side and back up. My fingers slid through his hair and down his neck, and he felt so good, so solid and warm and delicious. The sounds of the ocean, of kissing, of just the two of us blended together. I hoped Sully could hear. I hoped this would be one of the things he'd remember when his hearing left him completely.

I don't know what time it was when we stopped. It had been a long time since I'd had a make-out session like that. Far too long.

"I told Audrey I'd be back tonight," Sully said, dropping a kiss on my chin.

"Okay." We just looked at each other for a minute. "I think you're probably the best person I know, Sullivan Fletcher."

"Does that mean we're a thing?"

"Yes. We're a thing."

He grinned, and my heart tugged. Then he got off me (alas), started the engines, and underneath the majestic sky, he took me home.

27

ON WEDNESDAY, THE CLINIC was slow. There seemed to be a feast-or-famine aspect to work here—we were either slammed, or we were twiddling our thumbs. So far my only patient had been a four-year-old hotel guest with a rash that was, I suspected, caused by a change in laundry detergent and not because he'd been stung by 999 invisible jellyfish, as he reported.

"That could be the cause," I said somberly. "It's unusual to find jellyfish in pools, especially the invisible kind. But if it is that, this cream will help."

His mother smiled and thanked me, and I tousled the little guy's hair, told him he was extremely brave and gave him a dolphin sticker. Another satisfied customer.

I went to the counter to fill out the forms. Gloria pretended I was invisible.

Okay, enough. "Gloria," I said, "don't you hate when two women have a really nice friendship going on, and then that friendship is ruined because of a guy?"

It took her five full seconds to look at me. "I'm sorry.

I just happen to think that what you did to Robert was really horrible."

"What did I do?"

"He was there for you when you went through this—" she made finger quotes "—'bad time,' and then you dumped him when *he* was the one who needed a little moral support."

"Did he happen to tell you what my 'bad time' was?" I asked, also using finger quotes.

"No. He still respects your privacy. He said you were feeling insecure."

"That's one word for it. A man broke into my home, beat the shit out of me, tried to rape me and was going to kill me. With a knife."

Her face drained of color, and her mouth fell open. It was satisfying.

"So yeah. I was probably a little needy after that. After I got out of the hospital. I was probably a little jumpy because they never caught him. As far as our breakup, that was all Bobby's doing. Ask him about a coworker named Jabrielle."

Gloria was frowning now. She started to bite a fingernail, then stopped.

"Here's the last thing, Gloria. I'm glad not to be with Bobby anymore. I really am. I'm very happy these days. If you guys are having fun together, good for you. I honestly don't care. But lose the bitchy attitude. Don't be one of those women."

My phone buzzed in my pocket, allowing me to exit on a high note. "Excuse me," I said and walked to the lounge.

It was Audrey. "Hey," she said. "Have you heard from Poe?"

"No. Isn't she at the boatyard?"

"She was. She got a phone call, and she just flew outta here. She had her bike, and she was really upset."

"Did she say who it was?"

"No. She just started crying and ran." Audrey paused. "She was really, really upset."

My free hand was clenched. "Okay, honey. If you see her or hear from her, let me know, okay? Thanks for calling."

There was only one person who could have that effect on my Poe.

Lily.

I called my mom at the hotel, but Donna answered the phone. "She just went home, sweethaht," she said. "Said she had to speak to Poe."

My mother didn't answer her cell. I called the house, but there was no answer.

Something bad had happened. Something with Lily. I closed my eyes and sent up a silent prayer to our father. *Let her be okay. Watch over Poe.*

Not that he'd been very good at watching over anyone.

I must've looked distressed because when I stuck my head in Amelia's office, she said, "Oh, no. Are you all right?"

"I need to leave. Family emergency."

"Call if you need anything."

"Thanks, Amelia." I ran out to my little car, glad it was raining and I hadn't ridden my bike. I drove as fast as I dared, my heart thudding, my brain shutting the door against any of the big, horrible thoughts that banged on it.

I got to Mom's in record time and ran inside. My

mother sat at the kitchen table, a notebook and the big old phone next to her.

"It's Lily," she said without preamble. "There was a fight at the prison. She stabbed another inmate."

"Oh, God." I sank into the chair next to my mom. "Is she okay?"

"The other girl had to go to the hospital. Should be all right. But…" My mother tilted her head to look out the window, and it was a few seconds before she spoke again. Her voice was steady when she did. "Lily's in solitary. The fight added years to her sentence. At least five, the lawyer said."

I closed my eyes.

My sister would miss the rest of Poe's fragile childhood. Would miss her first date, prom, college applications, turning eighteen, maybe turning twenty-one. She'd miss Poe getting her license, falling in love.

"What did you tell Poe?" I asked.

"I didn't get a chance to talk to her," Mom said. "The lawyer called her first. I tried her, but she's not picking up."

"Audrey Fletcher said she tore out of the boatyard, really upset."

"Ayuh. I just got off the phone with Sullivan. I'm guessin' she's gonna try to get back to Seattle and see her mother."

"Well, we live on an island, Mom. She can't go far." I took a deep breath. Thunder rolled across the sky. "Call Jake Ferriman and tell him not to take Poe anywhere."

"Good idea."

"Call the police, too. Just so they know. Have them alert the marina that a blue-haired girl might be trying to get a ride to Portland."

"Smaht." She gripped my hand. "Thanks, Nora. I'm glad you're here."

"I'll check my place, okay? Maybe Poe went there." I tried to sound calm, but in reality, I was trying not to throw up.

Oh, Lily. You were so close to getting out. You had only a few more weeks! What the hell have you done?

Mom got up and called Jake. I called Poe, but it went right to voice mail, so I left a message, then texted the same thing.

I know you're upset right now. Call me, honey. I love you.

"Let me know if you hear anything, Mom," I said. She nodded, and I went back to my car and drove to Oberon Cove, pulled into my little space and ran down the dock. Boomer jumped up from where he was lying on the top deck and woofed happily.

"Poe?" I said, bursting into the house. "Poe, honey?" I checked my room, her room. I'd picked her flowers the last time she slept over—three nights ago—and they were still there, dahlias and orange geranium leaves.

Rain started to fall, hard and angry. *What did you do to my girl, Lily? How could you?*

Poe wasn't on the top deck, either.

"Come on, Boomer," I said, and he followed me down the stairs, back into the car.

I called my mom, told her I was going downtown and would take a look around for Poe, check in with the storekeepers and lobstermen.

Wait a minute.

I called Sullivan. "Where's Luke?" I asked tersely.

"He's power-washing the Donovans' sailboat. I can

see him from here." We both knew why I was asking. "Any luck yet?"

"No. Sorry, Sullivan."

"It's all right. You had to ask. I'll keep an eye on him."

"I'll talk to you later."

"Good luck, honey."

The endearment brought tears to my eyes.

At the ferry, I showed Jake a picture of Poe I had on my phone—her and Audrey, from the sleepover—to make sure he knew who was missing. "I'll keep an eye out," he said, hitching up his pants.

"Thanks, Jake."

I went into the bookstore and Lala's and the restaurants, and asked the same questions each time. *Have you seen this girl? She's upset. Her name is Poe. Blue hair. Ask her to call her aunt or grandmother if you see her.*

The last stop on the street was the general store and post office. I braced for Teeny Fletcher's bitchery.

"Teeny, my niece—"

"I heard all about it. Audrey just called me." She looked at me with that sour face. "Good luck finding her. Let us know if you need anything."

I blinked. "Thank you."

I got back in my car and gripped the steering wheel hard. Where else could I look? The high school? I guess she might go there. The grammar school playground, maybe? Boomer wagged his tail and snuffled my ear. "Not now, buddy," I said, pushing his big head away.

I glanced out at the harbor. Tide was dead low, just about to change. The moon was full, so it'd be awfully high tonight.

And then I knew. I knew where she was.

I floored it through town, down Perez Avenue, past the high school, down Route 12, which had never made any sense to me, since the island didn't have eleven other routes.

Past Mom's house. Donna's car was there. Good. I kept driving to where the road ended a few hundred yards past our place, at the edge of the state forest, got out and started running, Boomer cantering joyously behind me, jowls flapping, tail like a banner. The rain soaked my shirt, making it flop against my ribs.

I should've let someone know where I was going. But there was no cell service way out here, and I wasn't going to waste time by going back.

Through the forest, my old friend. A blue jay squawked, ratting out my presence to all other wildlife. I saw a flash ahead—a fox, maybe, or a rabbit. I came out of the woods onto the rocks, my feet sure and fast, Boomer right beside me, the best dog ever, the Dog of Dogs. The waves were loud, the water dark gray.

There it was. Our cave.

"Poe!" I yelled. "Are you in there?"

No answer. If she wasn't here, I had no idea where to look. But I'd keep on looking until I found her, damn it.

"Poe?"

Boomer barked.

I climbed down the rocks and went in, the cold, mineral smell of rock mixing with the sharp smells of the sea.

She was lying in the fetal position on the little plateau in the back of the cave, where Lily and I once told each other stories.

"Oh, baby," I said, my feet crunching on the pebbles as I went to her. "I'm so sorry." Wrapping my arms around her, I pulled her against me, feeling her heave with sobs. She was so light, just like Lily had been. "I'm so sorry," I said.

"How could she do this?"

"I don't know, honey. I don't know any details."

"She *stabbed* someone! She'll never get out now!"

I just rocked my niece and kissed her head. Boomer barked from outside, too wary of the water to come down. The waves were lapping at the entrance now. We'd have to wade out. "We need to get out of here, sweetheart," I said. "The tide's coming in."

"I don't care," Poe said. "I don't care about anything." She curled against me as if warding off a blow, and her sobs shook in and out of her.

"I'm so sorry, honey," I murmured. "I wish I had more to say than that, but I am. I know you miss her."

A thin wail came out of Poe's mouth.

"I do…but I *don't*, Nora," she sobbed, looking up at me, her face twisted in pain. "I told her the last time we talked that I wanted to stay here. That she should come back and live with Gran and we could all be together, and she said that wasn't gonna happen, and I… I didn't *want* to go back to Seattle. I told her I wanted to stay here, and now she'll never get out, and part of me is… is…glad." Her voice rose on the last word, going silent as she cried and cried and cried.

"Oh, baby," I said, hugging her harder. I closed my eyes against my own tears and tried to think of something to say, something that would put things right.

There was nothing. All I could do was be here. The tide had risen enough that there was water in the mouth of the cave. Our pants would get wet, but who cared? I stroked Poe's hair and her studded ear, and rubbed her back.

"I hated it here when I first came," Poe said, pulling back from me and wiping her eyes, smearing her eyeliner. "It's so boring. But it's so…safe, too." She sucked in a shuddering breath. "I don't want to live with my mom. I love her so much, but I'm glad she can't take me away. I'm a bad daughter. She must hate me. That's why she stabbed that other person. So she wouldn't have to be with me because she's so mad."

Poe broke down again.

"No, sweetheart. No. You're the best thing she ever did, and she knows that. She's always loved you so much."

But there was some truth in Poe's words. It wasn't that Lily hated her own daughter…but somehow, in the wrong way, she was giving Poe what she needed, and making sure it couldn't be undone. Stay in jail, and Poe was safe from her.

The same way my father had left us forever. Not to punish us…but maybe so he'd limit the damage.

Oh, Lily.

If there was any doubt my heart was broken, it was gone now.

When the water seeped into my shoe, I knew we had to go. I took a breath and looked up.

There were the words. My mouth opened.

Still here after all these years.

The memory flashed like lightning. A little girl's hand, scraping words into the cave ceiling, tracing them over and over again. Our laughter bouncing off the cave walls. Lily's hand in mine, her braids bouncing as we ran back home through the woods.

"Poe," I said, "I think you should live with me instead of Gran."

Her crying stopped abruptly.

"Yes," I said. "I think that's the best idea."

"In Boston?" she said, her voice small.

"No. Here. On the island."

It could work. I'd be full-time at the clinic. I had enough for a hefty down payment on a house. I had all that furniture in storage, just waiting for me to make a home.

Poe had moved enough in her life. She already had friends—well, one, anyway. She was already enrolled in school.

"Yes. Live with me. We can still see Gran all the time, but you belong with me, honey. Here on the island."

Because I didn't want to be the girl who'd left Scupper anymore. The one who had to run away to find herself. The one who—let's face it—had been playing a part for a long time. Not completely; there were things about my Perez self that were genuine. But God, it had been so much work, that person in Boston! Bobby's girlfriend, the organizer of outings, the most cheerful of the cheerful, the most hardworking of all. I'd been trying too hard for too long.

Here, I wasn't perfect all the time, not so polished, not so concerned with making the world love me.

Here on Scupper, people *knew* me.

After all this time, I was really myself.

And so was Poe. She didn't stomp all the time, she'd let go of a lot of her anger, she had conversations with people, a job, a friend and a genuine sweetness.

This was where we were meant to be.

"Are you sure?" she asked, her blueberry eyes full of hope.

"Completely. I love you, you know."

"You do?"

"I do."

She hugged me, the poor little bird, and I hugged her back, long and hard. "Come on. Gran's a wreck. We have to get back."

The tide was up to my knees now, the mouth of the cave halfway full. "Looks like we're gonna have to swim for it," I said. Our phones would be ruined, but who cared?

"I don't think so," Poe said.

"Well, it's that or drown." I smiled. "You can do it. I'll be right there next to you."

And so we waded in, holding hands, the numbing water stealing our breath, and on the count of three, we went under and pushed off, kicking and reaching. Though the salt water stung my eyes, I opened them to make sure Poe was right there with me.

For just a second, she was Lily, my lost sister now found in her daughter, baptized anew in the harsh bite of the clear, cold Maine ocean.

MY MOM WAS fine with Poe living with me, even if her eyes did fill with tears when I told her.

"I guess that's a good idear," she said.

"I'll still see you every day, Gran," Poe said, pulling the blanket closer around her shoulders. My mom insisted on wrapping us both up tight, and Donna was making coffee.

"Well, you don't have to come *every* day."

"I will. I promise."

"By the way, Gran is dating someone," I said, tilting my head at Donna. "Mrs. K and she are a couple."

Poe's eyes bugged out. "I have a lesbian grandmother? Oh, my God, I'm so cool!"

We all laughed, and I ruffled Poe's wet hair. Boomer's tail wagged, and he smiled his Dog of Dogs smile, glad that his womenfolk were all right.

Over the next few days, I made plans.

Amelia was more than happy that I'd be staying. We talked about benefits and hours, and I went back to Jim Ivansky, the real estate guy who'd found me the houseboat. Too bad I couldn't afford to buy that. Asked him to keep an eye out for a little house in town. I called my practice and gave notice and said, of course, I'd come back to visit. Roseline cried when I told her, then gave me some news of her own—she was newly pregnant, and just because I'd be living in Maine didn't mean I was getting out of godmother duty.

Sully... Sully gave me that ovary-destroyer smile when I told him I'd be staying.

"Don't get cocky," I said. "This has nothing to do with you."

"No, no, I'm just a happy side note here." He kissed me. "Very happy."

We still hadn't slept together—well, the right way, that was. But the girls were going to sleep over at my mom's this weekend, so hopefully that was about to change.

Five nights after I found Poe in the cave, I got a phone call from a number I didn't recognize. The area code, however, was 206.

Seattle.

"You have a call from an inmate at Washington State Women's Correctional Facility," the recorded voice said. "Press 1 to accept the call."

My hand was shaking. I pressed 1.

"Lily?" I whispered.

For a minute, there was no response.

"Tell her I'm sorry." My sister's voice, which I hadn't heard in years, cut my heart in half. "I'm so sorry. Take care of my baby, Nora. Take care of her better than I did. I had no business becoming a mother, but I love her, and I'm so, so sorry I couldn't be better."

"I will," I breathed. "I swear it, Lily. I'll take good care of her."

"I know you will," she said, her voice breaking. "I know."

Tears poured out of my eyes, and I pressed my lips together. "She loves you, too," I said. "She loves you so much."

The sound of my sister crying had always gutted me. It still did.

I wiped my eyes on my sleeve. "Are you okay, Lily?"

There was no answer. Of course, she wasn't okay.

"Hey," I said, my voice wobbling. "Guess what I found? In the cave. Remember? Remember what you wrote?"

There was no answer.

"You wrote 'Nora and Lily, together forever.' Remember that? I'll send you a picture of it," I said.

"I never… I never showed anyone our cave. I never did."

I bit down on a sob. "I love you, Lily. I love you. I love you. I love you."

I kept saying it until she hung up so softly I didn't know the connection had been cut. And even then, I kept saying it.

I love you. I love you. I love you.

28

THE MORNING OF Go Far, Be Strong dawned clear and blue, a stiff breeze coming off the ocean.

Xiaowen and I were running together—we kind of had to, as the organizers. We'd asked the high school cross-country teams to join us and run with the littler kids in a shorter run than the 10K for us older folks. Audrey had suggested they all wear superhero T-shirts, so the town green was dotted with Avengers, Batman T-shirts and the Superman symbol. One redheaded girl was dressed like Black Widow—it would be hard to run in leather, but she sure was rocking the look.

Audrey wasn't quite up for the run just yet, though she'd already committed to next year. She was walking the 3K, though, and wore a shirt that said Healthy Comes in Every Size. Poe had opted to walk with her, holding the Go Far banner. "Gotta stick with my friend," she said.

I was ridiculously proud of both girls. In fact, I couldn't look at them without tearing up. Poe saw and rolled her eyes, but there was a smile there, too.

Mom and Donna ran the water station and gave out race numbers to last-minute registrants. A lot of the hug therapy gang was helping, too—Mr. Carver, the weepy widower, Jake, Bob Dobbins, who kept shooting confused looks my mother's way.

"How's it going?" came a voice, and I smiled and turned. Sullivan Fletcher.

"Heya, handsome," I said.

"Hey yourself."

We smiled stupidly at each other the way only two people who've had wall-banging sex can. Oh, yeah. Wall-banging, then nice and slow in bed…and then later on in the kitchen. Medals should've been awarded to us both, thank you very much.

He leaned in and kissed me.

"Old people kissing!" Poe said. "Look away, look away!" Audrey laughed.

The other night, he'd come over for dinner at the houseboat, Poe was still at Mom's for now, though we'd be moving to a house come the end of summer if my offer was accepted. Sully and I had been sitting on the top deck, drinking wine and watching Boomer lick the mint leaves, and I laughed at something Sully said. He leaned forward and clicked his phone. "Got it," he said.

"Got what?"

"Your laugh. It's on record now. It'll go in my best-things file."

My heart, my ovaries, my everything turned into a puddle of lust. We'd barely made it to the bedroom.

"Hello," said Amy. She was wearing a T-shirt with a race number pinned to it. Boomer got up to greet her and licked her knee.

"Hey, Amy," I said. She seemed okay with me dating the father of her child. Then again, she'd moved on long ago.

In fact, Amy wasn't so bad. She was, I'd found, just a normal person, no longer queen of the Cheetos. Just a mom with two kids, trying to do her best and earn a living. She wasn't the only one who'd judged people back in the day. Ironic, that the fat girl and the prom queen were now almost friends.

"You running the 10K, or the five?" Sully asked.

"The ten," she said. "Obviously. It's only six miles. Are you, Flabby?"

"Sorry, I missed that," he said.

"I said, 'Are you, Flabby?'" she repeated in a loud voice, overenunciating.

"Sorry. Didn't catch that."

"I *said*—oh, I get it. You're joking. He's joking, Nora. It hardly ever happens, so enjoy it now."

Sully smiled.

I loved him, of course.

Funny, how easy that could be. When you found the right person, there was no hiding of flaws…there was just trying to do better. There was the comfort of admitting your weaknesses and trying to get past them. The knowledge that no one needed you to be on all the time, always fun, upbeat, attentive… He only needed you to be yourself. The security in knowing someone loved simply being with you.

I'd registered for a sign language class with him and Audrey this fall in Portland. It looked like I'd be needing it.

I squeezed his hand. "I need to get up front with Xiaowen," I said.

"Good luck," Sully said.

"See you at the finish," Amy said. "But I ran in school, so… I might be home by then. Oh, snap!"

I laughed, too.

Xiaowen was the master of ceremonies, being much better with a microphone than most people on earth. She welcomed people, called a few out by name, talked about how everyone could aspire to physical strength and good health and should feel free to work out with her, and only dropped the f-bomb four times.

People loved her (of course), laughing and clapping. In the crowd, I saw Richard Hemmings, the guy from Jitters. Hmm. I had a sneaking suspicion he might be here to see my friend, though she was playing dumb so far.

"Let's get it started," Xiaowen sang. "Go far! Be strong! Get your asses moving!" The starter gun went off, and a big cheer went up from the crowd. No more gray…just color everywhere, the blue of the sky and ocean, the flower boxes and planters, the brightly painted doors of Main Street, the riotous mix of T-shirts as we surged forward as one.

All of us, together.

WE RAISED MORE than fifteen grand for a health initiative for kids in grades six through twelve. Cooking and nutrition classes, some new equipment for the gym, obesity prevention, all that good stuff. The picnic on the green afterward featured burgers and hot dogs, but also vegetarian burgers, whole-grain buns, salads and fruit. Moderation in all things, as my favorite teacher in med school used to say.

"Is it okay if I sleep over at Audrey's?" Poe asked me.

"Fine with me if it's fine with Gran," I said. My mom said it was.

"Guess I won't see you tonight," Sullivan said. "I'll be making popcorn and watching *The Fault in Our Stars*."

"You lucky thing. That's okay. Xiaowen's supposed to come over, anyway."

"That's right, Sully," Xiaowen said, punching his arm to get his attention. "And you know how we bitches are. We put each other first, right, Nora?"

"Word," I said.

"Please stop trying to be cool," Poe said.

"Sorry," I said, standing up. I'd cleverly been on setup crew to avoid having to clean up. Six miles was two more than my usual four, and my muscles were starting to cramp up. "I'm heading home to shower and probably nap. See you later, gang. Great job today. I'm proud of everyone."

"Oh, God, she's crying again," Poe said.

"Just got something in my eye, that's all," I answered, smiling at her. She patted my shoulder.

As Boomer and I made my way through the crowd, I was a little surprised at how many people I knew, summer folks and locals alike. Amelia, who had donated a large chunk of what we earned, waved, looking like she was at the Derby with a big, beautiful beige hat adorned with a huge ivory bow. I waved back, then bumped right into someone.

Bobby.

"Hello," he said. Gloria stood behind him, hands on her hips.

Boomer, faithless ho that he was, began wriggling

and whining to be acknowledged. "Hey, Boomer," Bobby said, his voice softening a little.

"What a surprise," I said.

"How are you?" he asked.

"I'm fine."

He looked constipated, so I knew something was up. Ah, here it was. Gloria gave him a sharp jab in the back.

"Uh, Nora," he said, "I'm very sorry for misrepresenting you to Gloria."

"As you should be." I folded my arms.

He sighed the sigh of a man forced to do something against his will.

"And why *did* you lie, Robert?" Gloria asked.

Another sigh. "I was trying to make myself more interesting than I actually am."

"Ooh," I said in admiration. "Gloria, wow. Well done."

"Thank you."

Bobby rolled his eyes.

Hard to believe I once felt so lucky to be with this guy, the self-centered ass. "You're dating out of your league here, Bobby. Good luck keeping her."

I started off, then felt a hand on my arm. "I'm sorry, too," Gloria said. "I have a shitty track record with men, and I thought dimwit here was gonna be different, so I was defensive and believed his bullshit."

"I'm hardly a dimwit," Bobby grumbled.

"Shut up. Anyway—" Gloria shrugged "—I hope we can... I don't know. At least work together like we did before."

"You bet," I said. "Come on, Boomer."

There was such a freedom in truly not caring.

I drove home, let Boomer out of the car and watched as he raced into the woods, nose to the ground.

The pine-salt air felt so good to breathe. The tide was high, the water calm, baby waves lapping at the edges of the cove, the wind rustling the long grass of the meadow. From somewhere in the woods, Boomer barked twice.

I'd miss the houseboat, that was for sure. But Poe had been isolated enough, and even if Collier Rhodes would let me buy this place (and if I could afford it), it was too isolated for my niece. Jim Ivansky, the nice Realtor, had found a house in town for me. Something permanent. My furniture, so carefully and joyfully chosen, was waiting, and Poe and I could buy new stuff, too. It would be *our* house. Our home.

God. My muscles were definitely seizing up now. I let myself into the houseboat, put my bag on the counter and found myself face-to-face with Luke Fletcher.

He was high. Pupils like pinpricks, a muscle in his face twitching. With one hand, he was scratching his arm.

In the other hand was a knife. The big knife for chopping vegetables.

For a second, all I saw was white. My mind emptied completely. I was just gone in a wave of fear so big and absolute that there was no room for anything else.

And then I was back, in my kitchen, wearing my running clothes, feeling the gentle rock of the houseboat.

With a knife-wielding junkie.

"What can I help you with, Luke?" I asked. My voice was calm.

"Where do you keep your prescription pad?" he asked.

"At the clinic. What have you taken?" My legs felt wriggly with adrenaline.

"I need something. Vicodin. You got Vicodin?"

"I don't keep drugs here. Are you okay? Do you want me to call Sully?"

Wrong thing to say. He started tapping the knife tip against the counter. "Do you want me to call Sully?" he mimicked, same as he used to. "You think you're so *special*, don't you? You think I'm stupid. You think you can steal my family the way you stole my scholarship?"

"Oh, Jesus, not that again."

"Fuck you." He gave a little lunge forward, knife pointed at me, and the fear flashed, lighting up all the old hurts. I might've flinched, and I was definitely trembling now.

"I could kill you, you know," he said with a mean smile. "Bash your head in and dump you in the water and everyone would think you were a big fat bitch who fell."

"I guess that's possible." Ironically, I felt a flash of pity for Luke, this golden boy turned nothing.

"You're not staying here. You're not taking my brother and Audrey and brainwashing them. You stole enough from me. Get out on the dock, you fat bitch. Time for you to go."

Something snapped inside me.

The fear was gone, and in its place was molten fury.

"I didn't *steal* anything. I *earned* that scholarship. And I did something with it. I'm a doctor, you piece of shit. I help people. *You* were on the road to destruction long before you lost that scholarship. And you're right. It was yours to lose, and you lost it. You could've gone to another school, but you decided to get high and crash your car, and it was Sully who paid the price. Take a hard look around, Luke. You're a pathetic junkie living off his brother's generosity. So stop whining and get off my boat."

This time, he did lunge, and I jerked away, but not fast enough for a meth-stoked addict. He looped a strong arm around my neck and held me against him, knife at my ear. His breath was foul.

Poe. Mom. Lily. Sullivan. Audrey. Xiaowen.

Luke wrangled me out the door, so he could bash my head in on the dock, I guessed. Unfortunately, I had a problem with that plan.

The second we were on the dock, I elbowed him in the stomach, bit his arm as hard as I could, turned and heel-palmed his face, feeling the crunch of cartilage as I smashed his nose. He yelped and fell back onto the dock, and I stomped on his nuts as hard as I could, getting a scream.

Guess that self-defense class had been worth every cent.

Then there was a blur of black and brown and a snarling so ferocious, for a second I thought it was a bear.

But it was Boomer, who sank his teeth into Luke's arm and shook it so hard Luke looked like a rag doll. The Dog of Dogs. I watched for a second, then said, "Boomer! Off!"

He obeyed, a meaty growl in his throat, his teeth exposed. "Don't move," I said to Luke. His sleeve was wet with blood. Kinda hard to feel bad about that. "Boomer, good boy. Good boy. Stay."

Going inside, I took my phone out of my bag and dialed 911, asked for cops and an ambulance. Then I got my first-aid kit.

After all, I was a doctor.

Epilogue

A YEAR LATER, Poe got her driver's license, and we threw a celebration party, since it had been her third try. Mom and Donna, Sullivan and Audrey, Xiaowen and Richard (Georgie, the hotel owner, turned out to be gay).

We'd decorated in yellow and crimson—Gryffindor colors, of course. Streamers dangled from the porch, and we had Harry Potter paper plates and napkins. Reading Harry Potter had been my one requirement for Poe to live with me, I'd said, and she grudgingly opened the book, only to fall under its spell immediately. Like the rest of the world, thank you very much.

Poe's other friends were here, too—Bella Hurley, daughter of the former Cheeto Carmella Hurley, and Henry McShane, who had a huge crush on her, as well as six or seven kids from the track team, as Poe had taken up running. So had Audrey. She'd shot up four inches this past year, now that her Cushing's disease was cured, and dropped a lot of weight. She was happy and lovely, and I adored her. I wouldn't be surprised if she was in line to win the Perez Scholarship, her grades were so good.

Even Teeny Fletcher was here. She'd finally acknowledged that Luke had crossed the line. And yeah, she'd be my mother-in-law pretty soon. We'd never be best friends, but we could get along.

I'd thought Sully might kill Luke that day. Somehow, he'd gotten there before anyone else and had started beating his brother to a pulp until I forced my way in between them. Between Sullivan and Boomer—and me—Luke had hardly been a threat at the moment.

Luke was now in jail and sober, too. Sully said if he saw his brother on the island, he'd drown him himself.

But late one night as I sat out on the deck alone, I realized something.

If Luke *had* killed me that day, I would've died not on a dirty street in Boston, wondering about who'd take care of my dog, but with a heart full of love for Poe, my mom and this place. I would've died full of color, not grayness—the blue sky, the deep green of the pines, the mercurial colors of the ocean, the pink-and-apricot sunsets. I would've died knowing what it was like to be loved by a truly good man.

"You're the bravest person I know," Sully had said to me that day, and he held me for a long, long time. His eyes were wet when he pulled back.

The bravest person. I'd take it.

A roar of laughter came from the porch where the teenagers had settled. My niece's hair was pink now, and it suited her. Our eyes met, and her smile was everything.

Lily was still in jail. Poe talked to her almost every week; Lily had been better about calling. My sister wouldn't talk to me on the phone, but that was okay. I'd talked to the prison doctor about medication, and she said she'd work figuring out the right balance of medication and therapy for my sister. Otherwise, I stayed out of it, realizing Lily needed to find her own way.

I sent her a picture of the carving.

Nora and Lily, together forever.

And we *were* together, more now than in the past two decades, because Lily was with me in the form of her child. I didn't know what would happen when she got out...but you never knew what life held. I had never expected to be back here, after all.

The fragrant pink roses on the side of our little house were in full bloom, filling the air with their smell. I looked up at the sky, so blue and clear today.

Somewhere up there was my father. *Watch over us, Daddy*, I thought. *Take care of Lily.*

"Happy?" Sullivan asked.

"Happy," I signed back. While his lip-reading was excellent, I didn't think he should have to do all the work all the time. Besides, signing was fun. Sully's hearing had slipped away significantly this past year. He didn't complain. He never did.

And the sign for *happy* was to place your hands in front of your chest and gesture outward while you smiled. A glad heart, overflowing with love.

Which, now that you mention it, was exactly how I felt.

Dear Lily,

Poe is doing so well in school. She came in third to last in the cross-country meet, and at the end, she sprinted across the finish line, and you should've heard us screaming for her! Mom just about had a coronary. I felt like she won the Olympics.

It's late here, and I can smell wood smoke. The waves are breaking on the rocks, hissing over the pebbles on their way back into the ocean. Pretty soon, it'll be too cold to sit outside at night for very long.

The stars are so bright tonight. Until you can come home and see them for yourself, I'll look at them for you.

Love,
Nora

* * * * *

Acknowledgments

MANY, MANY THANKS to Julia Kristan, RN (and also my beloved godchild), for her help in procedure and terminology, especially in the ER scenes. Thanks also to Mighty Jeff Pinco, MD, for always being willing to give medical advice on anything from my skin rashes to how fast a car would have to be going to kill me if I were on a pizza run and jaywalked. You're the best, Dr. J! Any mistakes are mine, all mine.

Thanks also to:

Firefighter Kori Kelly, who shared her experiences with hearing loss and auditory processing disorder; my interns: Jessica Hoops and Lillie Johnson, who did such good and thorough work for me over the past two summers; Jennifer Schulten, founder of the Go Far program, which has inspired thousands of kids to get outside and exercise, learn the joys of teamwork and see just how far they can go in life; Wendy Xu, creator of Angry Girl Comics and sensitivity editor extraordinaire, for her help with the character of Xiaowen; my friend the great writer Sherry Thomas for allowing me to borrow her name; the PlotMonkeys—Huntley, Karen, Shaunee and Jen—who make me laugh till I'm sore and whose wonderful writerly advice improves every book. And special thanks to my book club, who insisted that Tweety be included in a story.

I am ever indebted to the wonderful team at Harlequin, headed up by my editor, Susan Swinwood, with huge thanks to Dianne Moggy, Michelle Renaud and all the people who work so hard on my books. Sarah Burningham at Little Bird Publicity dazzles me with her enthusiasm, creativity and energy. And thanks to the amazing Mel Jolly for remembering everything I forget and doing everything I can't.

Maria Carvainis, my agent, has held my hand for more than ten years now. Madame, thank you for your faith in this middle child. Thanks also to the warm and wonderful Elizabeth Copps and Martha Guzman at Maria Carvainis Agency, Inc.

The spouse of a writer is required to endure long silences when the writer is thinking, non sequiturs in almost every conversation, distraction, eavesdropping, discouragement and a lot of nonsensical babbling. I am absolutely positive no one handles this better than mine. Thank you, honey.

Thanks to my daughter and son, the lights of my life, for being yourselves. I love you more than I could ever say.

And thank you, readers. Thank you for giving me the gift of your time. It means the world to me.

A funny, frank and bittersweet look at sisters, marriage and moving on, from the *New York Times* bestselling author of the Blue Heron series,

KRISTAN HIGGINS

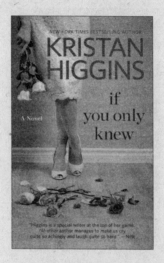

"[An] emotionally compelling story [and] perceptive study of love, marriage, sisterhood, and loyalty. A powerful, emotionally textured winner."
—*Kirkus Reviews*

Order your copy today!

HQNBooks.com

PHKHIYOK0420